WE LEAD

WE LEAD

(ARK ROYAL, BOOK IX)

CHRISTOPHER G. NUTTALL

ISBN 13: 9781542340977
ISBN: 1542340977

http://www.chrishanger.net
http://chrishanger.wordpress.com/
http://www.facebook.com/ChristopherGNuttall

Cover by Justin Adams

http://www.variastudios.com/

All Comments Welcome!

DEDICATION

To my beta-readers. I couldn't do it without you.

Thanks, guys!

CGN

PROLOGUE

Published In *British Space Review,* **2216**

Sir.

In their recent letters, the Honourable Gordon Cameron and General Sir David Anilines (ret) both asserted that Britain - and humanity - has no legal obligation to go to the aid of the Tadpoles, even though human ships were attacked and destroyed during the Battle of UXS-469. They claim that we can pull back and allow the Tadpoles to face the newcomers on their own.

I could not disagree more.

The blunt truth is that the newcomers attacked a joint task force composed of ships belonging to both ourselves and the Tadpoles. They made no attempt to open communications; they merely opened fire (which is, in itself, a form of communication). Their attack came alarmingly close to capturing or destroying over thirty warships from five different nations, including the Tadpoles. They followed up by invading a number of Tadpole-held star systems, culminating with a thrust at a major colony that would, if captured, have opened up access to tramlines leading towards Tadpole Prime. Those are not the actions of the innocent victims of unthinking aggression. They are the actions of an aggressor.

We do not know - we have no way to know - what our new opponents are thinking. They may be so xenophobic that an immediate offensive is their only possible response to any alien contact, although the proof that we are in fact facing two unknown races seems to render this unlikely. Or they may merely be an aggressive, expansionist race taking advantage of the contact to snatch as much territory as possible. Given their technical advantages, we dare not assume that the whole affair is a simple misunderstanding. Nor do we dare assume that communications have merely been poorly handled and the matter will be solved through simple negotiation. We are at war.

From a cold-blooded perspective, fighting the war well away from the Human Sphere has a great deal to recommend it. Human colonies and populations will not be at risk. We can and we will trade space for time, if necessary; there will certainly be no messy political repercussions from military missteps so far from Earth. Keeping the war as far from our major worlds as possible cannot do anything, but work in our favour.

But there is another point - one of honour. We gave our word to the Tadpoles that we would uphold the Alien Contact Treaty. Are we now to welsh on the treaty we proposed and drafted? Are we now to confirm to the Tadpole Factions that humans are truly untrustworthy? And should we write off the deaths of over thirty thousand human spacers we can ill afford to lose? Their deaths cry out to be avenged.

No one would be more relieved than I, should we find a way to communicate with our unknown foes. But I have seen nothing that suggests that communication - meaningful communication - is possible. We may be dealing with a mentality that will refuse to negotiate until they are given a convincing reason *to* negotiate or we may be dealing with a race that we *cannot* talk to, whatever we do. The only way to guarantee the safety and security of the Human Sphere is to assist our allies and make it clear, to our new foes, that human lives don't come cheap. And if we are unable to convince them to talk to us, then we must carry the offensive forward and strike deep into their territory.

The galaxy is a big place. But it may not be big enough for both of us.
Admiral Sir Tristan Bellwether, Second Space Lord (ret).

CHAPTER
ONE

Captain Susan Onarina opened her eyes, feeling oddly lazy. She'd served in the navy long enough to feel that she *should* be jumping out of her bunk and hurrying to the mess before her first shift began, but she wasn't on her ship. The ever-present background hum was gone. Instead, she was lying in her old bed in her old room, back in London Town. She took a breath and smiled in anticipation as she breathed in the familiar scent. Her father was cooking downstairs.

She glanced at her terminal out of habit, but there were no priority messages demanding her immediate attention. HMS *Vanguard* was in good hands, apparently. The latest set of refits were going smoothly. Susan wished, despite herself, that she was back on her ship, but she knew she'd had to take *some* leave or the ship's doctor would have complained. And besides, she'd had to spend several weeks at the MOD, being debriefed after Operation Unity.

Which makes a pleasant change from waiting to find out if I was going to be shoved in front of a court-martial board, she thought, wryly. She was still surprised she'd been promoted after relieving her previous command-ing officer of his command. *But it's still a pain when I should be back on the ship.*

She sat upright and looked around. Her room had always been small, but it felt smaller now she was a grown woman. The bed was barely large enough for her, even though she was used to bunking in Middy Country. Her father hadn't changed anything since Susan had taken the shuttle to the academy to start her training. The posters of Stellar Star - and two pop singers who'd gone out of fashion a decade ago - were still hanging from the walls. Her chest of drawers, on the far side of the room, remained untouched. She couldn't help feeling, as she swung her legs over the side of the bed and stood up, that her old clothes and possessions remained untouched too.

Better to donate them to the nearest charity shop, she thought, as she walked into the shower and turned on the water, allowing it to splash over her body. *It isn't as if I need them any longer.*

She allowed herself a tight smile as she washed herself clean, then stepped back into the bedroom and reached for her underwear. As a mixed-race child in London - and a poor one at that - her early life had never been easy, even though her father had taught her how to fight. Her first set of schoolmates had been poor too, all things considered; her *second* set of schoolmates had been wealthy enough to buy and sell a thousand of her, if they'd wanted to convert their trust funds to cash. They'd mocked and belittled the scholarship girl who'd never quite fitted in...

...But she'd proved herself. And that was all that mattered.

She finished dressing, then opened the top drawer and studied the photographs. The young girl she'd been - with a brilliant smile - had been replaced by a gawky adolescent, then by a newly-minted naval officer in a midshipwoman's dress uniform. She held the latter up for a long moment, realising just how far she'd come. *That* young woman hadn't known she'd have to relieve a commanding officer, let alone run the risk of being hanged. Shaking her head, she put the photograph back in the drawer and removed another one. Her parents smiled out at her on their wedding day. They hadn't known, either, that death would separate them in a few short years.

And being motherless didn't help either, Susan thought, sourly. *Everyone thought it was only a matter of time until my father remarried or got deported.*

She studied the photograph for a long moment, wishing she had more memories of her mother. A white woman with long blonde hair and a brilliant smile...Susan looked in the mirror, silently comparing herself to her mother. Her skin was dark brown, her hair was black, but their cheekbones were identical. She had her father's dark eyes in her mother's face. And maybe…

"Susan," her father called from downstairs. "Food!"

"Coming," Susan shouted.

She hastily returned the photographs and shut the drawer, silently promising herself that she'd come back after breakfast and clear them out. Too many of her old possessions were useless now, even though her father had preserved them. The clothes, the shoes, the handful of books and trinkets…she hoped, suddenly, that her father hadn't found some of her more embarrassing possessions. Grown adult or not, knowing that her father knew about them would be awkward.

The stairs creaked uncomfortably as she made her way down and into the kitchen. Her father's restaurant - and the apartment above it - was solid, but parts of it *looked* shabby, as only an old building could look. The handful of photographs nesting on the walls only made it look worse. She'd always been embarrassed to bring her friends home, fearing their reaction. And yet, the ancient building had survived the bombardment when so many others had fallen down, when the ground shook. Her father had had the last laugh.

She fell back into old habits as she entered, laying the table while Romeo Onarina - her father - stirred the pot over the stove. Susan had never been allowed to laze around as a child, unlike far too many of her schoolmates. She felt a flicker of embarrassment, mixed with shame, at just how badly she'd resented her chores as a child. And yet, they'd helped prepare her for boarding school and a naval career. Her father, bless him, had known what he'd been doing. She sat down and waited, smiling, as her father picked up the pot and carried it over to the table. The smell was heavenly.

"Best compo," her father said, cheerfully. "You'll love it."

Susan had to smile. Her father had been a soldier - and an acknowledged expert in turning inedible rations into something people could eat. He might not serve compo to his customers - she *hoped* he didn't serve compo to his customers - but she'd eaten quite a few makeshift dinners when she'd been growing up. Some of them had been surprisingly tasty, given what had gone into them; others, less pleasantly, had tasted of cardboard or worse. But he hadn't made her compo for breakfast, thankfully. Instead, the scent of brown stew chicken rose to her nostrils.

She leaned back and studied her father as he started to ladle stew into her bowl. He was black, his dark hair trimmed close to his scalp in a distinctly military manner. His dark eyes sparkled with amusement, even though he rarely smiled with his lips. It still felt odd to be taller than him, even though she'd matched and exceeded his height back when she'd turned eighteen. Part of her still felt like a child in front of her father.

Her father sat down facing her, then motioned for her to tuck in. Susan did, savouring the taste of chicken and spices. Her father ground his own, she knew, following a recipe he claimed had been handed down from his grandmother. Susan had only met the formidable woman once, during a brief visit to Jamaica, but she believed it. Her great-grandmother had been a remarkable cook.

No wonder the restaurant is so successful, she thought, wryly. *There aren't many places like it in London now.*

"Sandy was asking about you," her father said. "I believe he's *still* unmarried."

Susan snorted. Sandy Devonshire had been her best friend back when she'd been a child, before she'd won the scholarship to boarding school. They'd stayed in touch for a while - and even dated twice - before she'd gone into the navy and he'd been called up for National Service. But they'd gradually lost touch with each other after the war. She had no idea what had happened to him.

"I haven't heard anything from him," she said, finally. "Is he the *only* person to come calling?"

"A bunch of reporters turned up," her father said. "They were *very* interested in hearing stories of your childhood, so I told them about the quarry..."

"I hope not," Susan said. She'd been nine when she and a few friends had broken into the quarry and gone climbing. It had been a dare, but it had also been incredibly stupid. They'd been lucky not to be marched home by the police. "You didn't, did you?"

"I could have done," her father teased. "And I could also have told them about Aunt Dahlia's flowers…"

Susan groaned. "You didn't."

"Of course not," her father said. "I *did* tell them about your academic achievements, but they weren't so interested in *those*."

"Probably not," Susan agreed. She'd done well at Hanover Towers, but she'd lacked the connections necessary to *really* benefit from a boarding school for aristocrats. "Do you think they interviewed everyone?"

"I guess so," her father said. "There's quite a few older folk around here who'll remember you. To say nothing of your old school chums…"

Susan sighed. Mixed-race kids were unusual, particularly ones with immigrant parents. The Troubles had left scars in their wake, bad scars. She'd probably be remembered by people who'd never done more than pass her in the streets, just because her skin colour made her stand out. If her father hadn't been a soldier, if there hadn't been dozens of other former soldiers in the community, life would have been a great deal harder. And now…she was probably the most famous person to emerge from the community. She couldn't help wondering what would have happened if she'd faced a court martial instead.

Dad would have been in trouble, she thought, bitterly. *Everyone here is patriotic as hell.*

"I don't *think* you'll have to bribe anyone to keep your secrets," her father added. "Unless you've done something I don't know about…"

"I haven't," Susan protested. Even if she *had*, the community would probably close ranks against anyone who betrayed her to the media. "I was a good girl."

"Glad to hear it," her father said, dryly.

He leaned forward, meeting her eyes. "Why didn't you tell me what was wrong?"

Susan didn't have to ask what he meant. She'd sent him a brief message, when *Vanguard* returned to Earth after the Battle of UXS-469, but she hadn't given him many details. And she'd gone into custody on Titan shortly afterwards. Her father had contacted lawyers and generally made a fuss, but he'd gotten nowhere. Too many people in high places had warned him to keep his mouth closed until a decision - any decision - was reached.

"It was my problem," she said, finally. "You couldn't do anything to help."

"I thought fathers existed to fix their daughters' mistakes," her father said, dryly.

"I don't think you could fix this mistake," Susan said.

She shook her head. Her father wasn't the only father she knew who'd taken good care of his daughter. She knew a father who'd beaten up his daughter's boyfriend after he'd turned abusive - and a father who'd shelled out hundreds of pounds after his daughter had vandalised a war memorial - but *her* mistake had been on a very different scale. If, of course, it *had* been a mistake. *Vanguard* had come alarmingly close to being blown out of space when the Contact Fleet had been jumped. The medals she'd been given after she'd been officially cleared suggested that she had some new friends in high places.

"I would have tried," her father said.

"You can't fix everything," Susan pointed out. "I plotted and carried out a mutiny, technically speaking. They could have hanged me."

She sighed. Relieving a superior officer of his post - particularly under fire - was not encouraged. In truth, she was surprised she hadn't been told to quietly resign, thus balancing the need for reward and punishment. She hadn't dared to hope that she'd be left in command of *Vanguard*. It had simply never occurred to her that her actions would have created a political headache for the government, a headache that could only be resolved by confirming her as *Vanguard's* new CO.

And I'll probably be kicked out once the war ends, she thought, cynically. *If the war ever does end...*

"I would have tried," her father said, stubbornly.

He met her eyes. "You're not the only person to consider taking such steps."

Susan blinked. "*You* did?"

"Yes," her father said.

He looked down at the table for a long moment. "I didn't have a hope in hell of going to Sandhurst," he said. "When I joined the army, I was sent to Catterick for basic training and then assigned to the Yorkshire Regiment."

Susan nodded, impatiently. A penniless nobody from Jamaica, without connections...he'd have to do *very* well to win one of the coveted spots at Sandhurst. And he hadn't. Instead, he'd been trained and then slotted into a regiment. Jamaica had a long history with the British Army, but there was no specifically Jamaican regiment. Only the Ghurkhas and the Sikhs had *that* honour, for better or worse. It was still a matter of hot dispute.

"I did well, the first couple of years," her father added. "We were on patrol, operating from forward bases in Africa and the Middle East. Mainly pirate-hunting, though we got in a little barbarian-chasing too. I was fortunate enough to be promoted to corporal with a promise of a prospective promotion to sergeant, if I chose to throw my hat into the ring for NCO training."

"Which you had," Susan said.

"This was before my promotion to sergeant," her father said. He shrugged. "We get a new chap straight out of Sandhurst - a thick-headed second lieutenant with a chin so weak you'd think he'd go have it fixed. Talks like a cup of weak tea passing its way through my digestive system, acts like he wasn't even there a week before getting kicked out. Oh, and did I mention he was the third son of the Duke of Somewhere?"

"No," Susan said. She had a nasty feeling she knew where the story was going. Someone with such strong family connections would be virtually guaranteed a place at Sandhurst, regardless of his qualifications. "What happened?"

"Officers like that...everyone prefers they just stay in the tents, get drunk and claim the credit," her father told her. "It would have rankled, of course, but it would have been preferable. This one was too dumb to realise that he really should listen to his NCOs, if he insisted on exercising direct command. He changes everything because he thinks it should be different..."

Susan nodded. She'd met quite a few officers who'd insisted on stamping their authority on their ship as quickly as possible, even if their changes were largely cosmetic. It had been annoying, back when she'd been a junior officer. Now, she rather understood how those officers had felt. They'd needed to make it clear that they were in charge.

"And then we get into a firefight," her father added. "I'm meant to be leading the patrol, but thickhead decides to take command himself. Not his job, but...hey, he's the superior officer, so I swallow it. And then he leads us straight into an ambush, which gets us pinned down in a defile. The bastards can't get to us, but we can't get out either. Bullets are pinging everywhere and it looks bad.

"Thickhead decides to organise a mass charge, right up the side and into the teeth of enemy fire. Brave, I suppose, but fucking stupid. It's the sort of thing that only works if you have a patriotic scriptwriter on your side. Our body armour is good, but it's not *that* good. I put my foot down and he starts screaming at me, threatening everything from a whipping to being fired out of a cannon. And I start seriously thinking about putting a bullet in his brain."

Susan swallowed. "But you didn't?"

"The Household Cavalry showed up and drove the insurgents away before we could mount the charge or I could kill him," her father said. "Someone with more rank than I must have...*discussed*...the whole affair with him, because he was surprisingly quiet for the rest of the deployment. I think he took early retirement and left a few years later. He was certainly never put in command of deployed troops again."

"Good," Susan said.

Her father leaned forward. "You did the right thing in relieving your commanding officer of his post," he said. "But you did the wrong thing in not telling me."

Susan shrugged. "Would you have told *your* father, if you *had* shot the idiot?"

"I would have had to tell him *something*," her father said. He conceded the point with a sly nod. "But he wouldn't have been in any position to help."

"Neither were you," Susan said.

Her father sighed. "At least you survived," he said. His eyes twinkled. "And you're getting older. Any chance of a husband or children yet? I could do with grandchildren."

Susan shook her head. "I haven't met anyone, father," she said. "My career makes it harder to meet men."

"I met your mother while I was a serving soldier," her father pointed out.

"That's different," Susan said. "I'm a commanding officer on a battleship. The men I meet are either my superior officers or my subordinates."

"Then spend more time meeting civilians," her father said. "Should I ask Sandy if he wants a date?"

Susan would have blushed, if her skin allowed it. "*No*," she said, horrified. "Father…"

Her father's eyes sparkled with amusement. "Your mother would have approved of him," he said. "And he'd understand the demands of your career."

"I'm not interested at the moment," Susan said. "And I don't know if I'll ever be."

"There's more to life than serving in the military," her father said. He waved a hand around the kitchen. "I can swear to that, Susan."

Susan shrugged. She liked the restaurant - she'd spent most of her holidays waiting tables and cleaning after the doors were closed - but she didn't want to spend the rest of her life there. Too many of her friends *were* trapped in the community, even after the war; unable to leave, unable to build lives away from their childhood homes.

"Perhaps," she said. "But, for the moment, the navy *is* my life."

CHAPTER
TWO

"Keep your fucking head down!"

George ducked into the mud as a spray of bullets rattled over her head, trying to compress her body into as small a target as possible. She knew, intellectually, that the bullets weren't real, but the whole scenario was terrifyingly realistic. The exercise ground near Hereford was designed to push soldiers to the limit - and woe betide the soldier who treated the exercises as a *game*. They might not be shot, if they made a mistake, but they would have to face the wrath of the exercise coordinators and their superior officers.

And people have died out here, she thought, as the ground shook violently. She stayed low, praying it would be over soon. *Accidents happen.*

She glanced up as the shaking came to an end. A line of Royal Marines were running forward to take up defensive positions, their rifles at the ready. Everyone *knew* the enemy - the opposition force - was on the march. They'd be hit at any moment. She ducked down again as a pair of aircraft zoomed overhead, then cursed her own mistake as she realised they were friendly. The emplaced antiaircraft weapons to the rear would have fired on them if they'd been unfriendly.

And no one flies now if they can help it, she reminded herself. The HVMs and ground-based lasers were more than capable of blowing anything out of the sky, even a modern stealth aircraft. She'd seen simulations of wars between the Great Powers that ended up looking like a modern version of the First World War. *The enemy would slaughter our aircraft as mercilessly as we'd slaughter theirs.*

"Get up," Sergeant Roberts snapped, as he ran past. "Dig yourself a fucking foxhole!"

George nodded, scurrying forward until she was just behind the trench. Digging foxholes hadn't been covered in the academy, but she'd learnt hard lessons since she'd been seconded to Hereford. She wasn't quite sure why her superiors - and her family - wanted her to learn ground-pounder skills, yet...she had to admit part of her had enjoyed it. But the rest of her wanted a shower, a long nap and a flight back to HMS *Vanguard*. The battleship had been a hard posting, harder than she'd anticipated, but she'd been *clean*. Right now, George was covered in so much mud that she suspected she'd need a series of showers just to dig down to her bare skin.

She pulled her entrenching tool from her belt and set to work, digging into the ground. The marines were digging with terrifying speed, putting together a trench that looked more sturdy than her own pathetic efforts. She gritted her teeth and worked harder, wishing she'd had longer to pre-pare. It was impossible to forget that each of the marines had at least three years experience, far more than herself. As far as they were concerned, she was little better than a raw recruit.

"Incoming," someone shouted.

George dived into the foxhole, cursing the puddle of water at the bot-tom, as mortar shells landed around their position. Dirt tumbled into the hole, mocking her. Water dribbled down afterwards, slowly flooding the bottom. Her boots were good, she knew, but she could still feel water soaking her feet. She'd have to be careful, she reminded herself. She hadn't run the risk of bacterial infections since she'd escaped boarding school.

Where the gym mistresses were all frightfully keen, she recalled. She'd enjoyed playing games, but some of the other girls had considered gym a foretaste of hell. If you weren't a player - and a good player at that - the gym mistresses *hated* you. *What does it say about them that drill instruc-tors are nicer people?*

She smiled at the thought as she carefully lifted her head and peered south. The enemy was somewhere in the distance, hidden behind a thicket of trees. They'd be probing north, if the intelligence briefing had been remotely accurate, searching out the Royal Marines before they mus-tered a counterattack. And they already knew where the marines were, she reminded herself, sharply. No one would call down a mortar strike at random and expect it to hit someone.

Someone moved, behind her. She turned to see Sergeant Roberts, hugging the ground. He was a short burly man, so immensely muscular that she was tempted to suggest that he had muscles on his muscles. She found him a little intimidating, even though he lacked the near-sadism practiced by her gym teachers. He'd certainly made it clear that he would be treating her just like any other recruit, despite her youth, sex and family connections. And the hell of it, she knew, was that he was right. The Royal Marines couldn't afford weak links, even in their naval liaisons.

"Get your com out," he growled, pitching his voice low. "They'll be coming soon."

A rattle of gunfire, in the distance, underscored his words. George nodded, then pulled the terminal off her belt and checked the datanet uplink. Thankfully, the exercise coordinators had decided that enemy jamming would be ineffective - this time. The close-air support network opened up in front of her, showing her exact location on the map. She let out a sigh of relief as she entered her ID codes, then settled down to wait. It wouldn't be long now.

She cursed her digging as the ground quivered, wishing she'd been allowed to join the marines in their trench. But no, she'd been told to dig her own foxhole and hide in it. The marines were skilled diggers, she knew; she wouldn't have got in their way...she sighed, pushing the thought out of her head. Sergeant Roberts - and his superiors - no doubt had their reasons, even if they didn't make sense to her. Besides, she *was* meant to pull her own weight.

An odd silence fell over the battlefield, broken only by bursts of gun-fire in the distance. She thought she heard another aircraft, but there was nothing in the grey sky when she looked. A couple of marines hurried past her, expanding the trench to create an escape route, if necessary. She'd been surprised when she'd first seen them doing it, two months ago, but she'd learnt hard lessons since. Trying to escape by running on the surface was just *asking* for a bullet in the back.

The marines glanced at her, jabbed a finger towards the escape route to confirm she knew where it was, then headed onwards. George sighed. Three months of training with the marines, three months of tagging along…and they still hadn't warmed up to her. They were polite enough, she supposed - she'd heard worse in Middy Country - but they weren't very welcoming. She wasn't sure if it was because of her sex or because she'd been forced on them at the last moment - or because they didn't expect her to make it. Maybe it was her sex. There were no female Royal Marines.

But they've obviously worked with women before, she thought, sourly. *Everything from intelligence agents to liaison officers.*

The gunfire grew louder. George peered towards the trees, seeing shapes flittering forward and into the muddy field. The enemy was advancing slowly, pushing forward…they *definitely* knew the marines were there. But they might also hope that the marines had been killed by the bombardment, clearing the way across the battlefield. She tensed, placing her terminal by the side of the foxhole and aiming her rifle. Maybe she wasn't as good a shot as the marines. She could still take down a few enemy soldiers before they had to retreat…

She braced herself, careful to keep her finger off the trigger. Sergeant Roberts had warned his squad, in graphic detail, *precisely* what would happen to anyone who fired before he issued the order. George had no intention of drawing his wrath, not now. She had no way to be sure, but she had a feeling that her time on the exercise field was drawing to a close. And then? She honestly had no idea. Shipped back to *Vanguard* or…?

"Fire!"

George fired, automatically. The lead enemy soldiers dropped, their successors falling to the ground and taking cover as the marines opened fire. George searched for a second target, but saw nothing. A handful of enemy soldiers were still in the trees, but they were low…a rumble echoed through the air, sending more mud cascading into her foxhole. A trio of tanks were advancing north, straight towards the marines. The marines might be able to stop the enemy infantry, but the tanks…? Their bullets would just bounce off the tanks.

"Fitzwilliam," Sergeant Roberts snapped. "Call in a strike!"

"Yes, Sergeant," George shouted back.

Her fingers danced over the terminal, tapping in orders. She cursed the safety precautions built into the network, even as she ordered an immediate strike. But they were necessary. It wouldn't do to accidentally call in a strike on her own position. The command went into the network...she braced herself, silently praying that the strike wouldn't be aborted by some REMF sipping tea in an office several miles from the front lines. She'd never really understood the resentment some of the groundpounders felt for the Royal Navy - and the army's own uniformed bureaucrats - until she'd started training with the marines. As bad as her early days on *Vanguard* had been, they'd been wine and roses compared to training with the marines.

The notification popped up in front of her. "Ten seconds!"

"Call at two," Sergeant Roberts ordered.

George watched the seconds tick down to zero, hoping - desperately - that nothing would go wrong. Some of the strikes she'd called in had been disrupted, either by enemy counterbattery fire or long-range guns being retasked at *very* short notice. It awed her to think there was a whole network of guns, missile launchers, aircraft, drones and orbital bombardment stations waiting on her command, but she knew she wasn't the only Forward Strike Controller on the battlefield. Even without political interference, the network might decide that someone else - perhaps someone in danger of being overrun - needed the strike more than her...

"Two seconds," she shouted. "Two seconds!"

She ducked down as the missiles flashed overhead and slammed into their targets. The ground shook violently, the walls of her foxhole crumbling inwards until she was half-buried in the mud. She forced herself to remain still, even though her instincts were demanding that she scramble out before she was buried completely. Being hit by a piece of flying debris would be embarrassing, particularly as it would be a *real* injury. The British Army took safety seriously, but there was no way to prevent accidents on an exercise ground. Shit happened.

The ground stopped shaking. "Get up," Sergeant Roberts snapped. "Back to the next line of trenches!"

George pulled herself free of the mud and looked south. There was nothing but burning wreckage where the enemy tanks had been. Her head hurt, just for a second, as she tried to understand what she was seeing. She *knew* the tanks hadn't been real, right? Or perhaps the missiles hadn't been real? Or...she dismissed the thought as she crawled towards the escape trench, determined not to give the marines an excuse to hurry her along with a kick. The battlefield - partly simulated or not - was lethal. A mistake could get her killed.

And a simulated death will still be held against me, she thought. *And if others die because of me...*

She followed the marines, silently grateful for the hellish exercises they'd put her through when she'd arrived. Walking over the Beacons had been unpleasant - the old sweats had cheerfully informed her that she'd been steered away from the parts used by the SAS and Pathfinders - but it had built up her endurance. She might be cold, muddy and exhausted, but she could keep going. Behind her, she thought she heard the sound of engines. The enemy was clearly gearing up for another push. But Sergeant Roberts didn't seem bothered, so she did her best to ignore the sound. The enemy might be deterred by the missile strike.

We hope, she thought. *There's no one in place to call in a second strike.*

They reached the rendezvous point and stopped. Some enterprising soldier had set up a stove and was boiling water, allowing soldiers and marines to have a mug of tea. George removed her mug from her rucksack, found a teabag from her emergency supplies and joined the queue for water. The soldier's eyes went wide when he saw her, glancing at her muddy chest as if he wasn't quite sure if she was male or female. George resisted the urge to giggle as he stared at her. She could probably have passed for a man, if someone hadn't already known she was a woman. She'd never been particularly well-endowed.

She sat down and drank her tea quickly, allowing the liquid to warm her. It wouldn't be long, she was sure, before they'd be going out on the march again. A dozen different units - soldiers and marines - seemed to have arrived at the RV point simultaneously, their sergeants hastily reorganising them into new units. It was a test, she suspected. Soldiers could fight well in their original units, but could they fight when plugged into another unit? Better to find out on the training field than on the battlefield.

A hand landed on her shoulder. "Bearing up, Georgina?"

George scowled. Lance Corporal George Michelet - they shared the same first name, at least as far as *she* was concerned - was an ass. Or someone determined to needle her into doing better…she wasn't sure and she didn't really care. He reminded her of Lieutenant Charles Fraser, only Fraser had been pissed at her for her social standing instead of merely being a woman forcing her way into a man's world. The fact that George hadn't really been offered a choice seemed lost on him.

"I could go on for years," she lied. Her body was starting to ache, now she was sitting down, but she was damned if she was showing weakness. "How about you?"

"Make sure you eat something," Michelet told her. It was impossible to tell if he was trying to help or setting her up for a fall. "A little bird says we'll be on our way in five minutes."

George eyed him for a long moment, then dug a ration bar out of her belt and opened it. The bar tasted like cardboard, but she'd been assured it contained all the nutrients a soldier needed on the battlefield. She was surprised they didn't taste better. Civilians might be given the tasteless bars to encourage them to buy more regular food, but soldiers? They didn't have much of a choice about what they ate on the battlefield. She wasn't the only one eating, either. Soldiers knew to eat when they could.

Sergeant Roberts called them to attention four minutes later, then led the squad out on a long march. George forced herself to keep moving, even though the ache was getting worse. The battlefield was shifting, apparently. She wanted to look at her terminal, to download the latest update, but she knew she didn't have time. They reached a hill and marched up it, turning when they reached the top. Smoke was rising from the south, suggesting that the enemy had resumed its advance. She listened, but heard nothing apart from the beating of her heart. It meant nothing. Battlefields, she'd been told, always had odd acoustics. One unit might be under attack, yet its neighbours might not hear a thing.

"Dig in," Sergeant Roberts snapped. "The enemy is on the march."

He waved to George. "Get your terminal ready," he ordered, sharply. "You'll be calling down fire on the bastards, when they show themselves."

"Yes, Sergeant," George said.

She took the terminal out and hastily linked into the command datanet. It was patchy, alerts blinking up to warn her that the enemy jamming was finally taking a toll. She had to check and recheck their location four times before she was sure everything was correct, then sat down in the trench to wait. This time, at least, she could share with the marines. They didn't seem inclined to insist that she dig her own foxhole.

"Here they come," Sergeant Roberts said, ten minutes later. "Start calling down strikes."

George nodded, fingers flying over her terminal as the enemy columns came into view. A set of tanks, backed up by APCs…it was the sort of advance that no one had seen on Earth for decades, at least in the civilised world. Who *would* send tanks against a Great Power that could call down strikes from orbit? But…she hastily sent the orders, despite glitches in the command network. And then the response popped up in front of her…

Her blood ran cold. She'd fucked up. No, the *system* had been fucked. But it didn't matter whose fault it was, not now. She'd called down a strike on her own position!

"Get out," she screamed, desperately. The KEW was already inbound. It couldn't be stopped, even if she managed to alert her superiors. "Blue-blue! Blue…"

The marines didn't hesitate. They scrambled for the edge of the trench, clambered out and ran for their lives. George snatched up the terminal as she followed them, hoping they could get out of the blast radius in time. And then…

Her arms and legs snapped together, rendering it impossible to move. She tripped and fell, landing face-first in the mud. Cursing, she twisted her head to make sure she could breathe, then glanced backwards. The simulated KEW, apparently, had smashed the hilltop into a crater. The entire squad had been wiped out.

"Nice going," Michelet said, from where he was lying near her.

"Oh, fuck off," George said.

CHAPTER

THREE

London had changed, Susan noted, as she walked down towards Whitehall. Many older buildings had been repaired, since the bombardment and flooding in the war, but others had been rebuilt completely. A cluster of skyscrapers - resembling prefabricated housing rather than anything else - had been built along the Thames, providing living space for the government workers who dominated the centre of London. Others, she knew, had been erected on the outskirts of the city, re-housing the countless millions who'd been rendered homeless by the bombardment. They were soulless places, she'd been told, but they were better than the tent cities and refugee camps that had been so common in the years since the war. Hopefully, the combination of new housing and colonial incentives would be enough to push their residents out of the city.

She sucked in her breath as she entered Trafalgar Square. Nelson's Column had been knocked down during the bombardment, but it had been hastily rebuilt once the pieces had been located and patched back together again. Some people claimed that Nelson looked odd now, as if he was scowling at the nation he'd once defended, but Susan couldn't see any real difference. The *Ark Royal* memorial, erected on the other side of the square, was different, drawing her attention like a magnet. A chunk of the ancient supercarrier's hull, engraved with the names of all who'd gone down with her; a large statue of Admiral Sir Theodore Smith...she smiled as she saw the flowers, piled high beneath the statue. Britain might have almost forgotten Nelson - and far too many others - before the Troubles, but they would never be forgotten now. Admiral Smith had died to save the entire human race.

And now we're fighting beside our old enemies, she thought, wryly. *I wonder what he would have made of that?*

A small crowd of people were standing at one side of the square, exchanging shouts and insults with another - much larger - group. Several dozen policemen were also there, looking grim as the shouting grew louder. Susan listened, trying to make out the words as they blurred together into cacophony. One group was against the war, she decided; the other group had decided to mount a counter-protest. She turned and hurried onwards as more police vans began to arrive, armed policemen heading into the square. Peaceful protest was part of Britain's political tradition, one as old as British democracy, but violent protests would be squelched as quickly as possible. *That* lesson, too, had been learned in the Troubles.

She put the matter out of her mind as she approached the security barrier at the edge of Whitehall, manned by a pair of armed soldiers. There would be others in reserve, she knew, and probably more on their way from the nearby barracks, if the protest really *did* get out of hand. Whitehall had been bombed twice during the Troubles, then nearly flooded during the First Interstellar War. A degree of paranoia was only to be expected. She made sure to keep her hands in view as she approached the checkpoint, silently relieved she hadn't brought her service pistol. The Household Cavalry would take a very dim view of anyone carrying a weapon into Whitehall, even though she had a legal firearms permit.

The lead guard smiled at her. "I saw you on the news," he said. "You're *Vanguard*, aren't you?"

"I am her commanding officer," Susan said. She had to smile at his enthusiasm. "And yourself?"

"Household Cavalry," the soldier said. "We may be deploying to Nova Scotia or Britannia, but nothing's confirmed yet."

"It never is," Susan said.

She smiled in amusement. Deploying regiments outside the country - and off-world - was official policy, but certain units were harder to move than others. The Household Cavalry was unusual in that it was both a genuine fighting force *and* a ceremonial guard for Whitehall and Buckingham

Palace. She'd be surprised if its soldiers were ever sent off-world. The plans to build a palace on Britannia had been blown out of the water by the war.

The soldier checked her fingerprints and DNA, then made certain she had an appointment at the Ministry of Defence before giving Susan an e-pass and motioning her through the security gates. Susan approved, even though she knew there were plenty of officers, government ministers and bureaucrats who thought the rules didn't apply to them. Britain's enemies had worked hard to exploit gaps in the country's security, ruthlessly using blindspots and weakness to slip bombs into position. No one could be allowed through the defences until their identity had been checked and re-checked.

And even though the Troubles are over, she thought, *we can't take chances.*

Whitehall looked almost exactly as she recalled, she noted as she strode down towards the Ministry of Defence. The damaged buildings had been repaired, even though Parliament and the Civil Service could have worked out of their emergency accommodation for years if necessary. She wasn't sure how she felt about that, really. On one hand, it was important to make it clear that Britain would return to normal; on the other, the resources used to rebuild Whitehall could have been devoted to housing refugees from all over the country. But, in the end, the politicians had looked after themselves first.

She took a moment to pay her respects at the London Cenotaph, silently noting the inscription that stated that it was actually the *third* cenotaph. The first had been blown up during the Troubles, a symbolic strike against the British Government; the second had been ruined during the bombardment, almost certainly by accident. Nothing she'd heard of the Tadpoles suggested they would have targeted the London Cenotaph deliberately. They certainly wouldn't have understood its importance to humanity. The list of names - of men and women who had died on active service - seemed longer every year. She couldn't keep herself from searching out the names of people who'd died in the Battle of UXS-469, people she'd known during her career. Their bodies had never been recovered.

And probably will never be recovered, she thought, as she turned and strode towards the Ministry of Defence. The families of men and women who died in space rarely had bodies to bury. *Unless the Foxes recovered them for dissection.*

She reached the MOD and walked up the steps, holding up her e-pass for inspection. The guards checked her DNA again anyway, making sure she was authorised to enter the building. Susan rather suspected there weren't many spacers - or soldiers or even civil servants - who fitted her description, but she approved of the precaution. Getting into a military base was difficult, according to countless exercises, yet once someone *was* inside it was generally assumed that he had a *right* to be there. An infiltrator could do a great deal of damage before being caught, if he was inside the wire.

"Thank you," the guard said, when he'd finished checking. "Please place your terminal in the lockers, then wait in the lobby. You'll be escorted to the briefing room."

Susan nodded and walked through the gate into the lobby. It was larger than she'd expected, so luxurious that she half-wondered if she'd walked into an expensive hotel. The chairs were real leather, the wooden tables shining…a large painting of a scene from the Napoleonic Wars hung over the fireplace, an echo of a bygone era. Men on horseback, charging forward…even when the artist had painted, Susan suspected, the cavalry had already been on the brink of obsolescence. Charging into the teeth of heavy guns - or machine guns - would have been nothing more than suicide.

She put her terminal into one of the hidden lockers, then turned as she heard someone step into the lobby. A young woman, wearing a commander's uniform. Susan felt her eyes go wide as she realised the newcomer was a mixed-race child too, almost certainly Caucasian mixed with Asian. Faintly-tinted skin, dark almond eyes, hair a shade too light to be pureblood Chinese or Japanese…she couldn't help a flicker of envy, mixed with a dollop of fellow-feeling. *This* girl was exotic - and stunning - enough that she would have had almost no trouble in school.

The young woman came to attention. "Captain Onarina? I'm Commander Outlander, Admiral Fitzwilliam's aide. If you would like to come with me…?"

"Of course," Susan said.

She smiled to herself as she followed the younger woman through a twisting maze of corridors, all lined with expensive paintings. Judging from the name alone, she would have placed Commander Outlander as an asteroid dweller. The RockRats weren't known for caring about anything, but competence. Quite a few Chinese and Japanese engineers had fled to the asteroids when their governments had started clamping down once again. It was odd to see one in the Royal Navy, but perhaps it wasn't too surprising. The First Interstellar War had upset a lot of applecarts.

Commander Outlander stopped in front of a large wooden door, then held it open. Susan walked through the door, shaking her head in disbelief at the sheer opulence of the briefing room. It was *definitely* very like an expensive hotel, complete with a sizeable drinks cabinet and a uniformed servant waiting to take orders. Admiral Fitzwilliam, the First Space Lord, sat at a giant wooden table that looked old enough to predate the Troubles, flanked by Prince Henry and Admiral Soskice. Three others she didn't know sat beside them, a grim-faced man with dark hair cut close to his scalp, someone who was almost certainly a marine even though he was in civilian clothes and a woman wearing a captain's uniform and a perpetually vague expression.

"Captain Onarina," Admiral Fitzwilliam greeted her. "Welcome to the MOD."

"Thank you, sir," Susan said.

She took the seat he offered her and rested her hands in her lap. It was hard to escape the sense she was in trouble. If nothing else, she was almost certainly the lowest-ranked officer in the room. She'd expected a larger briefing, probably with a number of other commanding officers at once. Instead...it looked more like a private discussion. She couldn't help finding that a little ominous.

"I believe you've met Prince Henry and Admiral Soskice," Admiral Fitzwilliam said. He indicated the grim-faced man. "Rear Admiral John Naiser, Brigadier Percy Schneider and Captain Juliet Watson-Stewart."

Susan sucked in her breath. Rear Admiral John Naiser had commanded HMS *Warspite* during the Anglo-Indian War, practically winning the most significant naval engagement of the war single-handedly. And *then* he'd gone on to head the design team that had produced *Vanguard* and her sisters. Brigadier Percy Schneider had commanded Fort Knight on Vesy, then served with distinction during the war; Captain Juliet Watson-Stewart had *designed* most of *Warspite*, then gone on to revolutionise gravimetric technology…they were *legends*. Her mouth was suddenly dry. The entire Royal Navy looked up to them.

"John's promotion was only confirmed last month," Admiral Fitzwilliam said. "His return to fleet command is long overdue."

"Thank you, sir," Naiser said. Susan had always been good with accents, but she couldn't place his. She rather suspected that meant a lower-class origin. "It's a pleasure."

Prince Henry cleared his throat. "Perhaps we could get a move on," he said. "Time, tide and outraged family members wait for no man."

"Of course, Your Highness," Admiral Fitzwilliam said. There was a hint of droll amusement in his voice. "Susan, would you like something to drink? I'm afraid we may be here a while."

"So feel free to say when you need the facilities," Prince Henry put in. He winked at Susan, mischievously. "This is going to be a long meeting."

Susan nodded to the servant, then ordered tea. Admiral Fitzwilliam ordered a tray of biscuits, cakes and sandwiches, then tapped a hidden switch. A holographic starchart appeared over the table, red, blue and green stars linked together by yellow tramlines. Susan sucked in her breath as her eyes found the war front, surrounded by tactical icons. The enemy - the Foxes and Cows - had clearly made new inroads into Tadpole-controlled space.

Admiral Fitzwilliam leaned forward. "You can download a full strategic overview from the datanet," he said. "However, we do need to go over a number of points."

He pointed at two of the red stars. "Despite the success of Operation Unity and a series of follow-up raids, the Foxes have continued to bring pressure against a number of Tadpole systems. In two cases, they have successfully driven the Tadpole Navy out of the system and reinforced heavily, opening up lines of attack that will take them to Tadpole Prime. Based on what we now know about the enemy" - he nodded to Prince Henry - "we expect they will concentrate their forces and thrust towards

Tadpole Prime. As yet, of course, we have no idea when they will mount their offensive."

Susan nodded in grim agreement. The alien POWs - unlike the Tadpoles, back during the first war - were talking, but they apparently knew little beyond what their superiors felt they *needed* to know. It made sense, she'd been told, yet it was frustrating. There was no way to know what the alien leaders were thinking, ensuring that intelligence's best analysts were essentially guessing. They might be right about the alien plan to drive on Tadpole Prime...

...Or they might be applying human norms to aliens, thus being wrong with confidence.

"Assuming this is correct," Admiral Fitzwilliam added, "we may expect to see more and more alien forces diverted into jump-off locations for the planned offensive. That gives us a chance to go on the offensive ourselves, in tandem with our allies. The ultimate goal will be to punch our way through to the alien homeworld and force them to surrender."

"At the very least," Naiser injected thoughtfully, "it will force them to divert their fleets from the original front as we open up a new one."

"Correct," Admiral Fitzwilliam said. "The Tadpoles are, in fact, massing their own forces near Tadpole Prime. If the enemy weakens, they too will go on the offensive. We may see a repeat of the Battle of the Marne in space."

Susan nodded, thoughtfully. The Battle of the Marne had been studied, extensively, at the Luna Academy, even though it had taken place well before the first cosmonaut had been launched into space. The Germans, if she recalled correctly, had switched units from the west to the east, ensuring that they'd been caught in transit and unable to assist either front when the tide of battle turned against them. It was possible, she'd been warned, that something similar could happen in interstellar war. A scattered fleet might be defeated in detail before it had a chance to re-concentrate.

But the Germans didn't lose the war, not then, she recalled. *They just lost the chance to deliver a knock-out blow to either of their enemies.*

"Giving us a chance to crush enemy formations before they have a chance to re-concentrate their forces," she said, out loud.

"We certainly hope so," Admiral Fitzwilliam agreed. He smiled, as if he'd told a joke she hadn't heard. It made no sense to her. "What do you think of the concept so far?"

Susan hesitated. It wasn't as if she was surrounded by superior officers who'd never flown anything more complex than an office desk. Admiral Fitzwilliam was a war hero...they were *all* war heroes. Even Admiral Soskice had a sterling record for designing new weapons and putting them into play. There was no way they needed *her* to tell them the flaws in the plan, the little glitches that would make a theoretical concept utterly unworkable in the real world. Hell, they'd spoken in such general terms that it was hard to see any problems...

She looked up at the starchart and saw one. "The concept seems work-able, on the surface," she said. "However..." - she reached out and traced a line on the chart - "they would have ample opportunity to detect our fleet making its way towards their territory and shift units to face us. Their FTL communications system gives them a very definite unfair advantage. I don't think we could sneak a fleet up to their borders without being detected well in advance."

"We could sneak through the edges of their systems," Henry mused. "It isn't as if we haven't taken the long way around before."

"There would still be a risk of detection," Susan said. Admiral Fitzwilliam would *know* it, of course. Given interior lines of communica-tion, twinned with a FTL communications system, the enemy could blunt their offensive with ease. They might still lose, of course, but the costs would be high. The Royal Navy couldn't afford heavy losses. "I think..."

Her voice trailed off as it hit her. Captain Juliet Watson-Stewart...she shouldn't be present, not at a strategy meeting. Unless...unless...

"You think we don't *need* the tramlines," she said. "You think we have a way of getting there without using the tramlines."

Admiral Fitzwilliam smiled. "I told you she was smart," he said to Naiser. "And she's right."

Susan stared at him. Getting around the tramlines - moving FTL without following the whims of a poorly-understood network of natural forces - was the Holy Grail of modern science. Billions of pounds had been thrust into programs designed to find ways to avoid the tramlines.

But she'd never thought it possible, not until now. It had always seemed a pipe dream.

And FTL communications were a pipe dream too, she reminded herself. *We know they're possible now.*

He looked at Susan. "We think we can get a task force right into the enemy rear," he said, bluntly. "And no matter how swiftly they move forces from the front, they're still going to be in deep shit."

"And if we fail," Admiral Naiser said, "there's no way back. This may well be a suicide mission."

Susan smiled. "We lead, sir."

CHAPTER

FOUR

Captain Juliet Watson-Stewart took control of the holographic display, removing the starchart and replacing it with a string of equations that made no sense to Susan, followed by a line running between two gravity wells.

"I've been told to keep this simple," she said. Susan didn't miss the mixture of wry affection and resignation that flickered across Naiser's face. "Unfortunately, that means I'm going to have to simplify."

She paused for a moment, then went on. "An object's mass warps the structure of space - the greater the mass, the greater the warp. If you imagine space as a flat plastic sheet, the weight of each star leaves indents in the plastic - and, if the object is heavy enough, falls right through, leaving a tear behind. It's not a very good analogy, but it'll do.

"The warping eventually leads to gravity corridors running between sufficiently large centres of mass," she continued. "These corridors may actually play a role in holding the universe together - half the world's scientists think so, while the other half think they're nothing more than freak occurrences. Either way, we know that a low-level gravity field can be used to hop a starship along a tramline, while a high-level gravity field can be used to enhance a tramline to the point it becomes passable."

"Like the Tadpoles did," Susan said, just to show she was paying attention. "They opened up new tramlines and used them to attack us."

"Precisely," Juliet said. She nodded to the display. "Those tramlines, however, were always in existence. They were merely too weak to carry a starship without assistance. We - in the course of trying to unwrap the FTL communications system - stumbled across something a little more interesting. It is possible, it seems, to create a completely new tramline, if only for a few seconds. One just needs two gravity wells and a great deal of power."

"A *lot* of power," Naiser warned. "The output of every human battleship in existence would not be enough to produce a tramline."

"Thankfully, we can generate and store the power required," Juliet said. "However, it would be a one-shot device. Once you reached your destination, you would be unable to return by the same route."

Susan cocked her head. "You can't create the tramline permanently?"

"The power requirements rise towards infinity," Juliet said. "There are *some* theories allowing for creating and maintaining feedback loops, suggesting that it *is* possible to stabilise the tramline, but at the moment we're limited to a single jump. The tramline will fade into nothingness the moment you complete the trip."

"I see," Susan said. The Holy Grail...even being able to bypass the tramlines *once* would give humanity an *excellent* chance to catch the aliens by surprise. But if the operation failed, they'd have to fight their way back to safety, while the aliens threw more and more ships at them. "And this is how you plan to surprise the enemy?"

"Yes," Admiral Fitzwilliam said.

He retook control of the display and returned to the starchart. "The task force - we're still putting the details together with the diplomats - will proceed to New Finland, then head to UXS-566," he said. He tapped a dull red star on the edge of explored space. "According to our calculations, we should be able to jump from UXS-566 to ES-19...*here*. That will put the task force a mere four transits from the enemy homeworld, with two possible routes to follow to its destination. Assuming that the enemy detects your arrival in ES-19, you will still have several weeks before they can divert reinforcements from the front."

"Which doesn't include whatever they've held in reserve to defend their homeworld," Admiral Soskice warned. "They may have plenty of forces in reserve."

Susan nodded. Earth was hundreds of light years from the war front, but all of the Great Powers maintained sizable forces to defend humanity's homeworld. Earth had been attacked once, during the last war. Never again. There was no reason to assume the Foxes would have stripped their homeworld bare, just to push the offensive against the Tadpoles. The task force might encounter something it couldn't handle.

"If you cannot take their homeworld, we expect you to ravage their system and destroy their industrial base," Admiral Fitzwilliam said. "But if you *can* hold their system, if only temporarily, we believe we can use it to force them to surrender."

"Their natural response to a newcomer is a challenge," Prince Henry said. "To establish the pecking order, as it were. They'll surrender to us if we convince them they're beaten. And then the war will be over."

"So we have to give them a thrashing," Susan mused. "How very much like school."

Prince Henry's lips quirked. "In space and on the ground," he said, nodding to Brigadier Percy Schneider. "Assuming we can, the marines will be landed, with orders to dig in and hold. If they can't destroy our spaceheads quickly, they'll surrender."

"It seems there are a lot of assumptions in this," Brigadier Schneider observed. Susan had been thinking the same thing. "Your Highness, just how sure *are* you that they'll surrender?"

"Nothing is entirely certain," Prince Henry said. "It's quite possible that we've misunderstood what we've been told, even after capturing so many alien POWs. But even if we're completely wrong, hitting them in the rear will give us a realistic chance of either beating them or forcing them to retreat. Either way, we will be in an excellent position to end the war on decent terms."

Admiral Fitzwilliam met Susan's eyes. "Your opinion?"

"It sounds reasonable," Susan said, slowly. She rather suspected she would need to read through the datafiles before coming to any final conclusion. "And we have hedged a little, just in case the projections are wrong. Tearing the heart out of their industry will definitely shorten the war."

"They will also view it as dishonourable," Prince Henry said.

"Too bad," Schneider said. "Destroying their industrial base is the quickest way to end the war."

Susan was inclined to agree. Starships took months to construct, at least. A battleship like *Vanguard* required nearly two years, from the moment the keel was laid to the final fitting out and pre-release trials. Taking out the enemy shipyards would cut off their reinforcements, giving the human forces a window to crush the enemy and invade their home systems before the enemy rebuilt. And while the Foxes might view it as dishonourable, she found it hard to care. They'd *started* the damn war, after all.

"Admiral Naiser will command the task force, assuming we can get everyone else to agree," Admiral Fitzwilliam said. "Susan, *Vanguard* will serve as his flagship."

"Yes, sir," Susan said. The diplomats were going to have fun. *Everyone* wanted *their* officer to hold overall command. The Americans, the French, the Chinese...they'd all want to command the task force. And while Naiser was an experienced officer, he wasn't the only one. Sorting out the command structure would be tricky. "It will be a honour."

"Tell me that afterwards," Naiser told her. His lined face shifted into a tired smile. "You won't find it easy."

"Just remember to keep your hands to yourself," Admiral Fitzwilliam said. "Susan's ship is *Susan's*."

"You speak from experience," Admiral Soskice said. "Is Captain Pole still not talking to you?"

"We *did* get married, after she took early retirement," Admiral Fitzwilliam said. "And while we did separate, I don't think that was because she was my flag captain."

He glanced at Susan. "Don't be afraid to tell him to buzz off if he starts interfering in your command decisions," he added. "Captain Pole never hesitated to order me to keep my mouth closed."

Susan winced, inwardly. A captain was mistress of her ship, with sole responsibility for her fate. But when that ship played host to an admiral - or even another superior officer - it could lead to all sorts of problems. On one hand, an admiral had no right to issue orders to the ship's crew; on the other hand, what officer or crewman would *refuse* an order from his superior? She'd heard plenty of horror stories about toadying captains who'd allowed their admirals to believe they were allowed to micromanage their ships, as well as command their task forces. It wasn't going to be easy.

"I know my place," Naiser said, deadpan. "I'll stay on the flag bridge, if you don't mind."

"Not at all," Susan said.

"Percy" - Fitzwilliam glanced at Brigadier Percy Schneider - "will command the marine element. Ideally, he'll command the entire landing force, but we may have to compromise a little. The Americans and the French both have strong candidates for the role. Once you get down, Percy, you or the overall commander will have authority to accept surrender - or to offer it, if the operation goes belly-up."

"It will be an interesting challenge," Schneider said.

Susan nodded in agreement. The marines *had* landed on alien worlds before, back during the war, but this would be different. This time, the aliens were interested in the land, rather than the sea. There was enough space in the galaxy for humans and Tadpoles, but was there enough space for humans, Cows and Foxes? But then, she supposed, the two alien races *had* managed to work together. Unity, a world that was supposed to be shared between humans and aliens, had practically failed. The two settlements might as well be on different planets for all the contact they'd had.

"We will, of course, hash out the final details - as much as possible - over the next couple of weeks," Admiral Fitzwilliam said. "Susan, you'll be returning to *Vanguard* in five days - ideally, the refit will be completed within a fortnight. The task force should be assembled a week from then, hopefully. Unless the diplomats manage to screw the whole thing up..."

He shrugged. "John, you'll be boarding *Vanguard* at the same time?"

"It would be better to board *Vanguard* after the refit has been completed," Naiser said, after a moment. "Captain Onarina would probably prefer that my staff and I were somewhere else during the refit. I can stay on Nelson Base until then."

Susan resisted - barely - the urge to nod in agreement. *Vanguard* was far larger than *Warspite*, but she would still have found it annoying to cope with both the refit *and* demands from an admiral. Or, more likely, from his staff. It spoke well of Naiser, she decided, if he was prepared to accommodate her. And it probably worked in his favour too. He'd have more access to his future subordinates on Nelson Base.

"As you wish," Admiral Fitzwilliam said.

He smiled, rather thinly. "The downside is that you will also be joined by the press," he added. "A small selection of reporters will be offered the chance to accompany the task force, under the usual rules. Try not to insult them."

Oh, joy, Susan thought.

"I'll do my best," Naiser said. "But really...as long as they behave themselves, they should be fine."

"They'll be joining you after the refit," Admiral Fitzwilliam said.

He paused, looking from face to face. "I don't think I need to tell you," he said, "that this is top secret. We cannot hide the plans to dispatch another task force, but its ultimate destination is a secret. Officially, you'll be heading to Unity to reinforce the guard fleet there. I don't want a single *hint* to leak out from anyone in this room."

Susan frowned. "But if other governments know of it," she asked, "won't it leak out from them?"

"Only at the very highest levels," Admiral Fitzwilliam assured her. "Everyone below them is under the impression that we - that *you* - will be heading back to Unity. I don't want it leaking out until the task force is on the way."

"Yes, sir," Susan said.

It was unlikely, she knew, that there were any alien spies on Earth. The Foxes hadn't had *time* to convert humans to their cause, then slip them back into the Human Sphere. Even if they had, they'd stand out like sore thumbs. But it was quite possible that an alien picket was lurking somewhere near Earth, watching fleet deployments and monitoring radio broadcasts from a safe distance. They might just pick up on the fleet's *true* destination and send a message home.

And it will take us two months to reach UXS-566, she thought. *They'll have plenty of time to set up a welcoming committee.*

"Political considerations, of course," Admiral Soskice said. "The government's majority is slimmer than it might wish."

"That is true," Admiral Fitzwilliam confirmed. "We have to be careful."

Susan kept her face impassive. She had a nasty feeling that *that* discussion was well above her pay grade.

"Losing the fleet would be awkward," Prince Henry commented, dryly. "The public will probably be *very* concerned. And the media will have no trouble finding a bunch of so-called experts to condemn the plan."

He sounded bitter. Susan wasn't surprised. Prince Henry had been hounded by the media from the very day he was born, his life relentlessly scrutinised and every single one of his decisions called into question. He'd been tormented so badly that he'd joined the navy under a false name, then withdrawn from the Royal Family and accepted a post on Tadpole Prime, where there were no reporters. His children had grown up there, not really aware that they were part of the Royal Family. Hell, from what he'd told her, they weren't even on the Civil List.

Not that they need it, Susan thought, dryly. *An Ambassador's salary is quite enough.*

"I have no doubt of it," Admiral Fitzwilliam said. He rose. "John, you and I will discuss the finer details this afternoon. You'll want time, I assume, to chat with Captain Onarina?"

"Of course," Naiser said. He looked at Susan. "Would you care to join me for dinner tonight at the Royal Horseguards?"

"It would be my pleasure," Susan said. She'd heard good things about the Royal Horseguards, although she'd never been. Apparently, the hotel - inside the security zone - had a first-rate restaurant. Her father would pretend to sulk if she went, she knew, but she wasn't really being offered a choice. "What time?"

Naiser glanced at his watch. "1700? I'll book a table, then let you know."

"Yes, sir," Susan said. A working dinner would be tolerable. "I'll meet you outside."

"And I would like to invite you for coffee after this meeting," Prince Henry said. "Although we won't be going any further than the cafe across the road."

Susan nodded. She could murder a cup of coffee. Besides, she'd been hoping for a chance to chat to the prince and find out just how *certain* the xenospecialists were about their claims. If the aliens were truly driven by their own biology...

But women check out men and men check out women, even though it's rude to stare and it makes people uncomfortable, she told herself, dryly. *That's biological.*

"Percy, I'll be speaking with you later," Admiral Fitzwilliam said. "Is there any other business?"

"I plan to brief Captain Onarina on the new weapons mix," Admiral Soskice said. He arched an eyebrow. "I trust you will make yourself available?"

"I'm staying in London," Susan assured him, simply. She was curious, despite herself. She hadn't heard of any *radical* new weapons systems, but the Royal Navy was good at keeping secrets. "I'll be available for the next five days before I head back to the ship."

"Understood," Admiral Soskice said. He glanced at Fitzwilliam. "I believe that's everything."

"Then I declare this meeting adjourned," Admiral Fitzwilliam said. "As I said, everything we discussed is top secret. I would be seriously displeased if the BBC were to pick up on it before it's too late."

Susan nodded, then followed Juliet out of the room. She wondered, absently, if Juliet would be accompanying the task force. The chance to talk to such a genius…she made a mental note to check as they met Commander Outlander outside. She followed the younger woman down to the lobby, then recovered her terminal and waited for Prince Henry. There were seven new messages, six of them concerning *Vanguard*. The seventh was from Sandy Devonshire. Susan hesitated, unsure if she wanted to reopen Pandora's Box, then clicked on the email. It was a dinner invitation for the following night.

Dad must have given him my contact code, she thought. She read the message again, shaking her head. She'd dated Sandy when they were both seventeen, the year before she'd headed off to the academy. It hadn't lasted, but…she wondered, absently, what was going through his mind. *A meeting with an old friend or something else?*

But she didn't have any plans, did she?

She considered her options for a long moment. There wasn't much in London she wanted to see, beyond a handful of old bookshops that had somehow survived the bombardment. She'd never been a theatre snob, even when the streets had been packed with people going to see the shows. And she'd had no plans for the following night. Why not?

Susan keyed in a message, accepting the invitation, then looked up as Prince Henry appeared. He'd donned a heavy coat and a hat that hid his features, just enough to protect him from any marauding reporters. Susan doubted there would be many of them inside the security zone, but she didn't blame Henry for being paranoid. Reporters had come very close to ruining his life.

He gave her a tired smile. "Shall we go?"

"Why not?" Susan asked. Life on Earth - in London - couldn't be easy for a man who'd spent the last decade on Tadpole Prime. Cold, muggy, expensive and crowded…Earth looked like hell. "It's just across the road."

CHAPTER
FIVE

George had decided, long ago, that some complete bastard had decided that communal showers had to be as embarrassing as possible. Showers at Hanover Towers, thankfully, were single-sex; showers in the Royal Navy's Luna Academy put men and women together, relying on them to be professional when faced with temptation. But she had to admit it had prepared her for showering with the marines. She didn't feel particularly self-conscious as she washed herself, rivers of brown water and mud splashing down and vanishing into the pipes. It wouldn't leave her feeling *clean*, she knew from grim experience, but it was better than nothing.

They're preparing for the trials and tribulations of going on campaign, she thought, careful to avert her eyes as she stepped out of the shower. *And readying them for the deprivations they will have to face.*

She smiled at the thought. Her uncle had told her, back when she'd been a child, that there was no technological reason for the water restrictions onboard a large starship. Recycling the water wasn't hard - and besides, there was no shortage of comets that could be mined for water-ice if the ship was running short. But it allowed the Royal Navy to offer increased water rations as a reward for promotion, or even for good work. It was basic manipulation and it worked very well.

A dozen marines were dressing outside the shower, either preparing for the next exercise or heading straight to the barracks to catch up with their sleep. They paid no attention to her as she dressed, even though she looked more feminine than she had in weeks. She wasn't sure if they were being polite, if it was a quiet admittance she'd earned her place or if they were merely too tired to care. Some of the stories she'd read, while preparing to join the marines on exercise, had suggested that the sergeants put something in the water to dim the libido. Others insisted that the men were simply too tired to care. But then, there *was* a small town only a five-mile walk from the base. She would have been astonished if there wasn't a brothel somewhere down there.

She dressed hastily, then glanced at herself in the mirror. The green uniform made her look thin - she'd lost a lot of weight over the last month - while her face looked oddly skeletal, almost inhuman. Her black hair, cut close to her scalp, looked thin, as if she was on the verge of losing it. She could easily have passed for a teenage boy, if she'd wished. Shaking her head, she walked out the door. She should have time to get some sleep before the *next* series of exercises began.

And hopefully avoid the rest of the squad, she thought. No one had been remotely happy at how they'd been taken out, even though it hadn't *really* been George's fault. To be killed by their own side was embarrassing. *They won't wake me up just to yell at me some more.*

A young man wearing a lieutenant's uniform was waiting for her. "Complements of the CO, Ms Fitzwilliam," he said. "You're to report to him at once."

George tried hard not to groan. She was tired and sore...she needed food and sleep, perhaps not in that order. And the bloody exercises were due to continue for another fortnight...it was just like being on deployment, complete with bad food, worse sleeping quarters and the prospect of getting killed. But she knew better than to ignore the order. The base CO would be pissed. All her chances of promotion would vanish like a snowflake in hell.

"Thank you, sir," she managed. The young man looked depressingly fresh for someone who was supposed to be on deployment - or at least *pretending* to be on deployment. She felt a surge of hatred that was shocking in its intensity, a desire to just kick him in the nuts and swear blind it was an accident. "I'm on my way."

She scooped up a bottle of water as she made her way down to the doors and out into the open air. Night was slowly falling across the Brecon

Beacons, the sun vanishing behind the mountains that had tormented her for the last month. There were soldiers out there on SAS Selection, she knew, trying to make their way across the exercise ground before night fell completely. She'd had enough problems, merely working on the liaison course, to know she didn't have a hope of passing Selection, even if she'd been allowed to apply. The SAS, too, was an all-male unit.

Dering Lines Army Base looked oddly shabby, for one of the most important infantry training grounds in the United Kingdom. There was no escaping the sense of *age* around some of the barracks, even the ones that had been hastily erected to cope with the influx of new recruits - and conscripts - during the First Interstellar War. A dozen armed guards were clearly visible, marching to and fro; others, she knew, would be patrolling the fence or manning the guardpost at the gates. There had been a time when soldiers had gone unarmed on post, but that had changed after a series of terrorist attacks during the Troubles. Now, the guards had live weapons and the authority to use them if they believed they were under attack. It had come in handy during the Bombardment and its aftermath.

A flag fluttered in the breeze outside the main building, a stone construction that reminded her of Hanover Towers. The guards checked her ID, then pointed her towards the CO's office. She couldn't help noticing that the guards too looked remarkably neat and tidy for men who were supposed to be on deployment, one of them daring to throw her a 'come hither' grin that she ignored completely. But then, making a good impression was important too. The QRF on permanent standby in the nearby barracks probably looked a great deal nastier.

Looking good is not as important as being good, she thought. Her uncle and father had used to say that, causing no end of fights with George's mother. *And if mother saw me now, she'd faint.*

She sighed as she entered the outer office and announced herself to the CO's secretary. Her mother was a wonderful person, but there were times when George wondered what century her mother thought she was living in. She'd obsessed over George's coming-out ball, she'd insisted that George wore the finest clothes...even to the point of ordering her daughter to wear a wig, just to hide her short hair. It wasn't as if *George* was interested in winning a good husband, certainly not from the ranks of the aristocracy. All the *interesting* aristocrats had joined the army or the navy.

"You may enter," the secretary said.

George nodded and stepped into the CO's office. As always, there was a faint hint of impermanence about it, even though she rather suspected that very little had changed for the last fifty years. The table and chairs were designed to be broken down and transported from place to place, the filing cabinets sat on coasters that would make it easy for two men to move them down the corridor...the only thing that had changed, she thought, was the 'I Love Me' display on the rear wall. A dozen medals and commendations, all addressed to the CO; a set of photographs, some clearly from alien worlds...

Lieutenant-General Ball cleared his throat. George jumped, then hastily straightened to attention. She was worse off than she'd thought, she realised numbly. If she fell asleep on her feet, in front of the CO...she wasn't sure if that was a court-martial offense or not, but she was fairly sure it would earn her an unprecedented number of push-ups. The sergeants would have to invent some new numbers, just so they could give her them to do.

"Midshipwoman," the CO said. "I trust you have been enjoying yourself?"

George nodded, not daring to speak. Lieutenant-General Ball was an experienced combat soldier, someone who'd been in the army longer than she'd been alive. The army wouldn't have assigned him to the base if they hadn't felt he knew what was actually *important* - and what was nonsense dreamed up by some REMF in Whitehall. She couldn't help wondering if he classed *her* as a piece of nonsense dreamed up by an idiot. The training had been interesting - and even fun, afterwards - but she was starkly aware that she didn't even *begin* to match the Royal Marines.

"Glad to hear it," Ball told her. "You'll be pleased to hear that your orders have come down from London."

"Yes, sir," George said.

She wasn't sure, in truth, if that was actually good news. Hell, she wasn't even sure *why* she'd been given the training in the first place. Her uncle hadn't been very clear when he'd offered her the chance to study under the Royal Marines. Some of the marines had offered suggestions, ranging from the reasonable to the ribald, but none of them had quite made sense. If she'd wanted to join one of the handful of combat units women *could* join, she would have done it back when she'd turned sixteen, instead of joining the navy.

But I might have had to wait until I turned eighteen, she thought. *The army might not be so willing to take me when I was sixteen.*

"You're going to be reassigned to *Vanguard* as a liaison officer," Ball said. He gave her a droll smile. "I'm afraid this doesn't come with a promotion."

George blinked in surprise. A liaison officer? They'd had her running all over the Brecon Beacons just to make her a liaison officer? She'd *been* a liaison officer...well, she'd worked with the Royal Marines. She certainly wouldn't forget the hellish landing on Unity and the trek across the planetary surface in a hurry. If she'd known half as much as she did now back then...

She pushed the thought aside. Perhaps someone had decided she needed to train with the marines to be a *good* liaison officer. Or perhaps someone had something else in mind for her...she wouldn't know, she suspected, until the end of the next deployment. If she was going back to *Vanguard*...she had to smile. She would neither be First Middy nor a newcomer to the ship and her crew. Perhaps *this* time she would have a peaceful deployment.

There's a war on, idiot, she reminded herself. *And you're going to be serving on a battleship.*

Ball snorted. George dragged her attention back to him in a hurry.

"The good news is that you have four days of shore leave before you are required to catch a shuttle from London," Ball informed her. "I have been ordered to release you from my command and arrange transport to Cardiff, where you will be able to catch a train to your final destination. Your military card will take you anywhere within Britain."

George thought fast. It would take at least an hour to reach Cardiff, by which point the trains might have stopped running for the night. Coming to think of it, she had no idea just what the train service was *like* in Cardiff. The city had been devastated during the Bombardment and while she knew there had been a great deal of reclamation work, she'd heard that most of the survivors had chosen not to return. But the CO wouldn't plan to send her to the city if he hadn't thought she could make her own way from there.

I could hire a taxi for the drive to London, she thought. *Or find a place to stay in Cardiff.*

"Thank you, sir," George said. She made a mental note to check her terminal as soon as she left the base. Perhaps she could call a taxi from the nearest town, saving the military driver a long trip. And then she could make arrangements for a hotel in London. "Sir..."

She swallowed, hard. In truth, she wasn't sure she wanted to know. But her uncle had taught her the importance of facing up to the truth, whatever it was.

"Sir," she said. "How...how well did I do?"

Lieutenant-General Ball studied her for a long moment, his scrutiny reminding her of Mrs Blackthorn's expression after George had been accused - correctly - of playing a nasty prank on some of the younger girls. The headmistress had come very close to expelling her - and would have done, George suspected, if she hadn't had such strong family connections. She'd made George feel about an inch high.

And the lecture I got from my father only made it worse, she recalled. *I was lucky not to be grounded forever.*

"For someone who entered the training course with little practical experience in the skills taught to all soldiers, you did reasonably well," Lieutenant-General Ball told her. "Your shooting and unarmed combat skills were pitiful, but you learned quickly. Whatever basic training you did have wasn't *bad*, merely incomplete. Your academy training also prepared you for working closely with men - despite temptation, you made no attempt to take advantage of your sex."

George flushed. She'd been told, in no uncertain terms, that she would be treated as one of the boys - and that she was to *act* as one of the boys. Trying to use her feminine wiles - as if she'd had any, after tramping up and down the Brecon Beacons for hours - to get the marines to help her would get her kicked from the course and probably dishonourably discharged from the navy. She hadn't been inclined to argue. The Royal Navy had drilled strict rules on interpersonal relationships into her head from the day she'd first entered the academy.

"On the other hand," Ball continued, "you lack the endurance required of combat soldiers and, despite your best efforts, that is unlikely to change. You really came to us too late."

He met her eyes, evenly. "If you'd joined us in the normal way, you would probably have been binned by now," he added. "You're not lacking in determination and moral fibre, but you're physically incapable of meeting our high standards. You simply cannot carry as much as your fellows. A long march over the Brecon Beacons would probably kill you - or force your squadmates to decide between carrying you or leaving you behind. Either one might have proved costly."

"The spirit is willing," George mused, "but the flesh is weak."

"Correct," Ball said. "And as you know from experience, you don't get to shout *stop* in a combat zone."

He rose. "It's been interesting, having you here," he said. "And I wish you all the best in your future career."

"Thank you, sir," George said.

She saluted, then marched out of the office. The general's secretary might be a sour-faced prune - the administrative staff were treated as second-class citizens, as far as the army was concerned - but she was efficient. George's travel papers were already waiting for her, along with a brief outline of options for reaching London, Manchester, Edinburgh and Aberdeen. It looked as though there *were* late-night trains from Cardiff after all. Still, hiring a taxi would probably be quicker in the long run. She had the feeling she'd spend most of the trip snoring loudly.

"Collect your possessions from the exit barracks and change into civilian clothes, then report to the gatehouse," the secretary ordered, stiffly. "The jeep will be waiting for you there."

"Thank you," George said.

She walked to the barracks and recovered her bag from the staff. She'd been told to bring two sets of civilian clothes, as well as a handful of basic supplies, but most of them had been put into storage as soon as she'd reported to the base. Her terminal was sitting on top of her clothes; she clicked it on, watching as it linked into the datanet. Personal terminals were banned on the base, along with wristcoms and earphones. She'd never really understood the logic.

It felt odd, after wearing uniforms for nearly two months, to change back into her civilian clothes. The army clothes had been ill-fitting - she'd had to struggle to get bras that actually fitted her, not something she'd had to worry about in the navy - but they'd also made her feel part of something bigger, as if she actually fitted in. But now...she looked at herself in the mirror and sighed. Jeans, a shirt and a jumper...she looked like any other young civilian, perhaps one searching for her first job after completing her National Service. Shaking her head, she keyed a quick message into her terminal and headed for the gatehouse. If she was lucky, she'd be halfway to London by midnight.

And maybe Peter will be free, she thought. She'd exchanged a handful of messages with her boyfriend, but there'd been no privacy when she'd been using the public computers. Sexting had been completely out of the question. *We could meet in London.*

George shrugged as she reached the gatehouse. The guards processed her with commendable speed, checking her ID before altering it to make sure she couldn't swipe in and out of the base any longer. She couldn't help feeling oddly rejected, even though she knew it was absurd. No one was allowed to pass through the gates without clear authorisation from their superiors.

The army driver waved to her, cheerfully. "Where to, Miss?"

"The nearest town," George said, as she keyed her terminal. If there was a taxi firm there...if not, she'd just have to go to Cardiff. "And don't spare the horses."

"Of course, Miss," the driver said. Of *course* he would be flirting. She no longer looked like one of the boys. "We'll be there before you know it."

CHAPTER
SIX

"Susan," a voice called. "You look *very* different!"

Susan turned. That had been Sandy's voice, hadn't it? But for a moment, as she scanned the crowd, she didn't *see* him. And then she realised that the middle-aged man in front of her *was* Sandy. He'd changed. The gawky teenager she remembered had been replaced by a grown man wearing a black suit and tie, carrying a black briefcase in one hand. He looked muscular, like most young men who'd done two years of National Service, but it was clear that he was starting to put on weight. His brown hair was already starting to thin.

"Sandy," she said. "You look different too."

"Age comes to us all," Sandy said. He winked. "That and I can't afford expensive cosmetic treatments to regain my lost youth."

He looked her up and down. "You look better than I do," he added. "But that was always true."

Susan shrugged. As a teenager, she'd agonised for hours over what she should wear; as an adult, she'd pulled her one dress over her head and splashed a little make-up on her face. She had never been particularly vain as a child - and the navy had killed whatever tendency she'd had towards vanity as a cadet. Coming to think of it, so had boarding school. The one advantage of uniforms that came from a bygone age was that the richer kids weren't constantly flaunting their designer clothes in front of their poorer peers. And to think she'd hated the uniform at the time.

Sandy took her arm and led her down the street. "I was thinking we'd dine at the Raj," he said. "It's quite a good place to go, if you don't mind Indian food."

"I have no objections," Susan said. A lot of ethnic restaurants had been closed during the Troubles, but they'd had a revival recently. The Anglo-Indian War hadn't slowed it down, as far as she knew. She wasn't going to be accused of being unpatriotic merely for eating in an Indian restaurant. "Do you think we can find a table?"

"I called ahead," Sandy said. "They don't do reservations, but they often have empty tables while the crowds are at the theatre. It's a pain after they come out and start looking for somewhere to eat."

The Raj turned out to be a mid-sized restaurant staffed by young women wearing traditional Hindu clothes. They seemed surprised to see Susan, although Susan couldn't tell if they recognised her or if they were merely surprised to see an interracial couple. It *was* rare, something she regretted more than she cared to admit. The girls themselves were either the descendants of immigrants who'd assimilated or workers on a short-term work permit. She had to admit they were pretty enough to make her feel dowdy.

"It's traditional to order two or three dishes, then share," Sandy said, as Susan scanned the menu. "What would you like?"

Susan shrugged. There didn't seem to be anything particularly spicy on the menu, as far as she could tell. But then, she'd grown up eating her father's cooking - and he'd regarded chilli as a vital part of *everything*. Sandy ordered a couple of starters, then waited. Susan picked a couple of dishes largely at random, handing the menu back to the waitress. The food was important, but she was rather more interested in catching up with an old friend.

"So," she said. "What have *you* been doing since we last met?"

Sandy shrugged. "Two years of National Service, then a third year as a volunteer," he said, frankly. "The Reclamation Zones...they were a nightmare."

Susan leaned forward. "I've seen pictures," she said. "Was it really that bad?"

"Worse," Sandy said. "The tidal waves battered the west coast savagely, sending water ravaging east. Millions of people were killed, hundreds of thousands rendered homeless…we were pulling bodies out of the ruins every day. God alone knows who those people were, Susan. We never had time to do anything, but dump the bodies in a mass grave and cover them with earth."

Susan winced. It had become customary to assume, if someone had vanished during the Bombardment, that they were dead and gone, their body washed out to sea or dumped in a mass grave. Or eaten by wild animals. She'd heard stories of nature reclaiming entire towns, once the surviving population had been relocated. It would be decades, perhaps, before the mess was cleared up.

"And then we were struggling to clear up the mess," he added. "It was a real nightmare."

"It would have been worse if they'd won," Susan said.

"Probably," Sandy agreed.

Susan nodded as the starters arrived. "What are you doing now?"

"I went into business, working to reclaim the devastated lands," Sandy said. He gestured at his suit. "It pays…well enough for me to get this suit and tie."

"Very little, then," Susan said. "Or does that suit come from Savile Row?"

"I'll have you know it cost a couple of thousand pounds," Sandy said, in mock offence. He speared a piece of chicken with his fork. "There's quite a bit of money in reclaiming the lost towns and cities, Susan. You just have to know how to find it."

Susan lifted her eyebrows. "And where do *you* find it?"

"Depends," Sandy said. He nibbled his chicken for a long moment. "There's a lot of debate over how it *should* be reclaimed. We got the contract to rebuild a couple of seaside towns, after sifting through them for anything useful - or anything we can return to its owner. And we've been working on rebuilding some of the roads the army engineers didn't touch, back in the early days. *That's* hard going, let me tell you."

"You're doing well for yourself," Susan said.

"I saw an opportunity and took it," Sandy said. He smiled. "I went to work for the company after I was released from service, then clawed my way to the middle. You're talking to a regional director."

Susan cocked her head. "And you never married?"

"I was waiting for you," Sandy announced, deadpan.

"I'll have *you* know that I read engineering reports from men who think I'll be impressed if they constantly overestimate the time needed to repair the engines," Susan said. She jabbed a finger at him. "I know bullshit when I hear it."

Sandy shrugged. "I was in a couple of relationships," he said. "They never worked out. One woman dumped me for a wealthier man; I dumped the other when it became clear she was a gold-digger. You?"

"I've been too busy," Susan said. "Commanding a battleship leaves no time for romance."

"So it's not like Stellar Star," Sandy said.

"No," Susan said. She made a show of rolling her eyes. "If I did half the things *she* did, I'd be dishonourably discharged as soon as the court-martial board finished laughing. There's *nothing* realistic in that show, particularly not her chest size."

"No one watches it for realism," Sandy pointed out. "They watch it for beautiful women and strapping men."

Susan nodded. The Royal Navy had never been sure what to make of Stellar Star. She'd been on ships where the captain had quietly turned a blind eye to porn caches on the datanet, but exploded with rage at the mere thought of his midshipmen watching the latest season of *Stellar Star And the Magnificent Weapon*. On one hand, it did encourage youngsters to join the navy; on the other hand, it was so unrealistic that those youngsters were bound to be disappointed, once someone filled them in on the facts of life. *She* would have preferred them to be watching the shows the navy produced itself, but many youngsters found them boring. Realism needed to take a second place to entertainment.

She chewed the kebab thoughtfully, watching - with some amusement - as Sandy washed *his* down with cold water. The meat was spicy, but nowhere near as spicy as some of her father's more interesting dishes. She swallowed it, then tasted the chicken. It was more flavourful, but - again - it wasn't particularly spicy. Sandy seemed to feel otherwise.

"My company *is* looking for more personnel with military connections," Sandy said, as the waitress brought the main course and placed it on the table. "Would you be interested?"

Susan lifted an eyebrow. "Is this a recruitment dinner?"

"No," Sandy said, hastily. "But I would be remiss if I *failed* to bring the prospective opportunities to your attention."

"I think you need people with army connections," Susan mused. The military still controlled two-thirds of the reclamation zones. They made excellent training grounds for the young conscripts, as well as allowing them to help with the clean-up on the cheap. "I'm a naval officer."

"It would be fine," Sandy said. "Eastern Command likes people who speak the military lingo. Three years of National Service isn't enough."

Susan nodded, unsurprised. Every young man in Britain was supposed to serve his country for two years, yet National Service was considered the *least* of the service branches. Sandy might - technically - have been in the army, but the army probably didn't feel that way. A conscript, no matter how well he'd served, wouldn't be considered the equal of a volunteer, not socially. Sandy might have volunteered to serve for a third year, but he still wasn't considered a military man.

"The navy's my life," she said, finally. "I don't want to take early retirement."

"You might have to," Sandy pointed out. "What sort of prospects do you *have*, long term?"

Susan scowled. The blunt truth was that she had very few prospects - and she knew it. She had been unlikely to rise above captain even *before* relieving her former superior of command. Too many competitors, too few slots. Her family didn't have the connections to smooth her path to commodore, let alone the admiralty. She'd been lucky enough to be allowed to retain command of *Vanguard*.

And I won't be allowed to keep her for the rest of my career, she thought. It wasn't something she wanted to admit, but it couldn't be helped. *I'll either be promoted or pushed sideways.*

"I may never rise higher in the ranks," she said. "But that's not the point."

She sighed, wondering how she could explain it to a civilian. "Being in command of a starship is very different from anything else," she said. "I...I am solely responsible for a giant battleship. There's nothing you do that compares with it. You go into the office and work nine till five; I'm on duty all the time, even when I'm sleeping. I…"

"It sounds wonderful," Sandy said, sardonically.

"It is," Susan said. "I will eventually be pushed out of the command chair, I know. The Royal Navy dislikes leaving officers in command for more than a couple of years. But until then…she's *mine*."

She took a piece of *naan* bread and used it to wrap up the curry, chewing it slowly. It tasted different - better than the curries she'd eaten at her primary school - although it still wasn't particularly spicy. She was tempted to order the hottest thing on the menu, just to see what it was like, but decided it would be a waste of money. If she wanted something so hot that even *she* found it a challenge, she could just steal a precooked meal from her father's freezer and splash some of his homemade sauce on it.

"I did have another reason to ask you out," Sandy said, after they'd eaten their way through most of the main course. "There's some…uneasy questions rumbling through the corporate world."

Susan frowned. "I don't think *I'll* be able to answer them."

"There's the very real prospect of budget cuts," Sandy said. "Do you think that's likely?"

"I wouldn't know," Susan said. "I only know what I've read on the datanet."

She'd read a dozen political updates over the last couple of days, after Admiral Fitzwilliam's odd remarks, but the conclusions had been so widely varied that she'd found them completely useless. One analyst had insisted that the government's majority would remain strong, while two others had argued the exact opposite. Most of them had agreed that some things were going to change, but disagreed on what *would*. In the end, she'd done her best to put it out of her mind.

"But you're a serving officer," Sandy said. "Do you have any insights on the war?"

Susan kept her face expressionless. "I believe we will win," she said. "There's one alien empire facing both us and the Tadpoles. Their tech advantages are a problem, but we have faced that issue before and overcome it."

"Ah," Sandy said. "The *official* line."

"I have no reason to doubt it," Susan said, dryly. "The deceit regularly practiced by corporate hacks is largely absent from the navy."

"Idealist," Sandy charged, mischievously. He shrugged. "Jokes aside, it's rare for a corporate hack to *lie*. They just do their best to spin facts in their favour. I've fired people for spinning things so much that the essential truth is lost."

"How *honest*," Susan said.

"It's a matter of perception," Sandy said. "If we are seen as financially weak, our competitors will try to push us into situations that will tip us over the edge. It's in our interest to look strong, even if we're not. It helps keep us stable long enough to recover, as long as we're smart enough not to lie to ourselves."

Susan smiled. "Are you weak?"

"Not at the moment," Sandy said. "But if the government's budget is cut, for whatever reason, the knock-on effects might hurt us. So yes, we're trying to determine what might happen before it does."

"I think you'd be better off reading tea leaves," Susan told him. "The reports I read disagreed on almost everything."

"It would be cheaper too," Sandy agreed. He met her eyes. "Have you seen the protesters?"

"Yes," Susan said.

"There's a growing groundswell of discontent," Sandy said. "People thinking we should be investing more in Britain, rather than Britannia and the Royal Navy. Sending our ships millions of light years to fight a foe who poses no direct threat to us…they see it as a waste of resources."

"Better to fight over there than over here," Susan pointed out. "I was there when the Contact Fleet got jumped. The Foxes attacked without provocation."

She looked back at him. "Do *you* believe it's a waste? That we shouldn't be fighting the war?"

Sandy shrugged as he called for the bill. "From a strictly pragmatic point of view, Susan, we signed a treaty with the Tadpoles and we have to uphold that treaty. Doing otherwise will cause them to question our willingness to uphold *other* treaties. At best, they'll be disinclined to work with us in future; at worst, they may regard us as a prospective threat - again - and take steps to crush us. And, as you said, better to fight in their space than ours.

"From another point of view, we *are* wasting billions of pounds on fighting a war that could be better spent elsewhere," he added. "I could point to a dozen places in Britain that could use the investment. Hell, building more colony ships and freighters would be useful too, I think. From that point of view, the protesters have a point. The Tadpoles and our new enemies are distant. Our other problems" - he waved a hand around the room - "are in our face."

He paid, politely declining Susan's attempt to pay half, then rose and led her out onto the streets. Night had fallen; crowds of men and women were emerging from theatres and heading into the nearest restaurants. Susan followed him down towards Charing Cross, picking her way through the crowds. A line of policemen were positioned near Trafalgar Square, looking grim. The protesters, beyond them, were being confronted by a far larger crowd of angry civilians.

"Better to stay away," Sandy said, as they slipped up a side street. A number of policemen hurried past them, heading onwards to Trafalgar Square. "There's going to be trouble soon, unless I am very much mistaken."

"Probably," Susan agreed. There was a nasty feeling in the air, an ominous sense that violence was on the verge of breaking out. She hadn't felt anything like it since the last football match she'd attended, when the Royal Marines had played the Grenadier Guards on Britannia. Thankfully, the sergeants had put a break on the post-game shouting match before it had turned into actual violence. "We don't want to be arrested when the police squash the riot."

She followed him through a couple more streets until they stopped in front of a hotel, an old building that dated back over three hundred years. The doorman saluted, opening the doors for them. Sandy led her into the lobby, then stopped. Susan shook her head as she took in the golden statues and the animal heads mounted on the walls, silently recalculating her estimate of his earnings. The building was almost as luxurious as the MOD. It wouldn't open its doors to anyone who earned less than a hundred thousand a year.

"I'm staying here for the moment," Sandy said. His voice was suddenly serious. "Would you like to come up for a nightcap?"

Susan considered it, just for a moment. She knew what he had in mind and it didn't involve drinking. It had been a long time - a very long time - since she'd slept with anyone, let alone woken up in someone else's bed. Her body was suddenly intent on reminding her just how long it had been. It would be just a fling, she knew, something to enjoy before she went back to space...

"Of course," she said. She reached out and took his arm. "I'd like that."

CHAPTER
SEVEN

The bathtub, George decided, was large enough to float a small boat.

It was a bit of an exaggeration, she told herself as she lay back in the warm water, but the tub was definitely large enough for an orgy. Judging by some of the waterproof paintings on the wall, it *had* been used for an orgy. A dozen adults could have fitted comfortably in the tub, either relaxing in the hot water or enjoying themselves in other ways. She closed her eyes for a long moment, feeling the warmth slowly soaking into her body. Spending some of her trust fund on the Royal Hotel, the most expensive hotel in London, wasn't something she would normally do, but after training with the marines...

The terminal bleeped, once. She didn't even have to open her eyes or get out of the tub to answer. "Go ahead."

"A Mr. Peter Barton has arrived," a doubtful voice said. The receptionist had fawned over George as soon as she'd run her ID through the system, but Peter Barton probably looked a little more questionable to her eye. He'd be in hock for *years* if he tried to stay at the Royal Hotel. "Should we escort him up?"

Or call the police, George added, silently. The Royal Hotel had its own security staff, ready and able to throw out the riffraff. *They'd be happy to hold an intruder until the police arrived.*

"Please," she said, instead. "Buzz him into my suite when you arrive."

She kept her eyes closed until she heard the outer door opening, then opened her eyes and leaned forward. The escort - a man, judging by the voice - pointed Barton towards the bathroom door, then closed the outer door a little louder than strictly necessary. George concealed her amusement with an effort. Barton had either forgotten to tip or given an insufficient amount.

"Come on in," she called.

Barton opened the door and stared. "That's a swimming pool!"

"Close enough," George agreed. She wondered, suddenly, if she'd gone a little too far. He couldn't even *begin* to pay for the suite. "Get undressed and get into the water."

She smiled as she watched him take off his clothes. Barton probably wouldn't win any awards, but there was a rough edge to him that appealed to her, even though she knew her mother and sister would be horrified. It was a shame, almost, that she couldn't bring him as her guest to a family event, but the family would be shocked and he'd feel completely out of place. The romantic in her wondered about running off with him, somewhere; the practical in her pointed out that they'd never be able to stay together, but they might as well have fun until their final, inevitable, separation.

"You look different," Barton said, as he climbed into the bath. "Are you all right?"

"Thinner and stronger," George said. She wasn't about to admit that she'd ordered a large meal as soon as she'd arrived and eaten so much she'd nearly been sick. "The marines made me work for a living."

"I hope they're giving you hazard pay," Barton said. He swam over to her and kissed her, wrapping his strong arms around her upper body. "You're *really* quite thin."

"I don't think they know which department is meant to be paying me," George said. "I might have to do battle with the bureaucrats just to get my pay."

"Take a few of your new friends along," Barton advised, as he ran his hands up and down her body. "They can intimidate the beancounters into giving you what you earned."

George had to smile. "You managed to get down to London without trouble?"

"I was *in* London," Barton said. He smiled back at her, then pulled her closer. "Do you want to hear the news or make love?"

"Make love," George decided. It had been over two months since they'd last met, let alone had a private room. "You can tell me afterwards."

It was nearly two hours before they removed themselves from the bath, had a quick shower to wash away the traces of their lovemaking and ordered food from the kitchens. George felt almost human again, the pleasant glow of sex warming the parts of her the water hadn't been able to reach. Maybe their relationship wouldn't last - she *knew* it wouldn't last. She could still enjoy it for the time being.

"I don't believe the prices here," Barton said. He sat on the bed, gloriously naked. "How can *anyone* justify spending over two hundred pounds on a whole lobster? Or a chicken pie?"

"The people who come here are so wealthy they think nothing of it," George said. She'd never stayed at the Royal Hotel before, but she'd heard stories. Some of them had probably not been meant for her ears. "There are places where the total dinner bill is well over a thousand pounds."

"It's insane," Barton said.

George shrugged as she heard a knock on the door, then tapped the switch to unlock it. The maid didn't seem surprised by their nakedness. She merely placed the tray of food on the wooden table, took the tip George held out to her and then retreated, as silently as she'd come. Barton looked embarrassed when George turned back to him, even though he'd served in the navy long enough to be used to sharing the facilities. Perhaps it was different if one wasn't on a warship.

"That girl's skirt was so short I could see her bum," Barton said. He sounded astonished. "I...how does she walk around in it?"

"I could wear something like it," George offered, wickedly. "Would you like that?"

Barton flushed. "I'm afraid to cough in this place," he said. "I might break something."

"Don't worry about it," George said. She'd heard that the maids could be induced into guest bedrooms, if offered a sizeable tip. One of her distant relatives had been braying about it at a party she'd attended, although she hadn't understood most of the details at the time. "They'll have everything insured so completely that they can be replaced within the day."

She passed him his plate, then settled down to eat. "Why were you in London?"

"I was taking the mustang exams," Barton said. He held up his hand in salute. "You're looking at the latest officer-cadet!"

George grinned. "I thought you weren't interested!"

"I saw the light," Barton said. "Apparently *someone* told the chief that I was officer material, so I was put in for the exam. I spent the last month studying for it" - he paused, dramatically - "and yesterday I was told I'd passed!"

"Well done," George said. She was genuinely happy for him. "You should have told me."

"I wanted to surprise you, if I passed," Barton said. "And I wasn't sure what would happen if I failed."

George forced herself to remember. Mustangs - crewmen who became officers - were given a two-year course at the academy, rather than the four years she'd endured. The mustangs already *knew* the fundamentals of life in space. She wasn't sure what would happen to him after he was commissioned, assuming he passed his final exams. It was hard to imagine a mustang going into Middy Country.

Although it would have been very useful, she thought, seriously. She hadn't enjoyed her stint as the New Meat *or* as the First Middy. *Someone who knew they had nothing to prove.*

"I'm sure you'll do fine," she said. She sobered as a thought struck her. "You're not going to be heading back to *Vanguard*, are you?"

"No," Barton said. "I have orders to report to the academy in three days."

George felt an odd twist in her chest. Of *course* Barton wouldn't be going back to *Vanguard* - and even if he did, they couldn't carry on their affair onboard ship. Charles Fraser - her tormentor turned friend - had been right, when he'd pointed out that she was technically his superior officer. Having a relationship with him during shore leave was marginally acceptable. Having one onboard ship would earn them both a dishonourable discharge.

And yet…and yet, she knew she'd miss him.

"You'd better write," she said, jabbing a finger at him. "I expect to get a message from you every time I return to Earth."

Barton nodded. "Likewise," he said. He paused. "Are you allowed to write messages?"

"You can write," George said. "I wasn't allowed to receive messages during my first month, but…it might be different for you. You're already used to life on a starship."

She sighed. The academy's policy had seemed outrageously unfair, particularly after she'd been forced to write a letter home each weekend at Hanover Towers. Mrs Blackthorn had paced the classroom, reading the letters as they were written and making sure that nothing bad was said about the school. It had always surprised her that none of the wealthy or well-connected parents had complained. But then, she rather suspected that most of the parents had had the same treatment in *their* schools.

But the academy was different. Cadets had to learn, the hard way, that they would be out of touch with their friends and families for months, if not years. Their universe would shrink to the underground warren for the first six months, allowing them a chance to become accustomed to the claustrophobic conditions on a starship. And if they really couldn't hack it, they'd be released and sent home. The Royal Navy couldn't afford crewmen and officers who were unable to tolerate cramped working conditions.

And that's why a lieutenant's cabin seems so splendid, she thought, dryly. She'd been in Fraser's cabin a couple of times, back during her second cruise. The cabin had been small, but compared to Middy Country it was paradise. *The former midshipman is used to sleeping in a cramped room with five or six others.*

"We shall see," Barton said. "You can write me messages that will be held in the buffer, if necessary."

"Likewise," George said.

She finished her meal and put the plate back on the table. "Are you aiming at command yourself?"

"I'm not sure," Barton said, putting his own food aside. "The advisor I spoke to suggested I'd need to move off warships, if I wanted command responsibility. There are quite a few slots open on asteroid stations and mining ships. But being an XO doesn't sound too bad either."

He shook his head. "I'm not that old, am I?"

"I'll bring you a nice cup of warm milk and tuck you in," George teased. "And help you hobble to the bathroom in the middle of the night."

Barton smirked, then launched himself at her. George jumped aside, then darted around the room as he chased her. He caught up with her near the bed, pushed her onto it and started to tickle her mercilessly. George giggled, despite herself, as his fingers ran over her body, seeking out her most ticklish spots. And then he was on top of her, pushing her down...

"Give up?"

"Never," George said. She pretended to snap her teeth at him, then started to run her fingers down his back. "You'll have to do better than that."

"I'm young enough to catch you," Barton said, pulling back so he could start tickling her again. "You can't escape."

"Hah," George said. She forced herself forward, a trick she'd learned from the marines, then rolled over and off the side of the bed. "Bye-bye."

Barton snorted. "I'm really not that old."

"You're four years older than me," George said. She slipped up and sat next to him. "I don't think that'll hurt your chances *that* much."

"It depends," Barton said. "Either I'll be considered too old by the time I make lieutenant or I'll be charged with being stuck in Middy Country for *years*."

"Only if they don't read your file," George said. She wrapped an arm around his shoulders. "I think you're worrying over nothing."

"I hope you're right," Barton said.

George nodded. *She'd* been allowed to enter the academy at sixteen, but she'd been a special case. It was more normal for cadets to enter the academy at eighteen, after completing an extra two years in school. And the average age of a newly-minted midshipman was twenty-two. A midshipman who was twenty-eight - or older - would raise eyebrows. Barton would have the same problem as Charles Fraser, only worse. His superiors would wonder if he was incompetent, merely because he hadn't been promoted. They'd have to read his file to know he'd been commissioned at twenty-eight.

And what does happen, she asked herself, *to commissioned mustangs?*

"That's enough about me," Barton said, seriously. He tickled her back, pushing her towards him. "What about you?"

"I'm going back to *Vanguard* as marine liaison," George said. "I don't know if that means I'll still be serving as a midshipwoman too."

Barton frowned. "That's odd," he said. "Normally, there isn't a dedicated liaison officer."

"I worked with them," George reminded him.

"Just as a shuttle pilot," Barton pointed out. "You weren't actually *meant* to be fighting with them, were you?"

George shrugged. Fraser had insisted on her actually working *out* with the marines, although she knew they'd been holding back when they'd sparred with her. But she knew that wasn't what he meant. She *hadn't* been intended to crash-land on Unity, let alone join the marines as they fought the aliens. It simply hadn't been her day.

"If there is a dedicated officer…"

Barton's voice trailed off. "If there is," he said after a moment, "someone must expect a major deployment. I wonder where you're going."

George frowned. "I was just called back to the ship," she said. The notification she'd been given had been short on actual detail, let alone hints on what *Vanguard* would be doing in the future. "The refit must be nearly completed by now."

"And the ship will be heading back to the war," Barton said. "Perhaps they intend to retake one of the occupied systems."

"Maybe," George said. She didn't have access to any classified information - her uncle would have gone ballistic if she'd asked for a private briefing - but she knew that the only occupied worlds belonged to the Tadpoles. There were no land-based civilians to get in the way of orbital bombardment, if the aliens refused to surrender after the orbitals were captured. "But why would they *need* to?"

"There might be some industry on the surface," Barton suggested. He sounded as if he was grasping at straws. It wasn't a convincing argument and he knew it. "Something valuable enough to make landing an invasion force worthwhile."

"I think anything like that would have been destroyed before the world was occupied," George mused. "The Tadpoles wouldn't have left their tech around for the enemies to capture."

She considered it for a long moment. Any major enemy presence could be blasted from orbit, ensuring that there was no risk of losing a single marine. A handful of aliens might survive, if they were careful. But they wouldn't pose any threat, not on a Tadpole world. There was no logical reason to divert a marine division - or whatever - to hunt the remnants of the occupation force down. And yet, if Barton was right, *someone* expected the marines to be heavily involved in the next deployment.

"We might be hitting an alien world," she mused. "If we were to thrust upwards to UXS-469 and then into alien territory…"

"Perhaps," Barton agreed. He frowned, clearly unconvinced. "But you'd think we could force them to surrender, once we stripped the world's high orbitals bare. They wouldn't have a hope of keeping us from turning their world into ash."

"I suppose," George said. "Unless they're daft enough to think they can hold out under heavy bombardment."

She held him close for a long moment, feeling oddly conflicted. This was, if she wanted it, the perfect opportunity to end their relationship on a high note. Three days and nights of doing nothing, but making love… she smiled as she remembered the paintings in the bathroom. Some of the acts looked physically impossible, unless the participants happened to be contortionists, yet some of the others…they looked like fun, if they tried. And then, she could allow the letters to dry up until they were separated completely. He wasn't exactly a poor catch. There would be other women in his life.

And yet, part of her didn't *want* to let go. She liked him, in and out of bed.

Don't be fucking stupid, she told herself, firmly. What were they? *Romeo and Juliet?* A thousand bad stories and worse movies told her that their relationship had no future. *You come from different worlds. What sort of future could the two of you have?*

She kissed his chin, torn between the hope he'd do something worthy of a peerage and the grim awareness that it was unlikely. Even if he did… would her family approve? Or would they refuse to accept the match? She could argue it either way. Barton was hardly unintelligent, but he hadn't distinguished himself either.

"Three days," she said, out loud. They'd have fun, if nothing else. And they could have a more serious chat the day he left for the academy. If he found someone else, while she was gone, she wouldn't mind. She told herself she wouldn't mind. "I hope you weren't planning to leave this room for three days."

"Not at all," Barton said. His fingers traced lines around her breasts, making her gasp in pleasure, then reached down to stroke between her legs. "Food, drink, a bed, a bath…what more do we need?"

George smiled, then shifted until she was kneeling in front of him. "Nothing," she said, seriously. She held his manhood in her hand for a long moment, feeling him stiffen against her palms. "Nothing at all."

CHAPTER
EIGHT

"We've been cleared through the no-fly zone," the pilot said, as the helicopter flew over the Derbyshire countryside. "Ground-based defences are tracking us now."

"Good," Henry said.

He leaned back in his chair and watched as Haddon Hall came into view. It had been the county seat of a duke, if he recalled correctly, before the Troubles. Now, it belonged to the Royal Family as a holiday resort and emergency bolthole. Putting his family there wasn't the kindest thing he could have done, he knew, but it kept them away from both London *and* the never-to-be-sufficiently-damned media. It wasn't Tadpole Prime, with its warm beaches and relaxed attitude to life, yet there was plenty within the grounds to keep a trio of young girls occupied.

It was a beautiful building, he had to admit. An old manor house, surrounded by greenery; a lake, large enough to boat on…there were times when the perks of being part of the Royal Family made the whole hellish experience seem worthwhile. And yet, he would have given it up in a second, if he could. The price was far too high.

And they'll try to keep me from returning to Tadpole Prime, he thought, grimly. It didn't take a genius to see the writing on the wall. He'd been Earth's ambassador to Tadpole Prime for nearly a decade. Even if his country had no objection to him continuing in that role, other countries would want a chance to put their own man in. *I may have to find somewhere else to hide.*

The helicopter touched down neatly on the landing pad, a pair of armed guards hurrying over to check his ID before letting him pass through the gates. Haddon Hall looked innocent, but it *was* a high-security zone. No one was allowed to enter without proper clearance, countersigned by Henry himself. The media had already pitched a fit after two of their cockroaches had been roughed up by the guards. Henry found it hard to care. He'd never enjoyed being a prince and his daughters, no matter what the family claimed, were *not* princesses.

Well, not official princesses, he thought, wryly. *They're my princesses.*

He strode up towards the hall as thunder rumbled in the distance. It was going to rain soon, he suspected. Dark clouds were already drifting south. England was known for rain, but the Bombardment had done a *lot* of damage to the planet's weather systems. Even now, ten years later, the weather could change with remarkable speed. But then, he thought, that had always been true.

"Your Highness," the butler said, as he opened the door. "Your wife is in the front parlour, waiting for you."

"Thank you," Henry said. He surrendered his coat, then turned to walk down the corridor. "And my daughters?"

"I believe they went out riding this morning," the butler informed him. "They should be back at any moment."

"Before it starts raining, one hopes," Henry said. *He'd* ridden in the rain, but it wasn't something he would encourage his daughters to do. "Please ask them to come find me when they return."

He smiled as he walked down the corridor. Young girls were *mad* about horses - and his three daughters, apparently, were no exception. He'd insisted that they learn to take care of the beasts - feeding them, tending them, mucking out the stables - as well as learning to ride, despite their protests. Riding horses *almost* made up for having to leave Tadpole Prime and all the friends they'd made there. But he would be surprised, in all honesty, if they hadn't started to feel a little confined. Haddon Hall was hardly HMP Brixton, let alone Colchester Military Detention Centre, but they were rarely allowed to leave the estate. And there were no other children to play with, not on the grounds. They had to make their own entertainment.

"Henry," Janelle said. She sounded tired - and bored. "Welcome home."

Henry felt a stab of guilt as he gave his wife a hug. His daughters weren't the only ones who'd been dragged away from their home and friends. Janelle, the wife of the lead ambassador, had been an important person on Tadpole Prime. She was still an important person on Earth, Henry knew, but the price was a lot steeper. Despite his best efforts, he hadn't been able to prevent reporters from digging into his wife's past, or making mountains out of molehills. There was even a nasty rumour flying around that Janelle had had a relationship with Admiral Smith. And to think there'd been nearly forty years between them!

"I'm going back to space," he said, shortly. He didn't know how to sugar-coat the truth. His wife had been a spacer, before they'd married. She knew the facts of life. And yet, neither of them had been in the military for over a decade. "They want a liaison officer along for a joint offensive."

"There have to be others," Janelle said. But there was no real heat to her voice. She knew as well as he did that there were only a few experienced officers who'd also served as ambassadors. "When are you leaving?"

"A fortnight, I think," Henry said. It wasn't entirely true. He knew he couldn't stay at Haddon Hall for more than a few days. *Someone* would have to organise the xenospecialists as they readied themselves for the move. Hell, he'd have to decide who was allowed to accompany the task force and who was too valuable to risk. "I should have at least four days here."

"Good," Janelle said, tartly. "You can sit down with Victoria and explain the facts of life."

Henry blinked. "...What?"

"That she can't leave the grounds and that she can't have any of her friends come to visit," Janelle told him. "She threw a tantrum last night because Donald didn't invite her to his birthday party."

"He's hundreds of light years away," Henry protested. Donald - two years older than Victoria - was still on Tadpole Prime, as far as he knew. "How can she...?"

"She's eight years old," Janelle reminded him, sharply. "All she knows is that she's been dragged away from her home and dumped in a miserable place where there's no one to play with apart from her sisters and servants, the youngest of whom is at least fifteen fucking *years* older than her! She is not *happy* here!"

"And would she be happy," Henry asked, "if we sent her to Hanover Towers? Or Greenstones?"

"She's too young for boarding school," Janelle snapped. "And even if we did send her, would it be safe?"

Henry winced. He'd been sent to boarding school as soon as he'd turned twelve, four years older than his daughter. And it *hadn't* been safe. Sadistic teachers, nasty pupils who joked about beating up their future king...if he ever met one of the writers who waxed lyrical about life in a boarding school, he was going to take the headmaster's cane, sharpen the tip to a point and ram it up their backside. It was clear that none of those writers had ever *been* to boarding school. The schools were certainly no place for an eight-year-old girl.

Not to mention the reporters swarming around like flies, he thought, sourly. *And someone from the palace will try to convince the headmaster to cooperate with the media.*

He shook his head. He'd tried to remove himself from the line of succession, but Buckingham Palace had blocked him from removing himself completely. His sister would take the throne - she wanted it, the silly goose - yet if something happened to her, Henry and his daughters would be first in line. He hadn't managed to remove *them* from the line of succession either. And, with the government's majority slowly being eroded, some ministers would probably be tempted to use his daughters to divert public attention.

"I'll talk to her," he said, finally. "What about the others?"

"They're playing with horses," Janelle said. "But they miss their friends too. Is there no way we can invite others to play with them?"

Henry made a face. "It would cause too many problems," he said. He *could* try to invite some of the aristocratic children, but what did they have in common with *his* kids? "And bringing their parents into the hall would cause other problems."

"Of course," Janelle said, sardonically. "Is there nowhere else we can go?"

"Not unless you *want* reporters swarming around you like flies on rotting meat," Henry reminded her. "The security requirements alone would draw their attention."

He sighed. He'd spent a great deal of time ducking his father's... *requests*...that his grandchildren be formally presented at court. There was no way he would allow it, not until the girls were old enough to make up their own minds. Once they were presented, there would be no way to remove them from the Royal Family. Henry was a grown adult and yet even *he* had problems.

And it would be worse if I had nothing to do, but sit around and wait to be king, he thought, feeling an odd flicker of sympathy for his sister. She was in training for a job, but she could only *do* that job when her father died. It was quite possible that she'd be in her fifties when her father finally shuffled off the mortal coil, with children and perhaps even grandchildren of her own. *How long would it be before I was wishing my father dead?*

He pushed the thought aside as a maid entered, carrying a tea tray. His father wasn't a bad man, and he made a splendid king for ceremonial occasions, but he'd long since lost the urge to reform the monarchy. The parasites surrounding the crown had made sure of it, preventing him from changing anything. He was king, but king in name only. In truth, he was little more than one of those expensive dolls Henry's sister had used to play with. He spoke, but only as he was commanded; he dressed, wearing only what he was told to wear. Henry knew, all too well, why so many members of the family went off the rails. They were trapped in a gilded cage.

"Thank you," he said, as the maid poured tea. "We'll have dinner in the small room tonight, if possible."

"Of course, Your Highness," the maid said.

Janelle looked unhappy as the maid curtseyed and retreated, closing the wooden door behind her. Henry didn't really blame her. Servants had been a part of his life from birth, but people who weren't raised in upper-class households found them a little creepy. *Henry* knew, better than most, just how easily servants could *betray* their masters. Snow would fall in hell before he forgave his former nanny for publishing a book about his early years. The bitch had gleefully violated a non-disclosure agreement and gotten away with it.

Because they thought she made me sound like an idealised child, he thought, sourly. The book wasn't *exactly* a pack of outright lies, but the nanny had done a great deal of lying through omission. *I wasn't one of those Purity Sue's from Victorian storybooks.*

"There's no one here for me to talk to either," Janelle said. She took her cup and sipped thoughtfully. "I think I'm going to go mad."

"You can write emails," Henry reminded her. "Or..."

Janelle put the cup down, hard. Warm liquid splashed onto the table.

"You know better than that," she snapped. "There's no one here to talk to and you know it!"

Henry winced. Janelle had never been friendless, not until now. She'd been popular on *Ark Royal*, then the most important woman on Tadpole Prime...now, she had no one to talk to, save for servants who were unlikely to disagree with her about anything. And the servants might not even be *trustworthy*! Who knew which of Janelle's remarks would be spread across the datanet in less time than it took to make a cup of tea? Janelle was isolated and alone and...

"I wish I had a better solution," he said, finally. He *could* take his wife with him, couldn't he? But that would mean leaving his preteen daughters to the tender mercies of the Royal Family. They wouldn't be harmed, but they'd be trapped. "Do *you* have one?"

Janelle glared at him, but said nothing. Henry felt another stab of guilt, mixed with annoyance. She'd known what she was getting into when she'd married him. Maybe it would have been hard to extract herself from him beforehand, if she'd wanted to, but it should have been possible. He could have pulled strings to get her a posting somewhere far from Earth. The media would have given up on her eventually.

But imagining the life is far different from actually living it, Henry thought. He'd lost count of the number of gold-diggers he'd met at court. *And she can't leave without triggering a tremendous fight.*

The door opened. Victoria stepped into the room.

Henry resisted, barely, the urge to sigh. Victoria was wearing muddy jodhpurs and a straw hat that fell down over her eyes. Her shirt was wet - Henry glanced out the window and saw that the skies had opened, cold rain plummeting down to splash off the windowpane. And she smelt of horse. She clearly hadn't bothered to shower before coming to find him.

"Daddy," she said. She ran forward and gave him a hug. "Are you staying? I want to show you Trigger and Daisy and Flower and...the *Swallow* and..."

"I'll be staying for a while," Henry promised. His oldest daughter smiled so brightly that he thought a second sun had blazed to life. "What's the *Swallow*?"

"The boat," Janelle said. She sounded as if she was torn between amusement and disapproval. "They've been taking her out on the lake every day."

"She's *fantastic*, dad," Victoria said. "We went fishing and I caught a dozen fish and I threw them back into the water and James told me I could have had them for dinner and I thought it was cruel because the fish might have been a Tadpole and he..."

She broke off, gasping for breath.

"Breathe," Henry said, with some amusement. It wasn't *too* likely that any fish on the estate were secretly intelligent, but it was a valid concern on Tadpole Prime. Oddly, the Tadpoles themselves didn't seem to care about their children. Only a relative handful ever grew up into adulthood. "Did you have fish for dinner?"

"Fish are *sweet*," Victoria said. "We had pork instead. Pigs are *ugly*."

Henry had to smile. "I'm sure it was a good dinner," he said. The food at Haddon Hall would be first-rate, of course. Only the best for the aristocracy. "What else have you been doing?"

"We found a maze, but it was pathetic," Victoria insisted. "We couldn't get lost, no matter how hard we tried. It was easy to find our way out. And we tried to build a treehouse, but mummy wouldn't let us climb the tree... can we, dad? Can we?"

"I think you should listen to your mother," Henry said, firmly. Building a treehouse might be fun for teenagers, but dangerous for preteens. "Or you can ask James if he and the staff would like to build one for you."

"It wouldn't be the same," Victoria said. Her face fell. "We had a treehouse back home."

"You didn't build it," Henry said, trying to ignore the odd twist in his heart. *Home*, as far as Victoria was concerned, was Tadpole Prime. "You can try to build one when you're old enough."

"I miss my friends," Victoria said. She looked up, suddenly hopeful. "Can I invite them for my birthday party?"

Henry glanced at Janelle, helplessly. She raised an eyebrow, silently challenging him to think of an answer that wouldn't result in tears. Victoria's birthday was a month away, when he'd be halfway to enemy space. *He* wouldn't be there. And even if he was, there was no way Victoria could invite her friends. They were either on Tadpole Prime or scattered around the Human Sphere. Her ninth birthday would be the loneliest she'd ever had.

"I'm afraid they won't be able to make it," Henry said, finally. He wanted to tell his daughter a comforting lie, but what could he say? "They're a very long way away."

"That's what Patty said," Victoria reminded him. "And *she* made it back in time for Ling's birthday party!"

"Your friends are much further away," Henry told her. Patty was the American ambassador's stepdaughter, if he recalled correctly. He'd been recalled to Earth for consultations, taking his stepdaughter with him on the assumption he might not be allowed to return. But he *had* returned, just in time for the party. "And they can't come here."

"I hate this place," Victoria said. She kicked the seat. "It's cold and there's no one to play with!"

"You have your sisters," Henry reminded her.

"They're *babies*," Victoria protested. "*Children!*"

Henry wondered, absently, if he'd ever said that about *his* sister. He couldn't recall…but then, he'd never had the chance to get used to playing with other children. Victoria knew nothing of the social or political realities, not really. All *she* knew was that she'd had friends, a year ago. Now, she was trapped in a gilded cage, completely alone save for her younger sisters. The estate was large enough for a dozen children her age, but she could never go beyond the wall.

"I know how you feel," he said, hugging her. "But we can't go back until the war is over."

Victoria looked up at him. "And when *will* the war be over?"

"I don't know," Henry said. He didn't know if Victoria even knew what a war was. She certainly didn't know what it meant. "But when it is, we'll go home."

And he hoped, desperately, that he'd be able to keep that promise.

CHAPTER

NINE

"There she blows, Captain," the pilot said.

Susan put down the datapad and leaned forward as HMS *Vanguard* slowly took on shape and form. The giant battleship had been moved out of the repair yard and was now floating in space, just inside the security perimeter surrounding the shipyard. A blaze of light surrounded *Vanguard*, allowing her to see the handful of repair modules clustered close to her ship. It was hard to be sure, but - as the spotlights played over *Vanguard's* dark hull - it was clear that additional point defence clusters had been added to her defences.

"She's impressive," the pilot said. "You must be very proud."

"I am," Susan said.

HMS *Vanguard* looked like a giant dumbbell, although only an idiot would say that where her crew could hear. Four massive turrets at the prow, four more at the rear; her hull bristled with missile tubes, point defence weapons and sensor blisters. Her mighty drives were clearly powered down, but there was still a sense that she could leap forward and smite the enemies of Britain at any moment. A dozen shuttles were docked at various airlocks, suggesting that some of her crew were returning from shore leave; a handful of men were going EVA and inspecting the outer hull. Susan sucked in a breath, despite herself, as the battleship grew larger and larger until she was dominating the scene. *Vanguard* wasn't the largest starship ever built and put into service, but she was perhaps the most *advanced* ship for her size.

And the only bigger ships are the giant colonist-carriers, she thought. Even now, with a war on, the colonist-carriers were still carrying hundreds of thousands of settlers away from Earth. *Even the bulk freighters don't come close.*

The pilot cleared his throat. "We've been ordered to dock at Airlock One," he said. "Is that suitable?"

"It will suffice," Susan said, grandly. It wasn't a problem, although she knew that some commanding officers would interpret it as a snub - or a deliberate insult. Commander Paul Mason, her XO, knew how much she disliked pomp and circumstance. "Take us in as quickly as possible."

She'd seen the reports, in-between reading countless technological and sociological assessments Admiral Fitzwilliam had seen fit to forward to her, but seeing the battleship in person always took her breath away. Her eyes traced out the emplacements, noting the points where the newer weapons had replaced the old. Admiral Soskice had insisted that the latest generation of missiles had more range and destructive power than anything the Royal Navy had deployed before, but they were over a third larger than standard missiles. The entire missile tube structure had had to be pulled out and refitted before the latest missiles could be loaded onto the ship.

And they may still be ineffective against enemy point defence, Susan thought. Lasers and pulse cannons could take out missiles well before bomb-pumped lasers could pose a serious threat. *We'd have to fire hundreds just to be sure of scoring a hit.*

"Wow," the pilot breathed.

Susan followed his gaze. Dozens of worker bees - and men in suits - were swarming around Turret Four, adjusting the giant plasma cannons. Susan allowed herself a tight smile as a sheet of solid-state armour - the latest, she'd been assured - was bolted into place, providing protection against anything short of a focused nuclear blast. *Vanguard* could have wiped the floor with the fleets that had fought the First Interstellar War, she thought. Even *Ark Royal*, the heavily-armoured supercarrier, wouldn't have posed much of a threat.

Unless we were rammed, she thought. *Crashing a supercarrier into a battleship would destroy both ships.*

She scowled at the thought. She'd seen the footage of *Ark Royal's* last moments, everyone had. There was something obscene about the way two mighty ships had collided, the destruction ripping both ships apart in terrifying slow motion. The explosions had come late, too late. It was hard to escape the sense that one or both ships might have survived, even though she *knew* it was unlikely. Ramming was almost always fatal.

The shuttle shuddered, slightly, as it docked with *Vanguard*, the gravity flickering a second later as its onboard field matched the battleship's. Susan heard a low hiss as the airlock opened, catching a faint whiff of her ship's familiar scent as air blew into the cabin. She picked up her bag, slung it over her shoulder and headed for the hatch. It wasn't as if she had much to carry. She'd always travelled light.

Father drilled that into me from a very early age, she thought, ruefully. *And it came in handy, didn't it?*

She smiled at the thought as the inner hatch hissed open. There was no mistaking the heady scent of a warship that had seen combat, even though it was mixed with scents from the repair crews and new components that had been inserted into the hull. She closed her eyes for a long moment, feeling as though she was finally home. The dull thrumming echoing through the hull - the fusion cores, even though the drive was powered down - seemed to be welcoming her.

"Captain," a voice said. "Welcome back."

Susan opened her eyes. Commander Paul Mason was standing there, wearing a duty uniform that had clearly seen better days. She made a mental note to ensure he ordered a new one before Admiral Naiser and his staff boarded the battleship. Admiral Naiser would understand the realities, of course - he'd been a serving officer during wartime - but his staff might not be so forgiving. She didn't have *time* to correct them, even if she had the authority.

"Thank you," she said. She returned his salute, then shook his hand. "It's good to *be* back."

They fell into step, heading down towards the bridge and Susan's ready room. "I trust you had a pleasant time on the surface," Mason said. "Did they take it out of your shore leave?"

"Only a couple of days," Susan said. "I spent most of the last month at the Admiralty or the MOD."

"A terrible holiday," Mason said, wryly. "How was your father?"

"Growing insistent about grandchildren," Susan admitted. Mason was an old friend. She could talk freely to him. "He seems to think he won't have anyone to dandle on his knee."

"It isn't as if you're *that* old," Mason pointed out. "And you do have frozen eggs, don't you?"

Susan nodded. It was a standard precaution, one the navy offered for free. Men were invited to freeze sperm; women were invited to freeze eggs and embryos. Modern medicine had ensured that women could have children into their late seventies, but spacers faced the very real risk of radiation damage and other threats. If worst came to worst, she could have a child grown in an exowomb. But she wasn't sure if she could handle a child when she turned seventy.

I'm in my early thirties, she told herself, sternly. *I have plenty of time to get married or birth a child.*

She sighed, inwardly. A couple of generations ago, women who refused to have children - or put having kids behind their career - had faced social ostracism. Britain's native population had been in decline before the Troubles and, afterwards, motherhood had come to be seen as far more important. But now...she knew she could have both, if she wanted it. She just wasn't sure she *did*.

"*Fathers*," she said. She changed the subject before it could get any more embarrassing. "Did you manage to take a few days off?"

"Got to visit Sin City for a couple of days," Mason said. "Had to make some trades, though."

"Oh," Susan said. "Do I want to know?"

"It's growing wilder," Mason said. "But it still doesn't live up to memories."

Susan smirked. Sin City - the *original* Sin City - had been destroyed during the Battle of Earth. She rather doubted the Tadpoles had known what they'd hit, when they'd fired on lunar installations, but it hardly mattered. *Nothing* could have galvanised every spacer in the system into throwing *everything* at the invading aliens more than the destruction of Sin City and its semi-illicit pleasures.

And the new one is much more controlled, she reminded herself. *And it isn't really a bad thing, is it?*

She dismissed the thought as they stepped through the hatch and into her ready room. Mason had practically taken it over, like before. He'd turned the sofa into a bed and covered the desk in paperwork, both physical and electronic. A bottle of wine sat on the desk, two empty glasses placed next to it. And a giant hologram of *Vanguard* floated over the desk.

"I was lucky enough to pick up a bottle of Luna Picard 2200," Mason said, picking up the bottle to show her. "It may well be one of the few surviving bottles from that vineyard."

"I doubt it," Susan said. The vineyard domes on the moon had been damaged in the war, but not *that* badly. "It would cost a bomb if it *had*."

Mason shrugged, pouring them both a glass. "It cost more than I care to think about," he said. "Thankfully, the guy who was trying to outbid me fled the auction room before he had to pay."

"I don't want to know," Susan said. She'd never understood Mason's fascination with auctions. It wasn't as if he had any *use* for half the things he bought. Hell, getting them back to his home would be a struggle. "How much did it cost you?"

"I thought you didn't want to know," Mason said. He held out a glass to her. "To our departure."

"To our departure," Susan echoed. She took a sip, then frowned. "What sort of scuttlebutt have you heard?"

"Well, we're suddenly at the top of the list for supplies, we're stripping out the flag deck for an admiral and you've been busy on Earth rather than coming back here to retake command," Mason said. "It's clear we're going *somewhere*."

"Back to the war," Susan said, shortly. It was true enough. "But the remainder of the details are classified."

"Naturally," Mason said. "Speculating is half the fun."

He grinned. "Crewman Rogers is offering decent odds on a return to Unity," he added. "The runner-up is a trip to Tadpole Prime, followed by a push through to UXS-469 and alien space - if they refuse to come to terms, of course."

"You're going to have to have a few words with Crewman Rogers," Susan said. There was no way that anyone could eradicate gambling onboard ship, but it was far too easy for it to get out of hand. It was a shame there was no real way to rebuke anyone for gambling on the mission's goals. "Is he observing the limits?"

"I think so," Mason said. "I've made it pretty clear to him that going *over* the limits will end *very* badly."

Susan sighed. Gambling wasn't *precisely* against regulations, but there was a very real difference between the official and unofficial limitations. A crewman *could* gamble away his entire salary, even though there were supposed to be strict limits on what *could* be used as a stake. And no one wanted to go to a superior officer and admit they'd gambled away their entire paycheck for the month. They would be admitting to breaking regulations themselves.

And then they find themselves deeper and deeper in debt, she thought, grimly. *And if they're unlucky, they find themselves having to pay with something other than money.*

"Good," she said, coldly. She was damned if she was allowing *that* sort of nightmare on her ship. "Don't let him do anything stupid."

She leaned back in her chair and took another sip of the wine. Hanover Towers had made an effort to teach her about wine - apparently under the mistaken belief she was going to be a society wife who needed to be able to babble about grapes - but she'd never had the money to develop expensive tastes. Mason hadn't made a bad choice, she decided as the heavy liquid slid down her throat, yet it wasn't something she wanted to drink regularly. Which was lucky, she supposed. Her salary was very good, but she wasn't going to blow it all on expensive wine.

"And now," she said. "What have they done to my ship?"

Mason took a moment to gather his thoughts. "The damage we sustained in the last series of engagements has been repaired - again," he said. "I think the dockyard workers are getting pretty used to us, as this is the *second* time we've limped home. Much of the armour has been replaced with the latest composite, after we tested it extensively. We're now tougher than we were during our last deployment."

"Good," Susan said. "Can we stand up to a focused nuke?"

"The damage will be contained," Mason said. "They've also extensively modified the fusion cores and power distribution systems, based on our experience in the last year. Our drives are now better protected than they were, while the fusion cores are easier to fix while underway. The downside of all this" - he held up a hand - "is that efficiency isn't so high. I'll send the full report to your terminal."

Susan winced. Repairing the fusion cores was damn near impossible, at least away from a shipyard. If they could be modified to allow for onboard repairs...it was worth it, she supposed. She'd have to check the equations and projected power curves to be sure. The cores might need to be run constantly, putting more wear and tear on the system. But then, she reminded herself, anything that made it easier to repair the ship was worthwhile. A disaster that took out most of the fusion cores would probably take out the entire ship.

Or strand us, she added, thoughtfully. *And that would be the end.*

"I'll read the reports carefully," she said. "Weapons?"

"The new missiles, if the simulations are to be believed, may be better than we had expected," Mason said. "I've gone through the unclassified files very carefully - if they're right, the enemy may have some difficulty getting an effective lock on their precise location and taking them out. On the other hand, it wouldn't be the first time something functioned perfectly in the lab and failed completely in the field."

Susan groaned. "And we won't know until we fire them at the enemy."

She shook her head, tiredly. The boffins never bothered to account for *reality* when they did their trials. There was always *something* missing, something that *always* took a toll in the real world. She'd heard enough horror stories to be very wary of anything the boffins said until she'd seen it tested in the field.

"No," Mason agreed. "And the enemy may be putting their own versions into production too."

"True," Susan agreed.

"Our plasma cannons have been enhanced, again," Mason added. "They now pack an even bigger punch, with a longer range. We should be able to give the enemy a nasty fright, if they follow their standard tactics. They'll be in range before they know it. And our point defence is much more effective."

"But they can still sweep most of the guns off our hull," Susan said.

"I'm afraid so," Mason said. "We don't have a force shield *just* yet."

Susan nodded, ruefully. *Another* Holy Grail...and one that was supposed to be theoretically possible. But so far none of the boffins had managed to make one that was even remotely reliable. The shields simply couldn't stand up to anything.

And they can cripple most of our point defence once we enter weapons range, she reminded herself. It had happened before, despite their best efforts. *And there's nothing we can do about it.*

"We have stockpiled additional weapon pods," Mason told her. "But we can't refit them while under fire."

"Of course not," Susan agreed. She took another sip of her wine. "Is there anything else I ought to know?"

"Most of the newcomers seem to have fitted into the crew," Mason said. "Crewman Patrick Young has apparently deserted, as he is now five days overdue after going on leave to Sin City. I've notified the Shore Patrol and the Luna Police, as there is a *possibility* he might have simply lost track of time."

"He can try explaining that to the Senior Chief," Susan said, dryly.

It wasn't as absurd as it sounded. A person who plugged himself into a bliss machine - direct electronic simulation of his pleasure centres - could easily lose track of time. Men had been known to waste away in the machines, too lost in their own pleasure to realise that they were slowly starving to death. But a careful operator would ensure that his customers were hooked up to IV tubes, as long as their money lasted.

And if he is lost in bliss, Susan thought, *he may be unable to return to duty in any case.*

"Naturally," Mason agreed. He sighed. "If he doesn't report back within a couple of days, he'll be in deep shit anyway. The roster will have to be rewritten to exclude him."

"Handle it as you see fit," Susan told him. "And if he did decide to leave us, make sure he gets handed over for trial."

"Of course," Mason said. "Apart from that, there have been no major issues and only a couple of minor ones. All of them have been handled."

"Good," Susan said. She finished her wine, then placed the glass on the table. "Do you want to show me the changes before I resume command?"

"It will be my pleasure," Mason said. He gave her a droll smile. "Commanding *here* doesn't go on my record."

"Be glad of it," Susan said. Earth was a *long* way from the war front, but there was nothing stopping the Foxes from trying to strike at humanity's homeworld. *Vanguard* might have to power up and go on the offensive in a hurry. "If it *did*, we'd be in trouble."

CHAPTER
TEN

George felt sore - but in a good way - as the alarm bleeped, waking her up. For a long moment, she was confused before remembering that she'd set the alarm before climbing into bed. Their lovemaking had been particularly intense before they'd fallen asleep, she remembered, as she hit the terminal with one hand. They wouldn't be able to meet again for months, if not years.

Barton's head emerged from under the blankets. "What time is it?"

"1000," George lied. "Your shuttle leaves in twenty minutes."

Barton jumped up, rolling out of bed. "Where's my...?"

He broke off. "You lied!"

"Of course," George said. They wouldn't have been able to get to Heathrow in twenty minutes, even if they'd taken a jet. "It's 0800 and you need to have a shower and get dressed."

"Oh," Barton said. He rubbed his forehead as he stood. "Put your butt over here so I can slap it."

"Maybe later," George teased. She climbed out of bed and headed for the shower. "We both need to wash."

She wished, as she ran hot water over her body, that they had time for one final bout of lovemaking. But they didn't. Really, they were pushing things too close to the edge. He joined her a moment later, faint marks clearly visible on his back where her nails had dug into his skin. She kissed him lightly, then hurried back into the bedroom to order breakfast before getting dressed. They'd left the room so messy, she realised as she picked out her clothes, that the maids were not going to have fun cleaning it. She made a mental note to leave a huge tip before they headed to the space-port. She'd be coming back, but the maids would be cleaning the room before she returned.

"I've ordered a taxi too," she said, as he walked into the bedroom and reached for his underpants. "We'll be leaving in thirty minutes."

Barton nodded. "You don't *have* to come with me, not if you don't want to."

"I might as well," George said. "What would I do in London *without* you?"

The maid knocked before Barton could come up with a reply. George smirked, then opened the door. The maid carried in a large tray of break-fast, placed it on the table and retreated silently. George was starting to think they could give the marines lessons in sneaking about without mak-ing a sound. Barton shook his head after her - if anything, her dress was shorter than ever - and then stared down at the food. George knew exactly how he felt.

"Eat as much as you can," she said. God knew she'd had problems eat-ing on the day she'd first walked into the academy. He ought to understand the importance of eating better than the sixteen-year-old brat she'd been. "You'll need it."

Barton nodded and picked up a pastry. "Has it really been three days?"

"Yeah," George said. It had been strange; strange and delightful. Three days in the same room, with the same man...no wonder they'd lost track of time. "I'm afraid it has."

She munched her own breakfast, enjoying the mixture of tastes. It wouldn't be long before she was back on *Vanguard*, eating shipboard food. The cooks weren't *bad*, but naval food tended to be somewhat limited. And the less said about marine rations the better.

"It's been wonderful," Barton said. "Thank you."

"Consider it a gift," George told him. "I wouldn't be here if it wasn't for you."

"Maybe," Barton said. "But thank you anyway."

George sucked in a breath as she sipped her coffee. "You'll be on the moon, studying," she said. "And I'll be somewhere a million light years away."

"More like a few hundred," Barton pointed out. He smiled. "It doesn't really matter that much, does it?"

"No," George agreed. A hundred light years or a million…they were still going to be parted for a very long time. "I hope you won't be visiting Sin City *that* often."

"I'm meant to be studying," Barton said. "To learn how to act like an officer and a gentleman and a prat."

"Walk around with your nose high in the air," George said. "I don't think they'll have *that* much to teach you. You'll probably be commissioned by the end of the year."

"I doubt it," Barton said. "The commissioning rate for mustangs is only seventy percent, I think. The remainder get to become chiefs instead. I can't afford to take time off to enjoy myself."

"I thought the same too," George said. "This probably explains why I was at the bottom of my class."

Barton smirked. "I thought you did well enough to get *Vanguard*," he said. "She's hardly a garbage scow."

George shrugged. She hadn't done badly, she knew, but she hadn't been at the top of the class either. HMS *Vanguard*, she assumed, had been the luck of the draw. Or someone covertly pulling strings on her behalf. She knew from experience that both were quite possible.

"That's not the point," she said. She hesitated, unsure what to say. "I don't know what will happen in a year or two years or however long it takes you to get commissioned. And for me to return to the system. We've never been apart for so long, even if we didn't have any actual *privacy*."

She paused, struggling for words. "If you find someone else," she said. "Just…just tell me, ok? I won't blame you. I…"

Barton looked at her for a long moment. "Likewise," he said, finally. "And I won't blame you either."

George sighed. They'd never talked about the future. Hell, with a war on, there was a very good chance they might not *have* a future. Hundreds of thousands had already died, hundreds of thousands more *would* die… there was a possibility, a strong possibility, that the list of destroyed ships might eventually include HMS *Vanguard*. And if that happened, she suspected she would go down with the ship. A long-term relationship, perhaps even marriage…it wouldn't be on the cards until after the war, if they lasted that long.

But it hurt to tell him he could go, if he wanted. And she hoped he felt the same way too.

They finished their breakfast in silence. Something had gone out of them, George knew, even though she'd *had* to raise the issue. Perhaps, if they had the opportunity to make love one final time…she shook her head, knowing it would be different. She had no choice, but to wait and see what happened when she returned to Sol.

Her terminal bleeped. She glanced at it, surprised.

"My uncle wants me to meet him," she said, astonished. "Why?"

She'd met with her uncle two months ago, right before she'd been sent to the marines, but…it was rare for him to summon her directly. How had he even known she was in London? She cursed her slow brain a moment later. She'd been using her trust fund in London and her parents would have been notified. One of them had probably passed the message on to her uncle.

"Maybe he just wants to see you," Barton said. "You're his favourite niece, aren't you?"

"He has three children," George said, absently. She had butterflies in her stomach. If her uncle was willing to summon her, it had to be important. "He doesn't see any reason to favour *me*."

She sighed, crossly. "And I can't go with you to Heathrow," she added, passing him the terminal. "He wants to meet me at 0930."

"A lucky escape," Barton said, dryly. "You *do* realise you would have been driving back alone?"

George nodded. Perhaps, with the new tension between them, it was a good thing, even though it *was* an annoying coincidence. Or was it *really* a coincidence? Her uncle could easily have contrived to keep her from accompanying her lover to the spaceport, if he'd wished. But it struck her as rather pointless.

"I know," she said.

She kissed him goodbye once he'd packed, then scooped up her own bag and walked down to the ground floor. London was slowly coming to life, crowds wandering around as though they had somewhere to go. She frowned at the heavy police presence as she hurried through the streets to the Admiralty. There seemed to be more police on the streets than she'd ever seen, even during New Year celebrations. The guards greeted her when she reached the Admiralty, but insisted on checking her ID and fingerprints before allowing her to proceed through the gates. She knew she shouldn't be annoyed - it was their job - yet she couldn't help finding it annoying. There were only two days of leave left before she returned to her ship.

"Midshipwoman Fitzwilliam," a calm voice said. Her uncle's aide was standing by the door. "Your uncle is waiting for you."

George directed a death glare at the woman's back as she led the way up the stairs. There was no way to *hide* her connection to her uncle - Fitzwilliam wasn't *that* common a surname, certainly not in the Royal Navy - but she would prefer that it wasn't bandied about so casually by a woman who didn't seem to be anything other than beautiful. She knew she was being unfair, yet it was hard to be *reasonable* when her plans had been spoilt and the entire world had been reminded - again - that her uncle held the power of life and death over every spacer in the navy. And she wished, as she was shown into a large office, that she didn't feel as though she was being marched to the headmistress for a lecture.

"George," her uncle said. He was standing against the window, peering down at London below. "Thank you for coming."

"Your invitation suggested it was urgent," George said. She knew she should be politer, too, but she was *annoyed*. "And that I didn't have a choice."

The door closed behind her, loudly. She tried to ignore it.

"Your young man is on his way to the moon," her uncle said. He didn't look away from the window. "I'm sure he'll do well there."

George's eyes narrowed. "Did you get him the post?"

"I may have had a word or two with the examiner," her uncle said, casually. There was a faint edge to his voice that only someone who knew him very well would hear. "But I assure you he met the minimum requirements for the academy."

"You gave him the place to separate us," George snarled. Barton had been *proud* of his achievement. Her uncle...she clenched her fists in rage. How *dare* he? "You..."

Her uncle turned to face her. "You are not a twelve-year-old girl any longer," he said, sharply. "You are a twenty-one-year-old midshipwoman in the Royal Navy. Sit down, shut up and let me finish."

George sat, stunned.

"First, your boyfriend *did* meet the requirements," her uncle said. "I can prove that to you if you wish. I freely admit that I did put his name forward, but I would not have done that unless there was a reasonable chance of him completing the course."

"*Thank you,*" George said, tartly.

Her uncle shot her a sharp glance. "Second, certain…elements within the media *have* noticed your relationship," he added. "So far, it's stayed firmly in the pointless babbling sections of the datanet, but it won't be long before the tabloids decide it's actually creditable."

George scowled. "Those parts of the datanet also think we're descendants of space lizards who crash-landed on Earth a billion years ago," she pointed out. "What sort of credibility do they have?"

"You might be surprised," her uncle said. "Yes, a *lot* of the crap they spew out is obvious nonsense, but there are a few gems out there. I imagine someone at the Royal Hotel did a little research, then tipped them off. The tabloids *will* decide it's creditable sooner or later."

He met her eyes. "And even if it *wasn't* true," he added, "it would still reflect badly on you."

"Yes, sir," George said.

"Now," her uncle continued. "You have been separated, seemingly by chance. Should you meet again, you will do so as formal equals. And if you choose to develop a relationship then, you will have a fair chance of doing it without raising eyebrows."

George glared back at him. "And who *cares* about their opinions?"

"You were born into a powerful and wealthy family," her uncle said. He jabbed a finger at her chest. "Your father is an important government minister. Your uncle is the First Space Lord. Your more distant relatives include two cabinet ministers and nine members of the House of Lords. And you are, technically, in line to the throne."

"Assuming fifty-seven people die ahead of me," George snapped. "Is that ever going to happen?"

"One would hope not," her uncle said, dryly. "The point of the matter, *Georgina*, is that your conduct reflects badly on your family. No one cares what you do on shore leave, as long as it stays private, but they *do* care about something that might lead to scandal - and charges under naval regulations."

"Of course," George said. She tried to keep the bitterness out of her voice. "I could go to bed with five men or ten women and no one would give a damn, but do something that calls the family into disrepute…"

"Exactly," her uncle said. "Your little affair was right on the *edge* of permissible behaviour for a naval officer. Let me assure you that any court martial board would *not* choose to look at it kindly, particularly given the rest of your record. They'll be wondering if the problem with your midshipmen getting out of hand was because you were spending your off-duty hours with a lover!"

George flushed. "I wasn't!"

"I believe you," her uncle said. "How many others will feel the same way?"

He cleared his throat and went on, before George could think of an answer. "Now, your boyfriend is on the way to becoming a commissioned officer," he added. "And *you*, young lady, are going straight back to *Vanguard*."

George blinked. "Today?"

"If you wish," her uncle said. "But I believe your *assigned* slot is in two days."

He smiled, rather dryly. "The captain may welcome your enthusiasm, but you'll probably disrupt her planned schedule," he added. "Stay in London, attend a few shows or visit the shops…and keep your head down."

"Yes, sir," George said.

Her uncle sighed. "You may not have noticed this, but your 'career' is on thin ice," he warned, shortly. "You did well during your first cruise, George, yet you had all sorts of problems during your second. And while no *official* blame was attached to you, you ended up looking very bad. I believe that most *responsible* captains would have qualms about allowing you to serve as First Middy again, at least until you grow up a little. It might have been a mistake to allow you to enter the academy so early."

"It was not," George said.

She ground her teeth. Becoming First Middy so early in her career had been a fluke. If her reward for earlier service had come a couple of days later, Midshipman Simon Potter would have been First Middy. And he'd known it…she'd tried, as best as she could, but she knew she'd flubbed the test. Promotion probably wasn't in the books for the next few years, if at all.

"It may have been," her uncle said. "I know - you were a prefect at school and did a good job, by all accounts. But could you have done such a good job if you were younger than your peers?"

George said nothing. But she suspected he was right.

Her uncle shrugged. "Your current assignment serves two purposes," he said. "First, it is a step towards various other programs that are beyond your current need-to-know. Second, it is a chance for you to redeem yourself after several potentially disastrous failures. I don't think I need to explain to you that you're running out of chances. You *cannot* go on like this without hitting a *real* iceberg."

"Thank you," she said, finally.

"I hope you do understand," her uncle said. "Do you?"

"It isn't fair," George said. "Sammy…Sammy has had a whole string of affairs…"

"No one cares about her affairs," her uncle said. His lips thinned with cold disdain. "She is not exploiting her position to get men and women into her bed."

"Neither am I," George snapped.

"This is politics," her uncle said. "And in politics, perceptions matter so much more than *reality*. A lie can get halfway across the solar system before the truth has even got its boots on. You haven't been abusing your position. I know that - or rest assured we would be having a very different conversation. But the rest of the United Kingdom? *They* don't know the truth. You might be the seductress luring him into your bed. Or he might be the gold-digging seducer bent on tying you to him so he can exploit your position. Which version do you think will sell more tabloids?"

George flushed. She knew the answer to *that* question.

"Keep your head down," her uncle said, again. "Go explore London, then return to your ship and hope that the story never truly breaks. And I suggest" - he met her eyes - "that you do *not* discuss this with Peter Barton. He met the requirements for the academy and that is all that matters."

"Yes, sir," George said, reluctantly. "I...I understand."

"Good," her uncle said. "Hopefully, the next time I see you will be after a successful cruise."

"I hope so too," George said. She was torn between thanking him and cursing him. He was doing her a favour, but it didn't *feel* that way. It felt more as though she'd been called on the carpet. "I'll see you when I return."

CHAPTER
ELEVEN

"Welcome aboard, Admiral," Susan said.

Admiral Naiser nodded, his grey eyes tired. He didn't seem to like the ceremony anymore than she did, although he'd endured it without complaint. His staff seemed more invested in it than himself, something that Susan couldn't help finding amusing and pathetic at the same time. Anything that diminished a flag officer's status also diminished his staff. Probably literally.

"Thank you, Captain," Admiral Naiser said. "It's a pleasure to be back."

Susan nodded, reminding herself that Admiral Naiser had commanded the team that had designed and built *Vanguard* and her sisters. He'd been a hands-on manager too, according to her chief engineer. Admiral Naiser probably knew her ship as well as she did, if he'd been keeping up with the endless series of modifications, updates and repairs. She'd prepared a tour for him, if he had time to take it. Their departure date had already been moved forwards twice by the Admiralty.

"I've taken the liberty of arranging a drink in my ready room," she said. "My XO will show your staff to the flag quarters."

The admiral's lips twitched. "That would be delightful," he said, conversationally. "We have some small matters to discuss."

Susan glanced at Mason, then led Admiral Naiser down the corridor towards the bridge. A handful of hatches and inspection panels lay open, crewmen checking and rechecking every last component before *Vanguard* powered up her drives and headed for the tramline, but she was fairly sure Admiral Naiser wouldn't complain. He'd *been* a starship commander, then a shipyard CO. He *knew* that a battleship on the verge of departure was a very busy place. A politician from Earth might have a different opinion.

She opened the hatch to her ready room, then beckoned the admiral inside. Thankfully, she'd had a chance to clear up the room and generally make it look presentable, although there were still a dozen datapads and chips lying on the desk. Reading the reports, then checking them personally had taken most of her time over the last two days. She was damned if she was signing anything without checking it for herself, first. She'd made that mistake on her middy cruise and paid a steep price for it.

"Please, be seated," she said, as she picked up the bottle. "Finest scotch or finest shipboard rotgut? Or tea?"

"The rotgut sounds ideal," Admiral Naiser said. He settled into one of the chairs, looking surprisingly casual for an admiral. But then, he was experienced enough to know he didn't need to put on airs and graces either. "I haven't been on a proper starship for far too long."

Susan smiled as she poured them both a glass. The clear liquid had been brewed *somewhere* below decks, in a location that was officially a secret. Mason and the Senior Chief would turn a blind eye as long as the distillers were careful not to accidentally poison a crewman - or let him get too drunk. She hadn't really approved, when she'd been a newly-minted midshipwoman with her father's stern views on the dangers of drunkenness running through her head, but she'd come to realise that *someone* would put a still together with or without semi-official permission. Better to keep a sharp eye on it than try to come down like a ton of bricks.

"Thoroughly unpleasant," Admiral Naiser said, taking a sip. "I approve."

Susan sat facing him, crossing her legs. "I saw the latest set of updates," she said. "Are we really getting a trio of American battleships?"

"So it would seem," Admiral Naiser said. "The Yanks haven't quite decided if they want to divert the third to the war front or attach it to the task force, but we're definitely getting two."

"I see," Susan said. "I'm surprised they didn't demand command."

"They're already in command of the war front - or at least our contribution," Admiral Naiser said. "Giving them command of both the front *and* our planned offensive seemed a little much."

"Politics," Susan muttered.

"Quite," Admiral Naiser agreed. He made a disgusted expression. "And the hell of it is that we'll all get along fine, as soon as we leave orbit. But until then we'll be fighting over precedence and everything else."

Susan nodded in tired agreement. She'd served with dozens of foreign officers and while she'd gotten along with most of them, their political masters were another story. Everyone wanted the prestige that came with important commands, even if it caused friction with their allies. Thankfully, they'd had plenty of time to iron out the details between wars. The First Interstellar War *had* concentrated a few minds on what was really important.

"That's not the worst of it," the Admiral warned. "We're also getting *Vikramaditya.*"

Susan blinked. "The Indian carrier?"

"Commanded by someone who fought against us as a junior officer," Admiral Naiser confirmed. "We may have some diplomatic problems."

"Ouch," Susan said. It was a recipe for trouble. *Vikramaditya* was one of two Indian supercarriers, if she recalled correctly. Her sister had been blown out of space by HMS *Warspite* during the war, crippled beyond repair by a starship far cheaper than herself. The Indians had been humiliated, while all the other powers had taken note. "Surely they won't let disagreements get in the way of fighting a war."

"I'll do my best to spare you the headaches," the Admiral promised. "But there probably will be headaches."

He took another sip of his drink. "We should have the task force finalised and assembled within ten days, unless they change the departure date again," he added. He pulled a datachip from his pocket and slotted it into the nearest terminal. "So far, the veil of secrecy seems to be holding. We'll be departing for the front, as far as anyone outside the planning circle knows."

Susan had her doubts. Even if no one talked - and her father had dozens of stories about operations that had been spoiled because some politician talked to the media - there was plenty of evidence that the task force was going somewhere else, if someone put the pieces together. The handful of logistics ships, the repair crews that had been drawn from the various shipyards, the vast stockpiles of supplies...it all added up to the task force going where no man had gone before. *Someone* would put the pieces together, given time.

"I hope so," she said.

"I'll be commanding the task force from the flag deck," Admiral Naiser continued. He smiled. "You'll remain in command of the ship, of course. Hopefully, the command structure should be sorted out over the next couple of days. We'll be subdividing the task force into three smaller forces, ensuring that we cannot lose the entire command network if the shit hits the fan."

If someone takes us out, Susan thought. *Our enemies have probably been building better weapons too.*

She scowled down at her glass. HMS *Formidable* had been the pride of the fleet, a decade ago. That hadn't stopped her being crippled, then blown to atoms by a flight of enemy starfighters. *Vanguard* was far too heavily armoured to suffer a similar fate, but it was certain that the Foxes would be looking for a way to take the battleship and her sisters out as quickly as possible. And if they stumbled across one...

If we run into something that powerful, she thought dryly, *we're screwed anyway.*

The holographic display sprang to life. Susan watched, coolly, as the fleet details scrolled up in front of her, everything from communications protocols to tactical contingency plans. She knew better than to assume that everything would go by the book, once the fleet departed Earth. They'd be shaking the fleet down as they headed to their destination, working out how to turn their orders - and plans drawn up on Earth - into something practical. God only knew what the final disposition of the fleet would look like.

She frowned. "Can the Indian ships interface with ours?"

"I believe so," Admiral Naiser said. "There certainly *shouldn't* be any problems."

Susan nodded, slowly. Humanity's various navies had operated a degree of international standardisation, even before the first war, that would have shocked their ancestors. But starships might be crippled and lives might be lost if a Chinese component couldn't be inserted into an American starship and vice versa. All the bugs had been worked out during the first war, allowing human starships from a dozen different nations to fight as one. In theory, the task force should be able to fit neatly into a single formation. In practice...

We'll have to wait and see, she told herself, dryly. *As long as we can all talk to each other, we should be able to get along.*

"I'll be hosting a get-together once the rest of the task force is assembled," Admiral Naiser said. "You're invited, of course."

Susan smiled. She knew what *that* meant. Her presence was mandatory, barring utter catastrophe. Fortunately, a gathering of starship commanders wouldn't be as mind-numbingly boring as a formal ceremony for politicians. She hoped - prayed - that they'd avoid a formal send-off before they departed. Thankfully, the fact that everyone had been told they were going to the war front, rather than somewhere a little further away, made it unlikely.

"Of course, sir," she said. Even if her presence hadn't been mandatory, she would have had to make an appearance. She was the CO, after all. "I look forward to it."

Admiral Naiser didn't look convinced, unsurprisingly. "I'll be interested in your input," he said, instead. "And in your thoughts on the jump drive."

Susan lifted her eyebrows. "Jump drive?"

"That's what we're calling the artificial tramline," Admiral Naiser told her. "The designer wanted something technical, but her staff felt it would never catch on."

"It should be named after her," Susan said. "Surely...?"

"She doesn't want it named after her, apparently," Admiral Naiser said. "She's already looking at prospective future improvements to the system. A working FTL drive..."

He shrugged. "It almost makes you wish we didn't have to tell the others it exists."

"Yes, sir," Susan agreed.

It was frustrating, if she was forced to be honest. The nation that first managed to escape the tyranny of the tramlines...the possibilities would be endless. Countless star systems that were forever out of reach would suddenly become accessible, opening up whole new vistas for colonisation. But it wasn't to be. The rest of the Great Powers *knew* the jump drive was possible, even if they didn't know the details. They'd be pouring resources into their own programs, trying to match the British achievement before Britain laid claim to the closest systems.

She cleared her throat. "I will be happy to offer what I can," she said. "But it will have to wait until *Vanguard* is completely ready for deployment."

"Understood," Admiral Naiser said. "Do we have a timeline?"

"Five days, sir," Susan said. "I'm planning on the assumption that we'll need some extra time."

"Good thinking," Admiral Naiser said.

He finished his glass and put it on the table. "My staff and I will do our best to stay out of the way," he promised. "We'll be running through a series of fleet-level exercises to prepare for deployment, then start coordinating with the other ships as they arrive. Prince Henry, his staff and the press - horror of horrors - should be arriving in a week. Unless that changes too..."

Susan groaned, inwardly. She'd never had to deal with the media, at least not on her ship, but she'd heard countless horror stories from officers who had. Reporters rarely understood the realities of deep space operations, let alone combat. They expected the crew to be able to see everything in real time, as if the speed-of-light delay simply didn't exist. It didn't, on Earth, but it was a very real problem in deep space. And when they weren't demanding the impossible, they were demanding good food and spacious cabins.

"My XO will be happy to deal with them," she said. *That* was a flat-out lie. If half the horror stories were true, Mason would start plotting a mutiny of his own within the week. "We have already reserved space for both the xenospecialists and the reporters."

"You can't stuff them into storage cabinets," Admiral Naiser said, wryly. "And you can't tell them an airlock is a luxury suite either."

"No, sir," Susan agreed. "We've isolated a block of cabins for the reporters. They'll be reasonably comfortable."

Admiral Naiser grinned. "On a starship?"

Susan smiled back. She'd shared a cramped bunkroom with five other midshipmen, where there had been no privacy at all, then endured a claustrophobic cabin as a lieutenant. There hadn't been any real comfort until she'd made commander and by then she'd grown used to uncomfortable sleeping quarters. Hell, the captain's cabin had felt uncomfortably large the first night she'd slept in it. But for the reporters, no doubt used to large hotel rooms, the tiny cabins would seem a foretaste of hell.

Unless some of them are experienced embeds, she thought. She'd have to go through the files, if MI5 and the Admiralty had forwarded them to her. *An embed would know what to expect.*

"This should be an interesting voyage," Admiral Naiser said. He rose. "And I won't keep you any longer."

"My officers and I would be honoured if you joined us in the mess this evening," Susan told him. It was sincere. Admiral Naiser was a genuine war hero. "And I believe my engineer wishes to show you around the ship too."

"I've been looking forward to seeing the changes in person," Admiral Naiser said. He cocked an eyebrow. "And I'll discuss them with you in some depth later."

Susan rose, then watched as he headed for the hatch and stepped through. She almost offered to walk him down to his cabin, but stopped herself just in time. Admiral Naiser had helped to design and build *Vanguard*. He'd have no problem finding his way to the flag deck, let alone his cabin. She glanced at the status board, just to confirm that the last of the admiral's staff had boarded, then turned her attention back to the files. A number of omissions were clearly visible - the task force hadn't been *entirely* finalised - but *Vikramaditya* and her crew were included in the briefing notes. MI6, she noted, had added a great deal of detail that *hadn't* been included in the files the Indians had offered.

"Captain Rani Saran," she read, out loud. *That* was impressive. India had been a great deal more reluctant to allow women to join the navy than Britain, even after the Age of Unrest had finally come to an end. A woman who not only joined their navy, but reached command would be formidable. "Political connections…"

She made a face as she skimmed through the file. MI6 insisted that Captain Saran had only been promoted because she was related to three separate government officials, while the Admiralty thought her political connections were largely irrelevant. It was hard to be sure which of them was right, Susan thought. Hell, it was quite possible that *both* of them were right. India didn't have an entrenched aristocracy. Captain Saran's family connections might have helped her into the navy, but she wouldn't have been given a carrier without being extremely competent.

But Captain Blake got his command, even though he'd lost his bottle, she thought, sourly. *If his connections were enough to get him a command, why not hers?*

She read the rest of the file quickly. Captain Saran had studied in India, then Oxford. *That* wasn't really a surprise, although the number of Indian students attending British universities had dropped sharply since the war. Joined the Indian Navy at nineteen, three years before the First Interstellar War; commissioned into the service just in time to take part in the Battle of Earth. And then she'd served during the Anglo-Indian War on *Vikramaditya…*

No known political positions, Susan thought. The Indian Navy encouraged its officers to write about political defence issues, something it had copied from the Royal Navy, but Captain Saran had apparently published nothing about politics. *But certainly one of the loudest voices for an independent Indian defence policy.*

It was difficult to be sure. Captain Saran's career *might* have suffered because of the war, even though she'd been a mere lieutenant. It had taken her six years to earn a carrier command. But then, India only had one supercarrier. Susan knew, in the normal run of things, that she probably wouldn't have had a shot at *Vanguard's* command chair. Too many officers wanting their chance, too few command slots…Captain Saran was probably both competent and well-connected. The Indian Navy wouldn't have given her the carrier if they thought she couldn't handle it.

And she's probably tough too, Susan acknowledged.

It wasn't a pleasant thought. She'd read several books by the first women to serve in the Royal Navy, after the restrictions on female crewmen had been lifted. They hadn't had an easy time of it. Crews - male crews - had doubted them until they proved themselves. It would be harder, she suspected, in the Indian Navy. India had always been far more patriarchal than Britain.

She shrugged. Politics - human politics - didn't matter. All that mattered was winning the war before it was too late. And if Captain Saran didn't understand that, Admiral Naiser would have to appeal to her government before the task force left orbit. The task force couldn't afford to fight the aliens *and* itself.

"Commander Mason," she said, tapping her wristcom. "Report to my ready room when free."

"Understood," Mason said. He sounded relieved, although he hid it well. The admiral's staff would be keeping him hopping. "I'll be along as soon as possible."

"Good," Susan said. "We have plenty of work to do."

CHAPTER
TWELVE

"Wake up," a voice hissed. George started as someone prodded her arm. "We're almost there."

"Thanks," George muttered. She'd fallen asleep almost as soon as she'd transferred to the *Vanguard* shuttle. "Do we have some water?"

She opened her eyes, cursing as the light stabbed daggers into her skull. She'd gone back to the hotel, after her interview with her uncle, and proceeded to get thoroughly drunk, something that had clearly been a mistake. The sober-up she'd taken *should* have swept most of the alcohol out of her system, but the headache was still pounding away at the corner of her mind. She needed food, water and sleep, probably not in that order. But she knew she wasn't going to get any of them.

Stop feeling sorry for yourself, she told herself, as her companion pressed a water bottle into her hand. *You have a fucking job to do.*

The water tasted clean, too clean. George felt sick again, just for a second. The first leg of the journey hadn't been too bad, but the person who'd sat next to her on the second had spent most of the flight hitting on her... something she might not have minded, perhaps, if her head hadn't felt as though it was going to explode. And then she'd slept, but not enough. She thought she'd dreamt, during the flight, but she couldn't recall her dreams. Perhaps, just perhaps, that had been for the best.

You're a spacer, she reminded herself sharply, as a gut-wrenching quiver ran through the shuttle. *You have endured worse.*

She swallowed, hard. She'd spent part of the day composing a letter to Barton, only to give up when she'd finally realised that there was *no* good way to tell her lover - her former lover, perhaps - that the place he thought he'd earned had actually been given to him. How *could* she tell him? It would break his heart - or worse, if he blamed her for it. She'd deleted the final draft, in the end, then kept drinking until…the rest of the night was a blur. Part of her was surprised to discover that she'd woken up alone, before making her way to the spaceport.

A dull *clang* echoed through the shuttle as it docked with the giant battleship. She cringed into her seat as the pilot announced HMS *Vanguard*, running through a spiel that would have done a commercial aerospace company proud. It had been funny the first time, she recalled, but after two deployments and countless shuttle flights it had definitely stopped making her laugh. As if they needed their passports or the countless other civilian requirements for crossing an international border!

She gritted her teeth, then rose to her feet and retrieved her carryall before joining the small crowd of spacers and marines boarding *Vanguard*. No matter how carefully schedules were organised, she'd discovered on her first deployment, something *always* went wrong and spacers needed to be rushed around from place to place. The marines should have accompanied the rest of their unit, but they'd probably been on leave when the balloon went up. Thankfully, they hadn't missed departure altogether. George hated to think what would happen to someone who managed to do *that*.

Vanguard smelt old and new at the same time, she decided, as she stepped through the hatch and into the giant battleship. The drives sounded a little different - she couldn't determine if they were powered down or if someone had been adjusting the harmonics - but she knew it wouldn't take her long to get used to it. Spacers rarely noticed the hum after the first few days, prompting all sorts of questions from groundhogs. They sometimes even had to be *reminded* that the background noise was *there*.

"George," a familiar voice said. "Welcome home!"

George turned. Lieutenant Charles Fraser stood there, arms crossed in front of him, looking - as always - like a gorilla who'd been shaved and forced into a naval uniform. George surprised herself by smiling at him, even though he'd been an enemy before he'd become a friend. She hadn't realised how much she'd come to trust him until she'd faced the prospect of never returning to the ship.

"Charles," she said. She flushed a moment later. Maybe they were friends, but she still shouldn't address him by his first name where anyone could hear. "Lieutenant."

"You can be flogged for not giving me the proper respect," Fraser said, deadpan. He motioned for her to follow him down the corridor, allowing the rest of the shuttle passengers to depart in a steady stream. "I trust you brought some chocolate from Earth?"

George flushed. "I completely forgot," she admitted. She cursed herself, savagely. She'd *planned* to bring chocolate, but events had overtaken her. "Sorry."

"I'm sure we'll live," Fraser said. He met her eyes. "I have good news and bad news."

"Oh," George said. She wasn't sure she wanted to know. "What's the bad news?"

"It may actually be good news," Fraser said. "It depends on what you want to hear."

George sighed. "You've been demoted back to midshipman? I've been promoted to lieutenant? The captain has decreed that everyone whose name starts with 'G' gets an extra ration of ice cream at supper?"

Fraser beamed. "You're going to be bunking down with the marines!"

"What?"

"You're going to be sleeping with the marines," Fraser told her. He paused, dramatically. "I suppose that did come out wrong."

George bit down the response that came to mind. Friends or not, private or not, there were limits. "Why?"

Fraser shrugged. "Well," he said. "There's the small matter of you being their newly-appointed liaison officer. You can't do that if you're stuck on the other side of the ship, can you? And then there's the slightly more important factor of a new First Middy. Certain people thought it might be better if you weren't sleeping in Middy Country."

George felt herself flush. "I thought Simon or Paula would have got the job."

"Simon Potter and Paula Spurgeon both requested reassignment," Fraser told her. "I believe they both left shortly after you did. And with the other two idiots currently cooling their heels in jail, someone higher up the chain of command decided it would be better to bring in a completely new set of midshipmen."

"And that means you're still supervising them," George finished. "Sorry."

"Not as much as you might think," Fraser said. "Zak Smith - he's senior by over a year - is off *Queen Liz*. He knows most of the battleship ropes already. I've supervised, of course, but he hasn't made many missteps."

"I hate him already," George said. She wasn't entirely joking. A few more years of experience - of life - and she was sure she would have done a better job. "And I don't get to stay in Middy Country?"

"Like I said, you'll be bunking with the marines," Fraser said. He paused. "I'm not sure how the rest of your duties are going to pan out, really. You may find yourself serving as a gofer - or you may get the regular run of middy duties as well as everything else. Wait and see."

George rubbed her forehead as they resumed their walk down the corridor. She was screwed, unless...no, she was screwed. Her work for the marines would be noted, but it wouldn't count towards a prospective promotion; hell, the other middies would have an excellent chance to jump up the promotions ladder ahead of her...

And you screwed up, she reminded herself, sharply. *Even if you were an ordinary middy, promotion would come slowly, if at all.*

She glanced at him. "Did you manage to get some shore leave?"

"A little," Fraser said. "Not much, really. A brief flight to the moon and nothing else."

Sin City, George filled in.

Fraser caught her arm as they approached Marine Country. "I understand that you were training with them," he said. He looked her up and down, scrutinising her with an intensity that made her blush. "Just remember...they don't have time for deadweight here."

"I understand," George said. "Are we still going to be training together?"

"If you have time," Fraser said. "And if I have time too. I may be assigned to tactical in the next few days."

"Good luck," George said.

"Thank you," Fraser said. He smiled, rather thinly. "Report to Major Andreas. You may remember him."

The two marines on duty outside the hatch checked her ID carefully before opening the hatch, allowing her entry. Fraser nodded to her, then strode off in the other direction. George blinked - she'd expected him to accompany her - and walked into Marine Country. The air smelt different, the musty smell of too many sweaty men in too close proximity drifting down the corridor towards her. Marine Country was large, but their barrack-cabins were surprisingly small. George suspected she'd find some of them claustrophobic *despite* her experience on *Vanguard*.

She walked down to the CO's office and tapped the bleeper, then waited. The sound of exercise echoed down the corridor, men testing their skills in the fighting ring. She could hear sergeants alternately pushing the men to fight harder and reminding them, sternly, that some moves were banned for a reason. George had learned a great deal over the last eighteen months - from Fraser and the marines - but she knew better than to think she could take a marine in a fair fight. She'd have her ass kicked all around the ring.

And if I did win it would be suspicious, she thought. *I'd always wonder if they let me win.*

The hatch hissed open. Major Christopher Andreas was standing behind his desk, studying a holographic map covered in notations from at least three different countries. George stepped inside and saluted smartly, then waited for him to acknowledge her. Major Andreas would be a very busy man. She was surprised he was talking to her personally.

He looked up. "Midshipwoman."

"Major," George said. She wasn't sure what to expect. "Reporting as ordered, sir."

Major Andreas studied her for a long moment. "I received the reports from Dering Lines," he told her. "You did well, apparently, but not up to our standards."

"No, sir," George said. A dozen excuses rose to her lips, but she fought them down. The major would not be impressed by *any* of them, even if they *were* valid. "This was made clear to me."

"My two companies will probably be assigned to various support roles," Major Andreas said, after a moment. "We are a dedicated *space-trained* unit. Brigadier Schneider" - he chose to ignore the way George's eyes went wide at the name - "may find other uses for us, but there is no way to be sure. You will be expected to pull your weight. If you fail to do so, you may be left behind - either here or in enemy territory."

"I understand, sir," George said.

"You will live with us, eat with us, sleep with us and train with us," Major Andreas continued, coolly. "You will not find it easy. If I feel, when we reach our destination, that you are useless, you will be binned. Or, in your case, returned to Middy Country. The decision is mine and mine alone. Do *not* go whining to the captain or any of your relatives over it. I will not change my mind."

"Yes, sir," George said. From what her uncle had said, this was very much her last chance to shine. She didn't dare mess it up. "I won't let you down."

"We shall see," Major Andreas said. "You wouldn't be the first half-trained person who had to be brought up to speed at speed. Harder for you, of course, because you're a woman - still a girl, in many ways."

George kept her expression under tight control. He was trying to get under her skin, trying to see how she would react. She'd heard worse, she reminded herself, back on Earth. Hell, she'd dealt with prefects at school who'd abused their powers. Sergeants shouted, often so crudely she knew her mother would have fainted in horror, but they weren't *evil*. They just needed to know she could endure before they let her go.

She gritted her teeth, remembering the lecture she'd received the day she'd arrived at Dering Lines. A woman in the military would always face worse challenges than a man - that had been true of the navy too - but there were also very different dangers. Female soldiers had been gang-raped during the Troubles, their bodies beaten bloody and savagely abused, then left for dead. The officer who'd given her the lecture had shown her photographs, culled from the records. She could end up that way, he'd warned.

The Age of Unrest might be officially over, but large parts of the world were still dominated by savages.

And while the marines may push and prod, she thought, *they won't be the worst threat I might face.*

Major Andreas was still talking. She dragged her attention back to him with an effort.

"You will be tested," he warned. "You'll be tested, time and time again. And you will have to learn to cope with it - and to stand up for yourself."

He tapped a terminal at his belt. "And if you feel you can't endure it any longer, quit. It's no shame to back out before lives start depending on you."

George swallowed. "I understand, sir."

"Very good," Major Andreas said.

The hatch opened. A grim-faced man stepped into the cabin. He wore an unmarked uniform, but George could tell, just by the way he moved, that he was a sergeant. And probably a very good one. "Major?"

"Sergeant Tosco, this is Midshipwoman Fitzwilliam, our new liaison," Major Andreas said, nodding to George. "Take her to her bunk - we'll slot her into the beta shift for now, with space on the rota for her to work for me."

He made a show of glancing at his watch. "You should have at least five hours of sleep before you have to give up the bunk," he added. "Sergeant Tosco will put you on the training rota."

George kept her face expressionless. Hot-bunking was something she would have gladly foregone, if she'd had a choice. Even midshipmen were allowed a bunk each. But the marines thought differently. She'd have to get up and make the bunk each morning or the next sleeper would pull her out of the bunk and dump her on the deck. It had happened twice, back at the army base.

She saluted Major Andreas, then followed Sergeant Tosco out of the cabin and down the corridor to the barrack-cabin. It was larger than she'd expected, but the marines had somehow managed to cram over twenty bunks into a small compartment. Eighteen of the bunks were occupied by marines, several snoring loudly. She glanced towards the rear, where she knew the showers and toilets would be hidden, then slung her carryall into the locker Sergeant Tosco indicated. There was no lock, any more than there were shower and toilet curtains hiding the users from view. Privacy was an absolute joke.

"There are two uniforms waiting for you," Sergeant Tosco informed her, pointing into her locker. "Leave your middy uniform unless you are ordered specifically to wear it."

"Yes, sergeant," George said.

She checked the rest of the supplies, then undressed down to her bra and panties. *Someone* had done a good job, which was a definite surprise. She'd had to argue with ship's stores over the sizes she needed in the past, even though her measurements were a matter of record. Military-grade shirts and underwear…it would suffice, she told herself. It wasn't as if she had any alternative.

Good thing I was a middy before I went for training, she thought, as she clambered into her bunk. *I wouldn't be able to tolerate this at Hanover Towers.*

She smiled at the thought as she closed her eyes. Sharing a dorm with nine other girls had been a nightmare, or so she'd thought. They'd all had more room, in their beds, then she'd had to herself, ever since she'd gone to the academy. And *they* hadn't had to share their dorms with *boys*. And they'd been able to get up at seven in the morning, rather than six…

A hand tapped her shoulder. She jerked.

"Get up," a voice snapped. George stared for a moment, dimly realising that she'd been asleep. "Now!"

She rolled out of the bunk and dropped down to the deck. The marine's eyes widened in surprise as he saw her underwear - clearly, Sergeant Tosco hadn't bothered to tell him that he was hot-bunking with a girl - but he said nothing as George scrambled for her tunic and yanked it over her head, merely climbing into the bunk and closing his eyes. She wasn't sure, as she pulled on her trousers, if he'd done her a favour or not. Technically, *she* should have made up the bedding before he climbed in.

"Get out here," Sergeant Tosco snapped. He caught her arm and pulled her towards the hatch. "Move!"

George gritted her teeth as she stumbled into the next room. Thirty marines were standing around, stuffing their faces with food. George didn't feel like eating, but she knew she didn't have a choice. If she ran out of energy and collapsed, the major would kick her out of Marine Country and that would be that. She wouldn't get a second chance.

She sighed as she piled her plate, hoping she'd have time to eat it. The marines were looking at her, their eyes silently assessing her as she gobbled down the food. Their gaze wasn't sexual, she knew. In some ways, it felt worse. They were wondering if she could pull her weight on the battlefield…

She sighed, again. It was going to be a very long day.

CHAPTER
THIRTEEN

All things considered, Henry decided, the gathering had been moderately successful.

It had been boring, of course. Most of the commanding officers - starships and various ground units - had been warned, in no uncertain terms, to behave themselves. The dinner had been excellent, complemented with fine and expensive wines; the tactical combat exercises had yet to begin, ensuring there was no reason to fight. And so the various national officers were meeting their counterparts in a relaxed situation, far from their political superiors *and* the media. The chatting might be boring, but it laid the groundwork for a far more fundamental working relationship when Task Force Cromwell finally departed Earth.

His gaze swept the room, picking out faces and matching them to names. Commodore Kevin Hoover, the American who was the default second-in-command, chatting to Brigadier Percy Schneider; Rear Admiral John Naiser, speaking in quiet tones to General Horace Ross, the American in command of the ground forces. Henry made a mental note to speak to Percy Schneider at some point, if only to offer a few stories of the young man's father. They'd served together, back on *Ark Royal*.

He frowned in disapproval as he saw Juliet Watson-Stewart leaving the compartment - practically *fleeing* the compartment - hand-in-hand with her husband. He'd heard that Juliet Watson-Stewart wasn't *good* with crowds, but it was still annoying to watch her retreating in a hurry. And yet, it wasn't as if she was in the chain of command. Commodore or not, it had been quietly made clear to everyone that Juliet Watson-Stewart wasn't remotely suited to serve as a commanding officer. The fleet would need to be in very real trouble before she was allowed to take the helm.

"Your Highness," a female voice said. He turned to see an Indian officer standing behind him. Captain Rani Saran, if he recalled correctly. "Do you believe the Tadpoles will seek a separate peace?"

Henry took a moment to study her. She was roughly his age, according to her file, but she looked younger. Classically Indian features were mixed with lightened skin and dark hair that fell down around her shoulders. She was stunning, he had to admit, yet there was an edge to her posture that warned him there was nothing *soft* about her. He made a mental note to look up her recent publications, if she'd had any. Command of a supercarrier had probably ensured she hadn't had the time.

And this is a diplomatic nightmare, he thought, grimly. *What genius put an Indian carrier under the man responsible for killing her sister?*

"I think they would only consider a peace they could live with," he said, finally. "Coming to a meeting of the minds with the Foxes would be very difficult. The Foxes want unconditional surrender."

"They're either at your throat or at your knees," Rani said. Her lips twitched. "How very much like the Russians."

Henry kept his face impassive. She was making a political play, he suspected; he didn't have time to indulge her. There were Russian ships attached to the task force, their captains pressing the flesh in the giant compartment. Who knew how their crews would react to her slur?

"The Foxes would not give the Tadpoles a degree of autonomy," Henry said, instead. "They only came to an agreement with *us* because they realised that the galaxy was large enough for both of us. That might not be true of the Foxes."

Rani nodded. "But they're also taking a beating," she said. "They may suspect that *we* will fight the war to the last Tadpole."

"The Tadpoles don't have a choice," Henry pointed out. "There's no way they can escape being so close to enemy space, any more than India can move away from China. They have to fight if there's no other way to get a tolerable peace."

Rani gave him a long look, then nodded. Henry suspected he understood the *real* purpose of her question. India was making a major commitment by dispatching her lone supercarrier to the war, knowing that losing the giant ship would be disastrous. It was, on one hand, an attempt to rejoin the community of nations, but it was also risky. None of the Great Powers were interested in helping India rebuild her presence in space.

And their economy has been shaky since the war, he thought. *They may be unable to fund a replacement, assuming they haven't lost the taste for interstellar power projection.*

He made a mental note to discuss it with the Foreign Office as Rani continued to chat about the World Cup, the diplomatic version of talking about the weather. Perhaps something could be done to help the Indians, particularly something that might reflect well on Britain. But he had a feeling it wouldn't be done, regardless of the possibilities. There was too much suspicion and even hatred after the war.

"I think Brazil has a good chance of taking the cup this year," he said, instead. "But Poland is looking strong and Mars is putting in a team."

"The Martians won't be used to playing on Earth," Rani pointed out. "They'll probably be kicked out in the first round."

"I believe they're planning to spend the last couple of months before the cup training on Earth," Henry said. "And they might well be training in a habitat before then, where the gravity can be set to Earth-standard."

"Which is of questionable legality," Rani said. "They might be disqualified."

"Not if they put in a special request," Henry said.

He stopped as Admiral Naiser tapped for attention. "I know we're planning to leave in two days," he said. "And you'll all need time to recover from the evening's debaucheries. So I won't keep you here any longer than strictly necessary."

A faint series of chuckles ran through the air. No one was drunk, as far as Henry could tell, but most of the guests *had* drunk enough to give them a pleasant buzz. He would have drunk more himself, if he hadn't been keeping an paranoid eye out for reporters. The heir to the throne couldn't have a quiet drink without someone taking a photograph, then being barraged with long articles about how the prince should set a better example, etc, etc.

He pushed the thought aside. Admiral Naiser was still speaking.

"You've all been briefed on the planned operation," he continued. "And you've all been told the preliminary planned deployments. We will adjust them, if necessary, if our war games tell us that they don't actually *work*. And we're avoiding fancy formations that might just lead to an accident."

There were more chuckles. Fancy formations looked good, Henry had to admit, but they tended to be dangerous. *Standard* formations looked ragged, yet there was plenty of space to alter course in a hurry or simply tighten up to repel attack. Admiral Naiser, it seemed, knew the difference between looking good and *being* good.

"I do not pretend this will be an easy mission," Admiral Naiser said. "We have not launched a push into unexplored space since *Ark Royal* headed out on Operation Nelson. There is a strong prospect of being trapped, unable to retreat; there is a risk, as unlikely as it may seem, that we will be mouse-trapped and destroyed. Your governments are aware, all too aware, of the level of risk."

Henry felt Rani tense beside him. *India* had more at stake than anyone else, even the French or Germans. Hell, the Germans - at least - had added a battleship to the task force. The Indian carrier was dangerously vulnerable if an enemy battleship entered weapons range, no matter how much armour her crews had bolted to the hull. And losing her ship...

"I have not been awarded any medals for inspirational speeches," Admiral Naiser said. "And I will not try to inspire you now. What I *will* say is that this mission *can* win us the war, either by forcing them to bow the knee to us or by taking out enough of their industry to allow us to out-produce them. And our strike in their rear will be enough to force them to withdraw from the war front."

We hope, Henry added, silently.

"Ten years ago, humans stood together against a common foe," Admiral Naiser reminded them. "Now, we must stand together again. Our petty differences must be forgotten in the face of a threat to the entire human race. Tomorrow, things may be different; today, we must fight together. The fate of our entire race depends on it."

He saluted the gathered crowd, then turned and strode through the nearest hatch. Henry nodded in quiet approval. The Admiral's departure was a sign that the remainder of the guests could also begin to depart if they wished, although they didn't *have* to leave for several hours. He glanced at his wristcom, silently noting the time. The American, French, German and Indian commanding officers didn't have to be back on duty until morning.

"An inspiring speech," Rani said. "But do you think we can stand together?"

"We must hang together or hang separately," Henry said. "Right now, that is all that matters."

He watched her go, then frowned inwardly as a blonde-haired young woman separated herself from the crowd and walked towards him. She was about twenty-five, if he placed her age correctly, wearing a long green dress instead of a naval uniform. A civilian…? He tensed in sudden alarm as he saw the sensor bracelet on her wrist and the suspiciously innocuous necklace around her slender neck. A reporter…he gritted his teeth, reminding himself to be polite. He was too old to slug reporters, particularly ones who looked sweet and innocent.

They're the worst of the bunch, he reminded himself. *They're the ones who need to make a name for themselves.*

"I believe you served with my father," the reporter said. "Do you have a moment to chat about him?"

Henry blinked. A reporter whose father had served with him? He stared at her for a long moment, utterly unsure who she meant. It had to have been on *Ark Royal,* but as far as he knew his fellow starfighter pilots hadn't had children. And then the penny dropped. Penny Schneider very definitely took after her mother. *Kurt* Schneider had been tall, but dark.

And he'd be rolling in his grave at the thought of his daughter becoming a reporter, he thought, sourly. *There's no difference between reporting and whoring.*

"I could find a moment, if it's just about him," Henry said. The compartment was steadily emptying, but there were still dozens of people finishing off the alcohol. *And* the snacks that had been shipped all the way from Earth. "There are things I am not at liberty to talk about."

She inclined her hand towards the nearest hatch, but Henry shook his head and led her into a quiet corner instead. Being alone with a reporter was like being alone with a young woman, only worse. The latter would have the media reporting they were engaged before they even got to first base, but the former would lead to 'off the record' quotes that would be taken seriously by everyone, even though they were a tissue of lies. He eyed the bracelet at her wrist balefully as he leaned against the bulkhead, feeling a dull thrumming echoing through the giant ship. He knew from bitter experience that a skilled editor could forge anything, if it wasn't turned off to facilitate an 'off the record' conversation.

"You knew my father," Penny said. "What was he like?"

Henry's eyes narrowed. Penny wasn't *that* much younger than him. She would have had years with her father before his death. But then, she probably wouldn't have seen him as anything other than *dad*. Someone else might have a different perspective.

"He was a good man," Henry said, finally. There were details he wasn't going to talk about, even to Kurt's daughter. Perhaps *especially* to Kurt's daughter. She didn't need to know that her father had been having an affair before his death over Tadpole Prime. "He took care of his pilots, treated us" - he broke off, rethinking his next words - "treated us as though we mattered. And he never fawned over me when he finally found out who I was."

"Dad wouldn't have," Penny said. "He was never impressed with titles."

Henry shrugged. He wasn't sure *what* Kurt Schneider had been doing before he'd been called back to the colours, but the military tended to strip a man down to the bare essentials. It was hard to be impressed with fancy titles when no amount of aristocracy would make a difference between life and death. All that mattered, as far as he was concerned, was that Kurt Schneider hadn't treated him any differently from any other pilot.

"There isn't much more I can tell you," he said, flatly. "We didn't sit down to chat about our futures."

Penny lifted her eyebrow. "Why not?"

"We didn't know if we *had* a future," Henry told her. He frowned, trying to choose the right words. "How old are you?"

"Twenty-six," Penny said.

Henry frowned. "You're maybe a little *too* old to understand," he admitted. "Most of us starfighter pilots...we were big kids. Eighteen-year-old kids...I think the oldest, save for the Old Man, was twenty-two. Half of us were rushed through the academy and shoved into cockpits because the Admiralty was desperate. We were kids and some of us acted like kids, despite our training. Maybe we were being stupid, maybe we were storing up trouble for ourselves, maybe...what's the point of worrying about consequences if there's no chance of living long enough to face them?

"Your father...he was *our* father, in a way," he continued. "He kept us going, he led us into battle, he imposed some order...he was a good man. Maybe him having kids of his own gave him an insight into us that other officers didn't have...I don't know. The point is he was good to us. I wish he'd survived, but he died well."

He cocked his head. "Why do you ask?"

"I wish I'd known him better," Penny admitted. "I was a young woman, I thought; charming, sophisticated, worldly...of *course* my father knew nothing."

"A common delusion," Henry said.

"And now I think I understand him a little better," Penny added. "But I won't be able to tell him so."

Henry frowned. He'd never been very religious, although looking at the way the stars and planets interacted so perfectly made it hard to believe there *wasn't* a higher force responsible for ordering the universe. A deeply-religious person would probably have suggested that Penny would see her father again, one day; he wasn't sure, really, if he wanted to say anything of the sort. God alone knew - he smiled at the thought - which way she'd take it.

"Pass the lesson on," he said, instead. He met her eyes. "Are you the sole reporter?"

"I think I'm the sole embed," Penny said. "There's a bunch more reporters down near the flag deck."

Henry nodded. He'd avoid them like the clap.

"I do have other questions," Penny said. "What's it like, dealing with the Tadpoles?"

"Strange," Henry said.

He hesitated. "It's like talking to someone from a completely different culture, only worse," he said. "We say that humans are divided by a common language, but we don't even have *that* with the Tadpoles. They are so different from us that we can think one thing and they can think another. Their society is very strange, to our eyes; they find ours just as odd, threatening even. We have to triangulate every point with them just to be sure we're both talking about the same thing."

"Like talking to a child," Penny said, wryly.

"Or teenage boys talking to teenage girls and lacking the maturity to know that people can sometimes say the wrong thing by accident," Henry said. "I think we should be grateful that they prefer to live under the waves. There's little room for accidental contact and conflict. Long may it stay that way."

"We both live in space," Penny pointed out.

"But we have space to live in space, pardon the pun," Henry said. "The galaxy is big enough for both of us."

"So you're not a *Star Wanderer* fan, then," Penny said.

Henry snorted in resigned amusement. *Star Wanderer* was a relatively new show, he'd been told, featuring a crew composed of multiple alien races. He'd watched one episode, then given up in disgust. The producers had evidently never set eyes on a Tadpole when they'd crafted their crew roster - there were plenty of inexcusably inaccurate details - but that wasn't the worst of it. A Tadpole simply didn't *think* like a human. To have one sitting down for a friendly chat with his human comrades...

"I don't think we'll ever be *close*," Henry said. It was regretful, but it was true. And it was something he needed to make clear, time and time again. "We have certain interests in common, to be fair, but we're really quite different. Both of us would probably be more comfortable keeping our distances from the other."

"I see," Penny said. "Thank you for your time, Your Highness."

Henry watched her go, wondering just how much of their chat had been genuine. She *was* Kurt Schneider's daughter - he could check that, easily - but the rest? Had she been genuinely interested or was she trying to develop a relationship, one she could use to ask him more worrying questions? He had no way to know. He'd met too many reporters to relax completely around them.

And maybe you're being paranoid, he told himself, firmly. *Kurt's daughter is an established reporter. She doesn't need cheap tricks.*

But he knew, as he turned and headed for the hatch, that he'd never be entirely sure.

CHAPTER
FOURTEEN

"Status report," Susan ordered.

"All systems report ready, Captain," Paul Mason said. The XO looked up from his console and glanced at her. "Local space is clear."

"Shipyard command has cleared us to depart," Lieutenant Theodore Parkinson said. The communications officer worked his console for a long moment. "I have established a direct communications link to *Texas* and *Duquesne*."

Susan drew in a long breath. The majority of the task force had assembled just outside the shipyard, waiting for them. Nine battleships, three fleet carriers, over seventy smaller ships from a dozen different nations...it was the most formidable fleet humanity had assembled, save - perhaps - for the fleets that had fought the Battle of Earth. And those fleets, Susan suspected, would have been given a very hard time, if they'd had to face Task Force Cromwell. The battleship armour would have shrugged off most of the pre-war weaponry without even being scratched. Admiral Naiser had been entrusted with a terrifying amount of power and responsibility.

And if we don't make it back, Susan thought, *the war may be lost.*

"Bring the drives online," she ordered, pushing her fears aside. "And prepare to take us out of the shipyard."

A low hum echoed through the ship, growing stronger and stronger with every passing moment. Susan listened, knowing she'd grow accustomed to the background noise soon enough. Some engineers swore they could detect problems merely by listening to the thrumming of the drives, although Susan suspected they were exaggerating. But then, it *was* true that subtle drive problems *did* tend to change the background hum…

"Drives online, Captain," Lieutenant David Reed said. The helmsman looked excited. He'd been running simulations, of course, but nothing quite matched reality. It wouldn't be the first time the simulations had overlooked a set of major problems. "We are ready to depart."

Susan glanced at Mason. "Confirm that we have severed all links to the shipyard and that all shipyard personnel have left the ship."

There was a pause. "Confirmed," Mason said. "All non-crew are accounted for."

"Good," Susan said.

She allowed herself a tight smile. Stellar Star might be able to get away with *accidentally* kidnapping shipyard workers because she had to depart immediately, but the real world was rarely so accommodating. Any unintentional stowaways would be returned to the shipyard, of course, where a lot of sharp questions would be asked. An *intentional* stowaway… she wasn't quite sure what would happen to him. It would be largely unprecedented.

"Helm," she ordered. "Take us out."

The thrumming grew stronger as *Vanguard* inched forward, picking up speed as more and more drive sections came online. Susan keyed her console, bringing up the raw feed from the sensors monitoring the engineering compartment. It *looked* as though everything was perfect, but she kept a sharp eye on it anyway. A rogue drive harmonic at the wrong moment would completely ruin their day. And, with so many foreign ships in close proximity, it would be impossible to hide what had happened. Britain would be embarrassed in front of the entire world.

And I'll probably take the blame, she thought, dryly.

"Passing the inner defence layer now," Reed reported. "All systems nominal."

Susan nodded, slowly. It definitely *looked* perfect. *Vanguard* had never been the most manoeuvrable of starships - she handled like a wallowing pig, rather than a bird in the air - but she was picking up speed. And her helmsman was very experienced, capable of pushing her right to her limits. No one would ever mistake *Vanguard* for a light cruiser or a destroyer, but the battleship might surprise her enemies. Or her critics.

Funny how they stopped complaining about the cost when we discovered we needed her, she thought. Her lips curved in a moment of amusement. *If we hadn't started building battleships, the war would probably have been lost by now.*

She sobered, remembering a position paper she'd read while she'd been XO. It had been the Tadpoles who'd first started building battleships, rather than humanity. And they'd put *their* dreadnaught design into production at terrifying speed. The writer had wondered if humanity, far from being supremely innovative, was actually at risk of losing the innovations race. Fear of being effortlessly crushed had led to billions of pounds - and other currencies - being ploughed into next-generation weapons programs.

But there's also the risk of accidentally crippling herself, she recalled. *The armoured carriers were useless until they suddenly weren't.*

She leaned back as *Vanguard* slid into position, flanked by HMS *King Edward* and USS *Alabama*. The American battleship was larger than *Vanguard* - the Americans always seemed to build on a greater scale than anyone else - but she had a private suspicion that the design had its limitations. *Alabama's* power curves were so high that losing even a single fusion core might cripple the ship. And she was so massive that she might well draw most of the enemy fire. Susan couldn't help wondering, cynically, if the reason Admiral Naiser had chosen to fly his flag on *Vanguard* was because she might attract less fire.

Unless the Foxes remember us from previous engagements, she reminded herself. *They might see us as the more desirable target.*

"Full command datanet established, Captain," Parkinson reported. "Command datalink is up and running; tactical primary and secondary networks up and running. We are good to go."

Susan frowned. "No difficulties with the interface?"

"None, Captain," Parkinson confirmed. "We can talk to them without problems."

"As long as we can fight with them," Mason commented.

"There shouldn't be any problems, Commander," Parkinson assured him. "The datanet is designed to adapt to any problems."

Susan exchanged a glance with her XO. They both knew that command datanets could be weakened, if not crippled, in the real world. The enemy would do everything in their power to disrupt them, using everything from ECM drones to warhead detonations to create confusion. Directly *hacking* the command network was probably impossible, but *nothing* could be taken for granted. There were some downsides to standardising everything. One of them, she had to admit, was that someone who learned to crack one system would probably be able to crack others.

But we don't have a choice, she thought. *We have to fight together as one.*

"Signal from the flag," Parkinson said. "The task force is to proceed as planned."

Susan nodded. "Take us out in formation."

"Aye, Captain," Reed said.

Susan felt a flicker of cold ice running down her spine as the task force began - slowly - to pick up speed, heading straight towards the tramline. There was no reason to assume they were under observation, no reason to believe the enemy was massing to stop them, but she knew she wouldn't feel comfortable until the deployment was over. The die was cast, assuming they managed to pass the naval base without being redirected to the war front.

She closed her eyes for a long moment. She'd sat down last night and read through her will, trying to decide if anything should be changed. She had no direct heirs, no close relatives save for her father; no close friends who weren't already on *Vanguard* or serving somewhere in deep space. It was hard to decide who should inherit her possessions, such as they were, let alone her savings. In the end, she'd ordered the former to go to her father, with a request that he distributed them as he saw fit. The latter could go to the naval fund. Maybe the money would help a struggling family survive after the breadwinner was injured or killed.

"Captain," Reed said. "We will be crossing the tramline in five hours, forty minutes."

Susan opened her eyes. "Very good," she said. She nodded in approval. Admiral Naiser clearly wanted to move as quickly as possible, even though it would take six weeks to reach UXS-566. But then, they *did* have a lot of work to do, work that was better done away from their political superiors. "Commander Mason, please remind the crew that this is their last chance to record a message before we cross the tramline."

"Aye, Captain," Mason said.

Susan concealed her amusement at his tone. Everyone on the ship knew that they wouldn't have another chance to send a message home, not directly. Sending messages with homeworld-bound ships was easy, but it could take weeks - if not months - before they reached their destination and a reply came winging back. She still recalled with some embarrassment the time she'd received several messages from her father, only to discover that they were all the *same* message, sent in several different ways. It was one of the minor annoyances of serving away from Earth.

And far too many officers received a 'Dear John' message, she thought, sourly. *Their partners didn't even wait until they got home to break the news.*

She pushed the thought aside. The task force was on the way. And that was all that mattered.

––––––––

Commodore Solange Leclère, John Naiser considered, was beautiful, in the same sense a lion or a tiger might be considered beautiful. Honey-dark hair, dark eyes, perfect skin and a body her uniform didn't *quite* conceal...if he'd played for a different team, he had the feeling it might have been hard to deny her anything she wanted. Her file made it clear that she also had a mind like a steel trap, something that really wasn't a surprise. Beautiful or not, Solange would not have risen to command rank - and then to flag rank - without being extremely competent. The French, like the British, had learned hard lessons about aristocratic entitlement.

Although they'd insist they didn't have an aristocracy, he thought. *And they'd deny the suggestion they did have with vigour.*

"I see no flaw with the tactical plan, John," Solange informed him. "But I do wonder at the deployment decisions. Would it not be better to fight the fleet as a unit?"

"We certainly will, once we break into the enemy rear," John said, patiently. "But until then, we are better off subdividing the fleet into three sections."

"Sections that will be close enough to offer mutual support, if necessary," Commodore Kevin Hoover injected. "It might be smart, though, to adjust our deployments. *Texas, Alabama* and *Montana* have trained together before, fighting as a unit."

"Which is in direct contravention of the orders we have received from our superiors," Solange snapped. "We are a multinational force!"

"And Admiral Naiser can override such orders, if necessary," Hoover said. "There is political reality and there is military reality and the two don't always meet."

And you are asking this now, when we are still within communications range of Earth, John thought, in tired annoyance. *Someone* was playing politics and he wasn't sure who. Both officers, perhaps. *This should have been settled last week.*

He took a breath, cutting off Solange before she could speak. "I am aware of the advantages in having our three American battleships serving in the same unit," he said. "Those advantages are obvious. But we have six weeks to drill together, figuring out our strengths and weaknesses. I see no reason to change the tactical formation now. If we have *real* problems over the voyage, we will reconsider."

Solange looked pleased. Hoover looked irritated, rather than annoyed or frustrated. Had he decided to back down with good grace or was he planning to revisit the issue, once the task force had crossed the tramline? Was he playing politics for an audience back home or was he genuinely concerned with efficiency? There was no way to know. John couldn't help thinking that war had been a great deal simpler when Britain had been facing the Indians.

"You should all have received the first set of simulations," he said, changing the subject slightly. "The later sets will be put forward by my staff, sight unseen."

"Of course," Hoover agreed. "We wouldn't want anyone to teach to the test."

"No," Solange said. "That would be awkward."

John nodded. The simulations were deliberately designed to push the edge as much as possible, giving the enemy technological advantages that - he hoped - they didn't possess in real life. Their missiles were faster, their starfighters more agile, their sensors so capable that they could track operations in real time...if his crews could survive training, they should be able to handle any real-life threat. But there were also problems, he knew. If they underestimated the enemy at any point...

And there's always someone trying to play games, he reminded himself. *It wasn't that long since they had us flying through a trench to put a missile through an exhaust vent.*

"We will commence training as soon as we cross the tramline," he said. "Do you have any further concerns?"

"Merely that there will be limited opportunities for marine training," General Horace Ross said, curtly. "We can and we will drill as much as possible in VR tanks, but they're not *real* and everyone knows it. Ideally, I'd like a chance to carry out a full landing drill before we reach enemy space."

John considered it. "I don't see how, unless we take a week out of our schedule," he said, slowly. He could see Ross's point, but - at the same time - he knew they had to reach their destination as quickly as possible. "I was informed that your division had carried out landing drills before being dispatched out here."

"We did," Ross said. "*My* division. The French, Russian and Chinese troops - to say nothing of the Royal Marines - were not included. There will be problems, sir, that will not show up until we actually make the drop. And at that point, it will be too late to fix them."

"I see," John said. Landing troops on Unity had been unexpectedly complicated - and Unity hadn't been populated by aliens intent on slaughtering the invaders. The troops hadn't had to worry about ground fire, let alone the prospect of being overrun before they got their defences into place. "Why wasn't this concern raised during the planning stage?"

"It was," Ross said. "But the plan kept changing, along with the forces assigned to the operation."

That was true, John knew. He'd done his best to stay out of the diplomatic discussions and horse-trading concerning the forces assigned to Operation Cromwell, but it had been impossible to ignore the constant addition and removal of groundpounders, squadrons and even individual starships. His plans had needed to be reworked twice when several ships had been pulled at short notice. General Ross had had the same problem, only worse. There had been no opportunity to conduct an exercise before departure.

"Perhaps your division could carry out the first stage of the landing alone," he said, finally. It wasn't much of a solution, but it was the best one at hand. "The remainder of the groundpounders could be landed afterwards, once the spacehead is established."

"There will be political concerns," Solange pointed out.

"Not here," John said. Was the French government *eager* to see Frenchmen die on an alien world? Probably not, yet it *was* important for them to make a contribution. "We'll look for an opportunity to carry out a drill, General, but if we can't…your men will have to take the lead."

"Aye, sir," General Ross said.

John leaned forward. "We'll pick this up after we cross the tramlines," he said, before anyone could raise any other objections. "Until then…I declare this meeting at an end."

He keyed a command into the console. The holographic images snapped out of existence, leaving him alone. He shook his head, wishing - not for the first time - that he'd done his best to decline the post when it had been offered to him. Command of a multinational fleet would look *very* good on his resume - he hadn't stood on a command deck for nearly six years - but it was also a headache. Too many competing interests, too many political concerns…too many smart officers forced to uphold the demands of their political superiors, even though they *knew* they were nonsensical. He had to keep reminding himself that an officer who sounded like an idiot might not actually *be* an idiot.

If it had been up to me, he thought as he poured himself a cup of tea, *I would have finalised the task force and then drilled for a month before leaving Sol.*

He pushed the thought firmly out of his head. It simply hadn't been possible. Talking Earth's governments into parting with nine battleships had been hard enough, even though Earth *was* hundreds of light years from the front lines. The support ships - the logistics freighters, the marine landing craft - had almost been harder. If the task force had hung around in interplanetary space, burning through supplies as it carried out live fire exercises, *someone* would have started to insist on redeploying some of the ships to the front. And then the task force would have fragmented before the operation had even begun.

"But we're underway now," he told himself. "And they can't call us back now."

He shrugged, then tapped his terminal. A handful of messages rested in the buffer, most of them clearly unimportant. He'd read them later, when he had time. The remainder were more interesting. A personal good luck message from the Prime Minister, a formal copy of his orders from the First Space Lord and a couple of notes from his husband. He opened the latter and settled down to read, knowing he had only two hours to reply. And then there would be no hope of communicating in real time...

But the Foxes have FTL communications, he thought, grimly. It had shocked so many officers, when they'd first heard the news, that some of them were still in denial. *What will happen when we duplicate their systems for ourselves?*

He shrugged. Under the circumstances, it was the least of his worries.

CHAPTER
FIFTEEN

"On three, you go first," Lance Corporal Steven O'Brien muttered. "Ready?"

George tensed as they waited outside the hatch, feeling sweat dripping down her back. The body armour they'd given her fitted astonishingly well - all the more so given that the Royal Marines had yet to see the wisdom of designing body armour for people with breasts - but it was hot and heavy, along with the rest of the equipment she had to carry. The armourer had sworn that the armour would save her life, if she got into a firefight, but there were times when she almost considered the risk acceptable.

"Ready," she muttered back.

She braced herself as O'Brien started to work on the lock, hacking through the controlling circuits to open the door. He'd told her, when she'd been teamed up with him, that he'd been given a choice between trying out for commando training or going straight to jail, but she didn't believe him. A convict who showed promise was more likely to be assigned to a work gang then offered military training. But marines seemed to be fond of bullshit, of telling tall stories to see which ones she'd believe. It was something that alternatively amused and exasperated her.

O'Brien darted back as the hatch hissed open. George moved, raising her rifle into firing position as she rushed into the cabin. The nasty suspicious part of her mind was tempted to wonder if she'd been sent first so she would soak up any bullets, if there *was* someone in the cabin waiting for them. She swept the room, but saw nothing beyond a tiny bed and tinier set of lockers. O'Brien followed her in, covering her with his rifle; she checked the tiny washroom, then peered into the lockers. They were empty.

"Clear," she said, shortly.

"Good," O'Brien grunted. "Lieutenant, Cabin #343 is empty. We're proceeding to Cabin #344."

George followed him out of the compartment, not daring to relax. It had been a hellish three weeks, the marines poking and prodding at her, pushing her right to the limits of her endurance. She found it impossible to care, now, that she was sharing a bed with a man, or showers with a bunch of other men. Happiness, she'd discovered, was getting enough sleep at night. She'd said that to the sergeant and *he'd* told her that she was far from the first person to have *that* insight.

On command, she bent down and started to open the hatch, bypassing the terminal to access the control circuits underneath. It wasn't something she'd thought about, that often, back at the academy, but the marines expected her to be able to make repairs on the fly. She'd never been interested in following an engineering track, yet...

The hatch hissed open. O'Brien lunged in, weapon at the ready. George followed him, eyes flickering from side to side for a possible threat. There was nothing. She reminded herself, sharply, not to get complacent as she saw the same bunk and lockers from the previous cabin, mocking her. There *was* someone hiding in the section, she knew. They had to find him before he could escape.

"Lieutenant, Cabin #344 is empty," O'Brien said. "We're proceeding to Cabin #345."

"Understood," the Lieutenant said. "When you've checked 345, proceed upwards to Point Beta. The rat can't have gotten *that* far away."

George nodded as she followed O'Brien out of the cabin and peered down the corridor. The rat - a lone marine, hiding from his fellows - wouldn't be *easy* to find. Sure, he was within a defined zone, but afterwards? *Vanguard* was massive, with plenty of nooks and crannies he could use as a hiding place. Even the biggest marine was tiny on such a scale. A smart person who knew the battleship as well as her crew could remain ahead of any hunters for *hours*.

The third cabin was just as empty, save for a few hints that *someone* had been inside, using the bed. George puzzled it over for a second, then decided that a couple of crewmen must have turned the compartment into a secret love nest, assuming that none of their superiors would notice. They were probably right. She scanned the room anyway, making sure that nothing was particularly out of place, then walked out of the compartment and down towards Point Beta. O'Brien followed her, his weapon at the ready.

"You're relaxing too much," he warned, as they reached Point Beta. "The rat could be anywhere."

George nodded, curtly. Point Beta was nothing more than a set of hatches isolating one part of the hull from the next. A trio of marines guarded the outer hatch, checking their faces before allowing them to slip through; another two stood on duty by the inner hatch, their weapons at the ready. George wondered, absently, if the marines had bothered to guard the tubes, then told herself not to be stupid. The tubes were the easiest way to move around the ship without being seen. Of *course* they'd be guarded.

"Subsection C is next to be checked," the lieutenant on duty said. "Bill and Andy are already entering from Point Charlie."

"We'll move through from here," O'Brien said. George cursed inwardly, trying to hide her dismay. Her body was aching too badly. "Remind Bill and Andy they're not supposed to shoot us."

"I'll try," the lieutenant said, dryly.

George resisted the urge to cringe as the inner hatch opened, revealing yet another corridor and a handful of hatches. Friendly fire wasn't *dangerous*, not with training weapons, but Sergeant Tosco would give everyone involved thousands of push-ups: the shooter for being stupid enough to pull the trigger without making sure of the target *and* the target for getting shot. It was better than the base, where a negligent discharge brought a fine and a lecture from one's commander, but not by much.

And better than being shot during an actual fight, she reminded herself. *Body armour can't stop everything*.

The hum of the drives seemed louder as the hatch hissed closed behind them. She peered into the distance, her eyes narrowing as she saw the closed hatch. Bill and Andy would be on the other side, making their way down to her. But surely guarding the hatch would have made sense…she shook her head, remembering how few marines had been assigned to the search parties. The LT just didn't have the manpower to do more than isolate the subsection and sweep the compartments, one by one.

She glanced at O'Brien. "What happens if he stays ahead of us indefinitely?"

O'Brien shrugged as they reached the first hatch. "He gets to watch as the rest of us clean the barracks with toothbrushes," he said. "Unless he cheated and sneaked outside the exercise zone. Some bastard tried that back when I was a boot. The sergeant was not amused."

George nodded, sourly. It was never easy to know when cheating was acceptable and when it wasn't. There were times when she was encouraged to bend the rules and times when she was warned that any rule-bending would get her in very real trouble. But she was fairly sure that sneaking outside the exercise zone counted as the latter. The hunters weren't *meant* to be wasting their time, poking around like idiots.

The hatch opened. She swept the room with practiced ease, but there was no sign of the enemy. The compartment was clean and tidy, just waiting for a guest. She heard a hatch opening further down the corridor and sighed in annoyance. Bill and Andy had already completed their side of the subsection, then. They'd take great delight in rubbing it in once the entire squad returned to the barracks.

She turned and paced out of the cabin, weapon at the ready. A second later, a strong arm grabbed her and yanked her backwards, wrapping tightly around her neck. George kicked out, a second before she felt a knife pressed against her throat. She forced herself to stand very still as her captor held her firmly, cursing under her breath. There was no hope of escaping hours of mockery in the barracks, afterwards. She'd become a literal damsel in distress.

O'Brien burst out of the cabin, rifle raised. "Let her go," he snapped. "Now!"

"I walk out of here or the bitch dies," George's captor snarled. George shivered. It was a drill, but…there was a knife at her throat and accidents happened. "Back the fuck off, now!"

"Put her down and we take you alive," O'Brien snapped. His voice was harsh. He would have triggered the alert, wouldn't he? "We don't negotiate with hostage-takers!"

George moaned, despite herself. The pressure on her throat was growing unbearable. She was all too aware of the knife, ready to cut her open. O'Brien was right. Britain did *not* negotiate with hostage-takers. Better to kill the terrorists, even at the price of killing the hostages, then allow the scumbags to think they could take hostages to gain leverage. She knew all the agreements, all the possible situations she might face if she became a commanding officer in her own right, all the logical reasons to refuse to dicker…

…And none of them seemed believable, somehow, when it was *her* life at risk. She could *die* here, killed in a training exercise that went a little too far…Her heart raced as she struggled to breathe. She felt a warm trickle running down her legs as her bladder gave way. She could die…

"Slash," her captor said. "She's dead."

"Bang," O'Brien said. He jabbed his rifle forward. "So are you."

George gasped for breath as she was released. Her throat hurt… she touched it, half-expecting to feel blood. But there was merely a sore patch…she sighed, realising she had managed to embarrass herself. How many marines had been taken hostage? There had been some, she knew, during the Troubles, but most of them had either died quickly or managed to escape. Hell, their captors had *known* there would be no mercy, when they were caught. She wondered, as she adjusted her clothing as delicately as she could, just what the sergeant would have to say about it. Maybe there was a way she could have freed herself…

"Lieutenant, we killed the rat," O'Brien said. "Fitzwilliam was killed too."

"Metaphorically speaking, one hopes," the lieutenant said. "Report back to barracks and grab a shower. There'll be a post-exercise chat afterwards."

"Understood," O'Brien said.

He glanced at George. "Well," he said. "*That* could have gone better."

George nodded, stiffly. Technically, she'd been killed...it would look very embarrassing, afterwards. And while they *had* caught the rat...she looked at the rat, an older marine. He'd stayed ahead of them for hours, even though he'd been caught. That was more than long enough to do some real damage, if he knew what he was doing. The thought of someone managing to set off a missile warhead inside the hull was terrifying.

It's supposed to be impossible, she reminded herself. *There are dozens of safety systems built into the command modules.*

She scowled as she followed O'Brien back down the corridor and onwards to Marine Country. The rat bid them both farewell as they passed Point Beta, stopping to speak to a couple of his comrades. George had a nasty suspicion they were about to hear a detailed report of just how he'd stayed ahead of them...she sighed under her breath, knowing there was no way to avoid it. They needed to know what had gone wrong before they tried it for real.

Her uniform felt damp and icky, soaked with sweat and urine. She was hardly the first person to lose control of her bladder when she thought she was in danger - the briefing notes she'd read at the academy had made it clear that it happened there too - but it was still embarrassing. The marines might tease her, if they noticed. She undressed as soon as they entered the shower cubicle, putting her equipment to one side and tossing the filthy uniform into the basket. The marines did their own washing - she wasn't looking forward to *her* turn on that rota - but none of them would bat an eyelid. Filthy uniforms were alarmingly common.

"Five minutes," Sergeant Tosco shouted, as she stepped into the shower. O'Brien followed her at a more sedate pace. "Then come join us in the briefing room!"

George groaned. She would have sold her soul for a *long* shower - or a bath. Instead, she washed herself down hastily, then dried herself as the water cut off. Her pale body was married with scars and red marks, including a nasty-looking bruise on her face. The body armour had taken its toll too, sadly. She supposed she should consider herself lucky. She'd seen far worse scars, scars that refused to heal, on older marines.

She stepped out of the shower and dressed rapidly, donning clean clothes and picking up her equipment. *Someone* might make a fuss about her leaving it out, even though she was fairly sure O'Brien wouldn't have tried to steal it. Losing her rifle, even one loaded with practice ammunition, would *definitely* have landed her in hot water. She returned the body armour to the rack, then joined O'Brien as they walked into the briefing room. A dozen marines were already there, studying a hologram of the exercise zone. The rat was standing beside them, his fingers tracing out his path on the diagram. George took a hard seat and forced herself to relax. She'd screwed up and she knew it, but she would *learn* from it.

"An interesting exercise," Sergeant Tosco said, once they were all assembled. "What went wrong?"

"Insufficient manpower," the rat said. "As you can see" - he traced out a line on the map - "I was able to move from place to place without being detected. You *did* have the tubes fairly well guarded, but I got through one sweep by hiding in a spacesuit. No one thought to check it."

"Or to ram a bayonet into it," someone said, from the rear.

"A kick would have sufficed," the rat said, dryly. "I didn't run into trouble until I got into Subsection C, whereupon I found I was too close to a pair of determined searchers."

"Heh," Andy said.

"Silence," Sergeant Tosco ordered. "Continue."

The rat shrugged. "I got through the next hatch, only to run into another pair of searchers," he said. "At that point, I decided I was fucked anyway, so I tried to take a hostage. It failed."

George felt herself flush as several of the marines laughed. "We killed you."

"Yes, but I killed you," the rat said. "It wasn't a good trade."

"Probably not," Sergeant Tosco agreed. He raised his voice. "We took forty minutes to find and kill the rat. Forty minutes! Do you know how much damage he could have done in that amount of time?"

Too much, George said.

"Manpower was a problem," the rat said, again. "You just didn't have the numbers you needed to flood the exercise zone. I could and did double back from time to time. You couldn't even secure your rear."

"We trapped you," O'Brien said.

"Only because I couldn't leave the exercise zone," the rat said. "If this had been real, I would have sneaked out and left you wasting your time."

Bill held up a hand. "We were also deliberately limiting ourselves," he said. "I know we weren't meant to use shipboard sensors, but we didn't use our own portable devices too. Next time, we should sow sensors networks through the corridors and track everyone within the zone. At best" - he nodded to the rat - "our quarry wouldn't be able to move, allowing us to systematically search the area until we caught him. At worse, a single motion would be enough to betray his location and allow us to steer troops to him."

"Advanced sensors can fail," Sergeant Tosco pointed out.

"Yes, Sergeant," Bill said. "but we wouldn't be limiting ourselves if we were hunting for a *genuine* intruder."

"True," Sergeant Tosco agreed. He cleared his throat. "We'll be carrying out more exercises tomorrow, so I want you to get something to eat and then swap bunks. Expect some fun tomorrow."

"Great," O'Brien said. He sounded as though he meant it. "Thank you, Sarge."

"Dismissed," Sergeant Tosco said. "Except you, Fitzwilliam."

George gritted her teeth, but waited until everyone else had left the room. "Sergeant?"

"You got taken prisoner," Sergeant Tosco said. His eyes bored into hers. "What went wrong?"

"I heard the hatch opening outside," George said. She'd had a moment to think about it, thankfully. "It never occurred to me that it might *not* be Bill and Andy. In hindsight..."

"You should have been careful," Sergeant Tosco said. "And you should have fought harder, when you were captured."

"I had a knife at my throat," George protested. A twinge of pain reminded her that the knife had been real. "Sergeant...!"

"You were also a valuable hostage," Sergeant Tosco reminded her. "Hostage-takers have to be careful not to kill the golden goose, as it were."

His lips curved up into something that could - charitably - be called a smile, if she used her imagination. "Apart from that, how did you cope?"

"Well enough, sir," George said. She was damned if she was admitting weakness. To lose because she couldn't hack it was one thing, to lose because she simply gave up was quite another. "I could do it again."

"And you will," Sergeant Tosco said. "Get some sleep. Tomorrow, you'll be doing it all over again."

And everything else too, George thought. She shivered as she saluted, then headed for the hatch. *If this is what it's like for the Royal Marines, what is it like for the SAS?*

CHAPTER
SIXTEEN

"As you can see," Doctor Jane Lewis said, "the alien computer tech is actually roughly comparable to ours."

Henry allowed himself a thin smile as he studied his guests. Admiral Naiser was a friend, of sorts. Henry had certainly spent a great deal of time working with Naiser over the last couple of months, after *Vanguard* had returned from Operation Unity. But Commodore Solange Leclère was a newcomer, while Penny Schneider was a reporter. The former, at least, had a solid record in the French Navy. He still wasn't quite sure what to make of Penny Schneider.

"They do have their own quirks," Jane added, after a moment, "but they are far more comprehensible than Tadpole tech. I think we can be reasonably sure we are pulling intact datafiles from captured computers."

"Those that survived long enough to be captured," Henry added. "The Foxes were careful to destroy a number of cores that might have fallen into our hands."

"*Previsible*," Solange said.

"Maybe not," Penny pointed out. "Didn't we have considerable trouble drawing *anything* from captured Tadpole computers?"

"We drew enough to plan Operation Nelson," Admiral Naiser said. "A *wise* opponent would assume that the encryption protocols *would* be insufficient to protect their data, particularly if people with security clearances were captured too."

Henry nodded in agreement. "All of our cores are designed for self-destruct if there's a serious prospect of them being captured," he said. "Most of their computers seem to have been designed along the same lines."

He leaned forward. "We still don't know how they send messages at FTL speeds."

Solange frowned. "There are no *theories*?"

"There are a dozen theories," Admiral Naiser said. "But we haven't been able to determine which one of them is true, yet. Capturing an intact sample of the technology is an obvious priority."

"Of course," Solange agreed. "Can we *use* their technology?"

"Oddly, we shouldn't have any difficulty turning their technology against them," Henry said, dryly. "Most of their devices are quite simple, rather like a child's first computer toy. It puzzled us until we remembered that there are actually *two* races involved. They design their kit to be usable by both races. There's no reason why we shouldn't be able to use their kit ourselves."

He shrugged. "Of course, the more complex the device, the less likely we will be able to use it in a hurry."

Naiser met his eyes. "Because we don't speak the lingo?"

"And quite a few other issues," Henry said. "The Foxes and Cows seem to simplify everything to a remarkable degree, but we don't understand their cultural references and everything else they use to get along. We've been teaching a few contact specialists their language, yet there will be… issues…that will only become clear upon actual discussions."

"Hacking their systems is out, then," Solange said, wryly.

"For the moment," Henry said. He shrugged. "In theory, we could hack their systems; in practice, it probably couldn't be done under battle-field conditions."

He leaned forward. "I'd suggest having the marines start on exploring alien tech and how it works, but really…it's quite easy to understand."

"A more practical issue, of course, is their space-based weapons," Solange put in. "We know some of their weapons, but are there others?"

"We're not sure," Henry admitted. "Much of their tech appears to be equal to ours, but we know their starfighters are cruder than ours and their stealth systems effectively superior. I suspect that's a cultural trend, rather than a technological limitation - we expect to see them introduce superior starfighters fairly quickly."

"If they haven't already been seen along the war front," Naiser said.

Penny leaned forward. "How long would it take *us* to design and produce a completely new starfighter?"

"It would depend," Henry said, honestly. "If we were modifying a current design, we could probably iron out the bugs and get it into production within six months. Something completely new, perhaps something involving alien tech, would take longer. We might need upwards of two years to get it into production."

"We worked faster during the war," Solange said. "The *last* war, I mean."

Henry shook his head. "We bolted plasma cannons to Spitfires and Hurricanes," he said, shortly. "It boosted their firepower, but it didn't give them any other advantages."

He shivered, remembering the moment he'd ejected into space. A few microseconds either way and he would have died, vaporised by his own starfighter or killed by the enemy. It haunted his nightmares, sometimes. Janelle held him…he told himself to forget it as sharply as he could. There was nothing he could do about it now.

"There weren't any new *starfighter* designs until the end of the war," he said. "*Those* took longer to put together and deploy."

"And we know nothing about their tech base," Naiser said, coldly.

"Or what they think of innovation," Henry added. "For all we know, they have real problems in upgrading their technology. Or that they think they've already reached the top and don't need to go any further. Or…"

He shrugged, expressing his lack of actionable intelligence. It was hard to imagine *any* human power thinking it had reached the limits of the possible, but human nations *had* stagnated before. They'd lost the habit of innovation, of constantly questioning everything…eventually, it had weakened them to the point they'd been beaten by barbarians who *knew* they didn't know everything. Perhaps the Foxes were the same.

Unlikely, he told himself. *Their culture is a constant struggle for dominance.*

"So we expect the unexpected," Naiser said.

"They may well improve their missiles still further, just as we have," Henry said. "They're probably looking for ways to burn through armour too. And to upgrade their own armour."

"And put more battleships into space," Naiser said. "We really need to know more about their industrial base."

"Those details weren't recorded in their computer cores," Jane said. "They may well have believed we'd capture them."

Henry nodded in agreement. *Vanguard's* computer cores might be designed for self-destruct, if there was a realistic prospect of them falling into enemy hands, but that wasn't true of any private terminals or computers owned by her crew. MI5 had warned, constantly, of the dangers, yet Henry knew crewmen sometimes sneaked their own gear onboard. A basic encyclopaedia, something that the average crewman might never touch, would be terrifyingly revealing to alien eyes. And then there were books and movies and plenty of other items that would tell aliens far too much about humanity.

"Of course they weren't," Naiser said.

He looked at Henry. "Are you *sure* we can force the aliens to surrender?"

"I believe so," Henry said. "Our interviews with POWs make it clear. If we can prove our superiority, they'll show us their necks and surrender. I suspect they think we're cheating by continuing the fight."

"They're not interested in total war, then," Solange mused. "More like...more like the states that skirmished before the First World War."

"I think so," Henry said. "They don't seem interested in crushing their enemies, merely in assimilating them. Culturally, they're more like Rome than Dixie. Successful slaves earn their freedom, while their descendants rise to power. I suspect there's even a degree of honour given to those who rise out of slavery. They've overcome great challenges."

He scowled. "On one hand, they're probably not intent on exterminating us," he added, slowly. "But on the other hand, they're also probably determined to find a way to make us submit."

"And to stay submitted," Naiser said. "How will they react if we *pretend* to surrender?"

"Poorly," Henry said. "We need to watch for that, Admiral. They might be fooled the first time, but afterwards...they may see it as foul treachery."

"Joy," Naiser said. He smiled, rather dryly. "But at least we have a chance to hurt them."

Henry nodded. He'd seen the plans - or, at least, the basic outline, drawn up by planners in the MOD. They'd gone over the details again and again. If the aliens could be forced to surrender, well and good; if not, at least their home system would be stripped of its industrial base. And then...

"Let us hope so," he said. "Now..."

———

George stepped into the observation blister, closed the hatch and sank down on the bench, feeling too exhausted to move. Giving her an hour or two off was a joke, a cruel joke...except Sergeant Tosco had been quite serious. She was meant to go on guard duty in a couple of hours, yet...she didn't dare try to sleep. She'd either oversleep or wake up with a throbbing headache. Neither one sounded very pleasant.

The stars outside blazed down on *Vanguard*, mocking her. George looked back at them, wondering which of the points of light were actually starships. Probably none of them, she told herself. The task force was operating under stealth protocols, sneaking around along the edges of inhabited star systems rather than blazing through and announcing their presence to all and sundry. They were too far from the system's primary star for the task force's ships to reflect light.

We'll be dead on our feet by the time we reach our destination, she thought. *Or mad enough to make a blind drop if it will get us some sleep afterwards.*

She rubbed her forehead, feeling a layer of dirt and grime she hadn't been able to remove. A month of heavy exercise, of drill and drill until she was shouting out orders in her sleep, had taken its toll. Maybe she'd earned a little respect, but she didn't know. Part of her was starting to think that giving up was the only way forward. If she went back to Middy Country and kept her head down, or applied for transfer to a remote mining station...it would be a poor end to her career, but at least she'd *have* a career. Right now, she wasn't sure *what* she had.

A star twinkled at her. She blinked in surprise, genuinely shocked. Stars didn't twinkle in space, not when there was no atmosphere to produce the effect. Perhaps it *was* a starship, after all. Or perhaps she was too tired and she'd imagined it...she wondered, absently, what would happen if she just closed her eyes and rested. Perhaps Sergeant Tosco would understand if she crawled off to sleep...

He won't, a voice said, at the back of her head. *You can't sleep on duty.*

But you're not on duty, another voice said. *You can rest...*

The hatch opened. George looked up, then straightened hastily as the captain strode into the blister. She wasn't quite sure where she stood in the chain of command, now, but the captain was still the absolute mistress of her ship. There was something in the way she walked, a confidence, that George admired. Her skin colour hadn't done her any favours, George was sure, and yet she'd risen to command anyway. George couldn't help feeling a surge of envy, mixed with an odd resentment. The captain, at least, didn't have demanding relatives.

"Captain," she said. She stood on wobbly legs and tried to salute. "I..."

"Sit down," the captain said. She sounded amused, rather than angry. George cringed inwardly, hoping that the captain wouldn't send her to sickbay. It would be an admission of weakness, one she could ill afford. "How are you coping?"

George hesitated. One rule she'd learned at boarding school - the same school the captain had attended, if she recalled correctly - was not to complain. Grin and bear it might as well be the school's unofficial motto. But then, she'd also been expected to know the difference between problems that needed adult support and tattling. Getting it wrong could turn someone into a social outcast quicker than a starship could move between Earth and Luna.

"Well enough, Captain," she said, finally. "There's a lot to learn, of course."

She tried to smile, but she was afraid it was more of a grimace. It felt as though she'd studied everything under the sun, from basic weapons handling to electronic repair and engineering under pressure. She'd learnt to fly a shuttle at the academy, but the Royal Marine assault shuttles handled differently...and fly through hostile skies, crammed with antiaircraft

139

weapons ready to blow them into atoms. And then there was…too many things, too many skills she'd had to learn in a hurry. Her brain sometimes felt as though it was going to explode.

"Of course there is," the captain said. "Are you handling it?"

"I think so, Captain," George said. "They haven't kicked me out yet."

She sighed, looking down at the deck. Sergeant Tosco had grown sharper over the last couple of weeks, pointing out her errors more and more. She wasn't sure if that was a good thing or not. It might have been a sign that he was coming to respect her - or at least decided she wasn't a complete waste of space - but it also might be a red flag that her time with the marines was coming to an end. And yet…if they thought she was worthless, they'd kick her out. Wouldn't they?

"That's true," the captain agreed. "Would you prefer to return to Middy Country?"

George hesitated. If her record could be wiped, if she could start again from scratch…she shook her head, knowing it was nothing more than wishful thinking. There was no way she'd be allowed to start again, not after her failures. They would hang over her like a shroud until she left the navy or died in service.

"No, Captain," she said, wondering if it was the right choice. "I want to see this through to the bitter end."

———

Susan hadn't *expected* to meet Midshipwoman Fitzwilliam, not after she'd been transferred to Marine Country. The brief explanation for the midshipwoman's crash course in all things marine hadn't satisfied Susan, but she had a feeling that asking questions would get her nowhere. Major Andres would reject George Fitzwilliam if she didn't come up to scratch and that would be the end of the matter, even though it would make life difficult for the First Middy. George would have to be slotted back into Middy Country with as little disruption as possible.

If she was honest with herself, Susan was tempted to order that George *did* go back to Middy Country. She didn't know George Fitzwilliam *that* well - they moved in very different circles - but it was clear that her training was taking a toll. The younger woman looked thinner, almost *gaunt*. Susan could practically *smell* her from halfway across the small compartment, the stench of sweat and blood she recalled from the gym her father had helped to run, when she'd been a young girl. There was something almost *feral* about her, merged with a tiredness that made it impossible for her to see how informal she was being.

And yet, it was clear she was grimly determined to endure.

Susan studied the young woman for a long moment, wondering if she should raise the issue with Commander Mason or Major Andres. Her father, she suspected, would have advised the girl to quit, pointing out that a woman couldn't meet the minimum requirements for the Royal Marines. Indeed, George *hadn't* joined the Royal Marines, not really. A *dedicated* liaison officer would have started much sooner. There was a point, Susan thought, beyond which struggle was futile. If George couldn't meet the requirements no matter how hard she tried...

But it wasn't something she wanted to say, not really. The will to continue was important, the will to overcome each challenge...

No amount of will can make it possible for a man to knock down an iron wall, she thought, grimly. *But the will to keep going, whatever life throws at you.*

It was an odd thought. *She'd* overcome challenges, but she'd never taken on anything *quite* like this. George Fitzwilliam had been pampered, to all intents and purposes. She'd been the sort of girl Susan had hated, at school. The kind of person who thought that having aristocratic - and *very* well-connected parents - made them better than everyone else. And yet, she *did* have a stubborn determination to continue, whatever happened. Most of *those* girls had folded whenever they'd faced a challenge mummy and daddy couldn't save them from.

"Very well," she said, finally. "You may continue as long as you want to continue."

George gave her a tired smile. "And as long as Sergeant Tosco doesn't kick my ass out of the bunk and give it to someone else."

Susan hid a smile. George would be *horrified* when she realised just what she'd said to her captain, if she remembered it. Susan had known captains who would scream for the lash, if offered such disrespect. Hell, she recalled a particularly unpleasant jerk who'd demoted a lieutenant for grabbing his arm and yanking him out of harm's way. She couldn't remember what had happened to that captain, but she hoped it had been painful.

"Rest now," she said, feeling an odd surge of maternal feeling. What did mothers *do*, anyway? *Her* mother had died when she'd been very young. "When do you have to be back?"

George looked rebellious. "I can't sleep," she said. "I have to be on stag duty in an hour or so."

"I'll wake you in fifty minutes," Susan said, amused. "And then you can make your way back to Marine Country."

She smiled as the girl closed her eyes. George had definitely learned to sleep whenever she had the chance, probably back in the academy. Susan shook her head in droll amusement, then pulled her terminal from her belt and keyed it on. She had no shortage of paperwork to do, after the last set of exercises. And she wasn't due on the bridge for another couple of hours.

Sleep tight, she thought, as George shifted against her. *And wake feeling a little better.*

CHAPTER
SEVENTEEN

"Jump completed, Captain," Reed reported.

"Picking up a challenge from the guardship," Parkinson added. "They're pretty insistent."

"I'm not surprised," Susan said. In theory, it was unlikely that the Foxes could have sneaked around to approach the Unity System from human-controlled space, but it couldn't be ruled out completely. "Send our IFF, then forward Admiral Naiser's datapacket to Admiral Stirling and General Kershaw."

"Aye, Captain," Parkinson said.

She leaned back in her command chair as the tactical display began to fill with green icons, a handful patrolling the system while the remainder orbited Unity. The star system itself was still largely empty, save for a handful of asteroid miners probing the rocks for raw materials, but there were a dozen new stations orbiting the planet. Admiral Stirling was in position, theoretically, to block an enemy offensive into human space or provide support for the Tadpoles when - if - the enemy launched their attack on Tadpole Prime. Susan had her doubts about how well the plans would work out in practice, but she understood the political realities behind them. The gateway to human space could not be left open.

Except they could easily sneak past the guards if they tried, she thought, sourly. *And they know it as well as we do.*

"Picking up a signal from the guardship, Captain," Parkinson said. "They're clearing us to approach the planet."

Susan nodded, relieved. "Inform the flag," she ordered. Admiral Naiser had been cagey about just how *many* of his ships would go to Unity. The crew needed shore leave after six weeks in transit, but Unity hadn't been a good shore leave destination even *before* the Foxes had invaded the planet. "And then lay in a course to Unity."

"Aye, Captain," Reed said. "Course laid in."

"Message from the flag," Parkinson added. "The fleet is to remain in formation."

"Good," Susan said. "Take us out on command."

She allowed herself a moment of anticipation. There were enough ships orbiting Unity for a *real* war game, an exercise that would be far more informative than any number of computer simulations. And the marines would have their chance to practice an opposed landing. The only *real* danger would be being caught on the hop by an alien offensive, but all intelligence reports insisted that the aliens were focusing their attention on Tadpole Prime. Unity simply wasn't anything like as important.

And never will be, she thought, as she felt her ship picking up speed. *Even without the war, investment in this system was minimal.*

"Captain," Reed said. "We will be entering orbit in three hours, forty minutes."

Susan smiled. "Very good," she said, warmly. She glanced at her console. A proposal for a *real* war game had already popped up, although the admirals would have to have the final word. "Mr. XO, you have the bridge. I'll be in my ready room."

"Aye, Captain," Mason said. "I have the bridge."

———

USS *New York* was impressive, John Naiser decided, as he followed Commander Emily Sanderson through the maze of corridors from the airlock to the flag deck. The American battleship was larger than *Vanguard*, yet - he suspected - less capable of taking and absorbing damage. Her armour had been the height of technological advancement, when she'd been dispatched to Unity, but materials science had improved over the last few months. He made a mental note to check her stats and compare them to his designs as he was shown into Admiral Stirling's cabin. It was larger than his too.

The Americans always do it bigger, he thought, wryly. *But that makes their ships bigger targets.*

Admiral Frederick Stirling was about a decade older than him, according to the file; a balding man who'd commanded a cruiser during the First Interstellar War and then spent four years in the Pentagon before finally returning to space. He looked surprisingly fit for his age, John decided, and his sharp eyes suggested there was nothing wrong with his intelligence. The only black mark against him, in MI6's file, warned that Stirling was inclined to err on the side of caution. John would have hated that, when he'd been a starfighter pilot and then CO of a light cruiser, but the older man he'd become felt differently. Some risks had to be borne; others, perhaps, weren't necessary.

"Admiral," Stirling said. "Welcome onboard. Please call me Fred."

John nodded. "I'm John," he said. "And thank you for the invitation."

He allowed himself a moment of relief as a uniformed steward brought a tray of coffee and snacks. Admiral Stirling was his superior, by the international standards hashed out during the First Interstellar War, even though John commanded an independent formation. It could have been awkward, if Stirling had tried to assert command or even co-opt his ships for the ongoing war. There was no way either of them could appeal to higher authority.

"I don't see many people socially these days," Stirling said, a faint hint of a smile suggesting he wasn't entirely serious. "We *did* have a visitor from Tadpole Prime, but it was hard to hold any real discussions when we were wearing swimming trunks and bikinis."

John had to smile. "I'm sure it was a very productive meeting."

"I think there would be complaints if I insisted on *all* meetings being held in the swimming pool," Stirling said. "Perhaps if we swam in coffee instead."

He poured two mugs, then nodded to the plate of snacks. "Please, take what you like," he said. "My chef has been busy sourcing ingredients from the planet and turning them into little delights."

"Thank you," John said. He took a small cake and nibbled it doubtfully. There was too much sugar for his tastes. "What *is* happening on the planet?"

Stirling frowned. "Much of the population has gone to ground, those who refused to leave when the original task force pulled out," he said. "The remainder is working closely with us."

"Good," John said. "I'd heard it was a mess."

"Oh, it is," Stirling assured him. "Unity is not very united. But there isn't anything we can do about that without hampering the war effort, so..."

He shrugged, expressively. "I read the datapacket," he said. "Are you serious?"

John didn't need to ask what he meant. "Yes," he said. "We can put a task force in the enemy's rear."

"And without following a predictable path," Stirling mused. He keyed a switch. A holographic starchart appeared in front of them. "Their FTL communications *will* make life harder for you, won't it? They'll know they need to withdraw ships from the front sooner than you might expect."

"I'm counting on their withdrawal letting *you* know it's time to advance," John said. He tapped an icon on the display. "What *is* the situation?"

"The Foxes are pushing the Tadpoles hard," Stirling said. "Mainly through raids and skirmishes - my intelligence staff thinks they're gearing up for a two-prong advance on Tadpole Prime. The Tadpoles would either have to defend their homeworld, thus sacrificing the remainder of their installations, or try to defeat each prong separately. Either way...it could get bad."

John nodded in grim agreement. Human military operations - and the Tadpoles agreed - were based on the KISS principle: Keep It Simple, Stupid. Trying a two-prong operation, launched from two different systems, was asking for trouble, if only because it would be impossible to coordinate the two operations. It was the kind of tactic that wouldn't be found outside a bad simulator program. But a working FTL communications system changed everything. The Foxes *could* coordinate such an operation, if they wished.

And they'd have fleets entering the system from two different vectors, he thought, grimly. *It wouldn't be easy for the Tadpoles to choose which way to jump.*

"So far, the Foxes haven't shown any interest in resuming the drive on Unity," Stirling added, shortly. "That's good news for us, in some ways, but it's also worrying. The Foxes have almost certainly picked out Tadpole Prime as their priority target. I've been raiding their positions myself, but they haven't tried to return the favour."

"Perhaps we gave them enough of a drubbing to make them back off," John said.

"Perhaps," Stirling said. "But realistically, John, Unity isn't *that* important."

"True," John agreed.

It wasn't really arguable. Unity had a tiny population and almost nothing in the way of off-planet industrial nodes. The only thing that made the system important was its position, yet even *that* was useless - to the Foxes, at least - if they failed to secure their flank. They really needed to knock the Tadpoles out of the war before turning their attention to Unity. At the very least, he considered, they would need to block any renewed offensive from the Tadpoles, just to keep their lines of communication open.

And that won't be easy, he thought. *Tadpole Prime is heavily defended.*

Stirling cleared his throat. "I can't think of any good reason to deny you permission to proceed," he said. He smiled, thinly. "I'm not even sure if I have *authority* to deny you permission to proceed. I *wish* I was coming with you, but…"

He shrugged. "I'll have my spies keep a close eye on their formations," he added. "And if they start to withdraw, I'll give chase. But my logistics are pretty crappy right now."

"It's the same story everywhere," John said. "We just don't have enough freighters to support the war effort."

"Converting half of them into carriers or troop transports probably didn't help," Stirling commented, ruefully. "Building more will have to wait until after the war."

"We probably took too many STUFT ships," John agreed.

"I'll make what preparations I can," Stirling said. "The Tadpoles are being careful about mounting a full-on counterattack. I can't say I blame them, given how closely the Foxes have entrenched themselves to Tadpole Prime, but it is a problem. The diplomats are going to have fun."

John winced. "You can launch the offensive yourself," he said. "Can't you?"

"Theoretically," Stirling agreed. "In practice...? The Tadpoles might be very concerned, post-war, if we are the ones who liberate the occupied systems."

"Politics," John sighed. He'd become familiar with the political realities ever since he'd been promoted to flag rank, but they never ceased to grate. "I wouldn't have thought it was *that* much of a concern."

"We might still lose the war," Stirling agreed. "But...haggling with human powers is one thing, but haggling with the Tadpoles is quite another. No matter what the ambassadors say, I don't think we *really* understand each other."

He shrugged. "When do you plan to depart?"

John leaned forward. "Do you have time for some exercises? My tactical staff would like to hold at least one full-sized drill before we head to UXS-566."

"My staff will be delighted," Stirling said. He showed his teeth. "I look forward to kicking your ass around the system."

"My marines also need to carry out at least one landing drill," John added. "If we can do that, I think we can depart in a week. I take it there's no chance of shore leave?"

"There's nothing in the way of facilities," Stirling said. "But there are some lovely beaches, if you want to give your crews a day or two on the sand. It's their last chance for quite some time."

John nodded. "And there I was thinking you would have built an entire resort by now," he said. "My crews will be very disappointed."

"So were mine," Stirling said. "But right now? Digging in is far more important."

———

Henry wrinkled his nose as he stepped through the airlock, despite nearly a decade as a practicing diplomat. The smell - a strange mixture of fish, decaying flesh and something indefinably alien - pervaded the chamber, threatening to make him gag even though he was supposed to be used to it. But then, he reminded himself, it had been over a year since he'd set foot on Tadpole Prime. His memory had clearly faded.

Five Tadpoles were clearly visible in the water, swimming from side to side with a grace Henry could only admire. It was easy to tell that water was their natural habitat, that creatures that seemed surprisingly clumsy on dry land moved with ease and power under the waves. A sixth swam in a moment later, coming up the pipe that led down to the sea; two more followed, one splashing up and out of the water. Henry ignored the droplets of water flying through the air, knowing it was a friendly greeting. The meeting place - the swimming pool, the disrespectful called it - hadn't been used since Unity had been founded. Unity had been meant to serve as a joint colony, but the two races were largely incompatible. Neither group of colonists had been particularly interested in talking to the other.

He smiled as he saw the goldfish, trying to keep their distance from the Tadpoles. His daughters had been shocked when they discovered that Tadpoles considered goldfish a delicacy…Victoria, in particular, had been horrified. She'd *owned* a goldfish for three years before the poor creature had died. He'd had to swear, time and time again, that he'd given Golden a proper burial, rather than tossing the fish into the sea.

Henry pushed the thought out of his mind as he sat down by the poolside, splashing his feet into the water. There were diplomats on Earth who had never learnt to adapt to the new universe, to talking to aliens with very different physical requirements to humanity. *They* hated the thought of not wearing suits, of not sitting at tables, of not being treated like kings and queens…Henry had found it easy to adapt, simply because he'd had less to unlearn than the professionals. People might scorn at holding diplomatic talks while wearing shorts, swimming trunks or bikinis, but it worked. It wasn't as if the Tadpoles were entirely comfortable in the meeting place either.

The water rippled. Henry watched, impassively, as five Tadpoles surfaced. It was easy to see how they'd been mistaken for animals, the first time a human had set eyes on them. Their shapes were just too *alien*. And yet, he could spot the signs of high technology, the earpieces and voders used to communicate with humans. If that had been noticed, twelve years ago, countless millions of people wouldn't have died.

"I greet you," he said, carefully. It was always best to keep it simple. The computers translated - theoretically - but no one took the translations for granted. A tiny mistake could lead to outright disaster. "We intend to launch an offensive against our common foes."

He repeated his statement twice, using different words each time. It was the only way to be sure the Tadpoles understood what he was saying, even though he'd had to speak quite sharply to a number of ambassadors who'd mistaken the Tadpoles for mentally-disadvantaged children. Everyone who was anyone on Earth spoke English, something that made ambassadors lazy. It was hard for some of the professionals to comprehend that their words, no matter how carefully formulated, might mean something very different to their counterparts.

"This is understood," the Tadpoles said, finally. It was impossible to tell which one of them was talking. The computer-generated voice seemed to come from nowhere. He studied their faces for a moment, but none of them *appeared* to be speaking. "You have developed an enhanced gravity-manipulation effect generator."

Henry honestly wasn't sure if that was a question or not. Were the Tadpoles referring to the Jump Drive or something else? Sneaking into enemy space without one would be harder, but not impossible. And yet… deducing the existence of an FTL drive would have seemed one hell of a jump for humanity, yet maybe not for the Tadpoles. Their understanding of interstellar gravity waves had always been ahead of humanity's.

And they may have developed a jump drive of their own, he thought. *Even if they haven't, they now know it's possible.*

"We plan to hit the enemy rear," he said. He took a datachip from his shorts and held it out to them. "If they redeploy their forces, you will have an opportunity to counterattack."

The Tadpoles took the chip, then vanished under the water. Henry watched, wishing he had a way to listen to the debate. But he suspected that he wouldn't understand, even if he *could* listen. The Tadpoles were democrats in the truest possible sense. *Everyone* got a vote. Hell, there were even xenospecialists who believed the Tadpoles were inching closer and closer to a collective hive mind. Henry wasn't so sure - the

Tadpole Factions seemed to split regularly, whenever they became *too* harmonious - but it was a possibility.

He leaned back as the Tadpoles surfaced. "Engaging the enemy will bring risks," they said, finally. "Launching a counterattack could leave" - the computer refused to translate the next word - "homeworld defenceless."

Their only *homeworld*, Henry thought. It was the logical word. But logic was sometimes nothing more than a way to be wrong with confidence, when the Tadpoles were concerned. *They don't want to risk uncovering their homeworld.*

"The stalemate may be broken from the other side," he said. The Foxes would eventually try to take Tadpole Prime. And the Tadpoles had to know it. "They will eventually launch an attack too."

He sighed, inwardly, as the discussion raged backwards and forwards. *These* Tadpoles wouldn't be able to give him a final answer, he knew. Only the Grand Chorus on Tadpole Prime could do that. But...he sucked in his breath. The discussion would start about the same time Task Force Cromwell reached UXS-566. And maybe, just maybe, the Tadpoles would be ready to go on the offensive when the task force hit the enemy rear.

And even if they don't, he told himself, *Admiral Stirling can still move on his own authority.*

CHAPTER

EIGHTEEN

UXS-566 was a barren wasteland, orbiting a dull red star.

It was, Susan decided as the fleet probed its surroundings, so unimportant that hardly anyone would consider it worth visiting, certainly not *twice*. UXS-566 had only one tramline, a weak line of gravimetric force that would have been completely inaccessible before the war, and nothing beyond a handful of tiny comets that were barely worthy of the name. No planets, no asteroid fields…there was literally nothing to attract anyone, save for its location. An alien- star was a *mere* five light years away.

And yet the star doesn't have enough gravity to create a second tramline, Susan thought, coldly. *This system is forever useless without the jump drive.*

Admiral Naiser's face popped up in front of her. "Captain," he said. "The scouts report that the system is empty. I see no reason to delay any longer."

"No, Admiral," Susan said, after a quick glance at the tactical display. The task force was completely alone, as far as the scouts could determine. There was certainly no logical reason for the Foxes to be picketing UXS-566. "There's nothing to be gained by waiting."

She sucked in her breath. The task force had departed Unity and made its way towards UXS-566, a star system so far off the beaten track that there was no logical reason to go there. And that alone would worry the Foxes. Why would humanity send such a powerful formation into deep space, where it couldn't affect the war? Simple logic would suggest that humanity *did* think the deployment could affect the war. She knew that aliens were…well, *alien*, but they couldn't be *that* alien.

And they might be trying to invent the jump drive themselves, she thought. *We've certainly given them plenty of incentive to improve their Puller Drives. They may even have recovered intact hardware from the first engagement.*

"Then the task force will proceed to Point Suez," Admiral Naiser said. "And we will take every precaution to ensure that we are not detected."

"Aye, Admiral," Susan said.

Admiral Naiser's face vanished. Susan issued orders, then forced herself to relax as the task force slowly moved deeper into the unnamed system. She thought she understood, now, the sheer terror and hopelessness that must have gripped Admiral Smith and his crew, back when they'd found themselves trapped at the end of a string of tramlines. *Ark Royal* had cheated, in the end. It had been a desperate gamble, one that could easily have cost Admiral Smith his ship and humanity the war, but it had worked. Now...

Her eyes sought out the alien-grade tramline, a thin line of invisible force heading back to human space. What if it vanished? What if there was a sudden shift in gravity and the tramline simply popped out of existence? What if they remained stranded...it had been the plotline of a dozen books, back when the tramlines were new and humanity was alone in the universe, but there had never been any sign that the network might collapse. And yet...she told herself, firmly, that she was being silly. There was no reason to think that the tramline would collapse, let alone that it would collapse now.

"Captain," Reed said. "We are approaching Point Suez."

"Slow to all-stop," Susan ordered. She kept her voice calm. Her crew didn't need to hear her fears. "Once we're at rest, relative to the planned jump line, inform Admiral Naiser."

She felt her stomach clench uncomfortably. She'd had plenty of reasons to be nervous in the past, but this was different. This was like...like going into a vacuum chamber for emergency decompression training. *That* had been nightmarish, she recalled. Too many promising cadets had washed out of the academy because they couldn't handle vacuum training. She'd known she'd been safe, yet even *she* had had problems...

And it hasn't even started yet, she thought. *What will it be like when we activate the drive?*

"All-stop," Reed said. "We are at rest."

"Inform the admiral," Susan reminded him.

She studied the display for a long moment. The boffins who'd designed the jump drive claimed it would work, theoretically...but what if it didn't? None of the tests had included a large human fleet. What if a rogue gravity surge reduced the entire fleet to atoms? Or what if they found themselves in the middle of an alien fleet base? Or...she shook her head, firmly, as the engineering crews went to work. No doubt the admirals who'd watched in disbelief as ironclad warships cruised onto the water without instantly sinking below the waves had felt the same way. Technology advanced...

...And those who failed to adapt were left behind.

And sometimes we need to return to the past, she reminded herself. *Ark Royal* had been outdated fifteen years ago, permanently on the verge of being scrapped. And then, *twelve* years ago, she had been all that stood between humanity and a quick savage defeat. *The newer carriers have more in common with Ark Royal than Formidable and her sisters.*

She rose. "Mr. XO, you have the bridge," she said. The most optimistic projections suggested that it would be at least ten hours before the jump drive was ready. She needed to get some rest before they jumped into... into what? There was no way to know what they'd find at ES-19. "I'll be in my ready room."

"Aye, Captain," Mason said. "I have the bridge."

———

Commodore Juliet Watson-Stewart was in heaven.

She cared little for rank or for the niceties of interpersonal communication. The ass-kissing and brown-nosing tactics used by many of her fellow officers were a complete mystery to her, something she'd once found frustrating. But as more and more of her life was consumed by science, by finding an answer to all of life's questions, she had steadily stopped caring about how she appeared to others. She was an objective person in a world where far too many of her fellows were subjective, where something could be a compliment or insult based on tone and status and situation...all things she didn't understand. She simply didn't choose to waste her life on subjective matters. All that mattered was coming up with new theories, finding a way to test them and then turning the confirmed theories into realistic hardware.

"It's coming along nicely," Mike Johnston said. Her husband gave her a tight hug, heedless of the others in the compartment. "The power curves are forming exactly as you planned."

Juliet smiled as she leaned into his embrace. She'd never thought about love, not really, not even when she'd been a little girl whose mother had tried to read her soppy stories of how princesses found their princes and got married. Most men - and women - thought she was either boring or weird, depending on their mood. She was so introverted that she honestly hadn't realised that two-thirds of the men she met admired her looks, at least until it had been pointed out to her. But she found it hard to care about that either. Very few men or women could keep up with her, mentally.

Her husband couldn't either, not in the theoretical realm. But as an engineer - as someone who converted her concepts into practical technology - he was first-rate. And she loved him for it.

"The gravimetric flux appears to be intact," she said. She *had* tested the jump drive, of course. But taking so *many* ships through the tramline was new. "The power lines will need to be boosted."

She reached for her computer terminal and hastily input a series of ideas before they faded back into the background hum. Mike Johnston had told her that she was always thinking, even during sex, and he was right. Sex jogged her mind in ways she hadn't known were possible, at least until she'd started having it regularly. She wished she'd been allowed to fit herself with a direct neural link - her early work on computers had given her an uncanny insight into how the machines actually worked - but this was the next-best thing. Perhaps if she were to alter the gravity field to serve as a power sink...

"The charging should be finished in seven hours," a technician said. "However, the batteries may lose capacity."

Juliet tensed against her husband. Someone had broken her trance... she felt a hot flash of anger, mixed with frustration and annoyance. Mike

Johnston hugged her, then ordered the technician away. That was, Juliet considered, the *other* advantage to having a husband. He stood between her and the outside world, driving away everyone who would seek to interrupt her thinking. But now...she rubbed her forehead in annoyance. She wanted to see her theories at work, she wanted to be there in case something happened, but...maybe they should just have stayed at home. The asteroid research base crew were *far* more understanding of her requirements.

"It doesn't matter," she said, harshly. She was dimly aware that the technician had already fled, but she was talking more to herself than anyone else. "All that matters is that we have the power on hand."

She checked and rechecked the equations, knowing it was pointless. She'd outlined the theory; Mike Johnston had turned it into reality, after the theory had been run past the dozen other brightest minds in gravity research. There was no flaw, yet. Juliet liked to think it was perfect, but she knew better. There was no limit to scientific advancement, no limit to what could be achieved...no limit to theories that would eventually be proven outdated or simply wrong. People in the future would look back and ask, in tones of outrage, how she had been so wrong. Or merely so limited. Why not? She'd wondered at the limitations of *her* predecessors.

"Seven hours," she mused. There would be more power than *strictly* necessary, but the naval staff had insisted on building a degree of redundancy into the jump drive. Admiral Soskice had overruled her when she'd protested. "And then we get to jump."

She wasn't scared, not really. The equations were as close to perfect as she could make them, while the technology had been tested time and time again. She wasn't scared of anything going wrong during the jump. But afterwards...a part of her wondered if she would die, during the operation. She didn't fear death - her private research suggested there *was* a higher force ordering the universe - yet the prospect of not being able to continue her research was terrifying. Who knew what secrets would remain unlocked because she hadn't been the one to look for them?

Juliet shivered, just for a second, then retreated back into the safety of her own mind. The engineering crews could put the jump drive together without her direct supervision. And she could use that time profitably, very profitably indeed. Perhaps, just perhaps, if she meddled with the feedback loop, she could cut the power requirements…

———

"I hear things are proceeding well," Charles Fraser said, as he carefully manoeuvred the worker bee into position. "You seem to be surviving."

George rubbed her forehead, watching her console carefully. "It feels odd," she said. A low tremble ran through the tiny craft as it mated with the jump drive. "I feel less…worried now."

"Sounds like you've passed the hump," Fraser told her. "Can you check the module?"

"It looks fine," George said. Her console lit up as the automated systems confirmed it. "I think we can disconnect."

Fraser nodded, then put the worker bee into reverse. The craft glided backwards, allowing George to pick out the lights studding the giant framework. She shook her head, feeling the all-pervading tiredness threatening to return. It was odd, but she hadn't felt so tired since the drills on Unity. Maybe she was just getting used to it.

She smiled as she took in the jump drive. It looked like a giant framework studded with lights, just like the free-floating space docks she'd seen at the shipyards. And yet, it was far larger, tying the entire fleet into a single unit. The starships wouldn't be crossing the tramline - the artificial tramline - individually, but as a single unit. Thankfully, if they all hopped as one, there shouldn't be any risk of an accidental collision.

"I feel as though I'm finally getting somewhere," she admitted. "But I still have a very long way to go."

"Of course you do," Fraser pointed out, dryly. "You wouldn't be out *here* if they hadn't needed every qualified pilot."

George nodded. There had been no shore leave on Unity for *her*, unless one counted a parachute drop, a twenty-mile forced march and intensive shooting practice as something *relaxing*. She'd enjoyed the shooting practice and the parachute jump, but the march had been something to endure…the final stage, when they'd been trying to avoid the local militia, had been fun. The militiamen had remembered her.

And they learned their skills the hard way, she remembered. *The Foxes tried hard to hunt them all down.*

"It feels funny," she said, softly. "I feel like I'm skiving."

"I don't think the sergeants will hold it against you," Fraser said. "They'll just insist that you have to make it up later."

George sighed as she steered the worker bee back towards *Vanguard*. The giant battleship looked as though she was trapped in the framework, like a fly trapped in honey. Beside her, two other battleships were clearly visible; the remainder, some distance away, hidden behind their running lights. Tiny sparks glinting in the darkness of interstellar space suggested more engineering crews, checking and rechecking the struts before the task force jumped. George hoped - prayed - that nothing went wrong.

"I'm sure they will," she said, morbidly. "I just…I just can't wait to get on with it."

Fraser smiled. "Hard training, easy mission; easy training, hard mission."

"That's what they all say," George said. She shrugged. "How's the new First Middy coping?"

"Well enough," Fraser said. He didn't *quite* say 'better than you,' but George could hear the words hanging in the air. "I've largely left him to it now, though I *have* checked in from time to time. Middy Country seems to be doing well enough."

George winced. Fraser might not have rebuked her, but he might as well have done.

"He handled all the disciplinary issues remarkably well," Fraser added. "Although I dare say you would have no trouble giving someone a clout *now*."

"Now," George muttered.

She wished, grimly, that someone had outlined *all* the problems she would face, as a young midshipwoman with a far too well-connected family. Too young, in her case. In hindsight, perhaps she should have waited another two years before going to the academy. If - when - she left the navy, she was going to write a book outlining all her failures in gruesome detail. It would probably be banned on the spot, but the datanet had a habit of neatly circumventing censorship. And the advice she'd give would be very good indeed.

"It could be worse," Fraser said. "You know that four of the reporters have been sleeping their way through the crew?"

George laughed. "I suppose it could be," she said. "Should I be relieved they haven't tried to get into Marine Country?"

Fraser winked. "Depends," he said. "That redhead was *very* good in bed."

————

"The power curves are developing as predicted," Mike Johnston reported. "We are on track to jump."

"Understood," John said. He glanced at his aide. "And the task force?"

"Every ship has checked in," Commander Jackson Regal said. "The datanet is up and running, using both the hard connections *and* laser communicators."

John scowled, just for a second. The entire fleet was trapped within the framework. If they happened to jump right into the fire, they'd be sitting ducks. *Vanguard* and her consorts could absorb one hell of a lot of damage, but there were limits…particularly as they would be too close together to use *all* of their point defence systems. The projections suggested they should still be able to defend themselves, yet…

He pushed the thought aside. "Please inform your wife that we are about to test her theories," he said. He studied the console for a long moment. "We will jump in ten minutes."

"Yes, sir," Johnston said.

He turned to walk to the hatch. John watched him go, feeling a flicker of amusement mixed with envy. Mike Johnston and Commodore Juliet Watson-Stewart had a *very* loving relationship, a relationship so sweet that it made his teeth ache. And yet, there was no denying they were good together. Mike Johnston provided the technical expertise and interpersonal experience Juliet lacked, ensuring that she had unlimited funding to research whatever interested her.

And after proving that we can build a jump drive, he thought wryly, *only a complete idiot would cut the funding.*

"Admiral," Regal said. "All ships have acknowledged."

John nodded, curtly. For the first time since the discovery of the tram-lines, a human fleet was going to jump into the unknown. Long-range observation had confirmed that ES-19 had at least five planets, but there was no way to know if those planets were inhabited. There had been no radio broadcasts, as far as they'd been able to tell. He'd checked and rechecked the presence of a tramline before ordering the framework put together. Jumping to ES-19 and getting stuck there would be disastrous.

He waited, patiently, as the minutes ticked away. There was no need to hurry. They would make the jump as planned...

"Signal the jump crews," he ordered, finally. "Jump!"

There was a long chilling pause, mere seconds seeming to stretch out to minutes and hours...

...And then the universe went black.

CHAPTER

NINETEEN

Susan felt...*weird*.

The universe had dimmed around her, dimmed...she felt as if she needed to sneeze, as if the entire *universe* needed to sneeze. Her eyes were open, yet it was dark; she could hear nothing, but her ears *hurt*. And then the universe snapped back to normal, so violently that she nearly plunged out of her chair. The disorientation was so great that, just for a moment, she thought she'd had an awful nightmare, as if she'd woken up in shock...

She looked around, grimly. Half the bridge crew seemed to be unconscious; the remainder seemed to be in shock, their eyes flickering from side to side. There didn't seem to be any rhyme or reason, as far as she could tell. Mason was unconscious, as was Lieutenant Charlotte Watson...she cursed under her breath, hastily opening the compartment in her command chair to retrieve the emergency stimulant tab. Using it was a risk, she acknowledged as she pressed the tab against her shoulder, but there was no choice. Half the displays were blank, suggesting...what? Where *were* they?

"Captain," Parkinson said. "I...what happened?"

"Take the helm," Susan ordered. She found a second tab and tossed it to him. The drug was working its way through her system, giving her a burst of energy she knew wouldn't last more than an hour or two. She'd pay a steep price afterwards. "I'll take the sensor console."

This didn't happen during the trials, she thought, as she hurried to the console. *Did the sheer size of the fleet skew things, somehow?*

She put the thought aside for later consideration and checked the console rapidly, praying that the automatic systems had rebooted themselves. They had, thankfully. She checked the records, then waited nervously until the position-monitoring software pinpointed their location. The jump had evidently caused more disruption than anyone had predicted, she realised, but they *were* where they were supposed to be, drifting along the edge of ES-19. Most of the ship's systems were coming back to life as the framework disintegrated, but several departments seemed to be completely out of touch. Everyone inside might well be stunned - or dead.

The jump could have killed someone, she thought, numbly. There were horror stories about the first jumps through the tramlines, but *nothing* had been as bad as this. *Half the crew could be dead.*

"Local space appears clear," Parkinson reported. Beside him, Reed let out a loud moan. "I think we're safe, for the moment."

Susan nodded, sourly. None of the boffins had been able to answer what was, to her, an all-important question. Would the Foxes be able to detect their arrival? The jump drive was a powerful gravity flux, after all. There was a small, but significant possibility that there would be an effect on the system's tramlines. And the Foxes might respond to the flux, if they detected it.

"Give everyone a tab," she ordered, stiffly. The alpha crew would need to sleep for several hours afterwards. It was frustrating, but there was no way to avoid it. "And then try to raise the admiral."

She cursed under her breath as she worked the console. Engineering had reported in, thankfully. A good third of their staff was comatose, but the remainder were already working to free *Vanguard* from the framework. Sickbay took several tries before a nurse took the call, informing Susan that several of the doctors were also stunned. Susan issued orders, then left the nurse with instructions to call her if the situation changed.

"Got a direct link to *Montana*, Captain," Parkinson said. "She's in the same state as ourselves."

Susan nodded, unsurprised.

She moved from officer to officer as they pulled themselves together, offering words of reassurance while silently praying the jump hadn't done any long-term damage. The steady stream of updates from the rest of the ship - and the task force - reassured her more than she cared to admit. Only two fatalities had been reported in the task force, both men who'd stumbled and fallen during the jump. So far, it seemed as though *Vanguard* had escaped any deaths.

"We're free of the framework, Captain," Reed reported. The helmsman sounded drunk. If there had been any other choice, Susan would have relieved Reed of duty and told him to sleep it off. "Drives and weapons systems appear nominal."

"Long-range sensors are picking up bursts of radio traffic from Planet Three," Parkinson added. "I'd say there's definitely a mid-sized colony based there, probably including some interplanetary installations."

We're on the wrong end of a tramline chain, Susan's thoughts insisted. *How much industry did they put here, so far from their homeworld?*

Oh, her own thoughts answered. *And what sort of threat do they pose to Tadpole Prime?*

"Launch two stealth probes," she ordered, banishing the thoughts. Her brain felt as though someone had stuffed it with cotton wool. Technically, it was the admiral's call to make, but she hadn't heard from Admiral Naiser. "I want a clear picture of everything waiting for us in the inner system."

"Aye, Captain," Parkinson said.

———

There were three great traditions of the Royal Navy, according to Winston Churchill: rum, sodomy and the lash. John Naiser had practiced all three of them with varying degrees of enthusiasm, back when he'd been a starfighter pilot and his life expectancy had been measured in weeks, but he'd never felt quite so bad - afterwards - as he did now. His head felt as if he'd drunk himself senseless, then woke up in a police cell charged with so many offences against public order that he wasn't even going to be walked past a judge before winding up in a work gang. If it had been an option, he would have gone to bed, taken a sedative and slept it off.

But that isn't an option, he thought, as the holographic images sprang into life. *There's too great a risk of being detected.*

"That could have gone better," he said, once the entire command staff had arrived. "It was not a very pleasant experience."

"British understatement," Commodore Kevin Hoover said. The American sounded punch-drunk. "Very droll, sir."

Captain Paddy Hicks had a different question. "What happened?"

"The gravity flux wasn't precisely calibrated, apparently," John said. Juliet had been completely unaffected, apparently. He wasn't sure if that was a blessing or a curse. "We did have similar experiences on *Warspite's* first cruise, if...rather less unpleasant."

He shook his head in annoyance. No one had been entirely sure, afterwards, just how many of their problems had stemmed from faulty calculations, work done before any *real* tests had been carried out...and outright sabotage. Not that it mattered, in the end. The results *had* been much the same. Hell, they'd been worse. *Vanguard* and the rest of the task force had been battered, but at least they hadn't lost main power. *That* had been bad enough in friendly space. Losing power in *enemy* space would be utterly disastrous.

"That isn't a problem at the moment," he continued. "The framework is burned out, most of its components rendered into dust. Our engineers will sweep up the reusable components, then atomise the rest. There is no way back the way we came."

"Onwards to death or glory," Kevin Hoover said.

"Quite," John agreed.

He keyed his console, showing the live feed from the stealth probes. He'd known admirals who would have pitched a fit, when one of their subordinates showed initiative, but he wasn't one of them. Captain Onarina had done exactly the right thing. The feed from the probes had been very helpful, both in confirming the presence of two tramlines *and* in zeroing in on the populated planets and asteroids. Most of them, he suspected, were utterly irrelevant to the enemy war effort. But there *was* a major problem.

"The enemy doesn't have *many* defences in orbit around Planet Three, as far as we can tell," he said. They all knew the blunt realities of modern war. This far from the planet, it was impossible to be certain they'd seen *everything.* "What it *does* have is a mid-sized cruiser, roughly *twice* the size of *Warspite*."

"Not much of a problem," Captain Rani Saran observed. The Indian looked wretched, her dark eyes shadowed. John would have wondered if someone had blackened her eyes if he hadn't seen the injuries on his own flag deck. "We can take her."

"Unless she has some hyper-advanced weapons system we've never heard of, we can take her," John agreed. "We'll have to sneak up on her, of course."

He scowled. A cruiser wouldn't have any trouble outrunning a battleship. The Foxes would have to be utterly insane to fight when they were outgunned so badly - he tried not to think about the number of times the Foxes *had* picked a fight they were bound to lose - but if they chose to run instead, screaming a warning...

"*Vanguard* and *her* task force will attend to the planet," he said, flatly. "The remaining elements of the task force will proceed, in full stealth, to Tramline One and hold position near the least-time course from Planet Three. If our calculations are correct, that's the shortest route to their homeworld."

"And also the route they will use to dispatch any reinforcements," Commodore Solange Leclère pointed out.

"Indeed," John agreed. "And that poses another problem."

He studied the starchart for a long moment. There was no way to know the enemy dispositions, at least until a fleet of enemy warships arrived to push matters. Logically, the Foxes would hesitate to dispatch more than a handful of ships from their homeworld, at least until they determined the scale of the threat. But if they responded quickly, if they sent a full-sized fleet to ES-19, he would have no choice but to engage it. He *couldn't* leave that threat in his rear.

"The scouting units are to be detached," he added. "One scouting element is to proceed through Tramline One, the other through Tramline Two. They are to follow standard stealth procedures at all times. Bear in mind that the enemy have *very* good sensor-stealth systems - we can expect their sensors to have advanced too. *They* know more about what they have to break than we do.

"If we find a worthier target on the other side of Tramline Two, we will proceed through Two instead. If not, we will proceed as originally planned."

He glanced at Hoover. "You will assume command of Task Force 7.2 and 7.3," he said. "If the enemy ship makes a break for the tramline, intercept and destroy her."

"They shouldn't see us until it's too late," Hoover assured him.

John kept his face impassive. War was a democracy in the truest possible sense. The enemy, that dirty dog, had a vote. The Foxes could do something in the next few hours that would upset all of his plans. Hell, there *was* a substantial time-delay between the task force and Planet Three. For all he knew, the enemy ship had already started retreating towards Tramline One.

Or she might try to run to Tramline Two, he thought. It was unlikely, given the relative positions of the two tramlines, but it was possible. The aliens wouldn't have any choice if they spotted Hoover waiting for them. *And they could have already sent a message for help.*

"We will move in thirty minutes," he said, tersely. "If there are any further problems, inform me at once."

"Of course, Admiral," Solange said.

John nodded, but he wasn't particularly reassured. The real work was about to begin...

...And things had *already* started to go off the rails.

————

George couldn't help a flicker of *Déjà Vu* as she opened the compartment, clicked on the light and peered inside. It was empty, as far as she could tell. The occupants had clearly decamped to sickbay, even though the crew had been ordered to remain where they were unless they were seriously injured. She scowled, logged the compartment as empty and then backed out, as carefully as she had come. Hopefully, the occupants hadn't heard the orders, instead of either choosing to disobey them or being badly injured.

She rubbed her forehead as she closed the hatch. *Her* headache wasn't bad, compared to some of the others, but it was still an omnipresent distraction. The jump-sickness - some wag had already coined the name - seemed to strike at random, making no distinctions at all between male or female, young or old...or anything, really. George had a headache, Corporal Lewis hadn't had anything...and Sergeant Tosco had been laid up so badly that Major Andres had ordered him to stay in his bunk. That, more than anything, worried her badly. She couldn't imagine *anything* stopping the sergeant.

And if it had happened at school, she thought as she opened the next hatch, *some of the students would have been delighted.*

It wasn't anything to be pleased about, she told herself sharply. A third of the Royal Marines were either unconscious or too badly affected to do anything, beyond staying in their bunks and hoping it cleared up soon. It was why she'd been sent out alone, along with most of the other marines. There were just too many compartments to check for them to go in pairs. At least they weren't in enemy territory. She would have hated to search an enemy ship without armed backup.

She cursed as she found the light and clicked it on. A middle-aged man was bent over a table, moaning. He'd thrown up badly, she noted as she keyed her terminal to alert the others; he didn't look injured, but it was clear that he was definitely suffering badly. At least he hadn't choked on his own vomit, unlike the poor bastard who'd been asleep when the fleet jumped. Thankfully, one of his roommates had caught him before it had been too late. She gritted her teeth and hurried forward. He started to turn his head, then stopped.

"Relax," she said, pulling him back. His nose was bleeding, but it didn't look broken as far as she could tell. "You're safe now."

The man moaned, twisting against her. He was wearing a naval uniform, but one too fancy to wear on a day-to-day basis. It was too clean to be real. And he didn't have any rank badges or gold braid. A reporter then, she decided. Someone trying to look militaristic without actually attending the academy and being commissioned. The nasty part of her mind was tempted to leave him, but she knew better. Major Andres would be furious. So would the captain.

He shuddered, his hands flapping helplessly in the air. His eyes were half-closed, as if he was trapped in a nightmare. George hesitated, then

167

slapped him across the face as hard as she could. He jerked violently, his body going limp, then opened his eyes wide. George frowned as she saw an ugly red mark taking shape on his face. Perhaps she shouldn't have slapped him so hard.

He's a reporter, part of her mind insisted. *He'll tear your life apart because it'll boost his fucking ratings for a day.*

But he doesn't deserve to be assaulted, another part insisted.

"An angel," the man croaked, hoarsely. His voice was raspy, as if he hadn't drunk anything for days. "You're an angel."

George rolled her eyes as she positioned him carefully against the bulkhead, then looked around for a water dispenser. She was surprised he'd even realised she was *female*, thanks to the marine uniform and hair-cut. The uniform hid her breasts remarkably well. She found some water and held it out to him, then smiled as he drank it in great gulps. Hopefully, he wouldn't need a stimulant. Her supply was running out.

"Fuck," the man managed. "What happened?"

"We jumped," George said, tersely. She knew better than to talk to a reporter any more than strictly necessary. The asshole couldn't be trusted. Maybe he was an embed, maybe he knew the ropes and rules of military journalism, but he still couldn't be trusted. "The shock was unpleasant."

"Brilliant," the man said, sarcastically. "I'll be the sole reporter who doesn't have a write-up ready for his publisher."

George rolled her eyes. Assuming the fleet followed a least-time course back to Earth, the idiot would still have over three *months* to put together something that would satisfy even the most *demanding* boss. If she could satisfy her teachers at school - who rarely granted extensions without the most *solid* grounds - he could satisfy his editors. And then they'd probably change half of it to suit themselves.

I'll probably discover I'm a blonde bombshell with huge tits, she thought, wryly. The respectable newspapers and datanet sites were reasonably honest, but there were plenty of fringe publications more interested in titilla-tion than real news. *They wouldn't dare to print it otherwise.*

"I'm sure you'll be fine," she said, taking back the empty cup. "How are you feeling?"

"Foul," the reporter said. He looked down at his uniform jacket. It was stained, something that George couldn't help thinking made it look a little more authentic. "My head hurts, my eyes hurt and I need to change my shirt."

He winked at her. "Are you going to help me shower?"

"I think you've definitely recovered," George said, dryly. She had a suspicion that telling Sergeant Tosco that she'd stopped to help a reporter shower would result in so many press-ups that the poor sergeant would have to invent some new numbers. "Don't leave the cabin..." - she looked around, silently noting that the reporter had a nicer cabin than Fraser or anyone else below Commander Mason - "and try to stay calm. We're on the move now."

The reporter looked up, dimly. "To where?"

"The enemy, I assume," George told him. She smiled as his face rapidly paled. "We made it. We're in enemy space."

She paused, just for a second. Provoking him might be a mistake, but...she didn't want to stop.

"And now we have to win or die," she added. The reporter looked as if he was going to be sick again. "Victory or death."

CHAPTER

TWENTY

"Coming up on Planet Three," Reed reported.

"No sign we've been detected," Lieutenant Charlotte Watson added. "Their orbital defences appear to be quiet."

Unless they're quietly tracking us and preparing a surprise, Susan thought. Admiral Naiser had put her in tactical command, knowing that she would be in the best position to conduct the engagement. It was a challenge, but it was also dangerous. *If they caught a sniff of us, they might be trying to lure us in closer.*

It wasn't a pleasant thought, even though she was fairly certain that Planet Three and the lone enemy cruiser couldn't stand off the task force. The Tadpole fleet that had attacked Earth *had* been spotted on the way in, spotted and tracked by a lone destroyer. It had been sheer luck that the fleet had been detected in time for Earth's defenders to take up position to defend the planet, then drive the alien fleet away. Space was so vast, she knew, that an entire alien fleet could be lurking in the darkness, just waiting for her. Groundhogs might talk about hiding behind planets, but as long as the aliens were careful they didn't need to do more than keep their drives and active sensors stepped down to remain undetected.

"Hold us steady," she ordered. Three battleships were pretty much unbeatable odds for a single cruiser, as long as the battleships got into weapons range before the cruiser saw them coming. "Tactical?"

"Weapons locked, Captain," Lieutenant-Commander Jean Granger said. "Enemy ship will enter effective missile range in seven minutes."

Susan nodded, silently running through their possible options. Ideally, they'd want to get into *energy* range before opening fire, relying on the main guns to take out the enemy ship quickly and cleanly. There was no way a light cruiser could mount the sort of armour necessary to survive *one* battleship, let alone three. Unless, of course, she was armoured with something Susan had never heard of…she shook her head in annoyance, dismissing the thought. If the Foxes had made such a breakthrough, the war was already on the verge of being lost.

But if she sees us coming and wheels about, she thought, *we may have to chase her down.*

She cursed under her breath as the range narrowed. If the cruiser had her drives stepped down, there was no way she could bring them up in time to escape. But if she had her drives on stand-by, she might *just* be able to get out of Susan's missile envelope before it was too late. Hell, if her drives were already at full power, she could thumb her nose at the task force as she avoided engagement completely. Susan rather suspected a *human* crew would not be at full alert - they *knew* there was no danger of being attacked - but would the Foxes feel the same way?

Keeping the ship on alert puts wear and tear on the equipment, she reminded herself. *But if they suddenly found themselves under attack, wear and tear would be the least of their worries.*

The alien ship took on shape and form, a flattened arrowhead that reminded her of British or French light cruisers. She was bigger - it looked as though she mounted a *Warspite*-class primary gun as well as the usual armaments - but it was impossible to guess at her power. A handful of possible scenarios scrolled up in front of them as the tactical analysts struggled to make sense of what little data they had. Susan scanned it briefly, then dismissed the memos with a shrug. They weren't telling her anything she didn't already know.

That cannon could do real damage if they hit one of the carriers, she thought. *Or a cruiser, if they decided to waste their shot. But it won't damage us.*

She reminded herself not to be complacent as the range closed steadily. The aliens weren't running basic sensor scans, something that perplexed her, but their passive sensors would detect the task force soon enough. Unless it *was* a trap...she scowled as she surveyed the orbital display, as if glaring at the device would be enough to bring any lurking alien ships into view. The aliens might be careless, this far from the front, or they might be baiting a trap...

"Entering sprint-mode missile range," Jean reported. "Two minutes to energy range."

Susan nodded, impatiently. The latest set of improvements, she'd been told, enhanced *Vanguard's* effective energy range considerably. She'd had the chance to test them against drones, during the long voyage from Earth, but not against actual alien starships. Plasma bolts lost their effectiveness after a certain range, no matter how much power was fed into the magnetic bottles. If the aliens were *very* lucky, they might just be able to escape with a scorched hull.

"Signal the other two ships," she ordered. "We will open fire at effective energy weapons range, unless the enemy alters position."

"Aye, Captain," Parkinson said.

Susan braced herself. Three battleships, firing in unison? That cruiser was dead, if they managed to get into effective range. She'd be blown to atoms before she even had a chance to realise she was under attack, let alone fight back. And yet...she knew the chances of being detected were rapidly climbing higher and higher. They *couldn't* get much closer without the enemy reacting, surely...

The display changed, sharply. Red icons blinked into existence, centred around the alien ship. "Captain," Parkinson said. "The enemy ship has seen us! She's powering up her drives!"

We caught her at standby, Susan thought. The aliens hadn't been *entirely* senseless, she noted coldly. *They're flash-waking their drives.*

"Bring up our own sensors and sweep the area," she ordered, sharply. "Tactical?"

"Missiles locked," Jean said.

Susan thought, fast. The alien ship was already moving, if slowly. She might *just* get out of range before the battleships could engage her with energy weapons. It was frustrating, but there was no other option.

"Fire," she ordered.

Vanguard shivered as she launched her first barrage. A moment later, the alien starship returned fire, launching a pitiful handful of missiles towards the battleships. Susan watched them for a long moment, then relaxed as it became clear that there was nothing *special* about them. *Vanguard's* point defence units were already tracking them, calculating firing vectors and preparing to fire. The alien weapons didn't have a hope of reaching engagement range.

And even if they did manage to hit us, she thought, *the damage would be minimal.*

The alien crew had been shocked, she noted, but there was nothing wrong with their electronic servants. Point defence fire started at once, even though the missiles had been fired from practically point-blank range. The cruiser kept moving, picking up speed even as the first warhead detonated, sending a beam of deadly energy slashing into the ship. Two more followed, tearing great gashes in the alien hull. Susan watched, feeling a trace of sympathy, as the cruiser spun madly, her crew trying desperately to get out of range. But it was too late. Three more bomb-pumped lasers sliced into her hull, tearing deep into her innards. A moment later, a series of explosions ripped the alien craft apart.

"Target destroyed," Jean reported, dispassionately. "No lifepods detected."

Susan nodded, watching as the last alien missile vanished from the display. They'd been lucky. The aliens had been caught by surprise. Next time, it would be a great deal harder to take them out. Hell, a much larger incoming barrage would have caused far more problems for her point defences.

And they might have modified their own missiles too, she thought. *The arms race started the moment the war began.*

"Pass the word," she ordered, as sensor sweeps revealed a handful of weapons platforms orbiting the planet. "Destroy all their orbital defences, then launch surveillance platforms and survey anything that looks harmless."

"Aye, Captain," Parkinson said.

Susan smiled, coldly. Crew morale had suffered after the jump, after so many officers and crewmen had been stunned or rendered comatose. No one - on *Vanguard*, at least - had suffered any lasting effects, but it had still been frightening. Now...morale would be restored, once it sank in that they'd blown away an alien starship and captured an alien world with almost contemptuous ease. They'd need it, she knew. The next engagement would be far harder.

And they might already have sent a warning up the chain, she thought, grimly. One of the orbital installations might be the FTL communicator, for all she knew. The marines would inspect anything that wasn't trying to fire on the task force. *The alien homeworld might already know we're here.*

"Captain," Jean said. "Orbital space is clear. I'm not picking up any ground-based defence systems."

Susan frowned, although she wasn't too surprised. Ground-based systems were expensive - and largely ineffective, unless produced in vast numbers. Earth, Britannia and a few other worlds got that level of investment - the remainder, smaller and poorer, had to rely on orbital weapons platforms. It wasn't *that* much of a risk. Orbital defences could fight enemy starships well before they entered bombardment range.

And I suppose it's proof that the alien economy is not that different to ours, she thought, with a flicker of grim amusement. *They're not prepared to expend vast sums of money - or whatever they have that passes for money - on building pointless defences.*

She sobered. The jump drive had proved its worth, particularly if the jump shock effect could be curtailed. All of a sudden, planetary defence planners had a whole new problem to worry about. Formerly, they'd known attackers had to come through the tramlines; now, attackers could come from anywhere within ten light years. Hell, for all she knew, it might be possible to hop all the way to Earth, jumping through star systems that weren't connected to the tramline network. Defence planners were going to have a fit when they found out how the universe had changed.

Admiral Naiser's face blinked up in front of her. "Good work, Captain."

"Thank you, sir," Susan said. She was a little surprised Admiral Naiser hadn't chosen to command the operation himself, even though she saw the logic. It wasn't as though he wasn't experienced in such manoeuvres. Tiny *Warspite* had taken out a fleet carrier an order of magnitude larger than herself. "I believe that orbital space is now secure."

"Understood," Admiral Naiser said. "And the planet itself?"

"It poses no threat, as far as we can determine," Susan said.

She waited, unsure what the admiral would say. The planet *was* harmless, as far as her sensor crews could determine. There was nothing to be gained by dropping rocks and bombing the world back into the Stone Age. But Admiral Naiser could order an all-out bombardment if he wished. It would be a perfectly legal order. Hell, it would receive a great deal of popular support. Humanity had lost a great deal of its compassion, for better or worse, during the Age of Unrest.

But Admiral Smith refused to allow planetary bombardment when we were fighting the Tadpoles, she reminded herself. *Killing soldiers is one thing, but slaughtering defenceless civilians…*

She gritted her teeth, feeling her headache starting to return. The injection was wearing off, slowly but surely. She would need to return to her cabin soon, before she collapsed on the bridge. By then, her ship had to be safe. There didn't *seem* to be any other warships in the system, but it was impossible to be sure. The task force was far too isolated for her comfort.

"Hold position," Admiral Naiser said, finally.

————

Planet Three, Henry considered as he rubbed his pounding forehead, was the sort of planet that would make any survey ship captain very happy indeed. It could have easily passed for Earth, although it was clear that the planet hadn't birthed any intelligent life form. Two-thirds water, one-third land…the person who claimed settlement rights, under other circumstances, would wind up very rich indeed. But Planet Three was already settled, a dozen large cities resting along the coastline.

All settled by Foxes and Cows, he thought. The xenospecialists were already going to work, but a cursory look had told him that the planet was very similar to worlds humanity had settled. Chances were the colony wasn't *that* old, he thought. There was little reliable data on enemy breeding habits, but there didn't seem to be many factories or spaceports on the surface. *This is still a stage-one colony world.*

Admiral Naiser looked at him. "Your recommendation, Your Highness?"

Henry scowled. If Admiral Naiser was still feeling any discomfort, he was hiding it very well. It was very annoying. They were roughly the same age, after all. Coming to think of it, Admiral Naiser had been a year ahead of him at the academy, learning to fly starfighters before his deployment to HMS *Canopus*. Henry couldn't help feeling a flicker of envy. The admiral had a genuine naval career, not something that could be snatched away at the whim of his family. And he...

And he was getting off track. "The world is largely harmless," he said. "It contributes nothing to the enemy war effort. There's nothing to be gained by turning it into a billiard ball. I say we just finish checking the orbital installations, then leave it alone."

Admiral Naiser met his eyes. "And what happens if the FTL communicator is down there?"

Henry glanced at the live feed from the analysts. Hundreds of farms and small communities had been identified, along with a handful of more modern installations, but nothing really stood out. If the FTL communicator was on the surface, it was very well hidden. There wasn't even any radio chatter, let alone anything more advanced. He found himself morbidly impressed by their discipline. The alien communications network would have gone silent, the moment they realised that they were under attack, yet he would have expected a few more leaks. A number of civilians had kept using their radios during the Battle of Earth.

Which would have gotten most of them killed if the Tadpoles ever took the high orbitals, he thought, wryly. *The Foxes seem to be a little more careful.*

"I can't pick out a place it might be," he pointed out. "Can you? Or do you want to search the whole planet?"

Admiral Naiser gave him a dark look. Henry concealed his amusement with an effort, even though his headache was growing worse. Searching the whole planet was the sort of idea a *politician* would put forward, rather than an experienced spacer. There were nearly half a *billion* square kilometres to search...and limiting the search to land, leaving the oceans alone, wouldn't make it much easier. It was hard to comprehend just how big a planet truly *was*, on a human scale, when starships crossed hundreds of light years regularly. And yet finding something on the surface might be completely impossible.

"Point," Admiral Naiser said. He sounded oddly amused. "Is there anything to be gained by destroying the handful of installations on the surface?"

Henry shrugged. "From a military point of view, no. We're not planning to land troops, are we? Convincing them that they're beaten isn't necessary, not here. And even if we did, we'd have to beat them on even terms. Stamping on them from orbit isn't going to impress them, let alone convince them of our superiority."

"Very good," Admiral Naiser said. He keyed his console. "Captain, the planet is to be carefully watched, but otherwise left alone. The marines will inspect the remaining orbital installations and see if some of them - any of them - are interesting."

"Yes, sir," Captain Onarina said.

She sounded relieved, Henry thought wryly, as he settled back into his chair to await developments. He didn't really blame her. There was a nasty streak of anti-alien feeling running through the human race, a call to unite humanity against the rest of the universe. If Admiral Naiser *had* ordered a mass bombardment, it was quite possible he would have been given a medal when he returned home. Admiral Fitzwilliam wouldn't be pleased - he'd served under Admiral Smith, who'd insisted on fighting a civilised war - but he might be overruled by Parliament. Parliament was far too used to ordering punitive strikes against rogue states that thought Britain was a push-over.

And this war began with a sneak attack, as far as we are concerned, Henry thought. The Foxes thought differently, but their opinion didn't count. *There's a strong call to make sure the Foxes can't threaten us any longer, even if it means committing genocide.*

He shuddered at the thought. Humanity had known atrocities, from the casual destruction of entire towns and villages to mass slaughters, from forced population relocations to deliberately starving refugees to death...there had been far too many atrocities during the Age of Unrest, atrocities casually carried out by both sides. And yet, the deliberate extermination of an entire race would be an order of magnitude worse. Worse than the destruction of Carthage, worse than the Holocaust, worse than the Purging...it would be utterly impossible to defend.

But people will try, he thought. There were elements in Britain - the Humanity League, in particular - who considered him a traitor, just because he was an ambassador. They thought the Royal Family should lead a crusade against all inhuman elements. *If they see this as a war to the knife, there will be no mercy.*

He felt cold. *And if we start slaughtering their populations*, his own thoughts added, *they'll start slaughtering ours.*

The console bleeped. "Admiral, we inspected the orbital installations," a voice said. "We didn't find anything inexplicable. They were just basic communications relays and surveillance systems. Very primitive."

"Understood," Admiral Naiser said. He glanced at Henry. "Onwards, then."

"Yes, Admiral," Henry said. "Onwards."

CHAPTER
TWENTY ONE

Susan wrenched herself out of sleep, cursing under her breath.

The nightmares had been unpleasant, yet all she could remember - upon waking - was a dark looming presence and a sense of doom that had chilled her to the bone. She should have expected it, she reminded herself. Bad dreams were a known side-effect of the stimulant she'd taken, hours ago. And yet, the sheer intensity of the feelings had caught her by surprise. She'd been convinced, at some level, that she was going to die.

She sat upright, feeling sweat running down her body. *That* hadn't happened, if she recalled correctly, since she'd graduated from the academy. They'd made her work hard to keep in shape, preparing to serve on a starship. She shook her head as she swung her legs over the side and stood, feeling oddly wobbly. Maybe a good third of her crew would be feeling the same way, she thought, as she headed for the shower. They'd all taken similar drugs to recover from the shock.

And if that happens, our ability to fight is going to be limited, she thought, as she checked the status display. *The jump shock got all of us.*

It wasn't a pleasant thought. *Vanguard* and her consorts were steadily making their way towards Tramline One, altering their course to ensure they didn't jump into a predictable location in the next star system. There was no sign of any enemy presence, save for the handful of miners. Even they had gone dark. And yet she knew an entire fleet could be lurking out there, with a third of her crew disoriented. Perhaps she should suggest that half of her personnel be sedated, if they had to use the jump drive again. They might be spared the worst of the shock.

She undressed rapidly, cursing her decision to get into bed without doing more than removing her shoes. She'd been in no state to take command, even if they *did* run into an alien fleet intent on slaughtering them. And Paul Mason hadn't been much better off. Jean Granger would have had to take command, if the battleship had to fight. Susan promised herself, grimly, that they'd be carrying out more exercises for junior officers. God alone knew how many billets would need to be replaced at short notice, if they had to jump again.

The shower bleeped as she stepped inside. She felt a pang of guilt as she keyed her command code into the system, overriding the water restrictions. Cold logic told her that there was no *need* for any actual limitations, not when almost every last drop could be recycled, but old habits tended to stay even after they were no longer necessary. It hadn't been *that* long since she'd had strict limits on water consumption.

She closed her eyes as the warm water washed over her body, stripping the sweat from her skin even as it woke her up. They'd completed the first part of their mission. The Foxes now had to react to a large enemy fleet in their rear. *And* they'd killed an alien ship without getting their paint scratched, let alone taking more substantial damage. They had nothing to be ashamed of, not now. And yet, the nightmare still haunted her.

You had nightmares when you went to boarding school too, she told herself, sharply. She shut off the water, allowing it to drain. *It's normal to worry when things change.*

The intercom bleeped. "Captain, this is Parkinson. There's something here I believe you should see."

Susan scowled. "Understood," she said. It didn't *sound* like a cloaked alien fleet. "I'm on my way."

She donned a fresh uniform, checked her appearance in the mirror and hurried out the hatch, passing a pair of marines. Even *they* looked... *wretched*, somehow, even though she couldn't put her finger on it. She hadn't seen anyone looking so downcast since she'd completed her final set of exams, years ago. And she'd passed...so had the others, if she remembered rightly. But everyone had been convinced that they'd failed.

The bridge seemed quieter, even though Tramline One was clearly visible on the display, a line of gravitational force lancing out of the primary star. Admiral Naiser had decided to take a calculated risk by bringing the fleet so close to the star, although the risk of being singed was minimal unless they went a great deal closer. But the risk of sensor disruption was a great deal higher. The star put out enough radiation to blind some of the more sensitive sensor drones protecting the fleet. Finding an elusive alien fleet - if one existed - would be a real challenge.

"I have the bridge," she said, automatically. "Mr. Parkinson. What have you found?"

"This, Captain," Parkinson said. He pointed to the display. "The tramline was behaving oddly so close to the star, so I did a more detailed sensor scan. I found this."

He tapped an icon, surrounded by smaller icons. "I don't know what it is, Captain, but there's a gravitational flux around it."

Susan frowned. "Does it pose any danger?"

"Unknown," Parkinson said.

"It might be a bomb of some kind," Jean put in. "Or it might be designed to manipulate the tramline in some way. Perhaps using it to signal messages from star to star."

The FTL communicator, Susan thought.

Her mind raced. Was it possible? One of the *theories* certainly *suggested* that the Foxes had found a way to send messages up and down the tramlines, although she'd observed enemy tactics that suggested they didn't *need* the tramlines to send FTL messages. Or was it something else? An experiment to enhance the tramline? To gain access to alien-grade tramlines? Or...

We have to take it intact, she told herself.

She studied the display for a long moment. Parkinson had already vectored one of the stealthed drones towards the device, allowing them to take a closer look. It wasn't actually that large, no bigger than a standard tourist shuttlecraft. And yet, it clearly *wasn't* a shuttlecraft. It looked more like a communications satellite. Or was she thinking that, she asked herself, because she wanted to *believe* it was a communications device? Capturing an intact FTL communicator would be a real feather in her cap.

"Inform Major Andres that he is to dispatch a team of marines to inspect the device," she ordered, finally. It would be easy to manoeuvre the device into the shuttlebay, but she was unwilling to take the risk. A bomb that size could do real damage to her ship. It would have to be placed into one of the freighters, if one could be spared. "And once it is confirmed safe, it is to be removed from the tramline and transported to the fleet."

"Aye, Captain," Granger said.

Admiral Naiser is supposed to be asleep, Susan thought, as she took her command chair and studied the display. *Let him rest for a little longer, if necessary. We can handle the mission ourselves.*

———

"Take us in very slowly," Sergeant Tosco ordered. His voice sounded odd through the spacesuit's radio - the shuttlecraft was depressurised - but there was no mistaking his sharp tone. "We don't want to trigger anything unpleasant."

Teach your grandmother to suck eggs, George thought, rudely. She might not be a marine, but she'd taken the xenotech course at the academy, back when it had first been introduced after the war. *I know what I'm doing.*

She kept the thought off her face, even though he couldn't see her face behind the suit, as she steered the craft towards the alien device. Sergeant Tosco had been in a foul mood, ever since he'd been allowed to leave his bunk. Clearly, *he* thought that his near-collapse and pounding headache was a sign of weakness. The fact that George - almost certainly the weakest person in Marine Country - had endured the jump with only a mild headache had rubbed salt into the wound. He'd been snapping at everyone over the last few hours. She would have been more annoyed if he'd been the only one, to be honest. Two nasty fistfights had broken out and two *more* marines had had a very unpleasant shouting match before their superiors had intervened.

Jump shock didn't do us any favours, she thought. *But we survived.*

Up close, the alien device looked like a giant satellite from a bygone era. A pair of giant panels waving in space, a handful of power cores and other devices...she puzzled over them for a long moment, before noticing the command core. It *had* to be a command core, she was sure. Her sensors reported that the gravimetric flux was stronger around the device, although it didn't seem to be harming her craft. That proved nothing, she told herself, sharply. The gravity field might be tiny, but it was linked to the tramline. It was possible it could get a great deal stronger very quickly.

Corporal Robertson leaned past her. "What *is* it?"

"As you were," Sergeant Tosco growled. "George, hold us at rest relative to the device."

"Yes, Sergeant," George said.

There was no such thing as 'dead stop' in space, but she could and did hold the shuttle still, relative to the device. She couldn't help thinking, as she waited to see if the device would react to their presence, that the device was as near to still as was possible in space. If it was linked to the tramline, perhaps it was permanently held in position…she'd heard of something like that, theoretically, but it had never led to workable hardware. Perhaps someone *could* lock onto the surface of space itself and…

She shook her head, making a mental note to look it up when she returned to *Vanguard*. It was probably nothing, but who knew? She turned her attention towards the sensor console and frowned as she realised that the device hadn't reacted to their presence at all. No sensor sweep, no recorded message telling them to keep their distance…not even a self-destruct. In truth, she wasn't sure if that was good or bad. The *real* surprise might come when they tried to sneak into the command core.

"I'll take the lead," Sergeant Tosco said. "Smiles and Sammy will accompany me."

George nodded, keying a command into her console as the three marines headed for the hatch. Smiles - she didn't know his real name - was a good man in a fight, she'd been told, while Sammy had spent half his time examining the captured alien technology. He knew more about alien technology than anyone else, save for the xenospecialists parsing out its secrets. George was torn between envy and concern. She wanted to join them, but she knew the risks. Out there, wearing thin spacesuits instead of armour, the marines would be vulnerable as hell.

The hatch opened. George kept a wary eye on her sensors, remembering the contingency plans they'd gone over before leaving the battleship. If there was a power surge, if there was any sign of trouble, she was to turn and run, leaving the others behind. She'd tried to argue, but she knew - deep inside - that there was no alternative. If something went wrong, they wouldn't have time to do anything more than save themselves.

She frowned as the three men drifted closer to the command core. If they managed to get in…then what? Hacking the alien system should be possible, but the mystery device was a complete unknown. They might not be able to figure out how to shut it down. And then…a freighter was already being prepared to carry it, according to the latest update. The scientists could study the device a long way from anyone else. And then…

See what it is, she thought, as Sammy managed to open the alien hatch. *And then find out what we can do with it.*

Her radio crackled. "It's pretty simple," Sammy reported. "Plenty of redundancy built into the system."

"They must have seen you coming," Robertson said. "How much of it can you damage before it explodes?"

"Ha fucking hah," Sergeant Tosco said. "Stay off the channel unless you have something useful to contribute."

"The command nodes are beyond us," Sammy said, after a moment. "But I think we can power it down."

George tensed. She'd heard horror stories about researchers who'd pushed the wrong button while working with xenotech. The Foxes - and the Tadpoles - had to obey the same laws of science as humanity, but they still had different ways of looking at the world. Logic could not be trusted, she reminded herself, when dealing with alien technology. Something that was obvious, to a human mind, might look very different to an alien. And the *off* switch on xenotech might be in completely the wrong place…

The shuttle rocked. Just for a second, she honestly thought she'd imagined it. She was in space, not flying through a planetary atmosphere. There was no *turbulence* in space. But the gravimetric sensors *had* picked up a gravity wave, striking the shuttle like an ocean wave might strike a boat. She'd never seen anything like it, no one had. And the device, it seemed, was powering down.

It struck the shuttle with a gravity wave, she thought. She tapped her console, hastily reporting the incident to her superiors. *What if they managed to turn it into a weapon?*

"The device has powered down, I think," Sammy said. "I suggest we move it away, now. If it was linked to another device at the far end, it isn't any longer."

"Good thinking," Sergeant Tosco said. "George, attach a line and take us away."

"Yes, Sergeant," George said.

And wondered, as she carefully towed the device away from the tramline, just what they'd managed to find.

———

"My wife is still studying the device," Mike Johnston said. "But, as near as we can make out, it's an FTL communications hub."

John felt a glimmer of triumph, mixed with concern. "Are you sure?"

"There are some parts of the technology we haven't been able to unravel, yet," Johnston assured him. "It would be easier if we had direct access to the device."

"No," John said. "I can't afford to lose you *or* your wife."

He sighed inwardly as he studied the live feed from the freighter. The logic of allowing Juliet Watson-Stewart and Mike Johnston to accompany the task force was undeniable, but - in truth - both of them were really too valuable to be considered expendable. John had no illusions about himself or his subordinates. None of them, with the possible exception of Prince Henry, were truly important. But Mike Johnston and his wife shouldn't have been risked.

"The command system is clearly designed to handle communications," Mike Johnston said, after a moment. "It's actually very simple, compared to a datanet node. I'd say their bandwidth is actually quite low. I'd have wondered if this dated all the way back to the pre-space era if I hadn't known where it came from. Really...it isn't much more advanced than sending emails. Trying to send a simple photograph might blow the entire system."

John cocked an eyebrow. "Are you sure?"

"We may be misunderstanding what we're seeing," Johnston admitted. "As near as we can tell, there's one big trunk - sending messages along the tramline - and several smaller ones, all seemingly linked to distant units. I think their gravimetric science went in a different direction to ours. We looked at ways to improve our access to tramlines, then to create our own; they assumed that was impossible and started finding ways to piggyback messages onto the tramlines. And then they started forming mini-tramlines between the device and subordinate units..."

His voice trailed off. "Or it may be something completely different," he added. "We've barely scratched the surface of the possible. But yeah, this *is* an FTL communicator."

John smiled. "Can it be duplicated?"

"Not in a hurry," Mike Johnston said. "We don't understand the science behind it yet."

"I see," John said.

It wasn't a pleasant thought. He'd been a very junior starfighter pilot when *Ark Royal* had returned to Earth, bringing a captured alien ship with her. The debate about how alien tech should be integrated into the Royal Navy had been savage, although the war had ended before it had gotten too far out of hand. *Warspite* had been commissioned and launched after the war. Her maiden voyage had illustrated the problems facing the navy quite nicely.

He pushed the thought aside. "Can you tell me something useful?"

"I think the devices *have* to be fairly close to stars," Mike Johnston said. "If nothing else, launching a ballistic missile down the tramline will effectively take out the communications hub. It might be worth doing in every system we enter, sir."

John considered it. If they did - if the system had a giant vulnerability that could be exploited - it would tear holes in the alien FTL network. And yet, that would make it harder for the aliens to recall their forces from the war front. He wasn't sure if that was a good or bad thing, yet. It all depended on what they encountered in the next two star systems.

"Good point," he said, finally. "Can the system be jammed?"

"Not with present-day tech," Johnston said. "Juliet does have some theories, but turning them into reality may be beyond us."

"Then we will proceed," John said, firmly. "And we will take steps to cripple their network..."

He paused. "What about a computer virus? Something that might take down the entire network?"

"This isn't a movie, sir," Johnston said. "The worst we could do, if we hacked the system, would be to send insulting messages to them. There just isn't the bandwidth for a proper viral assault."

"Pity," John said. "Keep me informed of progress."

"Of course, sir," Johnston said.

John smiled. Finding the FTL transmitter, as they prepared to cross Tramline One, was a stroke of luck. But would their luck hold?

We make our own luck, he thought, as he studied the star chart. *And even if they know we're here, now, it will take them time to react.*

CHAPTER
TWENTY TWO

Civilians, Susan had often thought, didn't comprehend the sheer *vastness* of interplanetary space.

She forced herself to lean back in her chair and wait, patiently, as the fleet crawled across the system, heading for the closest tramline. ES-18 - the astrographers had declined to add any name to the system - had no habitable planets, but it *did* have four tramlines, two of which seemed to lead towards the enemy homeworld. If the projections were correct, either route would lead through two more star systems before linking up again just before the enemy home system. A series of hops, she suspected, would give them a reasonable chance to make it back to UXS-469 without being intercepted.

Except we have to draw them towards us, she thought, grimly. *And we don't dare stop before we reach their homeworld.*

It felt...tiring. The crew had recovered from the jump shock - and two-thirds had had a proper rest - but she found it hard to relax. There was no way to know what might be coming towards them, what sort of enemy fleet might be racing towards ES-19. How much did the aliens even *know* about the situation? How many ships had they even *seen?* And had they deduced the existence of the jump drive? There was no way to be sure. She would be happier, she knew, if she actually *saw* the aliens. As it was, the sensation of being watched refused to fade. She wanted to believe she was imagining it, but...

The task force wasn't really *trying* to hide. Passive sensors would have no trouble tracking their course, even though ECM would make it hard for anyone to get a solid count of their hulls. It was possible, she supposed, that the aliens believed that most - if not all - of Admiral Naiser's ships were little more than sensor drones. Hell, they *knew* humanity's sensor decoys were good. Sending three battleships to the back of beyond to create a false impression was precisely the kind of trickery they'd expect.

She glanced down at the latest set of reports, torn between boredom and a grim awareness she ought to be *glad* to be bored. The reporters were prowling the decks, hunting interviewees like aristocrats hunted deer and pheasant; the xenospecialists were examining the FTL communicator, trying desperately to understand how it worked when it seemed to defy half of their understanding of gravimetric science; her various departments were insisting that they were fighting fit, ready to take the war to the enemy...

A *ping* echoed through the bridge. "Captain," Parkinson said. "Long-range sensors are picking up a small enemy formation. They're heading directly towards Tramline One."

Susan sucked in her breath. That was *fast*. "Alert the admiral," she ordered, grimly. The alien FTL communicator had proved its value, again. "Time to intercept?"

"Three hours, assuming they maintain their current course and speed," Parkinson said. "But I don't think they'll seek an engagement."

"You may be right," Susan said. There were only nine alien ships, none of them larger than a heavy cruiser. One of the ships *might* be a converted freighter - the aliens needed carriers too - but the others were small ships, the kind of units that would be deployed to shadow an invading fleet while stronger formations were assembled. "If they get a solid look at us, they're not going to risk closing to engagement range."

She frowned. There was no way to know *just* how much the ES-19 aliens had detected, but she was fairly sure they'd seen three battleships. Nine smaller ships didn't stand a chance, if they came into engagement range. But then, perhaps it would be possible to lure the aliens onto her guns. She'd done it before, back during the first series of engagements.

Done properly, the aliens might be fooled into thinking they could close safely.

"Raise the admiral," she ordered, slowly. "I've had an idea."

––––––––

John Naiser was no stranger to daring operations. He'd killed a carrier through sheer balls - although, to be fair, the Royal Navy would barely have noticed if *Warspite* and her crew had been blown out of space. Hell, the odds were rather more firmly on his side than they'd been during the Battle of Clarke. But there were dangers too, he had to admit. The Indians had been civilised, even though they were mounting a bid for power. He suspected the Foxes would be less inclined to treat POWs kindly.

"That's the plan," Captain Onarina said. "We should be able to give the aliens a nasty surprise."

"So it would seem," John said. He didn't want the aliens shadowing the task force, even though they were *meant* to know the task force was punching up towards their homeworld. If they got an accurate count of his ships, they might decide they could afford not to withdraw from the front. "I'll pass the word."

He studied the display for a long moment, working out the possible vectors. The aliens *might* remain near the tramlines, calculating that he would have to close with them just to break through and cross the tramline. But if they wanted to get an accurate count of his ships, they would have to close with him themselves. *And* they should be able to do it without getting blown out of space, if they were lucky.

"Deploy drones too," he ordered. "We don't want them to notice that some of our ships have gone missing."

"Aye, Admiral," Captain Onarina said.

John allowed himself a smile as her face vanished from the display. He rather *liked* Susan Onarina, even if quite a few captains would give her the stink-eye for *daring* to relieve her former commander of duty. It wasn't the sort of precedent any Captain's Board would care to uphold, whatever sort of person had been relieved. Maybe he would have eyed her with more suspicion if he was still on a command deck himself. But there was nothing wrong with her tactical skill, he had to admit, nor her ability to take advantage of unexpected opportunities.

And if this fails, he told himself, *it won't cost us anything beyond time.* He sobered. Time was in short supply.

———

"The cloaking device is holding steady," Granger said. "But the enemy ships are sweeping space for trouble."

"Adjust the device to compensate," Susan said. "And alert me if they see through the cloak."

She watched, forcing herself to remain calm. The enemy weren't trying to hide, any more than Task Force 7.2 and 7.3 were trying to hide. It made it easier to track the enemy ships, but it also allowed the enemy to use their active sensors. And if they noticed that there was something odd with their returns, they'd deduce the presence of a cloaking device and know that Task Force 7.1 - or at least its battleships - was lurking under cloak, far too close to them for comfort.

The concept itself was simple. Logically, the enemy would want to close with the task force, at least enough to get a proper ship count. *Her* ships were hiding, positioned between the aliens and the task force. If the aliens kept advancing, they would impale themselves on her guns… assuming, of course, that they didn't detect her before it was too late. She knew, all too well, that far too much could go wrong.

"Their sweeps are intensifying," Jean reported. "But I don't think they've locked onto the cloak."

"Establish passive locks on their hulls," Susan ordered. "And prepare to fire on my command."

She scowled as the alien ships came closer. With the possible exception of the modified freighter - she assumed it was a carrier, given that it was holding position with the other ships - the enemy cruisers could easily escape the three battleships, if they saw the danger in time to reverse course. *Vanguard* and her two allies had stepped down their drives and sensors as far as they could - another advantage of the aliens using active sensors was that it made taking aim at them remarkably easy - but she knew the cloak wouldn't hold up forever. A sensor genius like Parkinson or Charlotte Watson would see through it, sooner rather than later. And then...

We see how many of them we can kill before they get out of range, she thought.

The red icons moved closer, their sensor sweeps blasting through space. There was something odd about their sensors, she mused, almost as if they were deliberately overpowering them. Perhaps they expected an ambush. Or perhaps they were trying to draw every last scrap of data they could, even though it was futile. Passive sensors would tell them more about the task force, at least until they got a lot closer. Commodore Hoover was holding the range open, daring them to pick up speed. It might annoy them to the point they threw caution to the winds and tried to close faster.

"Missile engagement range in seven minutes," Jean reported. "Energy engagement range in nine."

"Fire as soon as they enter energy engagement range, unless they detect us or reverse course," Susan ordered. She would be astonished if the aliens didn't spot them in far less than seven minutes. Their sensor sweeps were coming alarmingly close, even though *Vanguard* was doing her level best to pretend to be a hole in space. "Helm, prepare to ramp up the drives."

"Aye, Captain," Reed said.

Susan braced herself as the ships reached the edge of *Vanguard's* missile envelope, still coming closer...

...And then the display washed with red light.

"They've seen us," Jean snapped. "The cloak is fading."

"Fire," Susan ordered. "Helm, take us into engagement range!"

Vanguard belched a wave of missiles, targeted on the lead enemy ships. *King Edward* and *Alabama* followed suit a moment later, spreading their missiles across the other ships. The alien carrier seemed to hesitate, then launched two squadrons of starfighters even as the cruisers were scrambling to respond. Susan mentally tipped her hat to the alien CO - he'd clearly had his pilots ready to launch at a moment's notice - and then scowled as the alien ships returned fire. Individually, their salvos were pathetic; collectively, they posed a very real danger.

"Enemy missiles are targeted on *King Edward*, Captain," Jean reported.

"Move us up to offer point defence support," Susan said. Theoretically, *King Edward* could handle such a barrage without assistance, but Susan saw no reason to take chances with *Vanguard's* sister ship. It wasn't as if they had easy access to a shipyard. "Continue firing!"

"Aye, Captain," Reed said.

"*Alabama* is moving up too, Captain," Charlotte said. "Enemy starfighters are entering engagement range."

"Order the point defence to engage," Susan said.

She watched, grimly, as the alien starfighters closed in on her ship. Logically, she was dealing with second-line units...or reservists. Converted freighters that had become carriers rarely got the best units, at least in the Royal Navy. The aliens might feel the same way, or they might have trained up more starfighter pilots. God knew the Royal Navy could produce pilots far faster than either starfighters or carriers.

We go to war with what we have on hand, she reminded herself. *Not what we would like to have.*

The alien pilots might have been reservists - she cautioned herself, sharply, against assuming that she was correct - but there was nothing wrong with their skills. They corkscrewed through her point defence, firing madly and picking off dozens of point defence units before they were picked off themselves. There was no way they could do more than warm her hull, she noted, but they could weaken her defences. It was, she had to admit, the sole hope the alien squadron had...

"Captain," Jean said. "The enemy ships are closing on our position."

Susan blinked in surprise. The missiles had destroyed two alien ships and crippled a third, but the remainder were making no attempt to escape. Instead, they were closing rapidly, pushing their drives to the limits. Cold horror ran through her mind as she realised what they had in mind. They'd decided they couldn't escape, so they were trying to take three battleships down with them.

"Target them as soon as they enter energy weapons range and open fire," she ordered. The situation had just become very dangerous. Hell, the enemy ships were still firing missiles of their own - and, in moments, they would be in range to open fire with their own plasma cannons. "Take them all out."

"Aye, Captain," Jean said.

Susan gritted her teeth as the main guns opened fire, spewing plasma bolts towards the enemy ships. They weren't particularly well-armoured compared to *Vanguard*, she noted, but they were angling themselves to absorb as much of the damage as they could. Their bulk would keep going unless it was atomised...

A new icon flared to life as the aliens opened fire with their own plasma cannons. Lances of fire stabbed towards *Vanguard* and *Alabama*, *Vanguard's* hull quivering as the bolt slammed into her armour. Susan cursed under her breath, then looked at the status display. It looked as though the armour had absorbed the blast, but she knew it would have to be checked. A simple plasma lance had destroyed a carrier, seven years ago.

"The task force is launching starfighters," Parkinson reported. "They're racing to our assistance."

Susan shrugged. Starfighters were the fastest things in space, but the engagement would be over by the time they arrived. The converted freighter exploded under her guns, followed by two cruisers picked off by *Alabama*. A third cruiser nearly slammed into *King Edward* before the battleship's guns smashed her into atoms. And then a cruiser spun past *Vanguard*, bleeding plasma from her drive nodes. It seemed to have lost main power, so Susan ignored it for the moment. Either the crew would restart the power cores - in which case she would blow the alien ship apart at leisure - or they'd be trapped on a powerless hulk. They could be dealt with later, if they weren't simply left to die.

An alien starfighter slammed into the hull. Susan felt nothing, not even the tiniest quiver running through the ship, as the last of the alien pilots died. She wondered, sourly, just what the aliens had been thinking when they'd ordered the attack. Maybe they'd thought they couldn't escape. Or maybe they'd assumed they could do more damage than they had.

Or maybe their superiors would kill them, if they returned home failures, Susan thought. *If so, perhaps they sought a death in battle instead. Humans have done stupider things.*

"Status report," she ordered.

"Minor damage to hull plating," Mason said. "I believe damage control teams have it in hand. We've also lost seventy-two weapons mounts and sensor blisters."

"*King Edward* took a more serious battering," Parkinson added. He sounded grim. "She lost an entire armour plate to the aliens. Luckily, they didn't have the chance to get a missile into her hull."

"Inform Captain Tolliver that we will provide whatever help he requires," Susan said. A flight of starfighters roared past, too late to do more than provide comfort. "Scan the hulk."

"Aye, Captain," Charlotte said. She paused. "The ship is largely intact, but her main power is gone. I *think* battery power has taken over, but that won't last."

We must have crippled her power core, Susan thought. It was odd for a ship to lose power so suddenly. Her drives had spun right out of control before she'd lost them completely. *Maybe we hit something delicate...*

———

"Admiral, this is an opportunity," Prince Henry said. "That ship must not be destroyed."

John gave him a sharp look. "Are you aware of the risks?"

"Yes," Prince Henry said. He sounded confident, insanely confident. John didn't particularly dislike the prince, but there were times when he found him irritating. "I'm also aware that we can cow the aliens into submission."

"Really," John said. "And if you're wrong?"

"I can join the boarding party," Prince Henry said. "I would share the risks."

John wondered, briefly, if it would be worth going to jail if he punched Prince Henry in the nose. The prince had been a starfighter pilot - and he didn't seem to have matured since then, even though he'd been an ambassador. There was no way he could justify sending the prince with the marines - hell, he wasn't sure he could even justify sending the marines. He wasn't blind to the opportunity a drifting alien ship presented, but he was all-too-aware of the dangers. The aliens had redeployed one squadron to face them. It wouldn't be long before they dispatched others.

And he knows that I can't send him too, John thought. He knew he was being unfair - there was nothing in Prince Henry's war record to suggest he was a coward - but there was too much at stake. *He needs to stay here.*

"I'll dispatch some marines," he said, finally. It would be risky as hell, even if the aliens offered to surrender. The last major boarding action had been over ten years ago. It had surprised everyone, including the Royal Navy. "And *you* will concentrate on sending them the right signal."

"Of course, Admiral," Prince Henry said. He looked pleased. "I've already taken the liberty of asking the xenospecialists to draw up a suitable message."

John snorted, then glanced at the preliminary reports. *King Edward* damaged, *Vanguard* and *Alabama* hit hard...losing the point defence weakened the ships, even if the armour was untouched. The repair crews were already swarming over the battleships, but it would take time - time he didn't have - to complete the work.

"I suggest you make the message very clear," he added. "Because if the aliens greet the marines with loaded weapons, *I'm* going to blow that ship to hell."

CHAPTER
TWENTY THREE

"The message is pounding over the airwaves," Corporal Roberts said. "Can they hear it?"

"They should be able to hear it," Sammy said. "And they *should* be able to understand it."

George gritted her teeth as she piloted the shuttle towards the alien craft. They were far too close to its weapons for comfort, if the aliens decided to spit in humanity's eye. A point defence cluster could blow the shuttle out of space before she even knew she was under attack. *Vanguard* and the rest of the task force would take a terrible revenge, of course, but it wouldn't matter. The marines - and her - would still be dead.

The alien ship took on shape and form as George's sensors probed its hull. It reminded her of some of humanity's earlier designs: a collection of modules attached to a drive unit, crammed with weapons and sensor blisters. She couldn't help comparing it to a destroyer, although even Russian or Chinese destroyers looked smoother than the alien ship. Oddly, she was almost disappointed. *Tadpole* ships looked more alien, even though they too were bound by the laws of the universe.

And they found similar answers, she thought, wryly. *We won't have beautiful starships until we find a way to violate more of the laws of physics.*

"I'm picking up a beacon," she said, as a new light flashed on her console. "They're opening an airlock."

"Take us in," Sergeant Tosco said. His voice showed no trace of concern, let alone fear. The Foxes appeared to be obeying orders, so far. "If you can dock us properly, do so."

"Yes, sergeant," George said.

She took the shuttle closer, hastily evaluating the alien airlock. It wasn't *that* different from a standard human design, but she doubted it would be compatible with the shuttle. The Foxes hadn't been consulted when the international design teams had produced the standardised airlock - or anything else. She tensed as the gravity field flickered as she pushed the shuttle up against the alien hull, then activated the universal airlock. The marines had had plenty of time to plan ways to match airlocks, even if the minds that had devised them came from two different worlds.

"Reading an atmosphere within the airlock," she said, as hatches started to flow open. "It seems safe."

"Keep your helmets on," Sergeant Tosco told his men. "We don't *know* it's safe."

George nodded in agreement. The prospect of going through decontamination, when they returned from the alien ship, was unpleasant, but she knew there was no way to avoid it. In theory, an alien disease couldn't spread to humanity; in practice, there was no way to be *sure*. Besides, the Foxes had captured enough humans to allow them to experiment with creating species-specific biological weapons. Better to take precautions than accidentally release something lethal into *Vanguard's* ecosystem.

She took one last look at the sensors, fearing she might have missed something. But there was nothing. The alien ship was almost completely powerless, although she couldn't tell *why* it was powerless. A lucky hit *could* have taken out the power distribution network, she supposed. Something of the sort had happened on *Vanguard*, years ago. But the battleship had multiple redundancies built into her hull to ensure that losing one network didn't mean losing all of them. The aliens hadn't been so careful.

Their ship is smaller, she reminded herself. *There's a limit to how much redundancy they can build into their systems.*

The marines flowed through the hatch, weapons at the ready. George felt cold as she turned to watch them go, knowing they could easily be walking into a trap. Ship-to-ship boarding actions were rare, almost unknown. Only one alien ship had ever been stormed successfully in nearly two hundred years of spacefaring. And the aliens knew *precisely* which way the marines would come. Sweat trickled down her back as she reached for her rifle, silently grateful for all the times she'd been forced to practice while wearing the suit. If the aliens had treachery in mind, she'd make them pay.

And then die, she thought, as the minutes started to crawl. *And then the aliens will die, too.*

Her radio bleeped. "Fitzwilliam, come forward," Sergeant Tosco ordered. "The water's fine."

George relaxed, slightly, as she rose and walked to the hatch. Telling her that the water was fine was a way of telling her it actually *was* fine. Something else - anything else - would have served as a cue to hit the emergency alert, then cast off before the aliens had a chance to storm the shuttle. She stepped into the alien airlock - there was something oddly crude about the design, as if they'd hacked it out of solid metal - and through the secondary hatch, into the alien ship.

It seemed smaller than she expected, based on the hand-ful of hulks that had been examined during the war. George wasn't claustrophobic - a claustrophobe wouldn't have been allowed to serve, even on giant *Vanguard* - but she still found the alien ship a little oppres-sive. The light was tinted red, there was a faint heat haze in the air, the bulkheads were too close and there was something subtly *wrong* about the proportions, as if the world was slightly out of phase. It was a jarring reminder, if she'd needed one, that the Foxes were *alien*. They were not humans in funny suits.

The Foxes themselves were…she couldn't escape the impression that they were *grovelling*, prostrating in front of their captors. They were push-ing their heads into the deck, practically inviting the marines to step on them; they were wrapping their tails under their haunches, as if they half-expected to have them cut off. George was used to servants, to men and women who bowed and scraped in front of her, but this was different. There was something almost sickeningly servile about the whole display.

They know they're beaten, she thought, numbly.

She'd read the briefing notes, when she'd had a moment, but seeing it in person really brought it home. Humans would be resentful; humans would be planning an escape or finding a way to turn the tables, even though *Vanguard* was just waiting for an excuse to blow the ship out of space. But the Foxes knew they were beaten. They'd surrendered, far more completely than any human ever would. It boded well for the future.

Sammy's voder produced a hail of barking sounds. One of the Foxes rolled over, exposing his neck, then answered with more barking, mixed with a handful of English words. George stared in disbelief, more astonished that the Fox knew any English than at the mangled pronunciation. But she supposed it made sense. They'd need a way to communicate with any humans they captured, even if they hadn't expected to be captured themselves.

"Like a set of dogs," Corporal Roberts muttered.

George shrugged as the discussion continued, hoping against hope that the translation software wasn't misleading them. The Foxes *did* look like dogs, she supposed. She couldn't help thinking of the Jack Russell she'd owned as a child, the mischievous dog that had torn up the flower beds or chased rabbits all over the estate. And yet…she reminded herself, sharply, that the Foxes were thinking beings. Their familiar appearance was very - very - deceptive. Looks aside, they had almost nothing in common with their terrestrial lookalikes.

"But very dangerous dogs," she muttered back.

"I bet you owned a whole horde of dogs," Corporal Roberts said. "And went fox-hunting with them."

"Hah," George said. She *had* gone fox-hunting, once. The uncle who'd taken her and her sister had bragged about it - there was something political involved that she'd been too young to understand - but she'd just found it sickening. "I prefer man-hunting myself."

She rolled her eyes as she watched the conversation. The gentle teasing about her origins had been growing stronger over the last few days, although she wasn't sure if it was a sign of acceptance or a probe to check she hadn't been spoilt rotten. Some of the questions they'd come up with were insane. How was *she* to know if there was any difference between posh girls or common girls? She'd certainly never noticed any difference between men!

"The ship is ours," Sammy reported. "And we have willing allies."

"Just don't trust them completely," Sergeant Tosco reminded them. "Treat them well, but not too well. They could be recaptured just as easily."

George nodded in agreement. The Foxes didn't crush their enemies, not completely. They beat them, then integrated them. And yet, it was hard to see how they could integrate humans, let alone Tadpoles. Biology would prevent it.

They integrated another race, she mused, as she helped count the prisoners. *They probably think they can do it again.*

————

Henry sniffed as he boarded the alien starship, tasting something…indefinably alien hanging in the air. It was hard to describe, a strange mixture of spice woven into a *fleshy* smell that made him want to gag. He'd shared close quarters with starfighter pilots, back during the war, but *they* hadn't been so bad. The Foxes, it seemed, *liked* having the smell hanging in the air. Perhaps it reminded them of home.

"Your Highness," Engineer Jolene Anderson said. She was a tall woman, wearing naval trousers and a very loose shirt. Her skin glittered with sweat. "Welcome onboard the *Black Hunter.*"

Henry raised his eyebrows. "*Black Hunter?*"

"Our rough translation of her name is *Black Hunter Of Prey And Food*," Jolene said, seriously. "We decided to shorten it."

"A good idea," Henry said. He cocked his head as Jolene turned, ducking her head to pass through the hatch. "Is she in working order?"

"We have to replace one of the power cores, but otherwise she's in good shape," Jolene assured him. "From what they've told us, *Black Hunter* was being refitted after her *last* encounter with human starships before being hastily thrust back into the line of battle. They didn't have time to run the tests they should have run before clearing her to leave."

"Lucky for us," Henry said. "Did you recover anything from the computer cores?"

"Our hackers are working on them now," Jolene said. "The crew - the former crew - has been quite helpful, but we don't want to trust them *too* far."

Henry nodded in agreement. Everything they'd learned about the Foxes told them that the aliens submitted to superior force, submitted completely. They saw nothing *odd* about rearranging their hierarchy to put humans at the top - or the bottom - as long as the pecking order was properly sorted out. There was something oddly *Roman* about them, he thought, although even the Romans hadn't been perfect when it came to assimilating conquered populations. But then, the Foxes weren't human. They lacked the racism, religion, nationalism and other problems that plagued humanity.

He found himself staring as he followed her onto the bridge. The command deck looked absurd to his eyes: the commanding officer sat on a throne-like structure, peering down at his underlings from high overhead. The subordinates themselves were almost completely isolated, unable to even *see* their comrades. There were no holographic projectors, as far as he could see. Henry couldn't help thinking that the whole design was terribly inefficient, compared to a human bridge. And yet, the arrangement must have been meaningful to the designers. It would have been easy for them to come up with something more efficient, if they wanted it.

"The command and control systems aren't that different from ours," Jolene informed him, nodding to the places where human-designed computer cores had been fitted to the alien technology. "The prize crew should have no difficulty in controlling her."

"Very good," Henry said. He had no idea what Admiral Naiser would want to do with the ship, but it might be useful. "Did you find an FTL communicator system?"

"We believe so," Jolene said. "Commodore Watson-Stewart is already studying the computer files."

Henry took one last look, then allowed her to give him a brief tour of the alien ship. It was strange, very strange. Tadpole ships were completely alien, but *this* ship was just familiar enough to be disconcerting. The more he looked into cabins - he couldn't help thinking of them as *dens* - the more he realised that *hierarchy* was practically branded into the ship. A senior officer would literally look down on his juniors, only to be looked down upon himself by *his* superiors. The dim lighting - red enough to make him feel creeped out - only made the impression worse. He found his hand reaching for the pistol at his belt, several times, as they moved from compartment to compartment. It was a minor miracle, he decided, that no one had fired at shadows.

"Their power cores are actually slightly inferior to ours, Your Highness, but the design allows them to be fixed easily," Jolene told him, as they entered the engineering compartment. A team of human engineers were carefully removing parts of the alien system, following instructions from a single captured alien. "It reminds me of some of the modifications we made to *Vanguard*, really. The trade-off may not be as bad as it seems."

Henry nodded in agreement. Replacing a power core on a fleet carrier or a battleship was an absolute nightmare. The heavy armour surrounding the drive units had to be removed, carefully, before the power core could be disconnected and floated out into space. Making it *easy* would have given the enemy a perfect target, a weak spot on an otherwise near-impregnable hull. Henry was sure that humanity's enemies would take full advantage of such an opportunity.

"And we can replace theirs with one of ours?" He asked. "You're sure?"

Jolene gave him a sharp look. "It will not last forever, Your Highness," she said, rather tartly. "Frankly, the system will be weaker because we *cannot* lock the power core solidly in place without ripping chunks of the hull apart. But it will last long enough to be useful, I believe. We could easily fly her home without resorting to *Ark Royal's* parasite trick."

"Very good," Henry said. "Let me know if you find anything interesting."

Jolene smiled. It lit up her entire face.

"Your Highness, *this* is interesting," she said. She waved a hand down at the engineers. "All of this...*this* is how another intelligent race solves its problems. Some of their solutions are the same as ours, others are different. And their solutions open up new avenues for scientific research. There's enough here to spark genuinely *original* work back home."

"Assuming we get *Black Hunter* home," Henry pointed out.

"Even without the ship, there's a lot to take from her," Jolene said. "And we'll learn a great deal over the next few days."

"I hope so," Henry said. "We might need it."

————

George closed her eyes as warm water washed over her body, sluicing away the chemicals that had cleansed her skin of anything that *might* be dangerous. A blast of hot air followed, drying her within seconds. She walked forward, through a pair of airlocks, and into a small changing room. A pair of trousers and a tunic were already waiting for her, hanging from a rack. She glanced at her body in the mirror - thankfully, the chemicals didn't seem to have caused any reaction - then donned the clothes and headed for the hatch. The rest of the platoon were waiting outside.

"Very good," Sergeant Tosco said, as George joined them. "The boffins seem fairly certain there isn't any real risk, but…we have to be careful."

George nodded, sourly. Perhaps, if they were lucky, they could have proper showers later, once they went off-duty. She *could* sneak into one of the privacy tubes and use the shower there, if she was careful. It wasn't as if anyone would complain. She'd be alone, of course, but *that* wouldn't be a problem.

"There's no point in taking risks," Sammy agreed. He paused, dramatically. "Do we get the prize money?"

Sergeant Tosco smiled, rather thinly. "The Admiral has ruled that we get a *third* of the prize money," he said. "Technically, we only took their surrender. We didn't board the vessel and shoot everything until they gave up. *Vanguard* and her gunnery crews also played a role."

"So did the boffins who came up with the voder programs," Sammy said. "*And* the other ships too…"

"We have a third of the prize money," Sergeant Tosco said. "The exact *amount* of money will not be settled, I think, until we get home. There's…a certain disagreement over just how much *Black Hunter* is worth. It isn't as if we took a *Tadpole* ship."

"No," Roberts agreed. "We'd have a *second* war on our hands."

"For the moment, you'll each get a cut of the minimum amount," Sergeant Tosco said. "The full amount will be determined when we get home…"

"When the taxman can claim a share," Sammy muttered.

George shrugged. Technically, prize money was tax-free. But someone who won a great deal of money *could* be forced to pay taxes anyway, through some complicated legal system she didn't pretend to understand. She'd read some grumbling about it in naval journals, although it wasn't a big issue. Large prize awards were very rare.

And you don't need the money, she reminded herself. *You could easily give it up and never notice.*

"The bad news is that some of us may be going back onboard *Black Hunter*," Sergeant Tosco added. "Those of us with naval experience will be very useful, I am sure. The Admiral seems to have something in mind already."

Ouch, George thought. Her scalp itched uncomfortably. Maybe she had had a reaction to the chemicals after all. *We went through decontamination for nothing?*

"Report back to your bunks for a rest," Sergeant Tosco concluded. "You'll be back on your feet before you know it."

How reassuring, George thought.

CHAPTER
TWENTY FOUR

"I assume there was no permanent damage?"

"No, sir," Susan said. She was certain that Admiral Naiser knew the fleet's status as well as she did, but it was important to be sure. "The damage the task force took during the brief engagement has been repaired."

"Very good," Admiral Naiser said.

He tapped a switch. A starchart appeared in front of them, hovering over the table. Susan took a sip of her coffee - she needed the caffeine - as she studied the captured data. They'd had a rough idea where the tramlines led, of course, but the alien files showed just what was waiting for them. It didn't look good.

"They have a major naval base here, at ES-11," Admiral Naiser said. "That guards their rear flank, it seems. And its presence raises other questions."

Susan nodded. "Is there another hostile power out here?"

"We found no reference to one in the files," Admiral Naiser said. "Yet."

That, Susan knew, was all too true. There were literally *billions* of terabytes of data in the alien computers, ranging from navigational files to alien entertainment. For all she knew, a good third of the audio-visual files were alien *porn*! Surveying them all would take years, even with the best hackers in the navy. They might well have missed something important, tucked away in the alien files. If there *was* another alien race, pressing against the enemy rear...

"It beggars belief that they would have started a war with us, if they were threatened by another power," she pointed out. "A war on two fronts would be disastrous."

"True," Admiral Naiser agreed. "And yet, their behaviour is partly instinctive. They may not have thought better of it."

"Maybe," Susan mused. It would be *nice* to think there were potential allies nearby, although she knew better than to assume they were friendly. *The Seventy Maxims of Maximally Effective Mercenaries* - was quite right. Her enemy's enemy was her enemy's enemy; no more, no less. "Or they may just have put a naval base in place at a chokepoint, just to make sure their rear is covered. We did the same at New Russia."

"*After* we knew there was a major threat coming at us," Admiral Naiser countered.

"They *knew* that aliens existed," Susan reminded him. "*We* thought we were alone in the universe until suddenly we weren't."

She shook her head. In hindsight, she couldn't understand how her predecessors had made such an elementary mistake. *She* knew there were at least four other races inhabiting worlds not too far from Earth. They hadn't seen anything larger than a dog-like creature on a colony world. The chain of events that led to Earth birthing an intelligent spacefaring race had been so unlikely, they'd assumed, that they'd been practically unique.

"It may be the answer," Admiral Naiser said. "We'll have to plan on the assumption we won't find allies on the far side of enemy space."

He adjusted the display. "We have two options," he said. "On one hand, we follow the tramlines through ES-17, ES-15 and ES-12 to ES-11. We can *also* follow the tramlines through ES-16 and ES-14 to ES-12, then hop to ES-11. However, if we're reading the files correctly, the latter route would actually be longer because of the distance between tramlines. Worse, the enemy would have ample time to mass a force and send it against us."

"Or merely reinforce the defences at ES-11," Susan agreed. The Foxes didn't seem to *like* going on the defensive - *she* didn't like going on the defensive - but surely even *they* couldn't avoid military logic. If ES-11 fell, the task force would have a straight run to ES-1, their homeworld. "They know we *have* to pass through that system."

"It would be useful if they *did* send ships away from their defences," Admiral Naiser said, thoughtfully. "If we were taking out their FTL communications nodes as we advanced…"

"We'd also be telling them where we were," Susan said, as his voice trailed off. "They'd know which nodes were failing, wouldn't they?"

"The techs think so," Admiral Naiser said. He held up a datapad. "I couldn't make head or tail of half of what they said, but the gist of it is that the Foxes *would* notice. There's also a possibility that they *might* notice a gravity pulse running down the tramline when we jump into the system, like a string that's been plucked. If that happens…well, leaving the network in place and sneaking around is suddenly impossible."

"And they might even get an accurate idea of just how much *tonnage* is crossing the tramlines," Susan added. She shook her head, cursing the enemy under her breath. They were far too innovative for her peace of mind. "They'd know which way we were going."

"Probably," Admiral Naiser said. His voice suddenly hardened. "Which is why we're going to be splitting our force."

He adjusted the display. "We'll be dividing the task force into two formations," he said, bluntly. "Commodore Hoover will take one element into ES-16 and follow the tramlines to ES-12, while I take the other element into ES-15. We'll link up again in ES-12 and thrust together into ES-11."

Susan frowned. Dividing one's forces in the face of the enemy went against everything she'd been taught at the academy. It *would* upset the Foxes if they *could* monitor events in real time, but it still raised the spectre of one squadron being trapped and defeated in detail. And yet…it wasn't as if they couldn't avoid action, if necessary. They wouldn't be trying to hide, not really. No cloaked fleet would be able to get close enough to force engagement if they were careful.

And alter course regularly, she thought, morbidly. *They'll certainly try to do unto us as we did unto them.*

"Risky, sir," she said. It would confuse the aliens, yet it would *also* tempt them with the prospect of scoring a decisive victory. "We could cloak as soon as we crossed the tramlines, making it harder for them to track us."

She paused. "We don't *know* they can get accurate tonnage readings."

"No, we don't," Admiral Naiser said.

Susan met his eyes. "What if we sent destroyers through first, with orders to blow the FTL communications nodes before the remainder of the fleet crossed? We'd make it harder for them to guess what we were doing."

"And slow us down," Admiral Naiser said. "Each successive jump would cost us several hours, even before we started crossing the system itself. And there are other reasons to make a major commitment to both prongs."

He studied the console for a long moment. "If the files are accurate, both ES-15 and ES-14 have major colonies, both of which need to be rendered harmless. They will have strong incentive to keep us from hitting them."

"Hopefully drawing their forces out of position," Susan said. "And opening the way to ES-11."

"Maybe," Admiral Naiser said. "On the other hand, the fleet base at ES-11 is more important than the colonies, at least in the short term."

Susan nodded, sourly. Sure, the aliens *might* come out to defend their colony worlds. Human governments would certainly demand that the navy did precisely that, if humanly possible. But would the Foxes feel the same way? Cold logic would mandate abandoning ES-14 and ES-15, simply because they were impossible to defend without a major commitment. And the only way they could *make* that commitment was through divesting ES-11 of some of its defences.

"We'll do some damage to their industrial nodes, sir," she said, finally. She didn't envy the admiral. He would have to convince his subordinates that the plan was workable. "And give them a very hard time."

"Speed is still of the essence," Admiral Naiser said. He reached out and tapped the red-blue stars along the war front. "If they've started moving forces back now, they'll be on us soon."

"Yes, sir," Susan said. Her most pessimistic assessment stated that it would be at least a fortnight - more like three weeks - before recalled starships joined the fight for ES-1. But what if she was wrong? "There's too much at stake."

"And our captured ship may prove the key to getting into firing range without being detected," Admiral Naiser added. "If, of course, we can fly her properly."

"We'll find out, sir," Susan said. The prize crew would have plenty of time to practice - and a number of willing assistants. It still astonished her, but the xenospecialists had assured everyone that it made perfect sense. The POWs now considered themselves part of the human tribe. "They'll have plenty of time to work out the kinks."

"Then inform the fleet that we will depart in five hours," Admiral Naiser said. "That should give us enough time to sort out the new formations."

"Yes, sir," Susan said. She wasn't entirely happy with it, but the Admiral had made up his mind. Besides, she could see the logic. "*Vanguard* will be ready to depart on command."

"I expected nothing less," Admiral Naiser informed her.

———

"Congratulations, George," Sammy said. He stuck out a tongue as they walked onto the alien bridge. "Or should I call you *Captain*?"

George scowled. Technically, *she* was the senior naval officer on *Black Hunter*. Half the techs crawling through the alien hull were civilians - their habits driving their military minders to distraction - and most of the remainder were outside the chain of command. She honestly didn't understand why Commander Mason or another XO hadn't been assigned to *Black Hunter*...hell, there was no shortage of officers who were senior to her. But someone had left her in command...she wasn't sure if it was a backhanded compliment or a subtle insult. She was more expendable than many other officers on *Vanguard*.

And trying to give orders to the sergeant will be tricky, she thought. The marines had their own chain of command, with the senior marine reporting directly to the starship captain. But now...maybe it was just a fluke. Or maybe someone had thought she could be spared from other duties. *How am I meant to tell Tosco what to do?*

"You can call me *George*," she said, as she studied the alien throne. Command chair or not, she couldn't help thinking of it as a throne. "I haven't actually been promoted."

Sammy shrugged. "You're the senior naval officer on a starship," he pointed out. "That makes you the *captain*, whatever rank you actually hold."

"True," George agreed.

She shook her head. Two years ago - it felt like *decades* - she'd asked one of her instructors if there was a chance of becoming a CO within her first year on active duty. He'd told her that it would only happen if everyone above her dropped dead - and anything capable of killing so many crewmen would probably get her too. Being called *captain* while she was flying a shuttle had always struck her as absurd. Now...

You might be in command of an alien ship, she thought, *but you're also in command of the biggest target in the fleet.*

She sat down and studied the mismatched control systems. The alien technology wasn't *that* different from the gear she was used to using, but there were a *lot* of little discontinuities and things that didn't quite add up. It would get worse, she suspected, as they actually powered up the drive and headed deeper into enemy space. There was a chance, a very good chance, that they'd accidentally wreck the entire ship. The more she experimented with the systems, the more fragile they seemed.

A pity we can't use their controls directly, she thought. *They're not designed for human hands.*

"We got the weapons ready to fire," Sammy said. "But the tactical staff haven't quite managed to get them aimed in the right direction."

"Try to avoid firing on *Vanguard*," George ordered, dryly. "We'll be blown out of space before we can tell them it was an accident."

"I'll do my best," Sammy said. "But no promises."

George sighed and continued thumbing through the files, studying the starship's specifications. There was *definitely* something very crude about *Black Hunter*, although she had to admit it was effective. Her brief tour of the vessel had only deepened her sense that something was very wrong with anyone who lived in such an environment...she told herself, sharply, that humans and aliens could be very different. Humans were shocked when children were killed, even in horrific accidents; *Tadpoles* didn't even recognise their children as intelligent beings until they reached adulthood. The infant mortality rate on Tadpole Prime was, by human standards, utterly terrifying.

She looked up as Major Andres and Sergeant Tosco entered the bridge, then hastily rose to her feet and saluted. Captain or not, she doubted either of them would salute *her*.

"Status report," Major Andres ordered.

"We should be able to fly and fight, sir," George said, softly. She wasn't sure what the admiral had in mind for her ship. It wouldn't be *impossible* to sneak back home, leaving the rest of the task force to continue the advance. "However, we won't know until we power up the drive and take her out."

"And we won't know how she handles," Sammy added. "I think they deliberately surfed the drive field, overpowering the system to give them some extra nimbleness."

"Their beancounters must be less aggressive than ours," George muttered. *Surfing* a drive field was easy enough, but it put so much stress on the drive nodes that it shortened their projected lifespan significantly. Trying to warp one's drive field was technically forbidden, in the Royal Navy. It was only used if the crew were desperate. "If they really did overstress their nodes, one of them might explode sooner rather than later."

"I suspect their beancounters get regularly thrashed," Major Andres said, dryly. "They know their place."

He shrugged. "But you can accompany the fleet?"

"Yes, sir," George said.

"Unless there's a false harmonic in the drive," Sammy put in. "Realistically, sir, their system was never very good, even before the ship took a beating."

George kept her face expressionless with an effort. Sammy was right, yet he was undercutting her in front of their superior officer. She was sure, reasonably sure, that *Black Hunter* would have no trouble, once they powered up the drive. It wasn't the time to express her doubts.

But surely they would like to know the problems, if there are any problems, she reminded herself, grimly. *They'll need the problem list, just to make sure they know what could go wrong.*

"Then prepare to depart," Major Andres ordered.

"Yes, sir," George said. She paused. "Where exactly are we going?"

"Where we've always been going," Major Andres said. "The alien homeworld."

He smiled, rather coldly. "And make sure you know how to get off the ship," he added. "You'll need it."

George and Sammy exchanged looks. *That* didn't sound good.

———

Admiral John Naiser leaned back in his chair, as the fleet started to get underway, and wished for things he knew he couldn't have. A rug on a hot sunny beach, an impractical cocktail that defied gravity, a handsome man right next to him…they would have been preferable, he felt, to the catfight that had erupted between his senior officers. Half of them had supported his plan, the other half had loudly questioned its wisdom. And none of them had seemed inclined to shut up until he'd reminded them, loudly, that *he* was in command of the fleet.

Commodore Hoover didn't object, he thought. *But then, he got an independent command out of the deal.*

He reached for his cup of tea and sipped it, half-wishing he'd thought to ask the steward to put something a little stronger into the liquid. A stiff drink would have done him a world of good, except the Foxes would be straining every sinew to reinforce their defences before his fleet arrived. There was no time to get drunk, no time to do more than rest…he finished the tea, then rose and strode down the corridor to his cabin. The two marines on duty stepped aside to allow him to enter as he returned their salutes with casual ease.

It felt odd, John thought, to be in command of a fleet. He was travelling on a starship, but he wasn't *responsible* for her. Technically, he was nothing more than a passenger. And yet, he *was* responsible for the entire fleet. It was tempting, very tempting, to attempt to micromanage, only he knew - from bitter experience - that it would be dangerous. Quite apart from offending his flag captain, it would distract him from his *actual* duties. He was meant to concentrate on fleet tactics and operations, not supervise a single starship...

But now he felt helpless, even as his plan was put into operation. Splitting the fleet was a gamble, one that relied upon the captured data being accurate. The xenospecialists swore blind the Foxes would submit - and they had - but it only took one exception to the rules to cause absolute chaos. If *humans* were often unpredictable, even by other humans, why couldn't Foxes be unpredictable too?

He eyed his drinks cabinet, wondering just who'd decided that a fleet admiral needed a selection of expensive wines from across the Human Sphere. It wasn't as if he drank regularly, certainly not when on duty. Hell, the last time he'd drunk himself into a stupor had been shortly after HMS *Canopus* had been destroyed. He'd been the sole survivor, half-mad when he'd been plucked from the wreckage. No wonder he hadn't been able to return to starfighters after *that*.

A low quiver ran through the battleship as she picked up speed. She'd be crossing the tramline in hours, then plunging onwards into ES-15. And then...further, still further, until they reached ES-1. Enemy Star One. The alien homeworld.

Sleep, he told himself, firmly. *You'll be no use to anyone if you stay awake.*

CHAPTER
TWENTY FIVE

"Ballistic missile dispatched, Captain," Granger reported. "Impact with the FTL station in seventy-two minutes."

"Barring accidents," Mason commented.

Susan nodded, curtly. ES-15 wasn't particularly interesting, as star systems went; two rocky worlds, both of which would require extensive terraforming before anyone could live on them and a single gas giant, rather smaller than Neptune. The Foxes didn't seem to have done anything with it, as far as she could tell, although an entire community could be hiding on the gas giant's moons, completely undetectable as long as they were careful. She checked the live feed from the drones surrounding the task force, then smiled grimly. Nothing could come within engagement range without being detected.

"Set course for Tramline Two," she ordered. There were only two tramlines in ES-15, although they were far from useless. "ETA?"

"Forty-seven hours, assuming we don't push the drives," Reed reported. "We could push things a little harder."

Susan shook her head. "We can't risk leaving the logistics behind," she said. *Vanguard* could move faster, given time, but the freighters couldn't keep up. "Or the marines."

She leaned back in her command chair as the task force started to pick up speed. Forty-seven hours...she could relax, just for a while. There was nothing in the system, as far as she could tell, that threatened her ships. But there was no way to be entirely sure. If she was in command, on the alien homeworld, she would be scrambling everything she could to take advantage of the unexpected opportunity. Catching half the human fleet, hopelessly isolated from the other half...

They'd need to get very lucky, she told herself, sharply. *And even if they did manage to get a superior force into this system, we could evade contact.*

"Cloak us in twenty minutes, as planned," she ordered. "And then alter course."

"Aye, Captain," Granger said.

Hell of a gamble, Susan thought. She wasn't even sure it was necessary, although she understood the admiral's paranoia. A least-time course from Tramline One to Tramline Two would be completely predictable. *And we don't even know they're waiting for us.*

She glanced at Mason. "Mr. XO, how's our new friend coping?"

"They seem to have survived," Mason said. "And I *think* they're mastering the drive field."

Susan shook her head, honestly unsure if she should laugh or cry. The prize crew had fought desperately to control their vessel as she lunged from side to side, rather like a teenager taking a fast boat out on the choppy waters for the first time. Or riding a horse, something *she* hadn't done until she'd gone to boarding school. She hadn't envied the rich girls that much, she reassured herself, but she'd always resented their easy skill on horseback. The alien craft *did* seem to be settling down, she supposed, yet it was quite possible that the aliens would realise something was wrong the moment they saw her.

"Keep an eye on them," she ordered. "And inform me if anything goes wrong."

She brought up a starchart, studying the tramlines for the umpteenth time. Assuming the aliens had detected their arrival in ES-19, assuming the aliens had figured out what had happened to their task force...they had, of course. Even if they hadn't, she dared not assume anything less. No, the aliens knew the task force was in their rear. They simply *had* to be doing their best to block the advance before it was too late.

The fleet cloaked, then changed course as planned. Any watchful eyes would lose track of them quickly, Susan thought. There simply wasn't anyone close enough to the fleet to pick up what little escaped the cloaking devices. And yet...she knew it would be for nothing, the moment they crossed the next tramline. All she could do was hope - pray - that it would be enough to confuse the enemy.

She rose. "Mr. Mason, you have the bridge," she informed him. "It's time I toured my ship."

"Aye, Captain," Mason said. "I have the bridge."

———

Commodore Juliet Watson-Stewart was dimly aware, at some level, that the starship was moving, but it wasn't particularly important to her. She ignored it, just as she ignored the stream of unimportant messages that flowed in and out of her terminal on a regular basis. It wasn't *her* job to worry about flying the ship, even if she did hold a naval rank. She preferred to concentrate on raw science and leave the remainder to the other officers. Her husband could inform her if something was deeply wrong, something that actually *did* require her attention.

It was annoying, very annoying, to be denied access to the FTL communicator *or* the absurdly-named alien starship. Juliet cared little for her own safety - indeed, she found it hard to comprehend, these days, that there was a universe that might actually want to hurt her. The prospect of cracking two or three formerly unsolvable scientific mysteries was worth any risk, *she* thought. But Admiral Naiser, one of the few people she considered to be a genuine friend, felt differently. And while she still thought he was being a worry wart, she bowed the head to his insistence. The techs on the freighter and the alien ship could answer any of her questions.

The big mystery, as far as she could determine, lay in how the FTL communicator talked to alien starships. Working out the equations behind sending messages up and down the tramlines hadn't been hard - in some ways, it was an offshoot of her work on enhancing the tramlines - but how did they send FTL messages to their starships? Nothing smaller than an immense gas giant was large enough to produce a gravity well capable of forming tramlines...and even *her* imagination quailed at the thought of a starship large enough to intimidate Jupiter. Everything she knew about how gravity lines behaved told her that the aliens shouldn't be able to do what they did.

But they do it, she told herself, firmly. *And so the theory is incomplete.*

She studied the alien files carefully, wishing - not for the first time - that everyone made careful notation of *everything*. Humans were laughably imprecise about such details. So too, it seemed, were the Foxes. There were details she *knew* were missing, details the Foxes wouldn't have needed to include because *everyone* knew them...

A faint noise caught her attention. She took a moment to centre herself, then slowly pulled out of the trance. Her husband was standing there, looking tired. He'd been working on the alien tech too, probing through the elements that had been shipped to *Vanguard*. She didn't think he'd had any more success than herself.

"We found something," Mike Johnston said. "A faint harmonic resonance between the two systems."

He held out a datapad. Juliet took it, skimming the file with a practiced eye. He was right. There *was* a resonance. And that meant...she worked the problem for a long moment, trying to see it from an alien point of view. What had they created? And how did it work?

Ah, she thought.

She was barely aware of him gently rubbing her shoulders as she fell back into the trance, studying the files in the light of her new knowledge. Quantum entanglement? She'd studied the theories, of course, but it had never led to any useful technology. At least, not yet. But surely that would operate on an interstellar level...

Unless they focus it on the tramline, she thought. *It might just work...*

———

"Captain," Reed said. "We are approaching Tramline Two."

"No sign of any enemy presence," Charlotte added. "Local space is clear."

Susan nodded. The passage through ES-15 had proved uneventful. She'd toured her ship, had a nap and returned to the bridge, just in time to supervise the passage through the tramline. And yet, she knew time was ticking away. ES-13 might pose a far greater challenge.

And if they can track ships crossing the tramline, she mused, *they'll know exactly when and where we entered their system.*

"Launch the ballistic missile at the FTL station, as planned," she ordered. There was no point in delaying any further. "And take us across the tramline."

She braced herself as the task force jumped. The tactical display blanked, leaving them blind for a handful of seconds. Susan held herself steady, despite the utter confidence that a major enemy force was lurking nearby, in position to catch them with their pants down. She *knew* it was unlikely, yet cold logic proved no barrier to fear.

"Fleet command net re-established," Parkinson informed her. "Tactical combat network active; no enemy ships detected. I say again, no enemy ships detected."

"Ah," Charlotte said. "Captain, I think you need to take a look at this."

Susan shook her head in disbelief as the tactical display began to fill with icons. ES-13 was settled, *heavily* settled. There were no inhabitable worlds, as far as she could tell, but there were hundreds of thousands of asteroids, hundreds of them clearly inhabited. Her sensors were picking up dozens of drive fields moving between the asteroid belt and the two gas giants. There were at least two cloudscoops clearly visible through optical sensors, suggesting there might be others on the far side of the gas giants.

Admiral Naiser's face appeared in front of her. "Captain," he said. "We seem to have stumbled on an unexpected surprise."

"Yes, sir," Susan said. She couldn't have put it better herself. "This system is clearly important to the enemy."

"Yes," Admiral Naiser said. "However, we cannot waste time wrecking the system. It would take us weeks to strike all the important targets. *And* the collateral damage would be colossal."

Susan nodded in grim agreement. There was no way to isolate the habitat asteroids from the industrial asteroids, assuming they were actually separate. The aliens might easily have combined the two, as a number of human asteroid societies had done. It was galling to realise that they *could* put a real crimp in the alien industrial base, at the cost of committing mass slaughter and wasting time, time they didn't have.

"Yes, sir," she said, reluctantly.

"The fleet will follow an evasive path to Tramline Two, once we destroy the FTL communicator," Admiral Naiser ordered. "And we will return to this system later, if the war goes badly."

"Aye, sir," Susan said. She glanced at Granger. "Launch the missile. Take out the FTL system."

"Aye, Captain," Granger said. There was a pause. "Missile launched."

And let's hope they haven't stationed a starship near the communicator to protect it, Susan thought. A seeker warhead would have no trouble blowing an undefended platform away, but a starship could easily swat the missile out of space before it reached its target. *They must have realised what we're doing by now.*

She forced herself to relax as her sensors picked up more and more details she hadn't wanted to know. The system was heavily settled, more heavily than she'd thought. And yet, there was a surprising *lack* of fixed defences. The problems of defending an asteroid against a determined attacker were vast, but she would have expected *some* effort. Was she actually looking at a dissident star system? Or something the Foxes simply didn't consider very vital.

Which is insane, she thought. *This place has to be defended.*

Her concern grew as the fleet headed deeper into the system, giving the settled portions a wide berth. Finding nothing bothered her more than she cared to admit. Only a civilian would consider the prospect of hiding an attack fleet in a bunch of asteroids, yet the sense of impending doom was almost impossible to resist. They *should* be too far, logically, for the aliens to get a solid lock on them, particularly after they'd cloaked. But something was nagging at the back of her mind.

She glanced at Mason. "*Is* this one of their systems?"

"Drive fields match previously-observed enemy freighters," Mason reported. "I don't think we've encountered a fifth alien race."

Susan frowned. The Tadpoles had had multiple factions, some of which had been more hostile than others. It had proven possible to negotiate with some of the less aggressive factions. But the Foxes were a single nation, if the POWs were to be believed. They simply couldn't accept the idea of separate, but equal. Two nations were a war waiting to happen, as far as they were concerned. Perhaps this was just a relatively minor system, compared to others further towards their homeworld. Or maybe they'd just decided that it was pointless to attempt to defend the system and simply given up.

Which we did, once or twice, she thought. She'd studied history, back in school. Her tutors had drummed more of Britain's greatness into her head than she cared to admit. *Our plans to cope with a full-scale nuclear attack floundered on the simple fact that there was no way to cope with a full-scale nuclear attack.*

"Launch a spread of stealth probes," she ordered, grimly. "See what they can pick out from a closer vantage point."

She forced herself to relax, somehow, as the minutes became hours. The aliens showed no sign they even *knew* the fleet was there, something she was *sure* was absurd. Even if the techs were wrong, completely wrong, about the aliens being able to monitor the tramlines, they certainly should have picked up the fleet before it cloaked. And *something* had to have taken out the FTL communications nodes.

Maybe they sent their defence force forward and we killed it, she mused. *Or maybe it was withdrawn to ES-12.*

It was a pleasant thought, too pleasant. She cautioned herself, sternly, against believing it without more evidence. The aliens were *alien*. They might have decided the system wasn't worth trying to defend, they might be gathering their forces to defend the system, they might be…they might be doing something completely incomprehensible. All *she* could do was wait, as patiently as she could, for the hammer to fall.

And hope we can cope when it does, she thought.

"You're saying they've found a way to *fake* a gravity line?"

Commodore Juliet Watson-Stewart, John Naiser had often thought, had no sense of timing at all. If anything, she'd only gotten worse since she'd been relieved of her post on HMS *Warspite*. Hell, it said something about her tendency to fall into her own head that her backers hadn't made much of a fuss about her relief, even though it could have been used to score political points during the next catfight over budgetary appropriations. They'd probably been relieved, he suspected, that disaster had been averted.

And yet, in some ways, he was relieved she'd come to talk to him. It was a distraction.

"I believe they *do* manage to form a fake-gravity line," she said, slowly. "In essence, it's a *shadow* of a gravity line linking their ships to the FTL communicator. They...they effectively set up a wired connection between the ships and the communicator."

"Rather than broadcasting in all directions," John mused. It sounded rather cumbersome, but beggars couldn't be choosers. Given time, the system could probably be improved. Hell, *Warspite* had been an improvement on technology stolen from the Tadpoles. "If they lost the communicator, they'd also lose the ability to coordinate their fleets."

"On an interplanetary scale," Juliet agreed. "But there might be more than one communicator in a given star system. We still don't understand exactly how they're constructed."

Or how big a chunk of their economy each one absorbs, John thought. The catfight over funding the Royal Navy's proposed twelve battleships had been savage. Parliament had been reluctant to fund *eight*, let alone twelve. The Navy League had had to fight tooth and nail to secure the funding. *If those things are relatively cheap, they could replace them easily.*

He studied her for a long moment. "How much would it cost to build one?"

"Impossible to calculate," Juliet said, flatly. "There are aspects to the device we don't yet understand."

"Guess," John ordered.

Juliet gave him a resentful look that made her look strikingly *young*, a teenager whose father doesn't *understand*. "To duplicate the systems we *understand* would be relatively straightforward, using off-the-shelf components," she said. "The total cost would be little more than a hundred thousand pounds. However, you would *not* have a working FTL communicator. You'd have a fancy communications relay station and nothing else."

"I see," John said. It had taken him time to learn that Juliet hated to be pulled back into the real world. She was so single-minded that he sometimes wondered how she managed to get dressed in the morning. Her husband probably spent half his time playing nursemaid. "Can you not take a wild guess?"

"A million billion trillion pounds," Juliet said.

It was a joke, John hoped. It *had* to be a joke. Asking the politicians for that amount of money...he had to smile, even though it would probably have ended badly. Britain - and the rest of the Human Sphere - couldn't have funded such a program, not realistically. The Gross World Product was only two hundred trillion pounds or thereabouts.

"Let me know when you have a more *accurate* impression," he said. He doubted they could get even a small percentage of Britain's GNP, let alone the GWP. "I'll try to use what you've given me."

"Thank you," Juliet said. She looked vague, again. "I could move faster if I had access to the alien tech directly..."

"Definitely not," John said. Silently, he made a note to have a few words with Mike Johnston. He'd thought this particular matter was settled. "You're too valuable to risk."

Juliet gave him another resentful look. "*Captain*, I..."

The klaxons started to howl. John held up a hand as he checked his displays.

"It will have to be discussed later," he said. Red icons were appearing on the display. "We're under attack."

CHAPTER
TWENTY SIX

"Incoming craft," Charlotte snapped.

"Red alert," Susan ordered. The penny had finally dropped. "All hands to battlestations!"

"Battlestations, aye," Mason said.

Susan watched, grimly, as updates came in from all over the ship. *Vanguard* was ready to fight, when the enemy finally got a solid lock on the task force. It was clear that the enemy *did* have a rough idea of where they were, but from the way they were sweeping space it looked as though they didn't have a *precise* lock. They would, she knew, even if the task force remained cloaked. Their tiny craft would get close enough to spot the task force within minutes.

"Signal from the flag," Charlotte said. "*Black Hunter* is to withdraw to the edge of our formation."

Smart, Susan thought. *If they don't know we captured one of their ships, there's nothing to be gained by letting them know now.*

"The analysts can't determine just what we're facing," Mason said, quietly. The red icons on the display were sweeping closer, probing the edge of the task force's formation. "They read out as shuttles, rather than starfighters."

Susan leaned forward. Mason was right. The enemy craft couldn't be much larger than the average shuttle, although they were being handled as though they were starfighters. She puzzled over it for a long moment, wondering if they *were* facing shuttlecraft. The enemy could have improvised a defence, if they wished. But the average shuttlecraft - even a swarm of shuttlecraft - didn't have a hope of cracking her point defence and the aliens had to know it.

Unless they have something new up their sleeves, she thought. *We can't be the only ones to have advanced over the last year.*

"Continue to monitor their operations," she ordered, slowly. There was nothing else they could do, at least until the enemy zeroed in on them. "And stand by to engage the enemy."

She studied her displays for a long moment. Her ship was ready to fight, but how long would that last? Her crew couldn't stay at battlestations indefinitely. A few hours of tension would dull their edge, leaving them unable to man their positions effectively. She might have to send the secondary crews back to rest in an hour, if the shit hadn't hit the fan by then. It was clear there was no hope of evading the enemy any longer.

Those craft can easily keep a lock on us, she thought. *Outrunning them isn't an option.*

"Signal from the flag," Charlotte reported. "The task force is to drop the cloak and launch fighters in five minutes."

"Understood," Susan said. If the enemy craft, whatever they were, couldn't be outrun, they'd have to be driven away. She felt her eyes narrow as she contemplated the prospects. A shuttlecraft might be slower and less agile than a starfighter, but it had *far* greater operational range. "Ready the point defence, then prepare to engage."

She counted down the seconds until the cloak was dropped, wondering just how the aliens would react. Without the cloak, they could easily track the task force from a safe distance…they'd just need to fall back far enough to evade the starfighters. She silently saluted the enemy commander, even though she suspected the aliens had had a stroke of good luck. If the task force launched starfighters to drive the shuttles away, there was no way they could hide anyway. Starfighters were too small to carry cloaking devices.

"Signal from the flag," Charlotte said. Susan could hear the tension in her voice. "All units are to decloak."

"Do it," Susan ordered. On the display, the enemy ships were altering formation. "And bring up our active sensors."

"Aye, Captain," Parkinson said.

He sucked in his breath. "Those are either massively-overpowered shuttles or something we haven't seen before," he said. "Captain, those things are a specialised design."

Mason worked his console for a long moment. "A marine-class shuttle? They're planning to board us?"

"They're far *too* overpowered, even for the marines," Parkinson said. "I'd honestly say they were oversized starfighters."

Susan frowned as the alien craft altered course, settling into an attack formation. She'd seen patterns like that before, during training exercises when the pilots hadn't yet learnt that predictable formations meant certain death. There was no randomness, not yet. But the aliens had to be insane. Targeting starfighters was easy enough, even though they were tiny. Their bigger shuttlecraft would be picked off long before they became a threat.

And even if they're planning to ram us, she thought, *it's unlikely they can do any real damage.*

"*Formidable* and *Vikramaditya* are launching starfighters," Parkinson reported. "They're attempting to intercept."

Susan had to smile. It felt odd to know that her hull was being protected by Indian starfighters, even though the Indians had at least as much to lose as Britain, if the Foxes won the war. The Indian pilots were good, according to Admiral Naiser. Right now, that was all that mattered. If they could take the alien craft out before they could even *begin* to pose a threat, she would forgive them anything.

"The enemy craft are moving," Parkinson said. "I...*Jesus Christ!*"

Just for a second, Susan's mind refused to accept what she was seeing. The alien craft were moving fast, *impossibly* fast. Their acceleration curves were ludicrously good, better than starfighters or any human-designed shuttlecraft. Part of her mind insisted, frantically, that she was looking at an ECM-produced illusion, even though *that* would have horrific implications of its own. And the alien craft were blazing towards the starfighters...

"Reconfigure the point defence," she snarled. They'd been caught by surprise, she had to admit, but she was damned if she was just *letting* them get a free shot at her hull. "And fire as soon as they enter weapons range."

"Aye, Captain," Jean said.

"Enemy craft are firing on the starfighters," Parkinson said. He sounded shocked. "They're mounting ship-grade plasma cannons!"

Susan gritted her teeth as a dozen starfighters died. In hindsight, she suspected, there would be a great many questions as to why *humanity* hadn't thought of it first. Mating standard point defence cannons with a shuttlecraft, giving them ample firepower to drive right through a starfighter formation and blow it to hell...she cursed the aliens under her breath, even as three alien shuttlecraft were blasted out of space. They'd changed the balance of power in a single savage engagement.

Gunboats, she thought, darkly. The alien craft were still driving into the teeth of her formation. Behind them, she could see two *more* enemy formations lighting up their drives and coming forward. *Why didn't* we *think of that?*

"Enemy craft entering point defence envelope," Jean said. The icons started to blur until their exact position was no longer certain. "They're deploying standard ship-mounted ECM!"

"Reprogram the point defence to compensate," Susan ordered.

She felt sweat trickling down her back. *That* was, in many ways, a worse surprise. The gunboats weren't big enough to soak up more than one or two hits - they couldn't be heavily armoured if they were moving like starfighters - but if the point defence computers weren't entirely sure of their positions, they'd have to fire a dozen shots to be sure of killing a single gunboat. And, in the time it took to kill one, three more might have slipped through the defences and entered attack range.

And they can even deploy their own point defence against our counter-missiles, she thought, angrily. The alien CO had done *very* well. She had no idea how much the gunboats cost, but she doubted they cost more than a battleship. The aliens would come out ahead if they exchanged a hundred gunboats for a single capital ship. *They just turned the universe upside down.*

"They're closing in on *Formidable*," Parkinson reported.

"Move us closer to provide cover," Susan ordered. *Formidable* mounted formidable - her lips quirked - point defence, like all fleet carriers, but she wasn't anything like as heavily armoured as *Vanguard*. "Try to lure them on to us."

The aliens refused to be distracted. Susan gritted her teeth as seven gunboats raced towards the carrier, their point defence firing madly to keep the CSP away. Three vanished in tiny fireballs, picked off by the plasma cannons, but four survived long enough to fire their missiles into the carrier. Susan watched, horrified, as nine missiles slammed into *Formidable*, blasting through her armour and detonating inside her hull. The carrier staggered out of formation, plasma leaking from a dozen wounds...

"Captain Jones has ordered his crew to abandon ship," Parkinson reported. "They..."

Too late, Susan thought.

Formidable exploded, violently. Susan closed her eyes for a long moment, silently honouring her crew. She'd *served* on *Formidable*, years ago. The fleet carrier had been heavily armoured, but no armour in existence could have saved her. There hadn't been any time for her crew to get to the lifepods, which meant...she shuddered. Two thousand men and women were now dead. She watched as the remaining gunboats were swatted out of space, knowing that the aliens had come out ahead.

She clamped down on her emotions, hard. She'd mourn later. If there *was* a later.

"*Bunker Hill* has taken heavy damage," Charlotte reported. "*Verdun* has lost main power and..."

She broke off. "*Verdun* is gone, Captain."

"Signal from the flag," Parkinson injected. "The fleet is to close up and prepare to repel attack."

Susan cursed under her breath as the second enemy wave came into range. Gunboats, over seventy of them. They didn't have any more surprises - she hoped - but it hardly mattered, not now. The task force had taken a beating - losing *Formidable* would make it harder to mount an effective CSP - and it wasn't over yet. If *she* was any judge, *Vikramaditya* would be the next target.

"Signal from the flag," Parkinson said. "The battleships are to cover *Vikramaditya*."

"Move us forward," Susan ordered. She felt a flicker of bitter amusement. *Vikramaditya* was suddenly the most important ship in the task force. Theoretically, starfighters could be launched from shuttlebays; in practice, she knew it was impossible. Maintaining any sort of operational tempo would be hellishly difficult. "And prepare to repel attack."

She glanced at the status display, silently summing up their losses. *Formidable* and *Verdun* had been destroyed outright, both lost with all hands. *Bunker Hill* was badly damaged and unlikely to be able to continue, at least without major repairs; *Yamamoto* had lost a chunk of her armour, rendering her vulnerable if the enemy made another pass. *Her only chance for survival was the simple fact that there were bigger targets within the task force that might draw enemy fire.*

And we could take out a hundred of their installations, she thought, bitterly. *But we'd never be sure what we were actually targeting.*

"The analysts have finished reprogramming the point defence systems, Captain," Mason said. "They think they can do more accurate targeting now."

"Let's hope so," Susan said.

She studied the live feed from the analysts carefully, even though they were telling her things she didn't want to know about the enemy craft. The gunboats had been a *very* nasty surprise, one that had come close to beating the task force outright. Who would have expected ship-grade missiles mounted on such small craft? Starfighter torpedoes, even the latest versions, were nowhere near as powerful. It gave the aliens so many advantages that she hoped - prayed - that they were merely facing the first models. They *had* to get a warning back to the front lines before the gunboats started tearing their way through the defences and smashing onwards to Tadpole Prime.

"They may have been building them here," Mason said. "ES-13 is a long way from the front lines."

Susan hoped he was right. The Royal Navy did most of *its* secret research work in the Britannia System, rather than Sol, for the same reason. But she dared not assume that the enemy had hastily put their ships into active service when the task force had appeared in her rear. The attack had been too well planned for *that*. She rather suspected that the gunboats had been working up, in preparation for deployment to the front, before hastily being thrown into combat against her ships.

Maybe that's a good sign, she told herself. *They wouldn't risk showing them ahead of time - knowing they could be decisive - unless they had no other choice.*

She studied the display as the second enemy formation advanced, the third following at a respectable distance. It *looked* as though the aliens hadn't known where they were until it was too late, although they definitely knew *now.* She was surprised they hadn't concentrated their forces, giving them a far greater advantage. Perhaps their commanders wanted to claim the credit for the kill…she shrugged, tiredly. She'd take what she could get.

"The flag is redeploying the starfighters," Parkinson reported. "They're advancing against the enemy."

Susan winced. Starfighter pilots had always annoyed her - disciplining them had been a nightmare when she'd been Commander Air Group on *Formidable* - but she knew the flyers were about to take heavy losses. The poor bastards knew what they were facing, now, yet they hadn't had any time to train. Hell, half their squadrons were shot to hell, pairing British and Indian flyers together in improvised formations. She wished, suddenly, that Admiral Naiser had kept *Eisenhower* with the task force instead. British pilots had spent far more time exercising with their American counterparts, instead of the Indians. They'd known they might have to *fight* the Indians…

She gritted her teeth as the starfighters converged on their targets, firing madly. The gunboats had another advantage, one she hadn't appreciated until she saw their second formation engaging the starfighters. They could keep the starfighters dodging without altering course, trying their hardest to pick off the humans before they got into firing range and returned fire. It didn't *quite* render the starfighters useless, she acknowledged, but it limited them. And that was the last thing they needed.

"Order the main guns to engage as soon as the enemy enters range," she said. Her fingers danced across her console, forwarding the suggestion to Admiral Naiser. "We might get lucky."

"Aye, Captain," Jean said.

Susan watched, grimly. Flying too close to a heavy plasma bolt might *just* cause problems, even if the gunboats weren't hit directly. But they kept coming, regardless…

"They're entering point defence range now," Jean reported. "All ships are engaging."

"Switch to countering their missiles as soon as they open fire," Susan said. The analysts seemed to think that each gunboat could only carry one missile. She was no starship designer, but she tended to agree. There *had* to be a point of diminishing returns. "And list any gunboat that *does* fire its missile as a secondary target."

The aliens swarmed forward, trying to reach *Vikramaditya*. There was nothing subtle about their tactics, no attempt to hide their final destination. Susan watched, knowing that matters were out of her hands, as the task force poured fire into the enemy formation, picking off dozens of gunboats as they tried to reach engagement range. A handful even fired at long range, clearly trying to launch their missiles before it was too late…

"*Bunker Hill* is gone, Captain," Charlotte reported. "A lone gunboat rammed her."

"She must have triggered her missile at the last second," Mason commented.

Susan nodded, tightly. There would be time for a formal post-battle assessment afterwards, assuming they survived. Right now, the loss of an American cruiser was annoying, but hardly fatal. *Vikramaditya* had to be protected. And she knew, all too well, that the Foxes knew it too. Their third formation was already closing on the task force.

"That's the last of the second wave of gunboats," Jean reported. "They made no attempt to escape, even after launching their missiles."

"Weakening our starfighter formations," Mason growled. "We haven't taken losses like this since the *First* Interstellar War."

Susan nodded in grim agreement. The aliens might not succeed in destroying the task force, but in taking out *Formidable* and killing dozens of starfighters they had definitely *weakened* it. The repair crews were good, yet there were limits to how much they could do without a shipyard. It was possible, all too possible, that the offensive had just come to an untimely end. And if that were the case…

"The third formation is entering attack range," Charlotte warned. "All ships are engaging."

Susan exchanged a grim look with Mason. It didn't *look* as though there were any *more* alien formations out there, but that couldn't be taken for granted. Even if there weren't, the task force had been badly damaged. Losing *Formidable* weakened their combat power…

She watched as the enemy gunboats hurled themselves on her ships. A German destroyer was blown out of space, followed rapidly by a Brazilian frigate. This time, the enemy commander seemed more intent on weakening the point defences than pushing through to *Vikramaditya*. It wasn't a bad tactic, she had to admit. Stripping the task force of its escorts would make taking it out easier…

"Incoming attack," Charlotte snapped. "Five gunboats in attack formation."

"Swing point defence around to take them out," Susan ordered. The remaining enemy ships were closing rapidly, readying their missiles. Maybe they thought the battleship would make an easier target. It would certainly be impossible to *miss*. And they were the *last* gunboats. "Engage the enemy!"

"Enemy ships firing," Charlotte said.

"Point defence engaging," Jean added. "Captain, missile locks are failing!"

The entire ship shook, violently. Susan cursed out loud as half the consoles went blank, the remainder switching to emergency mode. The lights dimmed, then brightened. Her console flickered, red icons everywhere…

"Report," she snapped.

"We've taken major damage," Mason reported. His voice was very flat. "Main power is gone!"

We're dead, Susan thought.

CHAPTER
TWENTY SEVEN

"Just how bad is it?"

"Bad, Captain," Alan Finch said. The Chief Engineer looked badly shaken. "Three of the fusion cores have been totalled - one more is badly damaged, although still functional for now. We've been crippled."

Susan felt numb. *Vanguard* had been damaged before, but this... this was far worse. They were hundreds of light years from the nearest friendly star, trapped in an alien system that had already proven its ability to hurt them. Her ship could limp along the tramlines, she thought, yet it wouldn't be *hard* for the aliens to hunt them down. *Vanguard* didn't have a hope of making it home before it was too late.

She glanced into the engineering compartment. Dozens of engineers were scurrying around, opening hatches and removing damaged components. They looked industrious, but she knew - all too well - that they were only scratching the surface. Removing the power cores would be a far harder job. And, perhaps, one beyond them.

"Is there anything you can do?"

"Yes, given time," Finch said.

He tapped his console, bringing up a hologram of the drive section. "Two of the power cores can be dismantled *in situ* and removed, allowing us to replace them with units from the logistics ships," he said. "I'd *prefer* to borrow one of *King Edward's* power cores, but I suspect Captain Tolliver would object. Even if he didn't...removing the core in a combat zone would be asking for trouble. Given time, it should be doable."

Susan met his eyes. "How long?"

"If we work double shifts, and borrow some crewmen from the other ships, we should have it done in five to ten days," Finch said. "We've practiced breaking down a core before, but our drills always left out the emergency. Really, Captain, I'd advise going to a shipyard if we could."

"We can't," Susan said, bluntly.

Finch nodded. "The second problem is the damage to the armour," he added. "I'm going to have to buckle a replacement armour plate over the gash…which will be a weak spot, if they know what they did to us. Even if they don't, optical sensors will pick up the patchwork on the hull. They'll know *precisely* where to target."

"Let me worry about that," Susan said. She didn't have an answer, yet. Their only *real* hope was that the gunboats had been wiped out before they'd managed to report back to their superiors. "Right now, what can we do?"

"We can crawl," Finch said. "Captain, the remaining two power cores cannot produce enough power to let us fly and fight. We can cut power demands, to some extent, but we really need to replace one of the cores."

"Start now," Susan said. It was going to be a nightmare. She knew it. "And work as fast as you can."

"Aye, Captain," Finch said. "I'll keep you informed."

"Beg whatever you need from Captain Tolliver," Susan added. "And I'll countersign any other requisitions you need to make."

"Thank you, Captain," Finch said.

But we may still need to evacuate, Susan thought, as she strode through the hatch. *Vanguard* had been crippled. Her armour had absorbed blows that had killed a fleet carrier, but she'd still been crippled. *And if that happens, we will have to abandon ship.*

She resisted - barely - the urge to sag against the nearest bulkhead. *Vanguard* had been damaged before, but this…this was *fatal*. Or it would be, if the aliens managed to launch an attack before the repairs were completed. Maybe they could power the weapons - there were ways to cut all other demands - yet there was no way they could power the drive. Admiral Naiser might order her to abandon ship and transfer his flag to another battleship, rather than delay the advance any further. *Vanguard* would merely delay the rush to ES-12.

And if Commodore Hoover has run into his own problems, she thought grimly, *the entire operation might have failed.*

Over two thousand, five hundred dead, John thought.

He sat in his cabin, wondering how Admiral Fitzwilliam had been able to endure the thought of losing so many men. The Anglo-Indian War had been genteel, almost, but no one had doubted that the Indians would have killed *Theodore Smith* if they could. And yet, the losses of that war paled in comparison to the *First* Interstellar War. He'd never been a fleet commander, not until now. Had he made a mistake by splitting the fleet? Or had he run into something he couldn't have hoped to anticipate?

The gunboats were unpredictable, he told himself. But it wasn't very convincing. *We should have seen them coming.*

He picked up the datapad and surveyed it, thoughtfully. The analysts hadn't had *that* many problems working out the specs, once they'd had a chance to analyse the raw data thoroughly. Gunboats looked more like scaled-up starfighters than shuttles, they'd noted, although they were clearly designed for long-term operations. And they were built with off-the-shelf components, rather than anything new. It *looked* as through the Foxes had rushed a system into production, which might be their only saving grace. The gunboats his task force had faced might have been the only ones in existence.

We kept looking for ways to make starfighters smaller targets, he thought. In hindsight, the blind spot was terrifyingly clear. *They decided to go the other way and use larger hulls to carry all sorts of surprises.*

His door chimed. "Enter."

Captain Susan Onarina entered, looking tired. John didn't blame her. *Vanguard* had been badly damaged, almost crippled. Her captain was faced with the very real prospect of abandoning her ship to an uncertain fate or trying to nurse her home, if she couldn't be repaired. And *John* might have to order her to abandon her ship. No *true* captain would take such orders calmly.

"Captain," he said. He nodded to a chair. "How long?"

"Five to ten days," Susan told him. "If we're lucky..."

John made a face. He knew, better than most, just how hard it would be to either remove or dismantle the power core. Even the improvements worked out after a year's hard fighting didn't make it *much* easier. And yet, *Vanguard was* largely intact. If she could be repaired, if she could be brought back into the fight, he knew he'd be glad of her presence.

If, he thought.

"I see," he said. He tapped a switch, bringing up an image of the fleet. *King Edward* and *Alabama* had survived intact, along with *Vikramaditya* and thirty-seven smaller ships. It was enough firepower to wreck a star system, if they had time. But the aliens had delayed them and now - he was sure - they would be concentrating enough force to complete his destruction. "We need to link up with Commodore Hoover."

Susan's dark face was hard to read, but he saw her entire body tense. "Assuming everything has gone as planned, Kevin should be waiting for us in ES-12," he added. "It wouldn't take us more than a couple of days to reach him..."

"Unless he's run into problems too," Susan said. He knew *she* knew that *Vanguard* wouldn't be able to accompany the rest of the task force. "We won't know until we link up with him."

"No," John said. He met her dark eyes. "Could you repair *Vanguard* without the logistics ships?"

Susan looked back at him, evenly. "If necessary," she said. "Do you plan to leave us here?"

John felt a pang of guilt. Cold logic told him that he *should* abandon *Vanguard*, that he *should* take the rest of the task force to ES-12 and continue the mission. The entire operation could not be risked for a single ship, even *Vanguard*. And yet, he didn't want to abandon the battleship and her crew. The Royal Navy was *meant* to look after its personnel. Over a thousand years of tradition mitigated against it.

"I don't have a choice," he said, flatly. "The aliens cannot be allowed more time to organise a counterattack."

He saw a flash of betrayal in her eyes, mixed with grim understanding. She knew what he meant, even if she didn't want to face it. *Vanguard* was one ship. The entire operation couldn't be risked for her. And yet… he knew precisely how she felt. He wouldn't have willingly abandoned *Warspite* either.

"Transfer all non-essential personnel to *King Edward*," he ordered. He'd have to transfer himself, even though it felt as though he was running away. "The xenospecialists, the researchers…make sure all of your files are copied too. And then…"

He looked down at his hands. There was no way to know what might happen. *Vanguard* was a cripple, trapped in an alien system. There might be more gunboats out there, readying a final offensive. Or more *mundane* starships…he had no way to know. And yet…

"Those are your orders, Captain," he said. He felt almost as if a stranger was speaking with his voice. "You may have them in writing, if you wish."

"That won't be necessary, Admiral," Susan said. The *understanding* in her tone caused him another pang of guilt. "I will see to it personally."

"Thank you," John said. "And good luck."

————

"But I don't know why we have to leave," Doctor Linda Foster complained. "We're scientists!"

"And you're on a starship in the middle of a war zone," Henry snapped. Civilians! How the hell had Doctor Foster missed the impact? "This ship is not in a good state."

"My equipment…"

"Your equipment will be transferred later," Henry told her. He suspected it was a lie. The battleship's crew didn't have time to worry about scientific instrumentation. "But if you don't get on the shuttle, I don't know *what* will happen to you."

He rolled his eyes as he passed Doctor Foster to the marines, then checked the remainder of the lab. The boffins were supposed to be smart, but sometimes they had problems understanding the real world. There *were* things out there that could kill them…Henry had no idea *what* had hit *Vanguard*, yet it had clearly done significant damage. The battleship was in no state for a fight.

At least all the sensor and research data was copied to the rest of the task force, he thought, suddenly feeling very tired. *And Formidable...*

It wasn't something he wanted to dwell on. He'd hoped to serve on the *first Formidable*, over a decade ago. If he'd graduated six months sooner, he might well have been on the fleet carrier at New Russia, where she'd met her end. Now...another *Formidable*, commanded by a man he'd known during his service, was gone. Captain Jones had invited him to dinner twice, during the long voyage from Earth. They'd drunk and yarned about old times and...he'd never have that pleasure again. Jones was dead, along with his crew. And the name *Formidable* might be retired completely.

His wristcom buzzed. "Your Highness, your presence is requested at Airlock Five."

"Understood," Henry said. "I'm on my way."

He hurried through the hatch, closing it behind him. There was no way to escape the sense he was running away, even though cold logic told him there was no point in staying. *Vanguard* was doomed, if the Foxes rediscovered her before her power cores were replaced. He was no engineer. And his other military skills were *years* out of date. There was nothing he could do to make a difference...

Penny Schneider was waiting for him outside the airlock, held between two marines. "Your Highness," she said. "I volunteer to stay."

"And get yourself killed," Henry said, crossly. *Vanguard's* crew didn't have time for a reporter poking around, not now. "No."

"I won't cause any trouble," Penny insisted. "Your Highness..."

Henry took a moment to gather himself. Penny...was almost likeable, but she was still a damned reporter. She couldn't be trusted. And while he had no doubt that Captain Onarina would put Penny in irons if she caused trouble, it would just be a hassle the poor captain didn't need. Maybe Penny meant well. She was certainly on the list of reporters who'd been embedded with the military before, without blotting her copybook. But a crippled ship was no place for a civilian.

"No," he said, firmly. "You can catch up with the crew later."

If they survive, he thought, grimly. *Vanguard's* odds of surviving the next few days were very low. *Your chances of survival aren't much better.*

"Your Highness," Penny protested. "I…"

Henry looked at the marines. "Take her into the shuttle, cuff her to her seat if she gives you any trouble," he said. It would probably earn him some negative media coverage, but he found it hard to care. "And tell the pilot I'll be along in a moment."

Penny didn't offer any resistance as the marines marched her into the shuttle, much to Henry's quiet relief. He watched them go, then looked back down the corridor. *Vanguard* felt different, somehow…he closed his eyes for a long moment, wondering if he would ever see the battleship again. He'd grown to love the giant ship, even though he knew he would never serve on her, let alone *command* her. There was no hope of a starship command even if he returned to the navy.

I'm sorry, he thought. He wished he could stay, but he knew he couldn't. *I'll see you again.*

But, as he stepped through the hatch, he knew he couldn't convince himself that that was actually true.

———

George had been given orders she hadn't expected before, ranging from orders that made no sense to orders that were outright suicidal. But she'd *never* been ordered to abandon her friends and leave them behind to, at best, an alien POW camp. The Royal Navy - and the Royal Marines - left no one behind. And yet…

She stared down at the makeshift terminal in disbelief. *Black Hunter* had escaped notice, as far as she knew. The alien gunboats shouldn't have been able to see the ship, let alone report home…although she knew better than to take that for granted. And yet…and yet…she couldn't just abandon *Vanguard*. The battleship was her home. She had friends there…

"We have our orders, Captain," Sammy said. He was the only one who addressed her as *Captain*. "What do we do?"

George clenched her fists in frustration. There was nothing she *could* do. Major Andres or Sergeant Tosco would relieve her for disobeying orders, if she did. And it would be utterly pointless. Even if she did disobey orders, even if she *did* get away with it, she could do nothing to help *Vanguard*. The battleship had to be abandoned. If her crew managed to repair her...

If, she thought, sourly.

"Set course," she ordered, finally. She felt...odd, as if a stranger was speaking through her lips. "We'll leave when ordered."

"Aye, Captain," Sammy said.

George glared at his back. She knew better than to leave someone in distress. That had been hammered into her at the academy, even though she'd been taught to *win* at school. The Royal Navy didn't leave its people behind...

...But today, that tradition was going to die.

Hot tears prickled at the corner of her eyes. Her captain, her XO...her tormenter turned friend...were being left behind. And there was nothing she could do to save them.

"The task force is leaving now," Charlotte reported.

Susan sucked in her breath. *Vanguard* was...vulnerable. Admiral Naiser had done everything in his power to suggest that *Vanguard* was still with the task force, but there was no way to know if the *Foxes* were fooled. They might well have been able to sneak a cloaked ship up to the task force, close enough to tell that *Vanguard* had been left behind. And if that had happened, who knew *what* they'd do?

"Thank you, Charlotte," she said. "Continue to monitor the situation."

"Aye, Captain," Charlotte said.

Susan scowled down at her console. The irony, the bitter irony, was that her ship was largely undamaged. Her main guns still worked, her missile tubes were loaded, her point defence was ready to fire...but without power, getting even the point defence to work would be a nightmare. She'd known the figures, yet she hadn't really *comprehended* them until she'd had to work with far more limited power reserves. In hindsight, maybe that should have been included when they'd carried out emergency drills.

Too late now, she told herself.

She turned her attention back to the live feed from the stealth drones. The alien system was starting to take on shape and form, with a handful of industrial nodes clearly identified. A couple of mass drivers throwing rocks could do real damage, she thought, if she'd had the power to *run* them. And yet...she was fairly sure the aliens had *some* point defence mounted on their industrial base. They'd be insane to leave it unprotected when all hell could break loose at any second.

Mason leaned over to whisper in her ear. "All of a sudden, Captain, the plot of *Stellar Star and the Dark Star* makes a great deal of sense."

Susan had to laugh. The science behind *Stellar Star and the Dark Star* was somewhat lacking - the producers had gleefully ignored everything humanity had learnt about the universe - but the plot *did* make sense, now. Stellar Star and her crew, convinced they were going to die, had indulged in a massive orgy before their producer-mandated rescue via *deus ex machina*. Coming to think of it, it *was* what had happened on USS *Constitution*. The crew had been convinced they too were going to die.

"It isn't over yet," she said, firmly. "We've been in worse scrapes."

"Oh, yeah?" Mason asked. "Name one."

CHAPTER
TWENTY EIGHT

"As near as I can make out, Captain," Lieutenant Christopher Brookes said, "they massively overpowered a bomb-pumped laser."

Susan scowled as she studied the readings. "It would have to be *incredibly* overpowered," she said, thoughtfully. "Are you sure?"

"As sure as I can be without actually examining their hardware," Brookes told her. "The sensor records are somewhat lacking, but they *did* generate a *lot* of heat and focused it on our armour. Even so...it was sheer bad luck that they managed to do as much damage as they did. My best guess is that the first warhead was actually intended to clear the way for the second."

"Which would have killed us," Susan said. The drive section *might* have contained the blast, but it would have crippled the ship beyond any hope of recovery. "The second missile must have been lost."

"Or taken out in the first one's blast," Brookes said. "I have the impression, studying the records, that they hastily improvised an attack."

"They must have hoped to strike *Vikramaditya*," Susan mused. She met his eyes. "Is there anything we can do about these weapons?"

"Not without a shipyard," Brookes said. "There may come a point, Captain, when our armour reaches the point of diminishing returns. And if that happens, we may be in trouble."

"Science marches on," Susan said, briskly. She shook her head. "Let me know if you come up with anything new."

She acknowledged his salute, then headed for the hatch and stepped through. Mason met her outside, looking grim. And yet, for the first time in far too long, she saw a flicker of hope in his eyes.

"Mr. Finch reports that the second replacement core has been assembled," he said. "We should be able to power up both cores once the basic tests are completed."

Susan felt a surge of relief, mixed with fear. No one had ever dismantled and replaced a power core in space, let alone in *enemy* space. She'd spent the last six days silently praying that she hadn't made a terrible mistake in refusing to abandon her ship. Losing one power core was bad enough, but losing three…one completely beyond removal or repair…her ship and crew were still in terrible danger.

"Good," she said, finally. Mason knew her well enough to see her concern, but hopefully the rest of the crew couldn't. "Is there a reason you brought this to me?"

"I also caught Lieutenant-Commander Granger and Lieutenant Parkinson bonking like wild animals," Mason added. "Should I have a word with them?"

Susan sighed as they walked back towards the bridge. Technically, the lovers should both be in deep shit. Fucking someone in the chain of command, either above or below you, was flatly against regulations. But her crew had plenty of reasons, despite her reassurances, to believe that they would never see their homes again. There was little reason to worry about possible consequences if there was no hope of survival.

"Tell them I expect them to comport themselves professionally," she said, tiredly. At the very least, one of the two offenders should be transferred to a different ship. It was a problem she didn't need. "And if their… relationship starts interfering with their professionalism, I'll dust off some of the *really* old regulations and flog them."

"You would," Mason said.

Susan snorted. She understood the impulse, the desire to find comfort in another's arms, the desire to feel…*alive*. But it was a professional nightmare. If they had a falling out - or worse - there was nowhere for either of them to go.

"Yes, I would," she said, flatly. "It isn't hopeless *yet*."

She smiled, tiredly, as they walked onto the bridge. Both of the love-birds were manning their stations, carefully keeping their eyes on their consoles. Susan made a mental note to read them both the Riot Act later, if they refused to listen to the XO, then sat down at her console and scanned the updates. Finch had just finished the latest set of diagnostic checks, confirming that the power cores were properly emplaced. They certainly *looked* ready to go.

"Begin power-up sequence," she ordered, flatly.

"Aye, Captain," Mason said.

Susan forced herself to relax, even though she knew they were about to announce their presence to any prowling starships. Long-range sensors *might* pick up the surge of power, no matter what she did to dampen it. There was certainly no way she could power up the cloaking device! The wretched system would drain her batteries too quickly for her peace of mind.

"Core Three is powering up," Mason reported. "Mr. Finch reports that it looks fine."

"Good," Susan said. Maybe it was just her imagination, but the lights seemed to get a little brighter. "And Core Five?"

"Held in standby," Mason said. "She'll be powering up soon."

Wait, Susan told herself. If they'd missed something, if there was a damaged component that had escaped discovery, they were in *real* trouble. *Let them take it slowly.*

"Core Three appears to be fine," Mason reported. "Core Five is power-ing up now."

There was a long pause. "Core Five is only at seventy-percent power," he added, after a moment. "The engineers are looking for the problem now."

Susan cursed under her breath. Core Five...they *could* make it through the tramline, if Core Three was working. But it was a serious problem. Any unexpected demands on their power would be enough to finish them. She forced herself to wait, even though she knew they were now broadcasting their presence to the entire star system. There hadn't been any *sign* that ES-13 had any remaining mobile defenders...

Unless they were sent to ES-11, she mused. *That would be bad.*

"Captain, Mr. Finch is reporting a power blockage within the distribution network," Mason reported. "He says it'll take at least two days to fix, but we can move now."

"And we'll have to," Susan said. "We just told the aliens where we are."

She leaned back in her command chair. "Mr. Reed, take us along the pre-planned course," she ordered. "Miss. Watson, continue to monitor local space for any sign of the enemy."

"Aye, Captain," Reed said. A low rumble ran through the ship - it sounded wrong, somehow - as the drives came online. "We'll cross the tramline in three days."

"I know," Susan said. Making full speed wasn't going to be easy, at least until the engineers had completed their work. "Hold us steady."

She understood his feelings, but she had her reasons. She'd plotted the course herself, making sure they stayed well away from any known or suspected enemy positions. It added another day to their trip, but they wouldn't be following a predictable course. The enemy, once they detected *Vanguard*, would probably assume a least-time course to ES-12. It was certainly their *best* option if they wanted to catch a crippled battleship.

"We're on the move, Captain," Reed reported.

"No sign of any enemy reaction," Parkinson added.

"And let's hope it stays that way," Susan said.

But she knew, deep inside, that it wouldn't.

If Susan were forced to be honest, at least with herself, she might have admitted that part of her envied Lieutenant-Commander Granger and Lieutenant Parkinson. Two days of sitting in the command chair, waiting for something to happen, or trying to sleep in her cabin had left her on edge. The grim certainty that the enemy knew where they were - at least roughly - didn't help. Finding comfort - and peace - in someone else's arms would have been almost welcome, if she hadn't known she'd pay a price for it later.

And I suppose that makes Stellar Star and the Dark Star *the most realistic episode of them all*, she mused, as she returned to the bridge again.

She was tempted to take stimulants, although she knew that would be the worst possible choice. *The bar isn't that high, though.*

An alarm chimed. "Captain," Charlotte said. "I just picked up an emergency alert from our probes. A small enemy task force crossed the tramline."

"Which means they crossed the tramline forty minutes ago," Susan mused. Not for the first time, she cursed the speed of light delay. "Do we have a passive lock?"

"No, Captain," Charlotte said.

Susan forced herself to think clearly. The enemy shouldn't know where they were, unless *Vanguard* was being shadowed. It was possible, she had to admit. Stealth mode was nowhere near as effective as a cloaking device. And if that was the case, the enemy fleet could be vectoring towards them, hidden behind their *own* cloaking devices. But if it *wasn't* the case, the enemy had about as much hope of finding them as a farmer had of finding a needle in a haystack. Even if they assumed - correctly - that *Vanguard* was sneaking towards the tramline, they would still have an immense section of space to search.

And they may have escaped the admiral, she mused. *They came from ES-12, didn't they?*

"Launch two probes," she ordered, slowly. "If they're trying to set up an ambush, we should get *some* advance warning."

She glanced at Mason. "And sound yellow alert."

"Aye, Captain," Mason said.

Susan nodded as the drumbeat echoed through the ship, then glanced at the message. Five cruisers, three destroyers and two freighters...probably converted carriers, although it was impossible to be sure. Normally, they wouldn't have been any real threat to *Vanguard*, even though they could have kept the battleship under observation until other battleships or gunboats arrived. But now...she knew she couldn't hope to power all of her weapons, not until they fixed the remaining damage. They might just have a chance to cripple her.

And there might be more battleships we haven't seen, she thought. *Or gunboats.*

She waited, watching the updates from her crew. *Vanguard* had lost a third of her crew and it showed - reaction time was lower and some departments were badly undermanned - but she could still fight. Thankfully, the enemy hadn't caught them by surprise. But how long could they remain at yellow alert? She reached for her console and ran through a series of possible scenarios, trying to imagine which way the Foxes would jump. What *would* they do?

"Captain," Jean said. "The probes are detecting flickers of turbulence, directly ahead of us."

Susan swore. "Show me."

A faint red haze appeared on the display, large enough to hide a hundred battleships. There was no hope of isolating individual ships, not at that range, but at least they knew they were there. And that meant…

They must have someone shadowing us, ensuring that we couldn't escape, she thought, grimly. *And that someone kept a patient eye on us until we started to move.*

Her lips quirked in grim amusement. The enemy CO had to be hopping mad. *Vanguard* should have been an easy target. Instead, the battleship had started to move before his reinforcements had arrived. Susan had no idea if the Foxes had a god or if they believed the universe was completely random, but she could imagine the enemy commander cursing the fates. What should have been an easy target now wasn't.

"There's no hope of evading them," she said. "Let them think we haven't seen them."

"Aye, Captain," Jean said.

"And try to get a solid lock on their hulls," Susan added. She knew it was probably impossible, but it was worth trying. It might just give them a chance to launch a surprise attack, even though they *knew* where she was. Blasting unsuspecting alien ships might have seemed unsportsmanlike, once upon a time, but right now she found it hard to care. *Vanguard* was in no state for a prolonged fight. "Mr. Mason?"

"Captain?"

"Bring the ship to battlestations," Susan ordered. "Clear the decks for action."

She smiled, grimly, as sirens howled through the giant ship. They might be about to die, if there were more enemy ships they hadn't seen or one of the patchwork of repairs failed at a critical moment, but at least they'd go out swinging. And she was fairly sure she could take a bite out of the alien squadron, if it got too close. The experience would teach them a salutary lesson. Who knew? Maybe it would convince them to back off.

"I don't have a solid lock," Jean reported. "But I'm fairly sure I can narrow the targeting down a little."

"Hold fire until I give the order," Susan said. The possible target zone was *vast*. No one, outside very bad fiction, had devised starships several light-minutes across. There was no point in wasting time spraying vast regions of space with plasma fire. "And keep trying to lock them down…"

"Aye, Captain," Jean said. "I…"

She broke off as new red icons flickered into existence. "Captain, the enemy ships are decloaking," she added. "I'm picking up…"

Susan felt her heart sink as two unexpected icons appeared behind the enemy cruisers. Two *battleships*. *Enemy* battleships. "I see them," she said, quietly. *Vanguard* was doomed. She might have been able to take one battleship, but two? And the enemy cruisers and destroyers? There was no hope for either escape or survival. "Lock weapons on their hulls."

"Aye, Captain," Jean said.

We could surrender, Susan thought. They had the translation program. They knew how to speak to the aliens. But even if the aliens did take them prisoner, it wouldn't last. The Foxes would expect a degree of cooperation from her people that they couldn't offer. They'd be branded outright traitors, if Earth won the war. *And if they captured my ship, they'd learn far too much about us.*

She felt oddly calm, now that death was approaching fast. They'd been caught, but at least they hadn't been caught when they'd been a powerless hulk. And they could hurt the aliens before they died.

"Concentrate fire on the smaller ships as soon as they enter range," she ordered. "And then switch targeting to the battleships."

"Aye, Captain," Jean said. Another flurry of red icons popped into existence. "The enemy carriers are launching starfighters."

Susan glanced at her. "Not gunboats?"

"No, Captain," Jean assured her. "Starfighters."

They must intend to weaken us as much as possible, Susan thought. *I wonder if they're trying to preserve the battleships...*

She shook her head, dismissing the thought. It no longer mattered.

"Target them with point defence," she ordered. The enemy ships were steadily entering range, their starfighters zooming out ahead of them. Their commander wasn't even *trying* to maintain a CSP. "Helm, adjust our position to protect the weak spots, then alter course to keep the range as open as possible."

"Aye, Captain," Reed said.

It won't be enough, Susan thought. *They presumably don't have damaged drives...*

"Enemy ships are entering range," Jean reported, sharply. New icons appeared on the display. "Firing...*now!*"

Susan sucked in her breath as the main guns opened fire. An enemy cruiser shuddered, then exploded under her guns, followed by a destroyer. The remainder hastily started to reverse course, launching missiles that didn't have a hope in hell of getting through her point defence before it was too late. They'd clearly assumed that *Vanguard* was far worse off than she was...she smirked, then sobered as the alien battleships opened fire. A second later, *Vanguard* shuddered as their blasts slammed into her hull.

"They're pushing," Jean reported. "The armour is holding, but they're blasting away our sensor blisters..."

"Again," Susan said. It was a familiar pattern by now. Both sides knew too much about the other's capabilities. Why bother hacking through heavy armour when you could take out sensors and weapons instead? "Launch missiles, aimed at their drives and turrets."

She glanced at Reed. "Helm, spin the ship; bring the other turrets into firing position."

"Aye, Captain," Reed said.

"And link us to the stealth drones," she added. "I don't want to risk losing all of our sensors."

"Aye, Captain," Parkinson said. "Links established."

Susan gritted her teeth as the bombardment grew worse, both alien battleships slamming blast after blast into her hull. They were taking damage themselves, she noted, but not enough to make any real differ-ence. *And* they were trying to keep the range open, carefully prevent-ing her from trying to ram *Vanguard* into one of them. She wondered, absently, what would happen if two battleships collided, then pushed the thought aside. There was no time to do anything, but inflict as much dam-age as she could before the end.

"Turret Two has jammed," Mason reported. "Armour plating in zone nineteen is under heavy pressure. Damage control teams are on their way."

"Angle the ship so we can still bear on them," Susan ordered. Red lights were flaring up in front of her, warning that the armour was weakening in several places. *Vanguard's* innards were strong, far stronger than any fleet carrier, but it wouldn't be enough. "Concentrate fire on their turrets."

"Aye, Captain," Granger said. She paused as new icons appeared on the display. "Long range sensors are picking up..."

Susan stared. The alien battleships, so unstoppable a moment ago, had suddenly come under attack, heavy attack. Fire from eight *other* battle-ships were slamming into their hulls, a whole *fleet* of starfighters lancing past to sweep the enemy fighters out of space and wipe the enemy point defence out of existence. The alien battleships staggered, caught between two fires, then folded rapidly as they were battered into defenceless hulks. Moments later, they were gone.

"Picking up a signal," Parkinson said. He sounded stunned. "Captain, it's the Admiral!"

"Put him through," Susan said.

Admiral Naiser's face appeared in front of her. "Good afternoon, Susan," he said. "I trust we're not too late?"

"No, sir," Susan managed. It was suddenly very hard to speak. She'd *known* they were doomed. She'd *known* it. "You were right on time."

CHAPTER
TWENTY NINE

For once, Susan decided as she was piped onboard HMS *King Edward*, she didn't begrudge the navy's tedious ceremonies. *Vanguard* had come far too close to certain destruction - again - and she'd been rescued in the nick of time. She didn't blame Captain Tolliver for wanting to show off his ship and crew, even though she knew Admiral Naiser shared her own disdain for formal ceremonies. *King Edward* wasn't *quite* new, but she'd come off the slips a year after *Vanguard*, her construction delayed as the plans were updated after *Vanguard's* trials. And yet, she *smelt* new. There was still a whiff of the dockyards about her.

But by the time Susan was shown to the admiral's new cabin and a drink put in her hand, she was burning with questions that demanded answers.

"It's very good to see you again, sir," she said, as she sipped her drink. Clearly, Captain Tolliver's ship had a better class of rotgut. "But tell me... did you *plan* to use us as the bait in a trap?"

"If I had, Susan, I would have told you," Admiral Naiser said. Susan eyed him for a long moment, then decided he was probably telling the truth. Some admirals loved playing power games - it made her wonder what they got up to in the bedroom - but Admiral Naiser had always struck her as honest. "It was sheer luck that we discovered that they were sending a fleet to stomp on you."

Susan nodded, relieved. She wasn't sure what she would have done if he'd *admitted* to using her as bait in a trap - unaware bait in a trap - but it would probably have cost her *Vanguard*. The Admiralty would never let her get away with breaking an admiral's nose, certainly not after her *first* voyage. They'd think she'd developed bad habits and they'd probably be right.

Admiral Naiser tapped a console, bringing up a holographic display. "The enemy squadron was dispatched from ES-11 and passed through ES-12, luckily close enough for us to get a solid lock on them," he explained. "Given the prospect of crushing two of their battleships at minimal risk, I decided it was worth reversing course and shadowing them back into ES-13."

"And you linked up with Commodore Hoover first," Susan mused. "Did they have a pleasant trip?"

"They encountered nothing, beyond a mid-sized colony," Admiral Naiser said. "We've marked it down for later attention if we fail to convince the Foxes to surrender."

He shrugged. "And crushing two of their battleships will have weakened them," he added, frankly. "It gives us an opportunity to push into ES-11 and catch them with their pants around their ankles."

"Assuming they didn't scrape the battleships up from somewhere else," Susan said, although she knew it was unlikely. The Foxes wouldn't have wasted time trying to secure *every* system. That way lay madness - and a colossal waste of effort. "Do you have scouts already probing ES-11?"

"Yes," Admiral Naiser said. "And we are ready to push the fleet forward once we return to ES-12."

He met her eyes. "And now I need a honest answer," he said. "Can *Vanguard* fight?"

Susan took a moment to consider her answer. "We've replaced two of the three power cores," she said. "Barring another disaster, we have enough power to run our weapons and sensors. Replacing the systems we lost in the *last* engagement - and fitting more armour onto the hull - will take a few days, at most. After that...well, we're more than just a powerless hulk."

"But not in tip-top shape," Admiral Naiser mused.

"Good enough for government work," Susan countered. She smiled. "The only alternative is trying to sneak our way home."

"True," Admiral Naiser said.

He looked back at the display for a long moment. "I believe the fleet can return to ES-12 now, if *Vanguard* can keep up," he added. "And Captain Tolliver has extended an invitation to us to dine with him. I took the liberty of accepting on your behalf."

"Thank you, sir," Susan said. She wasn't *that* happy about it, but she knew there was no point in trying to object. Mason had the repair work well in hand. "I'm sure it will be a pleasant dinner."

"And I'm sure you'll have many stories to tell," Admiral Naiser said. He smiled, rather dryly. "I think they're all sick of hearing about *my* glorious victories now."

———

Captain Tolliver's chef, John decided as he wondered if he could eat another piece of pie or not, was a master of his craft. Tolliver was certainly wealthy and well-connected enough to poach him from a famous hotel, if the chef hadn't worked for his family before the oldest son had grown up and joined the navy. Having one's own chef wasn't a tradition John really approved of, but he had to admit it had its advantages. A good half - perhaps more - of the meal had been reconstituted, yet no one could have hoped to tell the difference.

And cooking reconstituted roast beef would have been tricky, he thought, wryly. *Perhaps the beef wasn't reconstituted.*

He pushed the thought aside and took another sip of his wine. Spacers preferred to draw a veil over where their food came from, certainly when there were civilians nearby. They *knew* it was perfectly safe, yet…civilians were such *doubters* about such things. Not, John supposed, that they could reasonably be blamed. There were still rumours of cannibalism in some of the refugee camps, after the Bombardment. It was possible, vaguely possible, that there was some truth in them.

"That was an excellent dinner, Captain," he said. "My compliments to your chef."

"I thank you," Captain Tolliver said. He was a middle-aged man, only a year or two younger than John himself. His ginger beard, grown in semi-defiance of naval regulations, made him look older. John *had* wondered if Tolliver resented being under John's command, but there had been no friction between them. "I'll make sure they are passed on to him."

"And mine," Susan said. "That was an excellent dinner."

"I hired one of the very best," Captain Tolliver said. "Anatole worked for my Aunt Dahlia before she and her estate were washed away during the Bombardment. Thankfully, Anatole survived and entered my employment."

"I regret I have, but one stomach to place at his disposal," John said, wryly. There had been a fashion amongst the aristocrats for cooks called Anatole, back before the First Interstellar War. He'd never cared enough to figure out why. "Is he really a refugee from France?"

Captain Tolliver smiled. "I have chosen not to inquire, sir," he said. "I prefer to keep my illusions intact."

He picked a small box off the table and opened it. "Cigar?"

John shook his head, but motioned for the other diners to take one if they wished. Smoking was a dangerous habit in space, even on a battleship. Besides, he'd never had the wealth to purchase any truly *good* tobacco. The best had come from Cuba, before the Bombardment had washed most of the island nation into the sea. Now, one could practically buy a destroyer for a box of Cuban cigars.

And the cigarettes I used to smoke in school were awful, he recalled. Smoking wasn't a health risk, these days, but he'd never grown to like it. *And two of the teachers smoked so heavily you just needed to stay downwind to smell them coming.*

He smiled at the thought, then cleared his throat. "Captain Tolliver, please invite the others to join us."

"Aye, Admiral," Tolliver said.

John kept his face impassive as a dozen holographic images flickered into view. Inviting Susan - and Commodore Hoover - to the dinner had been risky, even though there was no reason to believe the task force would come under attack. He hadn't dared invite Commodore Solange Leclère or any of his other subordinates, despite the risk they might see it as an insult. And they weren't the only ones involved. Even if *they* understood the military logic, their governments might not be so understanding. France,

India and Russia might believe - and not without reason - that Britain and America were manoeuvring to seize all the spoils of war for themselves.

A pity we will never get a world government, he thought. *Just organising a coalition war is hard enough.*

He waited until the last of the holograms had appeared, then spoke. "We received the updates from ES-11 as soon as we entered ES-12," he said. A holographic display appeared in front of the diners. The others would have already seen the reports. "ES-11 is quite heavily populated - and defended."

That was an understatement. ES-11-2 - the lone habitable world - was surrounded by shipyards, orbital industrial nodes and weapons platforms. ES-11-4, a large gas giant, had no less than four cloudscoops, along with what looked like a series of small colonies on various moons. It was impossible to be certain, but the intelligence analysts believed - judging from their briefing notes - that Planet Two had well over a billion Foxes and Cows living on its surface. John believed it. Planet Two looked to have been settled longer than Britannia.

"Our principal goal will be to destroy their industrial nodes and shipyards," he added, after a long moment. "We will not be occupying the planet's surface or striking at their colonies."

"What a disappointment," General Horace Ross commented.

"There's nothing to be gained by being drawn into a ground war," Prince Henry said. "If we take out the industrial nodes - and we will - the system becomes harmless, at least for the duration of the war."

John nodded. "Thankfully, they appear to have sent most of their mobile units forward to respond to our incursion," he added. "The largest single starship within their system is a heavy cruiser, unless we're missing something. We will assume the worst, of course, until we *know* they're not hiding an entire fleet somewhere within the system."

"And they'll also be trying to rush forces back from the front," Captain Tolliver commented.

"Yes," John agreed. "We must assume that they will be doing everything they can to block our advance."

He closed his eyes for a long moment, remembering the last time he'd studied the starchart in his quarters. He'd looked at it so often that the tramlines - and the least-time courses between the war front and the enemy homeworld - were burned into his mind. In theory, they still had time to punch through ES-11 and make their way to ES-1. But in practice...there were too many variables. The FTL communications system... he thought he'd taken it into account, along with every other surprise the enemy had shown them, but what if he was wrong? What if the enemy had another surprise in store?

We'll deal with it, he told himself, as he opened his eyes. *And we will survive.*

"We will cross ES-12 and launch our invasion of ES-11 as soon as possible," he added. "The basic operational plan is already loaded into the command datanet. Like I said, we will reduce the system's ability to threaten our rear and support their war effort before leaving."

He paused. "Does anyone have any concerns?"

"Merely that we only have two fleet carriers and three escorts," Captain Rani Saran said. "I took the remainder of *Formidable's* fighters onto my ship, but launching every starfighter in a hurry is going to be difficult."

"I can take half of them," Captain Mulhouse offered. "*Eisenhower*... alas...has far too many empty berths."

"See to it," John ordered. Rani had a point. British and Indian starfighters used the same components - and everything had been designed to be interchangeable - yet some of their flight routines were very different. If they'd had time, the problems could be smoothed out, but they *didn't* have time. "And see how many we can rotate through the escort carriers too."

"Not many," Rani said. "Even the biggest escort can only carry two squadrons."

"We could delay the offensive long enough to hold a proper set of drills," Captain Mulhouse suggested. "My crews have more cross-training, but not enough to speed up our fighter launch patterns."

"We don't have time," John said. He sighed. "Anything else?"

"Merely that we are running short of supplies," Commodore Peter Garrison grumbled. His image seemed to flicker with the force of his annoyance. "We may not be able to sustain the offensive much longer."

Hoover snorted. "Despite all the whining from the beancounters?"

"Yes, sir," Garrison said. The logistics officer leaned forward. "There are shortages in several vital categories. I have forwarded a full list to the command datanet."

John looked down at the table, crossly. The bureaucrats *never* seemed to understand that operational usage *never* matched predictions, particularly predictions drawn up by people who wanted to avoid spending money. He'd had to argue heavily to requisition as much as he had - and he'd had to forward some issues to the Unified Military Command - and it *still* wasn't enough. Running short of armour plate, sensor blisters, point defence weapons…the list of potentially devastating shortages was endless.

"We will attempt to limit our expenditure," he said, although he knew it was pointless. If they held back in a knife-range fight, they might not live long enough to use the *next* set of supplies. "And if we really do run short we'll have to break contact and evade."

"They can't *know* how we got here," Susan pointed out. "They'll have to assume that all of our ships are FTL-capable."

"Then we wouldn't be using the tramlines," Hoover countered. "They'll probably assume they missed an alien-grade tramline back in ES-19. Not impossible, I think, if the survey was cursory. We don't know *precisely* when they stumbled across that system."

John nodded. Humanity hadn't detected the alien-grade tramlines for decades - and even when they had, the working assumption was that they were inaccessible. It had taken the Tadpoles to show humanity just how dangerous that assumption had been. It was possible, reasonably possible, that the Foxes had made the same mistake. Watching them waste time trying to find a non-existent tramline would be amusing. But he didn't dare assume they *would*. They were depressingly innovative.

"That's not a concern at the moment," he said. "The principal concern is winning the coming engagements."

He leaned forward. "We've adapted our tactics in light of the enemy's latest innovation," he added, "but my tactical staff are concerned. Gunboats offer a number of advantages, none of which we even considered until it was too late. Launching shipkillers at point-blank range allows them to practically *guarantee* a hit, while their point defence makes them dangerous to starfighters as well as countermissiles. Their ECM, furthermore, make them alarmingly hard to hit.

"The good news is that we *can* use our main guns to thin the herd. We can *also* defocus our point defence weapons to some extent, giving us some extra *oomph*. The impact may not be enough to take the gunboat out - we don't have a solid read on their armour - but it should cripple them. We won't know for sure until we actually *do* it."

He looked from face to face. "The gunboats were completely new," he warned. "There's a *good* chance, a *very* good chance, that we won't see them again. They may well have been working up their squadrons in peace, in what they thought was a secure rear area, before committing them to the front. However, we dare not take that for granted. We must assume that future engagements will include gunboats and adapt our tactics accordingly.

"Furthermore, I will be detaching a stealth ship with orders to sneak back to the front," he concluded. "The Unified Defence Command must be warned. If any of you have dispatches you wish to include, have them forwarded to my staff by 1900."

"There won't be any response," Commodore Hoover warned.

"I think we have to proceed on the assumption we're still on our own," John agreed. There was no guarantee the stealth ship would make it back to Unity. The Foxes were certainly on the alert now. Merely avoiding all the *obvious* places to cross the tramlines would add *weeks* to the ship's journey. "But then, we knew that was true right from the start."

He rose. "We'll speak again in ES-11," he said. "Until then...good luck to us all."

———

Susan felt pleasantly full as she made her way back to the airlock and boarded her shuttle back to *Vanguard*, even though she knew they'd be going back into combat within a couple of days. She opened her datapad and downloaded the operational plan, opening the file and scanning it even as the pilot undocked from *King Edward* and took them back into space. It was bold, she had to admit, but it should be doable. Using *Black Hunter* as a Trojan Horse might *just* give the aliens pause.

Unless they think we cheated in some way, she mused. *Breaking their rules might encourage them to do the same.*

She put the datapad aside for later contemplation and leaned forward, watching as *Vanguard* came into view. Hundreds of engineers swarmed over her scorched hull, carefully removing the burned-out components and replacing them with new systems drawn from the logistics freighters. Commodore Garrison had a point, Susan had to admit. Their expenditure of just about everything was already well above projections.

Good thing no one takes them seriously, she thought. The shuttle altered course, heading towards the nearest airlock. *The projections are always far too optimistic.*

She keyed her wristcom as the shuttle docked. "Commander Mason, meet me in my ready room in thirty minutes," she ordered. The hatch hissed open. It smelt of *Vanguard*, not of any other ship. She couldn't help feeling that she was coming home. "We have an operation to plan."

CHAPTER
THIRTY

"Entering ES-11," Sammy said. "Transmitting our IFF...*now*."

George sucked in a breath, feeling dangerously exposed. Cold logic told her they were entire *light-minutes* from anything that could reasonably hurt her, but cold logic was out to lunch, leaving her uncomfortably aware that they were about to walk, buck naked, into a dragon's lair. They were, as far as she knew, the only humans in the entire star system.

"Let me know the moment they respond," she ordered, finally. "And then ready the ballistic projectiles."

"Aye, Captain," Sammy said. He sounded like he *meant* it. George couldn't help wondering just how he managed to sound convincing. "They should respond in a few minutes."

"Assuming we're right about how the FTL system works," George reminded him. "The boffins could be wrong."

"And then they'll come up with a better theory," Sammy told her. "I think..."

He broke off. "They sent a response," he said. "They've granted us permission to head to ES-11-2."

George felt cold. "Take us there," she ordered. "And keep our active sensors stepped down."

She couldn't help shivering as *Black Hunter* slowly moved away from the tramline and set course for her destination. Normally, even the massive sensor arrays orbiting Earth, Mars and Jupiter wouldn't have a hope of spotting a single starship crossing the tramline and entering the Sol

System. She'd studied the Battle of Earth at the academy, where she'd been told - time and time again - that it had been sheer luck the alien fleet had been spotted before it got into firing range. A day or two either way and the Tadpoles could have struck without anyone being aware of their presence until it was far too late.

But the Foxes could detect ships crossing the tramlines...

That must be how they detected the contact fleet, she thought. She still had nightmares, sometimes, about how close she'd come to death. *Maybe they even detected the survey ships when they stumbled upon ES-2. UXS-469 must have been completely useless, by their standards, but keeping an eye on the tramline would have been common sense.*

She wondered, absently, just how a working FTL communications system would change the universe. The Admiralty didn't have a hope of directing operations from Earth, not when it could take weeks to get a message from Earth to Unity or Faraway World. They had to give their subordinates wide latitude to do as they saw fit, then wait and pray until word finally arrived from the front. But if there *was* an FTL communications system, even a limited one...the Admiralty could watch over their shoulders and micromanage to its heart's content.

That won't be my problem, she told herself, sourly. She ran her hand along the alien throne, shaking her head tiredly. *This is the closest I'll get to actual command.*

She studied the display, wishing that the Foxes had seen fit to install holographic technology in their starships. It wasn't as if they didn't have the capability. Instead, she had to peer at flatscreen monitors like something out of the dark ages, so poorly designed that it was difficult to keep track of three-dimensional combat. The design puzzled her more than she cared to admit. It wasn't as if they were in the wet navy, for crying out loud! The Foxes *knew* that space was a three-dimensional environment.

ES-11 slowly revealed its secrets as *Black Hunter* crawled into the system. A heavily-defended - and populated - planet, a gas giant that was used as a fuel source as well as a secondary set of habitats...and a hundred or more asteroid settlements that hadn't been included on the captured files. Somehow, George wasn't surprised. The Royal Navy's charts of Sol, Terra Nova and even Britannia were permanently out of date.

Asteroids were so easy to settle - and the dwellers rarely bothered to wait for permission - that new ones sprang up every year. Oddly, it made the Foxes seem more *human.*

And for all I know, she thought, *the Tadpoles have the same problem.*

The timer pinged. "The fleet should be crossing the tramline now," Sammy warned, as Major Andres entered the command deck. "They'll be detected."

"Unfortunately," Major Andres agreed. "Let me know if they have new orders for us."

George felt a hot flash of resentment, mixed with grim understanding. Major Andres was *used* to taking command - and used to thinking of her as an unwanted tagalong. Maybe she was, technically, the senior naval officer on *Black Hunter.* In practice, he wouldn't think of her as his commander...and there was no way she could put him in his place. And really, she didn't blame him. Normally, the billet would have been passed to a lieutenant.

"They may expect us to help search for the fleet," she said, instead. "And if that happens, we're going to have to decline."

She turned her attention to the display, wondering just how far they could take their impersonation. The Royal Navy wouldn't allow *any* starship to enter orbit without making sure of the newcomer's *bona fides,* even though most people assumed that aliens couldn't pass for humans without making all sorts of mistakes. Did the aliens *know* they'd lost a starship? Did they think *Black Hunter* had been blown out of space? Had *Black Hunter's* consorts managed to get a warning off before it was too late? Or did they merely believe that the squadron had managed to escape certain death?

We're about to find out, she thought.

In a time of war, she doubted she could fly the lone survivor of a powerful squadron into the Sol System without having to answer some *very* hard questions. What had happened to the other ships, for a start. The Royal Navy - and the other human navies - had procedures to ensure that a surrendered starship was useless to her captors, but human error could easily lead to a ship being captured intact. And the Foxes, coming to think of it, had reason to be far more careful. They *knew* their captured personnel could - and would - switch sides, if captured. George had no idea how the Foxes managed to survive with their racial limitations, but there was no denying that they *had*.

Maybe it works in their favour, she thought, as the minutes ticked by. *They don't attempt to destroy their enemies and their enemies don't attempt to hold out after it becomes futile.*

"They just sent us another signal," Sammy said. "They're asking us for our sensor readings."

"Send them what we have," George ordered. *Black Hunter's* sensors were good - the boffins had made a fuss about not tearing them out of the hull before the ship was dispatched on her mission - but they weren't tracking the task force. "Don't give them any reason to suspect us."

She glanced at Major Andres, then back at the display. What would *she* do, if she suspected a ship had been captured and pressed into enemy service? Stop her right at the edge of the defence grid, she suspected; too close to the planet to escape, too far from the vital targets to be danger-ous. And yet, it would be risky. The starship's commander might decide to charge the defenders and go out in a blaze of glory, if he thought he couldn't hope to escape. But there was enough firepower orbiting the planet to take the ship out before it was too late.

"They're allowing us to come in," Major Andres commented. "Are you ready to escape?"

"Yes, sir," George said. The plan was weak, but it was the best one they had. "If they catch on to us before we've deployed the missiles, we're sunk."

"But we should be able to clear their range before it's too late," Major Andres said. "Right?"

George flushed. *She* was the naval officer. "Right."

"Good," Major Andres said. He made a show of glancing at his watch. "And as you have six hours before we enter engagement range, might I suggest you sleep for five of them?"

"Yes, sir," George said. She glanced at Sammy. "Inform me if anything changes."

"Of course, Captain," Sammy said. This time, he sounded a little more sardonic. "I believe Jon brought a VR suite, if you want a different form of relaxation."

"Remind me to have a word with him later," Major Andres said. "And I *suggest*" - his tone made it very clear that it was an order - "that you sleep."

"Yes, sir," George said.

The cabins on *Black Hunter* were largely unspeakable by human standards, although she was amused to note they were better than some of the foxholes she'd napped in on Earth. She had a small blanket in one of the holds next to the marines and considered herself lucky. Given time, she would have stripped out the alien cabins and turned them into something humans could use, but the odds were vastly against *Black Hunter* surviving long enough for that to matter. Her most optimistic set of assumptions ended with them limping away from the planet, desperately trying to link up with the task force before it was too late.

She lay down and closed her eyes, trying to sleep. Maybe she *should* ask to borrow the VR suite, if Jon had brought any programs she could use. It wasn't too likely. Most people used them for sexual fantasies, which were gender-specific. But it would be messy and public, something she couldn't afford. There were no showers on *Black Hunter* - the aliens seemed to prefer communal baths - and *nothing* that would wash away the damage to her reputation, if the marines saw her...

She must have fallen asleep, because the next thing she felt was Corporal Roberts shaking her gently. "George, get up," he hissed. "The Major's raging."

George cursed as she jumped to her feet, used the facilities and hurried to the bridge. Roberts hadn't dumped cold water over her, for which she was thankful, but she had to admit that it would probably have woken her up quicker. She'd forgotten to set an alarm...she glanced at her wristcom, gritting her teeth. If they'd been on *Vanguard*, in Marine Country, she would have had about a *zillion* push-ups coming her way.

"Captain," Major Andres said. He invested the word with so much sarcasm that George found herself flushing, again. "We are approaching our target."

"Yes, sir," George said.

She sat down on the throne and hastily checked the systems. The alien planet was growing closer, her sensors picking up more and more details. It was impossible to tell, yet, if it was a multiracial planet, with Foxes and

Cows living together in harmony, but it was clear that their population estimates might be an order of magnitude too low. Indeed, if she hadn't *known* ES-11-2 was a colony, she would have assumed it was the alien homeworld. The population density matched Earth.

And what, she asked herself, *does that say about their homeworld?*

Sammy entered the bridge and took his spot, relieving Corporal Hicks. "The targeting systems have been updating constantly," he said. "I have clear locks on all of our targets."

"Very good," George said. She studied the display for a long moment, wishing she could see the task force. It would have been reassuring, even though she knew it would also have meant that something had gone wrong. "Are you ready to begin launching ballistic missiles?"

"Yes, Captain," Sammy said. "The missiles are ready for launch."

George nodded, slowly. One reason for their slow progress towards the planet had been to keep the aliens from wondering why they'd slowed, when they'd nearly reached their destination. She didn't want *anything* to alert them, not now they were slowly approaching the edge of the planetary defence system. ES-11-2 wasn't as heavily defended as Earth, but there was enough firepower orbiting the planet to give *Black Hunter* a very exciting - and very short - time. And their window for offensive operations was starting to open.

"Upload the final targeting datapackets, then start deploying the missiles," George ordered. It was time to roll the die. "And ready defensive weaponry."

"Aye, Captain," Sammy said.

"And prepare to evacuate," Major Andres added. "This ship may not survive the next few minutes."

"See to it, Major," George ordered.

She had a suspicion she'd pay for that comment later - the look he gave her was *far* to reminiscent of her old gym mistress for comfort - but he merely nodded and keyed his wristcom, issuing orders. The memory made her smile, even though she'd been terrified of the old battleaxe at the time. If nothing else, life in space underlined just how pointless her life had been as a schoolgirl. Most of her achievements, in hindsight, had been mind-numbingly boring.

But we could throw Mrs Hawker at the Foxes, she thought, as the final minutes ticked down to zero. *And then they'd be begging to be allowed to surrender.*

"Missiles away, Captain," Sammy said. "No sign they've been detected."

George gritted her teeth. Too much depended on the enemy now. If they thought - perhaps rightly - that there was something odd about her ship, they might demand she hold position until she could be inspected. Or they might just do an active sensor sweep, which would pick up the missiles before they went active. Hell, there was no way she *could* let an inspection team board *Black Hunter*. They'd know something was wrong the moment they laid eyes on her crew.

"Picking up a signal," Sammy warned. "They're ordering us to hold position."

He paused. "Incoming starfighters!"

"Hold position," George ordered. The starfighters didn't seem particularly suspicious, as far as she could tell, but they might notice *something* when they made an inspection of *Black Hunter's* hull. If they spotted something out of place…she'd have to take them out quickly, knowing it would be far too revealing. "And track them on passive sensors."

She waited, grimly, as the starfighters came closer. They had no *reason* to go active, she told herself, but they also had nothing to gain from *not* going active. Their drive emissions marked them out as targets, whatever they did. Maybe, just maybe, their active sweeps wouldn't pick up the missiles. They *were* tiny objects in the endless sea of space…

The starfighters swept past, far too close to her hull for comfort, then vanished into the distance.

"Show-offs," Sammy pronounced. "All starfighter pilots are the same, whatever the species."

He smiled. "I once knew a pair of starfighter pilots on *Invincible* who…"

Major Andres cleared his throat. "I'm not sure George is old enough to hear this story," he said. "Coming to think of it, I'm not sure *I'm* old enough to hear this story."

George blinked, then realised he was trying to make a joke. She giggled, feeling the tension starting to evaporate. She'd never really understood why the marines joked in foxholes, but she thought she did now. It was a way of looking at death and laughing.

"Picking up another alien signal," Sammy warned. He looked up at her, his brown eyes worried. "They're dispatching a shuttle."

"Shit," George said. By her most optimistic calculations, the shuttle would reach them before the missiles entered attack range. She briefly considered trying to take the boarding party prisoner, but too much could go wrong. There would be someone on the shuttle in position to scream for help. *And* those damn starfighters were on their way back. "Stand by to engage."

She tapped the display. "We take her out *here*," she ordered. Plasma weapons weren't exactly light-speed weapons, but at such close range it wouldn't matter. The aliens would die before their sensors sounded the alert. "And then reverse course."

And hope they don't notice the missiles, she thought. They'd give the missiles a few extra seconds, perhaps. Just long enough for them to enter attack range and go active. *It might cost us our lives, but there will still be a chance for the plan to work.*

"Aye, Captain," Sammy said. His voice was very even, but she could detect a thin trace of anticipation. "Ready…"

George braced herself as the enemy shuttle drew closer. It looked more like a standard civilian model than a military design, according to the sensors, but she knew better than to take that for granted. The craft would probably have some armour, even if it wasn't obvious.

"Target the starfighters afterwards," she ordered. Maybe, just maybe, they could wipe out all the threats before it was too late. *That* would give them an excellent chance to escape. "Fire on my command."

She took a breath. "Fire!"

Black Hunter fired. The shuttle exploded, blotted out of existence before it even knew it was under attack. George cursed as the starfighter pilots threw themselves into a series of evasive manoeuvres, then spun around to take the offensive. They'd either suspected trouble, part of her mind noted, or they'd merely been on alert. *Black Hunter* was already pulling back, yet there was no way they could outrun the starfighters. Sammy opened fire, using the point defence to force them to keep their distance, but it wasn't enough. They closed to attack range and opened fire…

"The missiles have gone active," Sammy snapped. The display filled with alerts as the enemy active sensors came online, too late. The missiles were already flashing towards their targets. "I think we did it!"

"Good," George snapped back. The ship shook as plasma bolts slammed into its thin armour and burned through into the hull. Moments later, the power dropped sharply as one of the fusion cores was taken out. The end was approaching with terrifying speed. "And now we have to escape!"

She keyed her wristcom as she sprang up. "Abandon ship! I say again, all hands abandon ship!"

CHAPTER
THIRTY ONE

"Launch fighters," John snapped, as the task force decloaked. "All batteries, commence firing!"

He allowed himself a tight smile as the enemy recoiled. *Black Hunter* had done a *very* good job, her ballistic missiles tearing into the planetary defences. They were trying desperately to recover, but they wouldn't have time to do more than launch a handful of starfighters. His battleships were already advancing forward, their main guns and mass drives launching blast after blast into the enemy positions. They'd be too busy fending off his ships and starfighters to notice the mass driven projectiles, at least until it was far too late.

"*Eisenhower* has launched all her starfighters," Commander Janette Williamson reported, looking up from her console. "*Vikramaditya* is launching the remainder of hers now."

"Remind both ships to remain out of reach of enemy weapons," John ordered, as the enemy starfighters altered course to engage the newcomers. "We don't want to lose another carrier."

He glanced down at the display as his active sensors probed the system. It was *definitely* a bigger target than he'd realised, although - thankfully - most of what they'd missed during the recon flights appeared to be harmless. He marked some possible sites down for later attention, then looked back at the main display. *King Edward* and *Alabama* were exchanging fire with a massive alien battlestation, while *Texas* and *Montana* were crushing a second and the remaining battleships were sweeping orbital targets out of existence. As smash-and-run raids went, he had to admit, it had been terrifyingly effective. The defenders didn't have a chance to rally their forces before it was too late.

"Picking up several planetary defence centres on the surface," Janette warned. "They're firing mass drivers now."

"Return fire with KEWs," John ordered. A duel with ground-based mass drivers was likely to end badly, even though the enemy weapons were at the bottom of the gravity well. "And then warn the task force to attempt to stay out of range."

He winced as the alien battlestation struck *Alabama* a glancing blow, a second before parts of the battlestation's armour failed. The two battleships pressed their advantage ruthlessly, launching a stream of missiles into her weak spot. Moments later, the battlestation exploded into a cloud of debris, half of which plummeted towards the planet below. John cursed under his breath. Most of the debris was too small to do any real damage, assuming it survived its passage through the atmosphere, but a handful of pieces were alarmingly large. *And* they were out of effective range. There was nothing he could do about them.

"Signal the fleet," he ordered. The last enemy industrial node was gone. Their shipyards were already nothing more than atoms. "They are to withdraw to high orbit once the final targets have been destroyed."

"Aye, Admiral," Janette said. She paused. "*Clive* has been destroyed.

John glanced at her. "How?"

"She took a mass driver projectile dead on, Admiral," Janette reported. "There are no lifepods."

"Continue to target the PDCs," John ordered, after a moment. The aliens would probably have rigged up point defence to protect their installations, but he had a virtually unlimited supply of KEWs. "And order the remaining ships to pull back."

He watched, grimly, as a flight of alien starfighters swept towards *King Edward*, followed by a flight of craft that *could* have been gunboats. But they weren't, he noted, as his starfighters wiped them out. They were shuttles, practically helpless save for short-range lasers. The Foxes must have hoped - prayed, if they had a god - that one or two of them would survive the holocaust long enough to ram their targets. It was futile, John knew. After their engagement with the gunboats, his point defence crews had become *very* motivated.

"The last of the battlestations is gone," Janette reported. "I…"

She broke off. "Incoming starfighters!"

John blinked in surprise. "Where did *they* come from?"

"Unknown," Janette confessed. "They may have been launched by a cloaked carrier…"

"Send a spread of probes," John ordered. "*Find* that ship!"

"Aye, sir," Janette said.

John watched the display. A cloaked carrier, one they'd missed. And one with a captain cunning enough to wait until most of *his* starfighters were otherwise occupied. It must have taken nerve to send the starfighters in without power…He cursed under his breath as he tossed options around and around in his head. Had the enemy merely been lucky enough to escape detection or had he just stumbled into a trap? But it had already turned into a very expensive trap, unless the aliens had underestimated him. They'd given up a large percentage of their industrial base…

Maybe two cloaked carriers, he thought, as his sensors returned a more accurate count of the alien craft. *Their fleet carriers don't carry that many more starfighters than our own.*

"I'm picking up lifepods from the *Black Hunter*," Jeanette added. "Captain Fellowman is requesting permission to dispatch SAR shuttles."

"Granted," John said. Normally, he would have waited until the fighting was over, but the aliens were likely to want revenge. Besides, they might not recognise the lifepods for what they were. "And adjust our position to counter those carriers."

He studied the display for a long cold moment. If everything had gone according to plan, Commodore Solange Leclère and *her* task force should have hit the cloudscoops at the same time. There was no way to be sure, of course. The timing might have been flubbed…although, given that *Black Hunter* had caught the aliens by surprise, it was clear it hadn't been flubbed *that* badly. There was no way to be *sure* they'd taken down the FTL communications network completely.

"Aye, Admiral," Janette said. "The probes have yet to locate the enemy carriers."

John scowled. What did *that* mean? Had the carriers launched their fighters and then retreated? The alien starfighters didn't have any longer endurance than humanity's…the alien CO was taking one hell of a risk. Or had he decided to sacrifice his starfighters while preserving his carriers? Cold logic suggested it might be a good idea, but *John* wouldn't have cared to serve under any commander who considered it. Throwing one's men away would be disastrous for morale.

"Keep looking," he ordered. "And send a surrender demand to the planet."

"Aye, sir," Janette said.

It didn't matter, John thought coldly. The planet had lost its shipyards, its defences and its industrial nodes. It could surrender or not, as it saw fit. *He* didn't need to land ground troops to render the system utterly irrelevant. Assuming the war stopped, the aliens would *still* need ten years to rebuild what he'd destroyed.

And recover from the damage inflicted on their planet, he thought, grimly.

The thought caused him a pang. He'd never felt any particular concern over the standard policy for dealing with rogue or terrorist states - dropping KEWs until they thought better of it - but striking an alien world and threatening alien civilians *hurt*. There was no way to know just how guilty each of the dead were - and the laws of war cared little for civilians who lived near military installations - yet that wasn't the point. *Retaliation* was the only way to deter war crimes and - now - the aliens had more than enough excuse to strike back at a human world. It didn't matter, in the end, that he hadn't set out to cause a catastrophe. All that mattered was that the *aliens* wouldn't believe it.

And they'll want to deter us from doing the same thing again, he reminded himself.

He pushed the thought out of his head. If the operation succeeded, there would be time to sort the whole matter out during the peace talks. And if it failed…

If that happens, he thought, *I won't be alive to worry about it.*

Susan couldn't help feeling annoyed, at some level, that Admiral Naiser had dispatched *Vanguard* to the rear of the formation, covering the fleet carriers. It wasn't an unwise decision, she had to admit, but she'd already overheard some of the crew grumbling about their new position. She'd told them off, then pointed out that *Vanguard* could hardly resume her old position until the repairs were completed. The battleship's crew still had a lot of work to do.

"The enemy starfighters are approaching, Captain," Jean said. "They're coming in hot."

"And our starfighters are out of position," Susan agreed. The Foxes had timed it well, she had to admit. Either by good judgement or luck, they'd caught the carriers with only minimal CSP. "Swing us around to block their way."

It wasn't something she would have tried normally. A starfighter could easily evade a battleship, particularly if the battleship wasn't its target. But now…the longer they took to reach the carriers, the greater the chance the human starfighters would return to defend their motherships. No, they needed to push right through *Vanguard's* killing zone…

"They're entering range, Captain," Jean said.

"Open fire," Susan ordered.

She smiled, coldly, as the alien starfighters scattered under her fire. A dozen exploded and vanished from the display, several more swooped around as if they couldn't decide where they should be going. The remainder kept moving, zigzagging from side to side to make themselves harder to hit, clearly unaware that two-thirds of Susan's weapons were firing at random. A single starfighter wasn't a threat, not if it was knocked out of formation. And she'd already succeeded in killing the enemy formation.

"One rammed us," Jean reported. "The remainder are heading straight for *Eisenhower*."

"Bring us around to support her," Susan ordered. The two fleet carriers had plenty of point defence, but they were also far more vulnerable. Their crews had bare seconds before the enemy starfighters started launching torpedoes. "And continue firing."

She gritted her teeth as the aliens swarmed *Eisenhower*, four torpedoes slamming into her hull. Two more struck her landing bays, causing a chain of explosions that could have done real damage. The remainder of the alien starfighters lanced around, only to run into a hail of fire from the returning human starfighters. Susan felt her eyes narrow as she realised the aliens had no intention of running. They were fighting to the death.

"A starfighter just rammed *Vikramaditya*," Jean reported.

"No major damage," Parkinson added. Susan allowed herself a moment of relief. "But there's a second flight heading for her landing bays."

Susan watched, grimly, as the alien starfighters pressed their offensive. One made a dive for the landing bay, clearly intent on ramming the carrier, only to be picked off bare seconds from its target by a human starfighter. Susan wondered, absently, just who'd been flying the craft, then decided it didn't matter. Right now, all that mattered was staying together and killing as many aliens as possible...

...And then, suddenly, the last of the alien starfighters were gone.

"Local space is clear, Captain," Charlotte reported. She sounded rather annoyed. "Long-range probes have not found any trace of the alien carriers."

"They must have withdrawn," Susan mused. Under the circumstances, she found it hard to blame the aliens. They must have known there was no hope of preserving the system. Their carriers could fall back and pick up another load of starfighters. "Keep watching for surprises."

"Aye, Captain," Charlotte said.

"Signal from the flag," Parkinson added. "The task force is to complete recovery operations, then set a direct course for Tramline Two."

Susan nodded. Tramline Two was a dead end, although she didn't know if the *aliens* knew *she* knew that. She wouldn't, if the xenospecialists hadn't deciphered the alien files. If the aliens assumed that the task force was going to waste a few days bumbling around a thoroughly useless star system, it might just slow their response. The fleet would cloak, once it was out of sensor range, then head directly to Tramline Three. A lone ship could take out the FTL communicator before the remainder of the fleet crossed the tramline.

"Set course as ordered," she said. They'd remain with the carriers until relieved. Thankfully, no one could say they'd failed in their duty - or missed out on the fun. "And then stand down from red alert."

———————

Years ago, back when she'd been younger, George had watched an episode of Stellar Star where the heroine had found herself trapped in a lifepod with three of her bridge crew. It had served as an excuse for an orgy - nearly everything seemed to serve as an excuse for an orgy, in *that* universe - and the actress had looked rather disappointed to be rescued. But, in real life, the lifepod was tiny, smelly and dangerously claustrophobic. She was aware, all too aware, that a passing starfighter might mistake them for an enemy weapon and blow them out of space. Or, for that matter, that they might run into a piece of debris big or sharp enough to tear the hull and send them falling into vacuum. She'd donned her shipsuit and emergency mask, of course, but she knew they wouldn't provide much protection.

Perhaps I'm in hell, she thought, as she drifted against the bulkhead. She liked Sammy and the Major, but they weren't her first choice for companionship. *I'm in hell and I don't even know it.*

She felt trapped - and queasy - despite her training. There was no gravity in the pod, no way to tell up from down. The damned designers hadn't even bothered to include chairs, let alone something to distract them from their plight. All of a sudden, Stellar Star's orgy made a great deal of sense. If her boyfriend - it struck her, suddenly, that she hadn't thought of Peter Barton for a while now - had been with her, she would have suggested it. But she knew better than to suggest anything like that to either Major Andres or Sammy. Marine regulations against fraternisation were far stronger than anything on the navy's books.

"Forty minutes," Sammy said. He glanced up from his wristcom. "That's how long we've been out here."

"Shut up," George snarled. It felt longer, much longer. There was no way to look outside, no way to tell what was going on. Had the fleet won the day? Or were the Foxes carefully taking aim before using her pod for target practice? Would it have been *that* hard to include a gaming termi-nal? "I..."

"Take a deep breath," Major Andres advised. "There's nothing you can do any longer, so relax. Take a deep breath and try to meditate. Or sleep, if you can."

George wondered, tiredly, how he could be so calm. She'd had twenty-seven people on *Black Hunter*, despite the best efforts of the engineers to make the ship as automated as possible. Had they all made it off the ship in time? She had no doubt that *Black Hunter* was now nothing more than clouds of debris. If they were dead...she shook her head, numbly. She had no idea what she'd do if twenty-four people had died under her command. All of a sudden, her uncle's odder moments made a great deal of sense.

No one dies in Stellar Star, she thought, morbidly. It was astonish-ing just what difference friendly - and somewhat perverted - scriptwriters made. *They just get fucked. A lot.*

She started to drift downwards, her feet touching the deck. The deck...? She was so tired that it took her a moment to realise that they'd entered a gravity field. A dull thud echoed through the lifepod as some-thing banged up against it, followed by a low hiss. She reached for her pistol as the hatch started to open, silently preparing to sell her life dearly. There was no *way* she was going to be an alien POW. Behind her, the two marines also drew their weapons. They clearly felt the same way too.

The hatch opened. A dark face peered in. "I surrender," he - no, *she* - said, as she saw the three pistols pointed at her. Her accent was unmistak-ably American. "You're safe - really."

Major Andres leaned forward. "And you are?"

"Ensign Tanya Stedman, United States Navy," the woman said. She didn't look *that* much older than George, although her spacesuit hid everything below the neck. "Pilot officer, United States Shuttlecraft *Baseball Bat*, mothership USS *Montana*. You all want to come through?"

George exchanged a glance with Major Andres, then holstered her pistol and stepped through the hatch. The American shuttle was larger than *Vanguard's*, she noted, but empty. A chill ran through her as she realised that *they* might be the sole survivors. Or perhaps, she told herself in a desperate attempt to remain calm, there were other SAR shuttles out there. The planet, clearly visible through the cockpit, had probably been secured.

She glanced back at Tanya. "Did we win?"

"We won, honey," Tanya said. She looked from face to face. "I can't tow the lifepod, so I'm leaving it here. I hope that won't be a problem."

Major Andres snorted. "We can recover it later, if necessary," he said. "What happened?"

"We kicked the shit out of the orbital defences, thanks to you guys," Tanya said. She nodded to a younger man in the cockpit. "Close the hatch, then take us back to *Montana*."

"On the way," the man called back.

"We have to get to *Vanguard*," George said. She had no idea what would happen, when she returned. Technically, a ship had been lost under her command. She wondered, suddenly, what that meant for the prize money. It had already been paid out, hadn't it? "Is there a flight back?"

"My CO will see to it," Tanya assured her. "Until then" - she waved a hand at the chairs - "take a seat and enjoy the ride."

"Good idea," Major Andres said. He grinned, humourlessly. "When we get back to the ship, we'll have to work out what to tell them."

George groaned.

CHAPTER
THIRTY TWO

"It was my fault," Midshipwoman George Fitzwilliam said. "*Black Hunter* was lost under my command."

Susan carefully kept her face impassive. It would never do to give in to the urge to laugh. Poor George Fitzwilliam sounded as if she expected to be thrown in the brig, then marched in front of a kangaroo court and shot. Losing *Black Hunter* wasn't that much of a black mark on her record, but it still stung. *And* the starship had been practically irreplaceable.

"I believe the Admiral expected the ship to be lost," Susan said. She had no doubt that hundreds of people would condemn George for losing the ship, but Admiral Naiser wasn't one of them. *Black Hunter* had been interesting - Susan had no doubt that a more prolonged study of the ship would have revealed all sorts of useful details - yet punching their way into ES-11 had been rather more important. "He doesn't seem interested in punishing you."

George looked up. It struck Susan, again, just how *young* she was. Her family had done her no favours, Susan suspected, when they'd allowed her to go to the academy early. What she'd gained in early admittance had been more than outweighed by limited maturity and lack of experience. George had been knocked back down the promotions ladder, despite her family's best efforts. It was unlikely she'd ever climb back up again.

"I lost the ship," George said, her voice a mixture of hope and fear. "Captain…"

"The Admiral believes you did all you could," Susan said, "and his after-action report makes that clear. *Black Hunter* was not a Royal Navy starship, you were not a formal commanding officer, and you were given a mission that was almost certain to result in the loss of your ship as well as your life. Now, stop feeling sorry for yourself and buck up."

George swallowed, hard. "Yes, Captain."

"Very good," Susan said.

She allowed herself to show a little approval. Truthfully, George had done better than Susan had dared hope. The Foxes *should* have been much more suspicious when *Black Hunter* returned from the dead. Hell, they should have *known* their captured personnel would switch sides. It was in their nature! Susan had no idea how they managed to run a society where POWs effectively joined their captors, but she had to admit it did have its advantages. And yet, they should have known...

But she understood George, better than she cared to admit. Losing a ship was *always* painful, particularly for a first-time commander. Susan had believed, deep in her soul, that she would lose *Vanguard*, after her first return to Earth. She'd certainly had no reason to believe she would be returned to her command chair. But even *that* wouldn't have been as bad as knowing her ship had been destroyed. It wasn't uncommon for captains who survived their ships to be put on suicide watch. Too many had killed themselves after seeing to the safety of their crews.

She studied George for a long moment. Thankfully, the midshipwoman didn't seem *that* depressed. Tired, obviously; fearful, certainly... but probably not at risk of killing herself.

"The doctor cleared you to return to duty," she said, glancing down at the datapad on her desk. The doctor had reported bumps and bruises, but no serious injuries. "Do you want to return to the marines?"

"Yes, Captain," George said.

"Get some rest, then rejoin Major Andres," Susan said. It was an order, phrased as such. She rather suspected George would have gone straight to Marine Country if she hadn't been ordered to rest. She'd known too many girls who'd pushed themselves too hard at school and ended up burning out. "And, for what it's worth, I'm proud of you."

George brightened. "Thank you, Captain."

Susan frowned, inwardly. Was George *that* desperate for approval? Somehow, she couldn't imagine a girl growing up on a country estate to be lacking in self-esteem. She'd studied George's file, back when she'd been XO. The daughter of nobility, the niece of the most famous serving officer in living memory...George should have lacked for nothing. But it was clear that she'd learnt several lessons in her career, including the importance of *genuine* praise. Even Hanover Towers would have toadied to her, just a little. She might never have faced *real* hardship until she'd joined the navy.

Perhaps that's why they let her join early, Susan mused. *They knew she needed discipline before she turned sour.*

"And the prize money awarded to you and your comrades will stand," she added, pushing the thought aside. Admiral Naiser had ruled in their favour, although Susan knew the beancounters would whine and moan about it. *Black Hunter* hadn't been presented to the Admiralty, they'd say; Admiral Naiser had sent an irreplaceable prize into deadly danger and lost her. "I suggest you *don't* spend it all at once."

"Thank you, Captain," George said. The prize money was peanuts, compared to her trust fund, but she'd *earned* it. Susan rather understood. She'd done a paper route as a child, just to earn a little cash. It had always seemed better to earn rather than to receive. "What would I spend it *on*?"

Susan had to smile. There was nothing on *Vanguard* to buy, really. Everything George could reasonably want could be requisitioned from ship's stores. She could gamble, Susan supposed, although *that* was largely pointless. Most spacers saved their money for shore leave or put it in one of the Admiralty's long-term funds. They'd be able to retire early, if they were careful. Susan had heard of a couple of *Ark Royal's* officers who'd invested their prize money and retired millionaires.

Although they did have a vast sum awarded to them, she reminded herself, rather dryly. The Tadpole ship *Ark Royal* had captured had been a treasure trove of technology. *George didn't capture anything like as valuable.*

"There's always a black market between ships," she said. It was technically illicit, but wise officers turned a blind eye. "Or you could spend it on tuck."

George smiled. "I'd sooner go on shore leave again," she admitted. "I've always wanted to see Jupiter."

"You'll have to capture an enemy battleship single-handedly," Susan said. Getting to Jupiter was expensive, even though the Great Red Spot was one hell of a tourist attraction. But it was better than wasting the money on gambling. "Get some sleep, George. You need it."

"Yes, Captain," George said. She straightened. "And thank you."

She saluted, then turned and marched out of the cabin. Susan watched her go, feeling an odd flicker of affection mixed with amusement. George hadn't done badly at all, really. The Admiral certainly hadn't complained. But she was still fretting over it…Susan didn't really blame her, in truth. Good officers always wondered if they could have done better.

And great officers don't waste time worrying, she told herself firmly. *You have far too many reports to read.*

———

"This was their homeworld," Henry said, softly. "Originally…"

ES-4 was very similar to Sol, so similar that a casual observer might mistake one for the other. Seven planets, three of them gas giants; one of them smack in the middle of the life-bearing zone…under other circumstances, ES-4 would have been considered a prize. But long-range probes had made it clear that ES-4-2 was dead. Blackened cities dotted the surface, the entire ecology had been ruined…if there was any intelligent life left on the planet, it was very well hidden. The sheer level of radioactivity in the atmosphere was terrifying. It was as if all the worst nightmares of the last three hundred years had come out to play.

Admiral Naiser glanced at him. "And yet, they have practically *no* presence within the system."

Henry nodded. Traces of war were all around them - blasted settlements, wrecked asteroid colonies, even spacecraft from a bygone era - but there were no traces of living beings anywhere within sensor range. It was frightening to think that a spacefaring society could be obliterated so completely. He knew, of course, that *one* ship had managed to cross the interstellar gulf to keep the race alive, but still...

"They may feel the whole system is a tomb," he mused. "Or they may just have decided it isn't worth trying to salvage something from the ruins."

It felt odd, to him. If Earth had been wrecked, perhaps during the war, the colonies would have survived and eventually returned. Wouldn't they? There were other colonies within the Sol System. Earth herself could have been saved, given time...he looked back at the display and shivered. Was there *anything* that could cleanse such a poisoned atmosphere? In the end, the groundhogs had effectively exterminated themselves. And they'd taken the rest of the system down with them.

They stood together for a long moment, contemplating eternity. God alone knew just how many races had risen to greatness, then fallen into dust since the universe was born. Henry knew, deep inside, that he couldn't even *begin* to contemplate the vast gulfs of time between then and now. But if the Foxes *hadn't* blasted their entire society back into the Stone Age, if they hadn't had to make a risky interstellar crossing at STL speeds...they might have stumbled across Earth, before humanity was in any state to resist them. Or they might have crushed the Tadpoles instead...

We are so tiny on such a scale, Henry thought. *And it was sheer luck that we met the Tadpoles and the Foxes when we can face them as equals.*

He shivered. Countless experts had claimed, with wonderful computer models to back up their words, that any intelligent race would have filled the galaxy, a long time before humanity rose out of the primal sludge. They'd used it to prove that humanity was alone in the universe, something that had sounded convincing until humanity ran into another intelligent race. And yet, the Tadpoles hadn't been *that* advanced. Henry had heard theories that suggested intelligence was relatively new...or that something had destroyed hundreds of intelligent races so completely that there were no traces, millennia ago. He'd even heard theories suggesting that the laws of space and time were constantly changing, that only *now* intelligence was possible.

"There's nothing to learn here," he said, finally. "Not now. After the war, perhaps…"

"True," Admiral Naiser agreed. "And that means we push on to ES-1."

And to one hell of a battle, Henry thought.

The Admiral leaned forward. "Do you have anything new to contribute?"

"We have altered our surrender demands, based on interviews with the POWs," Henry said, frankly. They'd learned very little that was actually *new*, although it was good to have confirmation of some of the odder details. "However, Admiral, I believe we will still have to beat the shit out of them before they concede."

"As we planned from the beginning," Admiral Naiser said, tightly.

Henry looked at the starchart, floating over the table. They *should* have time to hit ES-1 before the alien reinforcements could arrive…he shook his head in frustration. The damned FTL communications system screwed up all their calculations. What if the Foxes had dispatched a fleet to the front just before *Vanguard* and her consorts had jumped into ES-19 and opened a whole can of worms? *Humanity* would have had to send a courier boat chasing after them, but the Foxes could merely call them back. There were so many variables that even his best projections were little more than guesses.

And they may believe they don't need to recall forces from the front, he thought.

He shook his head in annoyance. That couldn't be true. If the Foxes had enough mobile firepower to handle *both* fronts, the war should have been lost last year. They would have been able to punch through to Tadpole Prime, while pinching off Unity and positioning themselves for a drive into human space. No, all the logic - and prisoner interviews - suggested that the Foxes honestly *hadn't* known they were waging war on *two* races until the Battle of UXS-469. It still surprised him, given that the Foxes controlled a two-race empire, but perhaps it was understandable. They didn't seem to really comprehend that two nations - or interstellar powers - could actually get along.

Either they withdraw forces from the front, he told himself again, *or they don't. If the former, the defenders advance and push them all the way back to ES-1; if the latter, we beat the crap out of their homeworld and its industrial base. Either way, we win.*

"We'll be in ES-2 by tomorrow," Admiral Naiser said. Perhaps he was telling himself the same thing. "And then we will *know*."

"Yes, Admiral," Henry said.

He wished, suddenly, that he'd had a chance to send one final letter to Janelle. He'd been writing to her, of course, and the messages had been copied around the fleet to make sure they weren't lost with the ship, but it wasn't the same. None of *those* messages would get to Janelle before he did, unless another starship was sent home ahead of time. Janelle had been a naval officer. She knew the cold realities of interstellar travel. And yet...

And what will happen, he asked himself, *if I die out here?*

Angrily, he told himself not to worry. It was too late - *far* too late - to worry about the possibility of dying now. He'd known the risks long before he'd boarded *Vanguard* for the voyage to ES-19. And Janelle would cope, he was sure. He'd made certain - very certain - that she would have unquestioned access to his savings. Making sure he - and his children - weren't dependent on the Civil List had been plain common sense. The purse strings had been used to control far too many of his predecessors.

I will not die, he promised himself. *And if I do, she'll have a chance to keep the kids out of the public eye.*

But he knew, all too well, that it wasn't going to be easy.

———

ES-2 was something of a disappointment, John noted, as the task force crawled across the system. Three tramlines - five, if one counted the alien-grade lines - but no planets, asteroid or even comets. It was rare to encounter a G2 star without planets, yet ES-2 was completely alone. The Foxes must have wondered if the universe was playing a joke, he thought, when they'd stumbled across the tramlines and headed out to explore. But then, they'd also known that there *were* other inhabitable worlds out there. *Humanity* hadn't known that for sure until the first explorers had landed on Terra Nova.

"Admiral," Commander Jackson Regal said. "The first set of reports have arrived."

The Foxes would have had them by now, John thought, sardonically. The boffins had yet to devise a workable FTL transmitter, even though they had a piece of alien technology to study. *And their analysts would have had longer to study the files.*

"Put them on the display," he ordered. "And make sure they're forwarded to the fleet."

"Aye, Admiral," Regal said.

John pushed his annoyance aside as he studied the display. ES-1 *was* heavily defended, as he'd expected: orbital battlestations, a small fleet of starships and hundreds of automated weapons platforms. And yet…it wasn't anything like as heavily defended as Earth. His eyes narrowed in contemplation, matching what the scouts had picked up to what they'd been told by alien POWs. The Foxes, it was clear, had focused most of their attention on building a mobile fleet, rather than fixed defences.

It might not have been a mistake, he mused. He silently revised his estimate of the alien industrial base downwards. *Or they may have stripped the defences bare in hopes of punching through to Tadpole Prime.*

"I think we can take them," he said, out loud. Based on what he could see, he was sure of it. "We'll move with Plan Gamma, I think."

"Yes, Admiral," Regal said.

John barely heard him. Plan Gamma was simple enough - all the best plans were - but it needed to be updated, in light of the new information. *And* it needed to have enough room to cope with unpleasant surprises. The Foxes presumably knew the task force was on the far side of a tramline. They might have decided to hide some of their starships in cloak, just to lure him into a trap. It was what he would have done.

We never did run down those carriers, he mused. There were three large fleet carriers orbiting ES-1. *If they got here first, they'll have had plenty of time to load new starfighters and crews.*

"We'll try for a two-prong engagement," he said, after a moment. He should have enough firepower to win a straight match, although he knew better than to assume he could see *everything* the aliens had. Half of

Earth's defences were permanently cloaked. "Ideally, we want to trap their forces against the planet and crush them."

He leaned back in his chair. There were limits to how far he could plan the operation, he knew from bitter experience. Even a straight slogging match could end badly, if they tried to cling to an outdated operational concept. The Foxes could produce a very nasty surprise that would ruin his plans...there was no point, he knew, in trying to plan for everything. It was a losing proposition.

"Forward the operational plan to the ships, then schedule a holographic meeting for 1900," he ordered. It was a shame they couldn't meet in person, but they were in enemy-controlled space. "We'll discuss the planning then."

"Aye, Admiral," Regal said.

And then we will plunge right into their system, John thought. There was no time to try to be clever, no time to try to lure more of their forces out of position. He felt a flicker of anticipation, mixed with worry. *And then we win - or we die.*

CHAPTER
THIRTY THREE

"All stations report themselves to be at full alert, Captain," Mason reported. "*Vanguard* is ready to fight."

"Very good," Susan said. She would have hated to have to call Admiral Naiser and tell him that *Vanguard* needed to be held back. "Time?"

"Five minutes to cross the tramline, Captain," Reed said.

"No enemy presence detected," Charlotte added.

There wouldn't be, Susan thought. *They know where we're going.*

She studied the display, bracing herself as the tramline came closer. Following a least-time course to the tramline was a gamble, all the more so as the Foxes would have a chance to mount an actual ambush as the task force crossed the tramline. For once, it would be possible - even probable - that their ambush would succeed. There *were* scouts on the far side of the tramline, but they might have missed something. A mistake here could be disastrous.

But we don't have much time, she thought. *Barely a day or two before their reinforcements can arrive.*

"Two minutes," Reed said.

"Signal from the flag," Parkinson said. "Earth expects that every man will do his duty."

"How...appropriate," Susan commented. "Helm, take us across the tramline as soon as we reach it."

"Aye, Captain," Reed said.

Susan tensed as the last seconds ticked down, then clenched her fists as they crossed the tramline. The display blanked, as always. She felt sweat starting to trickle down her back as the sensors searched for potential threats…it felt as though it was taking forever…then relaxed slightly as the display came back up. There weren't any threats, as far as she could tell. Merely a star system that felt ominous, even though she *knew* she was imagining it.

"Jump completed, Captain," Reed said.

"Tactical scan is clear," Charlotte added. "Direct datalink established with scouts. No visible threat within sensor range."

They know we're here, Susan thought. *They must have been watching us in ES-2.*

"Signal from the flag," Parkinson injected. "The task force is to shake down, then head directly for Vixen."

"Do it," Susan ordered.

She thinned her lips in disapproval. Whoever had given the alien homeworld such an absurd nickname was going to be scrubbing toilets, when she caught him. Maybe humans couldn't pronounce the planet's *real* name. It was still no excuse for attaching an absurd moniker to the alien homeworld. And it ran the risk of encouraging the analysts to underestimate their enemies.

The display steadily filled with icons, blinked red, orange and yellow as the analysts sorted through the tidal wave of incoming data. Giant industrial nodes, orbiting shipyards, asteroid mining stations and settlements, cloudscoops…ES-1 was heavily populated, countless installations scattered over the entire system. Some of their industrial nodes seemed to be located amongst the asteroids, according to the analysts. Susan puzzled over that for a long moment, then decided the Foxes would be less concerned about enemy raiders. Their…alien…way of war didn't call for striking the enemy's industrial base.

But that's probably changed, given how badly we struck ES-11, she mused. *Or do they view us as uniquely barbaric for smashing harmless shipyards?*

"Launch probes," she ordered, shortly. "And keep a *close* eye on all possible attack vectors."

She leaned forward as the star system continued to reveal its secrets. Thirty enemy starships, including three fleet carriers...she hoped, despite herself, that they'd been the ships that had escaped them at ES-11. No battleships, oddly...had they dispatched their battleships to ES-12 or had they decided the front needed them more? Or were they lurking in cloak, waiting for a chance to spring an ambush. Admiral Naiser had planned to catch the enemy fleet against the planet, but if the enemy was careful the situation could easily be reversed and *he* would be pinned against the planet instead.

We can break off ahead of time, if we're watchful, she reminded herself. *And we can do immense damage to the system before they take us out.*

"Update from the flag," Parkinson said. "New tactical details for the offensive."

Susan glanced down at her console, then nodded. "We'll be ready," she said. "Commander Mason, ensure the tactical staff have the details."

"Aye, Captain," Mason said.

The minutes became hours as the task force continued its advance on the planet. There was no doubt the Foxes - and the Cows - knew they were coming, Susan thought. She wondered, absently, just what was happening on the world below. There had been panic on Earth, when people had realised there was an alien fleet inbound...what was happening, she wondered, in the warrens and fields on Vixen? Was there panic? Or were they relishing the chance to come to grips with a frustratingly stubborn foe?

"They're massing shuttles," Charlotte warned. She sounded doubtful. "At least, I *think* they're shuttles."

They may be gunboats, Susan thought. *And that would tip the balance against us.*

"Continue to monitor them," she ordered. Given time, a regular shuttle could be fitted with a warhead and turned into a suicide runner. She looked at Jean Granger. "And make sure the point defence crews are ready to resist gunboat attack."

"Aye, Captain," Jean said.

Susan kept her face impassive. The analysts had run all sorts of simulations, then forwarded their worst-case scenarios to the point defence crews. She'd watched their exercises, realising - as they lost the engagements time and time again - that the gunboats were a *very* deadly threat, even to a battleship. She hoped the analysts had exaggerated the gunboats as a threat, but she suspected she wouldn't know for sure until they met the gunboats in battle a second time...and by then it would be too late.

Not that they're the only threat, she thought, grimly. *Those battlestations pack one hell of a punch - and they're sweeping space with active sensors. We won't catch them on the hop a second time.*

"Signal from the flag," Parkinson said, as red icons flickered to life on the display. "All fighters are to launch, all battleships are to advance forward and engage the enemy."

"Understood," Susan said. On the display, green starfighters were racing forward. "Lock missiles and railguns on target, then fire at will."

"Aye, Captain," Parkinson said. "Firing...*now!*"

Susan felt a low rumble running through the hull as *Vanguard* fired the first set of long-range missiles. The other battleships fired a moment later, then reloaded their tubes and fired again, hoping to blanket the alien point defence in missile fire. Susan gritted her teeth as the aliens returned fire, launching missiles from the nearest orbiting battlestations and - seemingly - empty space. Putting missiles in orbit, programmed to remain quiet until ordered to engage, was an old trick. It looked, very much, as through the Foxes had overdone it.

"Captain," Charlotte said. "I'm reading over *five hundred* missiles heading towards us!"

"Stand by point defence," Susan ordered, curtly. The railguns were switching from target to target, blasting out streams of pellets that would be devastating to anything smaller than a destroyer. A number of orbiting missiles would be destroyed before they could bring up their drives and attack. "Engage as soon as they enter range."

She cursed under her breath as the automated platforms opened fire, pouring plasma bolts into their cloud of missiles. The railguns would get most of the platforms, she thought - a number had already been blasted into dust - but they'd provide cover for the battlestations, at least as long as they lasted. And they would soak up fire that would be better directed at other targets. Not that the battlestations themselves were any slouches, she noted grimly. Their point defence was even *more* effective.

They don't need to mount drives, she mused, sourly. The only upside was that the stations were easy targets, if they could get a missile into attack range. *They can cram more weapons and missile tubes into their hull.*

"Enemy missiles entering point defence envelope," Jean reported. "Point defence engaging…now!"

———

John watched, fighting the urge to bark useless orders, as the first wave of enemy missiles crashed into his defences. Hundreds died, dozens lived long enough to get into engagement range and detonate. He forced himself to watch, grimly, as the damage mounted; four destroyers and a light cruiser blown out of space, two battleships and a fleet carrier lightly damaged. It was less, in fact, than he'd expected, given the reported new warheads. Perhaps there hadn't been too many of those either.

Or perhaps they can only be mounted on gunboats, he thought. *They might be too large to fit on a standard missile.*

"Battlestation One has taken damage," Regal reported. "Battlestation Two appears to have escaped the first barrage…"

"Redeploy the starfighters to weaken her point defence," John ordered. The enemy starships, at least, were keeping their distance. Their starfighters were another story. "And then order the battleships to continue firing."

"Aye, Admiral," Regal said.

John barely heard him as more and more icons flashed up, flickered and died. The automated weapons platforms were largely gone, but the battlestations were *still* fighting despite soaking up a great deal of damage. Their point defence was good, *very* good. He'd hoped he wouldn't have to match his battleships directly against the battlestations, but it was starting to look as though he didn't have a choice.

"Battlestation One is weakening," Regal reported. "I think…"

He broke off as the battlestation's icon vanished from the display, replaced by an expanding sphere of debris. John leaned forward, trying to determine precisely what had happened. A nuclear warhead exploding inside the station, perhaps. The enemy's point defence had been weakening badly…they might have been unable to stop a missile before it flew into a gash in the hull and detonated. But it was impossible to be sure. There had been so many explosions in the vicinity that sensor readings weren't entirely trustworthy.

That's not going to be good for the population below, he thought, sourly. *Or for us, when we land the marines.*

"Order the fleet to come about and engage Battlestation Two," he ordered, instead. New alerts were flashing up in front of him, warning of the presence of ground-based defence stations. "And target the bases on the ground with KEW strikes."

"Aye, Admiral," Regal said. He broke off. "Sir, the enemy starships are withdrawing."

John wasn't surprised, not really. No alien starships had materialised out of cloak to strike at his rear. The enemy *had* to know he'd brought enough firepower to make his victory a foregone conclusion. No, the *smart* move was to fall back, slip into cloak and then wait for reinforcements to arrive. It was annoying - the chance to pinch off and crush a small enemy detachment wasn't one he wanted to miss - but inevitable.

"Detail a pair of scouts to track them," he ordered, curtly. The enemy carriers, at least, were largely harmless until they obtained more starfighters. "And launch another shell of probes to watch our rear."

"Aye, Admiral," Regal said.

———

"Captain," Jean said. "The enemy battlestation is targeting us."

"Open fire," Susan ordered.

Seven battleships opened fire as one, slamming hundreds of plasma bolts into the alien battlestation. It fought back savagely, its plasma cannons blowing point defence systems and sensor blisters off *Vanguard's* hull as it searched for weak spots, but it had to know it was badly outgunned. Susan suspected, although it was hard to be certain, that the alien armour was inferior to *Vanguard's*. But there was so much of it that it hardly mattered.

"Minor damage, section seven," Mason reported. "She's targeting us specifically."

"Continue firing," Susan said. They were locked in a death match now. "And keep firing missiles."

The hull shuddered, time and time again, as enemy weapons slammed into *Vanguard*. Susan watched, keeping her expression under tight control, as the damage started to mount. The battleship was tough, but even *Vanguard* couldn't endure such a pounding indefinitely. She had no idea what would happen if the patchwork repairs failed, yet she had a nasty feeling that it would be fatal. Thankfully, the drive section was on the other side of the hull from the bombardment.

"Captain, Turret Two has jammed," Mason said. "Damage control teams are on the way."

"Good," Susan said. She doubted they could do much, not when there was so much energy crackling over the hull, but she could hope. There was nothing else she could do. "Helm, alter course to allow Turret Two to bear on the targets…"

The alien battlestation started to disintegrate. The waves of incoming fire slackened, then fell off altogether. Susan stared, torn between relief and an odd kind of pity, as the battlestation died. There was no giant explosion, merely a series of small explosions and failures that ended in the entire structure coming apart. Giant chunks of debris rocketed in all directions.

"Tactical, target any piece of junk that looks like it's going to head into the atmosphere," Susan ordered. There were people who would probably call her soft, if they heard, but she had no interest in accidentally causing an atrocity. "Sensors, confirm that Battlestations Three and Four cannot target either us or the planned spacehead."

"They can hit us with missiles," Jean said. "We're out of effective plasma cannon range, even if they *can* bring their weapons to bear on us."

"But that wouldn't be true for shuttles," Mason commented. "Or…"

A new alert blinked up on the display. "*Texas* took a nasty hit from the ground," Charlotte reported. "They've mounted mass drivers on the surface!"

"The flag is ordering all ships to take the ground-based weapons out," Parkinson said. "And then commence bombardment."

Susan turned to watch as KEWs fell through the planet's atmosphere. A ground-based mass driver could pack one hell of a punch, enough to wreck a battleship or vaporise a smaller ship if it scored a direct hit. Hell, the Indians had deployed something similar to make the reconquest of Clarke difficult. But the Foxes didn't seem to have built enough of them to make a difference. Clearly, they'd reasoned that any enemy who got close enough to land on their homeworld would be unstoppable anyway.

And they probably expended as much resources as they could on building their fleet, Susan thought. *Orbital battlestations and ground-based mass drivers can defend a world, but they can't take the fight to the enemy.*

"The mass driver has been destroyed," Charlotte reported. She cursed, just loudly enough for Susan to hear. "They're deploying their shuttles into attack formation."

"Stand by point defence," Susan said.

She silently gave the enemy points for timing. *Vanguard's* point defence had been badly weakened, her hull scorched and broken in a dozen places. Her crew were experts at patching up the damage by now - they'd had plenty of experience - but there was no way they could repair the ship in time to stand off the alien shuttles. And if they were gunboats instead, the task force might be in deep shit.

"They're shuttles," Charlotte said, as the aliens crashed into the CSP. "They're not mounting any point defence."

Thank God, Susan thought. The Foxes were brave, but their desperate flight was futile. *They don't stand a chance of getting close enough to ram.*

"Signal from the flag," Parkinson said, as the last of the shuttles died. "The bombardment is to continue."

"Understood," Susan said.

The Royal Navy - and its counterparts - had learnt a great deal about breaking a heavily industrialised society during the Age of Unrest. It might have been nearly two centuries since Iran and Argentina had been brutally crushed from orbit, after pissing off their enemies one too many times, but the lessons remained useful. John had studied both campaigns in preparation for the operation, learning how best to weaken a developed world and prevent effective resistance. The Foxes might be alien, but they weren't *that* alien.

Spaceports and airports, rail lines and roads, bridges and ports...military bases and power distribution networks, he thought. KEWs were cheap, thankfully. Hundreds of targets had already been hit; hundreds more were still on the list, just waiting to be assigned to a starship for destruction. *We'll smash any hope of organised resistance for hundreds of miles around the spacehead.*

He told himself, sharply, not to get overconfident. The Foxes would be armed, according to the POWs. Even the *Cows* would fight, if they thought they had no other option. And while he knew he could blast anyone stupid enough to use a radio, it was impossible to locate landlines buried deep underground. The fleet could pick off any aircraft moving to attack the spacehead, but *that* wouldn't last. He couldn't afford to be pressed against the planet when the alien reinforcements arrived. There were mass drivers he couldn't reach, on the far side of the planet. They would pose a major headache if he kept his ships within range.

And there's another problem, he reminded himself. *We don't want them to feel we're cheating.*

It was an odd concern. The Royal Navy had long since lost any compassion for Third World fanatics. There was no point in showing compassion, they'd eventually realised, when law itself was turned into a weapon. And yet...here and now...they *had* to beat the Foxes on even terms. Cheating - making it impossible for the Foxes to actually mount a challenge - might cripple the entire mission.

But it feels absurd, he told himself. It went against everything the Royal Navy had learnt, for better or worse, in the wars. *And it is absurd.*

He pushed the thought aside. "Deploy the bombardment platforms," he ordered. Time wasn't entirely on their side. The sooner they landed and set up, the better. "And then signal General Ross. He may commence the landing as planned."

"Aye, Admiral," Regal said.

CHAPTER
THIRTY FOUR

George hadn't been entirely sure what to expect, when she'd walked back into Marine Country after her interview with Captain Onarina and seven hours of restless sleep in a privacy tube. A lecture from Major Andres about her conduct on *Black Hunter*, a million press-ups supervised by Sergeant Tosco, mockery for losing an entire starship in a mission…her imagination had provided too many possibilities. And yet, when she'd walked back through the hatch, she'd been pulled into a whole string of exercises and simulations that somehow blurred into mission prepara-tions. It had been so odd, to her, that it had taken her several days to realise that they'd accepted her.

And yet, as the shuttle undocked from *Vanguard*, she couldn't help wondering if returning had been such a bright idea after all.

"This is your captain speaking," the pilot said, as the shuttle jerked. "Please strap yourself in as this will be a very rough flight, with a high risk of someone trying to kill us. Ground fire is surprisingly strong, despite the best efforts of the tea-sipping spacers. And there are millions of pieces of debris falling down too."

George winced at his tone, silently cursing his mocking cheer She could have flown the shuttle - she'd certainly flown a shuttle on Unity - although she had been shot down over enemy territory. Now, with count-less Foxes below, all plotting an offensive against the human spacehead, she *knew* she was falling into danger. It was worse, somehow, to sit in the seat in full body armour, *knowing* that the slightest hit would destroy them. A glancing blow, something *Vanguard* would shrug off, would shred the shuttle into confetti.

She looked at the marines, wondering how they could be so calm. Didn't they *know* they could die at any second? Didn't they know they could be utterly vaporised by a single hit, before they even knew they were under attack? Didn't they know...she wanted to undo her straps, march forward and take the controls for herself. It would be better to die flying the shuttle than remaining trapped in a small box, waiting to either land or die. But she knew she couldn't do anything of the sort. She could only wait and endure it.

You flew in shuttles you didn't pilot before, her thoughts mocked her.

Yeah, she answered. *But not through unfriendly skies.*

The shuttle lurched, violently. George had no idea what had happened, but her imagination offered all sorts of possibilities. The pilot might have altered course to avoid a piece of debris, a warhead might have detonated far too close to the hull for comfort...she knew she'd never know, not until it was far too late. She gritted her teeth as the shuttle shook, repeatedly, as if the pilot was deliberately seeking out the worst patches of turbulence he could find. She'd flown a shuttle down to Tadpole Prime, a flight that had been thoroughly nightmarish, but this was worse. At least no one on Tadpole Prime had been trying to kill her!

She glanced at the marines. Some of them looked half-asleep, as if they didn't care what was happening; some of them were listening to music or audiobooks through their earpieces. A couple even looked to be praying silently; Sergeant Tosco was leaning forward, his eyes half-closed. George wasn't too surprised that the sergeant was unfazed by the bumpy flight, even the moment when the shuttle threatened to heel over completely just long enough to scare her to death. She couldn't imagine anything that could scare the sergeant.

"Landing in two minutes," the pilot warned. "Departure window is in five, so *hurry*."

"Understood," Sergeant Tosco said. He raised his voice. "Two minutes to landing!"

George nodded, even though sweat was dripping down her back. They'd practiced unloading the shuttle at speed, but she knew it was going to be an absolute nightmare. Sergeant Tosco had grumbled that the exercise planners always left out the emergency, even though the marines were all veterans of multiple combat drops. Hell, even *George* had experience on Unity, although she hadn't *planned* to crash-land. She hastily catalogued her share of the work as the shuttle bounced, so badly she almost threw up, then crashed down hard. Her straps snapped loose a moment later.

No one would have cared if I threw up or wet myself, she thought, as she pulled herself free and stood. Her legs felt weak. *They'd only care if I couldn't pull my weight any longer.*

"Go, go," Sergeant Tosco snapped. "Out, now!"

George settled her rucksack on her shoulders, then picked up one half of her box and half-dragged it towards the hatch. Sammy took the other handle and hefted it up, somehow managing to make it look easy. George rolled her eyes, feeling an odd flicker of envy. No matter how hard she worked, she'd never match any of the marines for raw strength. And even *they* were in awe of artillerymen. Sergeant Pink, who'd drilled unarmed combat into her head, had warned her never to get into a fistfight with an artilleryman. They were *strong*.

The smell struck her as soon as she emerged from the shuttle, a musty scent that reminded her of a garden hothouse. It was hot and moist, the wind shifting constantly to blow a multitude of smells towards her. She couldn't help thinking that the Foxes would probably find the heat uncomfortable, although she knew that might be wishful thinking. The warmth would have been more enjoyable in a bikini than body armour and BDUs.

She glanced around as Sammy pulled her out of the makeshift shuttle-field, towards a couple of markers that had been hastily erected by the first wave. They'd landed in the countryside, in the middle of what she assumed had once been a farm. A couple of dead bodies - both Cows - lay on the ground as they reported to the logistics officer, who checked their crate against a list and then pointed them towards a tent, surrounded by a number of mobile sensor systems. The first wave had also set up ground-based defence stations, including laser antimissile and antiaircraft systems. She hoped - prayed - that it would be enough to keep them safe.

"Seems reasonably organised," Sammy muttered, as they passed the crate to another logistics officer and hurried back towards the assembly point. "I've been in worse places."

George glanced at him, then looked around. Hundreds of shuttles were landing, unloading and taking off…the average time spent on the ground, it seemed, was barely five minutes, if that. Thousands of soldiers from a dozen different nations were running around, shouting in five or six different languages as the military police tried to sort them out. Behind them, a small row of light tanks and men in combat armour were making their way towards the edge of the spacehead. And, in the distance, she could see plumes of smoke rising into the air.

She shivered, despite herself. Each of those plumes marked a KEW strike, a place where a rock had fallen from orbit and destroyed its target. She knew the importance of crippling the enemy's ability to mount an immediate counterattack, but…she looked back at the dead aliens, lying on the ground. It was hard not to feel sorry for the poor creatures. They'd been minding their own business on their homeworld - and it *was* their homeworld, not a replacement - when they'd suddenly found themselves at ground zero. And yet…

War is hell, she thought, as she heard a trio of explosions in the distance. A missile lanced up, aimed at one of the shuttles. *And we're here, in the middle of it.*

She caught sight of Major Andres, barking orders as his men gathered around him. Sammy pulled her towards the major, just as two more senior officers appeared. One of them was a stranger, but the other was all too familiar…she had to keep herself from going up to him and saying hello. Brigadier Percy Schneider was, technically, her cousin. *Adopted* cousin.

And he's also a hero, she reminded herself. *That's why he was promoted so quickly.*

"All right, marines, listen up!" Schneider bellowed. "The Yanks have pushed out the engagement envelope as far as possible, so we're going to back them up and dig trenches for weapons positioning! I want two companies holding the line here" - he jabbed a finger around him - "and two more advancing forward to inspect the alien farm. *Watch* yourselves - the Yanks have already lost five men to improvised booby traps."

George shivered. The British military had a great deal of experience in finding and removing IEDs, but terrorists, insurgents and the just plain desperate kept coming up with interesting ideas to maim or kill British soldiers. Getting caught by a mock-IED on the training field was one thing - soldiers who set one off were often roundly mocked by their comrades - yet getting caught by a *real* IED would be far worse. She'd heard all the horror stories about soldiers having their legs - or genitals - blown off, about wounded soldiers who couldn't be rescued because they were trapped in a field of IEDs...

"Grab your tools," Sergeant Tosco ordered. "You have trenches to dig."

"Ouch," Sammy muttered.

George shrugged as she unhooked her entrenching tool and went to work. *She* would have preferred to search the alien farmsteads too, but there was no point in arguing. General Ross had plotted out the defences in some detail, according to the constant set of updates; fixed weapons and mobile tanks were moved forward as trenches were dug, ready to defend the spacehead. She needed to do her part before all hell broke loose.

She glanced up as she saw a series of flashes in the sky. The enemy were shelling them from a distance, trying to smash the spacehead. She was surprised they hadn't managed to mount a ground-based offensive yet, although maybe that wasn't a surprise. The continent was large, larger than Europe and Africa put together. Predicting their landing site would have required precognition, even if one assumed the spacehead *had* to be near to a city. The aliens would need time to get their forces assembled, then marched off to war.

Who gets there the first with the most, she mused. *That's who'll win the engagement.*

———

"And now it's a race," General Ross mused. "Who gets there the first with the most wins."

"Yes, sir," Brigadier Percy Schneider said. "And they're already scrambling to muster their forces."

He peered down at the live feed from dozens of stealth drones, spreading out in an ever-increasing radius around the spacehead. The Foxes were proving depressingly good at shooting them down, but they - and the orbital platforms - were still sending back enough imagery to confirm that the aliens were readying themselves for war. Nowhere in Britain - and perhaps not even in America - would have been *quite* so heavily armed. The aliens only needed a little organisation before they mounted their counteroffensive.

And a few hundred heavy weapons and tanks too, he added, silently. *They're going to need them before they have a hope of breaking our lines.*

"The scouts have already skirmished with the aliens," Ross commented. "They'll be forming a defensive line now."

He glanced at Percy. "You've served on Vesy," he said. "Do you have an opinion?"

"Nothing we haven't already discussed in the pre-landing briefings," Percy said.

He found it hard to keep his irritation out of his voice. Vesy was an alien world, true, but it wasn't *Vixen*. What was true of the Vesy might not be true of the Foxes - and the simple fact that *two* races lived on this world changed everything. The interaction between humans and Tadpoles had already produced all sorts of ideas, some of them remarkable. Who knew what the Foxes and Cows had produced?

"Warn the men, if you wish, not to take anything for granted," he added. "An alien weapon might not *look* like a weapon. Or something might set them off quite by accident..."

He shrugged. General Ross - a relative of the famed *Rhino* Ross, who had served with Percy's father - was a tough, competent officer. But he had the American prejudice against aristocracy in spades...prejudice Percy had to admit he would have shared, if he hadn't benefited from it so much. Being the son of a war hero and the adopted son of *another* had done wonders for his promotion prospects, but so too had his success on Vesy and Clarke.

"The plan is sound, General," he said. "All we need to do now is hunker down and wait for their response."

"Yeah," Ross agreed. "And what if they decide to launch nuclear-tipped missiles at us?"

Percy nodded, sourly. It was the *great* wild card. The xenospecialists insisted that the Foxes *instinctively* assumed that all races thought along the same lines as themselves - a mistake humans had been known to make too - but they could be wrong. And if they were wrong…if the Foxes had decided that humans didn't deserve the courtesies of war, thousands of soldiers might be caught in the blast and killed.

And we draw lines too, he reminded himself. *We think nothing of bombing villages in Africa, but refuse to kill Indian POWs.*

He scowled, inwardly, as he checked the latest set of updates. It was a common debate, usually raised by civilians who knew nothing of war. And Penny, he admitted quietly to himself. The villages in Africa harboured terrorists and insurgents, terrorists who paid no heed to the laws of war and were thus denied their protections; Indian POWs had fought - and been captured - according to the rules, therefore mistreating them was a war crime deserving of harsh punishment. It wasn't fair, Penny had argued years ago. The villagers were rarely given a choice when the terrorists moved in.

And perhaps she's right, he thought. *But no one cares any longer.*

"The shuttles have taken heavier losses," he said, "but we should be able to get everything set up by the time the enemy mount their counteroffensive."

"Quite," Ross agreed. "And if we assume the projections are accurate, we have two days - three at most - before the alien reinforcements arrive."

Percy nodded. He'd served on enough starships to understand that ETAs were precisely that - *estimated* times of arrival. There was no *guarantee* that the alien reinforcements would arrive on schedule. They might have decided to gamble and push their drives to the limit, risking a drive failure, or they might have decided to take it slowly and draw off reinforcements from other bases as they returned home. And the analysts might have fucked up the analysis completely…

"We can't help it, sir," he said, finally. They'd been committed from the moment they'd landed on Vixen. Pulling out now wasn't an option, unless the Foxes could be convinced to let them go. "All we can do is dig in and hope for the best."

"Then keep mustering the defences," Ross ordered. "I'll keep the scouts probing forward."

Percy saluted as he turned and left, although he wasn't sure just how *effective* Ross's tactics were going to be. Standard doctrine for dealing with a spacehead was to seal it off, bleed the landing forces and finally thrust forward to crush it below dozens of tank treads. But no one had ever actually tried the tactic in real life, not until now. Normally, anyone in a position to land troops and mount a ground offensive controlled the high orbitals. And that meant...

We'll find out, he told himself. Outside, he could hear explosions as alien shells were intercepted in midflight. So far, the aliens hadn't managed to bring enough artillery to bear on the spacehead. *And if they come at us before they're ready, all the better for us.*

––––––––

Night was falling by the time George and the marines were called back to the heart of the spacehead, passing lines of freshly-arrived soldiers, tanks and pallets of supplies. George felt sore and grimy - and yet oddly happy - as they were given rations and told to find somewhere to set up a stove. Corporal Rawlings collected the ration packs while Corporal Flynn produced a stove, a pot and a large kettle, then mixed them all together with various spices and sauces. The result - the compo - looked ghastly, but George had to admit it tasted better than the ration packs.

There were no tents, she discovered, as she used the makeshift facilities. She was too tired to give a damn that she was sharing the latrine with a bunch of men from far too many different nations. Given that she was covered in mud - and probably smelt foul - she rather doubted that any of them had *noticed* anything different about her. She stumbled back to the squad, then lay down on the mushy ground next to Sammy. The skies were alive with pieces of debris, falling into the atmosphere and burning up before they hit the ground. It was almost hypnotic, if she chose to ignore what it was. Pieces of junk that might survive the passage through the atmosphere, dust that would affect the planetary ecosystem, dead bodies - human and alien - falling to their destruction...

She sighed as she closed her eyes. If they were lucky - she hoped they were lucky - the orbiting fleet would have smashed anything that could pose a threat. If not...she'd been a child when the Tadpoles had attacked Earth, but she still recalled the fear. The entire world had come far too close to collapse. And now, with a genuine alien invasion underway, who knew how the Foxes would react?

And, on that thought, she fell asleep.

CHAPTER
THIRTY FIVE

"The enemy are definitely keeping their distance," Jean reported, as Susan peered over her shoulder. "But at least they don't pose a threat."

Susan wasn't so sure. It was true that the handful of enemy starships remaining within the system couldn't liberate Vixen, but it was *also* true that they could harass the task force or intercept and destroy any independent detachments that might be sent out to raid the remainder of the system. Merely bringing the fleet train *into* the system had been risky, even though there had been no choice. Engineers were, even now, scrambling over *Vanguard* and the other ships, transferring missiles and making - once again - hasty repairs.

"Keep an eye on them," she ordered, finally. The entire conflict seemed to have stalemated, for now. But it wouldn't last. Enemy reinforcements were already on their way. She didn't need an FTL communicator to know *that*. "Mr. XO?"

"The basic repairs have been completed, Captain," Mason said. "But Mr. Finch isn't confident that the makeshift armour will hold, if we engage the enemy a second time."

Susan scowled. "There's no way to improve it?"

"Not without a shipyard, Captain," Mason said. "We've locked the armour in place, but the hull plates aren't melded together. We can't do that here."

"We need a mobile shipyard," Susan grumbled.

She shook her head in annoyance. She'd seen proposals for something along those lines, but they'd never got off the drawing board. They would be too ungainly, the designers had said, too easy for a prowling enemy to pick off from a distance. And while she knew the naysayers were right, she had to admit a mobile shipyard would have been very helpful right now. There were limits to what Mr. Finch and his wonder-workers could do.

And if we were in a shipyard, with our rear open to space, she thought darkly, *a single missile would be enough to obliterate us.*

"We'll try to keep the vulnerable portion of our hull away from them," she said. It would be simple enough, in a straight battering match, but she knew the coming engagement could easily turn into a melee. "Jean, make sure the tactical computers are reprogrammed to take that into account."

"Aye, Captain," Jean said.

Susan looked down at the datapad, then up at the system display. Every instinct she had was calling for the task force to go on the rampage, to smash every last cloudscoop and asteroid mining station - and industrial node - within range. Tearing the guts out of the enemy's industrial base would make the outcome of the war inevitable, no matter what surprises and innovations the enemy had devised. And yet, she knew her orders. The task force had thrown down a gauntlet. They had to wait to see if the enemy would pick it up.

We may have called the dance, but we're dancing to their tune, she thought, resentfully. The plan had seemed perfect, on paper; now, she had her doubts. Trying to turn the enemy's culture and biology against them was one thing, but there were limits. *And who knows what they will bring to bear against us?*

"They should be here by now," she said, shortly. "Where are they?"

"We don't know when they set off," Mason pointed out. "Captain, they may not have *believed* the reports until we entered ES-18."

"It's possible, Captain," Jean added. "The early reports from Vera Cruz weren't believed until hard recordings reached Earth."

Susan shrugged. Back then, everyone had *known* there were no other intelligent races in the universe. But the Foxes *knew* that their enemies had access to tramlines they couldn't use...yet. They should have been *more* willing to believe in enemy fleets materialising behind their lines, not less. And yet...humanity had known the alien-grade tramlines existed, they just hadn't been able to use them. Maybe the

Foxes had reasoned there was *no* way anyone could reach ES-19 until it had become undeniable. They hadn't been wrong, either, until the jump drive had been invented.

"We'll see," she said.

She sat down in the command chair and studied the display. Everyone had assumed the Foxes would do everything in their power to mount an immediate counterattack, but what if they didn't? What if they were content to allow the stalemate to continue? Susan couldn't imagine being willing to allow an enemy power to control Sol, certainly not any longer than strictly necessary, but the Foxes might feel differently. They might even gamble on wear and tear breaking down her starships before mounting a counteroffensive of their own. *Susan* wouldn't have cared to try - there would be no way to be *sure* the enemy ships had been weakened - yet the enemy might try. They *knew* they were on the cusp between victory or defeat.

But they're not, she told herself, sharply. *Either we beat them and force them to surrender or we destroy much of their industrial base. We win, either way.*

She sighed. A *rational* species would be trying to negotiate by now, while it still had some bargaining power. But the Foxes weren't human… she cautioned herself, again, against thinking they *thought* like humans. They might be closer to humanity than the Tadpoles, but they weren't *human*. Their thoughts and actions were dangerously unpredictable. They might decide that throwing caution to the winds and launching an all-out attack on Tadpole Prime - or Earth - was the only way to win.

And if they do, she thought, *we still win.*

"All we can do is wait," she said. "And so we shall."

She grinned, rather humourlessly. "And organise another set of exercises," she ordered. "We may as well make use of the time, while we wait."

"Aye, Captain," Mason said. "Gunboats and battleships?"

"And long-range missiles," Susan added. "Everything we might reasonably expect to face, scaled up to the nines. We don't want to be caught by surprise when the shit finally hits the fan."

Vixen, Penny thought as she stepped off the shuttle, smelled odd. *Every* planet had its own smell, something utterly indefinable and yet unique, but Vixen had something *alien* mingled into its scent. It wasn't really a surprise, she told herself as she breathed in the smell. She'd stood on Vesy, years ago. That, too, had been an alien world.

"Step away from the shuttle," someone ordered. "We're moving supplies out now!"

Penny flushed as she hurried towards the markers that designated the edge of the makeshift spaceport. She'd been an embedded reporter for eight years, ever since her first cruise on HMS *Warspite*. She *knew* how to behave, yet...she'd made a rookie mistake. But how many people could really claim to have set foot on two alien worlds? Most civilians never even left *Britain*, let alone Earth.

The spacehead was a mess, a strange mixture of prefabricated buildings, tents and dozens of armoured vehicles. Thousands of soldiers were running around, unloading shuttles and transporting their supplies to the defence lines. She heard explosions in the distance as alien shells were intercepted, blown out of the air before they could reach their targets. She'd been told that the front lines were quiet, but the enemy were clearly still harassing the soldiers as best as they could. They certainly didn't want to give the humans any chance to relax.

We're on their world, Penny thought, as she slowed to a halt. She'd been told *someone* would meet her at the spaceport. *Of course they're not going to let us relax!*

"Penny," an oddly familiar voice called.

Penny turned and stared. A marine was walking towards her, wearing body armour and a helmet that concealed his face. He had a rifle slung over his shoulder, a pistol and a computer terminal at his belt...Penny was an experienced reporter, but it still took her several seconds to realise she was actually looking at a *woman*. And it took her longer still to recognise the face. The dirt and grime covering her features obscured them far too well.

She found her voice. "George?"

"In person," George said. Even the *voice* was different. "Long time no see."

Penny nodded, struggling to find something to say. George was, technically, her cousin - her *adopted* cousin. And yet, they'd never really socialised. George had been ten, if Penny recalled correctly, when Admiral Fitzwilliam had adopted Penny and Percy. She'd been fifteen years old at the time. George had been too young to be anything more than an acquaintance. And while George had grown into adulthood, Penny had been building her career.

She looked her cousin up and down. George looked…*messy*, her uniform stained with dirt and mud. And yet, she also looked *happy*. Penny shook her head in frank disbelief. She was no stranger to hardship - the key to get soldiers to open up to you was to share their lives as much as possible - but it wasn't something she really enjoyed. If she'd wanted to spend her life in the mud, she would have volunteered for the reclamation squads or the handful of military units that accepted women.

"You're looking good," she said, finally.

"Liar," George said. "I'm covered in shit."

She beckoned for Penny to follow her. Penny obeyed, remembering one of the big - and thoroughly awkward - family dinners she'd endured. George had gotten into real trouble with her mother, Penny recalled, because she'd gone out and played on the estate - messing up her clothes - rather than walking around like a little doll. It didn't look as though things had changed much, although George probably wasn't getting in deep shit for being muddy *now*. She was hardly the only person coated in mud.

I'll be coated in mud too, by the end of the day, Penny thought. Her boots were already muddy as she picked her way through the remains of the field. The ground had been torn up so thoroughly that there were hardly any traces of grass and crops left. Water pooled in places where tanks had driven through the mud as they made their way towards the front and into enemy territory. *And so will everyone else.*

"I haven't seen you in years," she said, truthfully. "How did you get down here?"

"It's a long story," George said. She didn't look back. "And really, I'm not sure where I fit in right now."

Penny nodded, thoughtfully. "And what is *really* going on?"

George stopped and turned. "What do you mean?"

"I've been to enough military deployments," Penny told her, "to know that the CO always gives me the best possible picture, whatever is actually happening on the ground. What's *really* going on?"

"I don't think General Ross would lie to you," George said. She smiled. "Do you think your *brother* would lie to you?"

"He's my brother," Penny said. "It's in the job description."

George smirked. "I lied to Anne so many times…"

Her voice trailed off. "You know she'd *hate* this place?"

Penny nodded. Anne Fitzwilliam looked and acted like a doll, a pretty princess with no thoughts or feelings of her own. Perhaps that was a little harsh, Penny thought, but she'd rarely seen anything to indicate that Anne was anything more than an extension of her social-climbing mother. It was hard, really, to believe that George and Anne were related. They were just so *different*.

But if George grew her hair long, she mused, *she would look a great deal more like her sister.*

George cleared her throat. "The truth…Anne couldn't *handle* the truth!"

Penny had to laugh. "*I* can handle the truth."

"Hah," George said. She shrugged, then turned away. "The truth is that we have established the defensive lines, as planned, and sent out scout teams, as planned, and are skirmishing with the enemy, as planned. So far, the enemy has declined to throw everything they have at us, *not* as planned. But we're fairly sure they're moving forces into position to hit us."

"When their reinforcements arrive," Penny finished. "Otherwise… they'd just be smashed from orbit."

"Probably," George agreed.

She stopped, just for a second. "I think it's going to be a bloodbath," she added. "I've been hearing stories…the Cows don't seem to fight, unless you force them into a corner, but the Foxes attack on sight. They're armed to the teeth, too. I heard a couple of Americans arguing that the Foxes were better armed than Texans. Antitank weapons, mortars…even plasma cannons."

Penny lifted her eyebrows. American gun control laws were so loose they might as well not have existed - and Texas had the loosest laws of all - but there were limits. Had the Foxes always expected an invasion? Or was it just their natural aggression demanding release? If the xenospecialists were right, the Foxes *always* existed in a state of low-grade conflict. It was how they sorted out the pecking order.

And aren't you glad humans don't settle things that way, she thought. *Would you have won your spot if you'd had to arm-wrestle Clark for it?*

"That's bad," she said, finally.

"Yeah," George agreed. "Penny, we took casualties from Foxes who are - effectively - civilians. What's going to happen when we run into more of their soldiers?"

Penny said nothing as they reached the command tent. It was instantly recognisable: armed guards outside, a handful of flags fluttering in the moist air...she wondered, absently, if it was actually *wise* to mark the tent for all to see. The Foxes could be flying their own stealth drones over the spacehead, quietly marking down targets for destruction. Who knew what would happen *then*?

They'll move as soon as the shit hits the fan, she told herself. *And then...*

"Good luck," George said. She smiled. "I'll be waiting outside."

Penny grinned. "What *are* you doing down here?"

"Right now, I appear to be a gofer," George said. She smiled, ruefully. "Believe me, it beats digging trenches - or latrines."

"I believe you," Penny said. "And I'll see you later."

———

"At the risk of sounding like a whiny little brat," Henry said, "I wish to protest at your decision to allow reporters to go down to the ground, but not me."

Admiral Naiser smiled. "You're rather more important than any reporter," he pointed out, dryly. "But your protest has been duly noted."

Henry sighed. Personally, he wouldn't shed any tears - he'd even raise a glass - if he heard that one or two reporters had been killed on Vixen. He wouldn't piss on a reporter who happened to be on fire, even the one or two reporters who weren't complete wankers who thought his private life was fair game. There was no fate horrible enough for a reporter...and yet he couldn't help feeling annoyed that reporters had been allowed to go down to the planet, without him.

"I'm not that important," he said, although he knew it was pointless. "The task force doesn't need me to survive."

"It *does* need you to negotiate peace, after the battle," Admiral Naiser said. "And your chances of survival are much higher on *King Edward*."

That, Henry admitted, was true. His prestige, at least as far as the Foxes were concerned, would be obliterated if he was captured. They'd certainly never take him seriously. And the giant battleship had a much greater chance of survival than the men on the ground. But it still felt *wrong*, somehow, not to share the danger. The whole operation had been *his* concept, even if it had been extensively refined during the planning stages. He *should* be down there with them.

"This isn't about my survival," he said, crossly. "Admiral…"

Admiral Naiser held up a hand. "You may appeal my decision, if you wish," he said. "But I will not change my mind."

Henry snorted. The closest superior officer was light-years away. Even if he sent an appeal direct to Unity, it would be weeks before any response arrived. And the officers there would hesitate to overrule the man on the spot, particularly given Henry's…odd…position in the line of succession. Admiral Naiser would probably be told to carry on the good work.

"Understood," he said, finally. "I'm just…bored."

"Be glad of it," Admiral Naiser said. He gave Henry a droll look. "Why did you become a starfighter pilot?"

"I liked the thought of fast starfighters and faster women," Henry said. It wasn't entirely untrue, but it was hardly a complete answer. Women had been throwing themselves at him for years. If they'd known about the gilded cage, perhaps they would have thought better of it. "I watched *Stellar Star: Carrier Commander* and fell in love."

Admiral Naiser looked disapproving. "And your family *let* you?"

Henry sighed. "They wanted me to take a different path," he said. "But none of them held out any real prospect for excitement."

He shrugged. "Why did *you* become a starfighter pilot? And why did you leave?"

"I and a…a friend were determined to sign up together," Admiral Naiser said. "And we did - we even managed to get ourselves into the same unit. And then he was killed on *Canopus* and I thought I needed a change."

"Ah," Henry said. "You didn't want excitement? Or romance?"

"I thought I was serving my country," Admiral Naiser said. "And I was right…"

The intercom bleeped. "Admiral, this is Hamish in Plotting," a voice said. "Long-range scouts have detected an alien fleet moving towards us."

"Understood," Admiral Naiser said. He sounded grim, even though everyone had *known* the aliens would counterattack as soon as possible. "Alert the fleet."

Henry glanced at the display, then sighed. "I'll go back to my quarters, Admiral."

"Stay here," Admiral Naiser said. He essayed a black joke. "You may as well see the missile that kills you."

"Thanks," Henry said. "I'll try to keep my eyes closed."

CHAPTER
THIRTY SIX

"Captain," Lieutenant Cathy Powell said. "I think you ought to see this."

Captain David Atwell looked up, sharply. HMAS *Darwin* had been on patrol long enough for him and his crew to get thoroughly bored, although he knew - all too well - that *Darwin* had no place in the line of battle. She had been on the brink of obsolescence even before the First Interstellar War and the only reason the Royal Australian Navy had retained her services was because of a simple shortage of hulls. The engineers could - and had - crammed hundreds of modern systems into her hull, but there were limits to what they could do. It was all too likely that *Darwin's* next engagement would be her last.

"Show me," he ordered.

Powell tapped her console. "There's a faint set of energy flickers here," she said. "I would have dismissed them as background radiation, but there's a definite *pattern* to the vibrations that *has* to be unnatural."

"And it's inbound from Tramline Three," David mused. Cathy was the best sensor tech in the navy, as far as he could tell. "That's the direct link to the front."

"Yes, sir," Cathy said.

David studied the display for a long moment, considering the situation. The Foxes *had* to be trying to sneak up on Vixen and engage the task force before it could react. There couldn't be any other explanation, unless Cathy had made a mistake. And that meant...

"Communications, send a priority-one signal to Admiral Naiser," he ordered. "Inform him that we have unwelcome visitors."

"Aye, sir," Lieutenant Raleigh said.

"Helm, prepare to adjust course," David added. *Darwin* was cloaked, but they'd be exposed as soon as they sent the signal. "Keep us close enough to shadow them."

"Aye, Captain."

David settled back into his command chair. Admiral Naiser had been right. The Foxes were coming to liberate their homeworld and drive away the human interlopers...

An alarm sounded. "They just swept us," Cathy snapped. "Active sensor sweep!"

They must have given up on sneaking around, David thought. *A human might have hesitated in hopes of breaking contact.*

"Drop the cloak," he snapped. On the display, brilliant red icons were snapping into existence. "Helm, reverse course..."

"Enemy starfighters inbound," Cathy said. "Captain..."

"Alert the task force that I do not expect to be able to avoid engagement," David ordered, bleakly. *Darwin* was far too close to the enemy fleet to escape. In hindsight, perhaps he should have...he gritted his teeth, dismissing the thought. Getting the word out took priority, even if it risked his ship. "And then bring us around. Prepare to engage."

"Aye, Captain."

———

Susan jerked awake as alarms howled through the battleship. She sat upright, hurled herself out of bed and slapped her wristcom while reaching for her trousers. "Report!"

"*Darwin* detected an incoming enemy fleet before being overwhelmed and destroyed," Mason reported. "They'll be on us in thirty minutes."

"Understood," Susan said. She'd hoped for more time. "I'm on my way."

She briefly considered a shower, but she doubted she had time to wash properly. Instead, she pulled her trousers on, then hastily buttoned up her uniform shirt before grabbing her jacket and heading for the hatch. Her instructors at the academy would have had a *lot* of sarcastic things to say about her appearance, she was sure, but *they* weren't the ones facing a large enemy fleet. She pulled her jacket on as she hurried down the corridor, passing a pair of marines as the ship rushed to battlestations. Maybe she *did* look unkempt. It hardly mattered when the ship was going to war.

"Captain," Mason said, as she stepped through the hatch and onto the bridge. A low rumble echoed through the hull as the drives came up to full power. "Admiral Naiser has ordered us to prepare to leave orbit on attack vector."

As planned, Susan reminded herself. *We don't want to get caught against the planet itself.*

"I have the bridge," she said, sitting down. "Status report?"

"All departments report ready," Mason said. "The fleet is gearing up to leave orbit now."

"Take us out with them," Susan ordered. "Long-range sensor report?"

"Twelve battleships, four fleet carriers and at least seventy smaller ships," Charlotte reported, grimly. "They're flying in such close formation that I don't have a solid lock on *all* of their smaller units..."

Susan's blood ran cold. Twelve battleships, four fleet carriers...this was no raid, but a cold-blooded attempt to destroy the task force. But then, she'd expected no less. The Foxes *knew* they had to crush the task force, preferably before it tore the system's industrial base to shreds. They must have departed the front shortly after the task force tore through ES-18, she decided after a moment. The enemy planners must have hoped they could reinforce their homeworld before it was too late.

It was too late, she thought. *But now...*

"Coordinate the datanet links with the remainder of the fleet," Susan ordered. "And be ready to move out on command."

"Aye, Captain," Reed said.

"Tactical combat links engaged," Jean added. "We have primary, secondary and tertiary links up and running."

"Very good," Susan said. It was going to be a battering match, one the humans might well lose. But they'd take one hell of a bite out of the enemy ships before they died. "Stand by to deploy ECM drones."

"Aye, Captain," Jean said.

Mason snorted. "The beancounters will throw a fit."

Susan had to smile, feeling a flicker of gallows humour. Sure, the beancounters *would* throw a fit about the expenditure, *if* there was anyone left to hear it. If there wasn't…well, battleships were *far* more expensive than even the most advanced ECM drones. And they took longer to build too. She would prefer to be lectured for wasting His Majesty's Government's valuable property than being blown away, along with her ship. It was unlikely they'd do more than moan at her, loudly. A court martial would require the bureaucrats to explain to a captain's board precisely *why* the ECM drones were considered more important than a battleship. It wouldn't go well for them.

"Signal from the flag," Parkinson said. "The task force is to leave orbit."

"Take us out," Susan ordered.

"Revised time to contact," Jean put in, as the fleet moved out of orbit. "Thirteen minutes at current velocity."

God help the people on the ground, Susan thought. *They're practically on their own now.*

She glanced at Mason. "Deploy damage control teams, as planned," she ordered. "And then ready the ship for close-quarter combat."

"Aye, Captain," Mason said.

Susan gritted her teeth. This was it, the final engagement. One way or the other, it was going to be the last. And then…

"Receiving updated targeting information," Jean said. "The freighter crews are moving into position now."

"Very good," Susan said. "Hold course and speed."

"Aye, Captain," Reed said.

———

"Well," Prince Henry said. "It seems that we were right."

"Barely," John muttered. "They must have pulled their reserves *right* off the front."

He stroked his chin, feeling stubble against his fingers. It was possible the Foxes had held back their main force for some inscrutable alien reason, but they couldn't be *that* alien. Only a complete madman would risk letting an alien fleet hold position in their most valuable star system indefinitely. John's contingency plans would ensure the destruction of most of the industrial base, even if the task force was smashed to rubble. No, they'd yanked forces back from the front...

And that gives Admiral Stirling a chance to give them hell, he thought. *Either they gave chase or they merely took the opportunity to recover the occupied star systems...*

He pushed the thought out of his head. There was no way to *know* what had happened, no way to be sure how much of the plan had actually worked. They'd done *their* bit - they'd forced the enemy to cope with a second front - and now they had to hold out until the end.

"Twelve battleships," he said. It was possible that their estimates of the enemy's industrial potential were *way* out, but twelve battleships was a significant force by any standards. "And they sent them here."

"They're desperate," Prince Henry said.

"Perhaps," John said. "Send the challenge."

He looked at Commander Jackson Regal. "Signal the fleet," he ordered. "Missile pods are to be deployed on my command."

"Aye, sir," Regal said.

"And starfighters are to be launched as planned," John added. There was no point in trying to be clever, not now. Half his starfighters would attack while the other half would defend, keeping the enemy off balance as much as possible. "And warn the fleet that there will be no retreat."

He leaned forward, studying the red icons as they advanced towards him in a ponderous mass of death and destruction. There was enough firepower in the enemy fleet to do *real* damage to Earth or Tadpole Prime, no matter how heavily they were defended. Hell, it had been sheer - and costly - luck that HMAS *Darwin* had detected the enemy starships before they could get into weapons range. John had been careful to keep his ships ready for combat, but no naval force could hope to remain on full alert indefinitely. Exhaustion would have worn his men out a long time before the enemy put in an appearance.

"They haven't responded," Henry said.

"I think I can understand what they're saying," John said, wryly. "*Oh yeah? Make us.*"

"Yes, Admiral," Henry said. "They need to be battered into submission."

Playground stuff, John thought. He'd grown up in a rough area, where disputes between schoolchildren had been settled with fists rather than reasoned discourse. The social hierarchy had been based on strength, not decency or popularity. *They haven't really grown up.*

But was that such a bad thing? Schoolyard fights had ended with bumps and bruises, not broken bones or dead bodies. He'd never fought to the death, not until he'd joined the navy; he'd never killed a man with his bare hands. But…he shook his head. It *was* bad. If one was strong, one held all the cards; if one was weak, one bent over and took it. As a child, he'd disliked the teachers who were supposed to be in control; as an adult, he couldn't help feeling sorry for them. They were caught between the need to maintain discipline and the need for a quiet life. The Foxes were shaped by their biology…

He shook his head as the timer reached zero. "Signal the carriers," he ordered. "All starfighters are to launch. I say again, all starfighters are to launch."

———

"Go, go, go!"

Flying Officer Mahubala Choudhury braced herself as the starfighter rocketed down the launch shaft and into interplanetary space. The craft's drives came online a second later, shoving her away from the giant super-carrier and out towards the alien fleet. They were already launching their own starfighters, an immense swarm of craft that threatened to over-whelm the human ships. She couldn't help noticing that the Allies were outnumbered two-to-one.

Her radio crackled. "So," Flying Officer Jonny Roberson said. "Drink and dinner tonight?"

Mahubala rolled her eyes. English pilots were the worst, as far as she could tell, although she had to admit that American pilots came a close second. Jonny Roberson hadn't been partnered with her for more than five minutes before he'd started trying to lure her into bed. Perhaps English pilots were allowed to do whatever they liked, as long as they put their lives on the line every day, but *Indian* pilots didn't have so much freedom. *She* had to be chaste if she wanted the men to respect her, even though *they* spent half their time chasing girls...

Maybe it's just a male thing, she thought. *Although their female flyers are just as bad.*

"Stay in formation," she ordered, as the enemy starfighters drew closer. "And watch my back."

"I'd pay money to watch your back," Roberson said. "You look *great* in your shipsuit."

"It could cost you your life," Mahubala said, dryly. The enemy starfighters were breaking up, half boosting onwards to engage the fleet, the other half slowing to engage the human starfighters. The odds were improving, slightly. "Engage tactical computers on my mark...*mark.*"

She keyed the firing switch as the enemy starfighters came into range, firing madly. They clearly had more faith in their plasma cannons than *she* did, although a decade of intensive research and development had reduced the problem of overheating plasma confinement chambers. She saw an enemy starfighter explode as she took a shot at it, then yanked her craft to one side as another enemy pilot sought revenge for the death of his friend. Roberson picked him off a second later, covering her back. She allowed herself to feel appreciation for as long as she dared - about half a second - and then swung into another set of evasive patterns. Flying a predictable pattern in the middle of a fight was asking to get killed.

"The bombers are punching through," the wing commander said. "All units, form up and cover them."

Mahubala nodded to herself. The bombers were blasting towards the enemy ships, trying to leave the enemy starfighters in the dust. Naturally, the starfighter pilots had different ideas and were giving chase...she picked off a careless flyer, then cursed under her breath as she saw a brother flyer die. Raman had been rude and unpleasant to her ever since she'd boarded the carrier - she had no idea *what* was wrong with him - but he knew how to fly. His death was a bad omen.

The enemy battleships opened fire as the bombers closed in, filling space with bolt after bolt of supercharged plasma. Their firing was essentially random, but they were firing so many blasts that it hardly mattered. A dozen bombers died as they closed to engagement range, four more died even as they fired their torpedoes. She had the satisfaction of watching an enemy carrier stagger under their fire a heartbeat before two more of her fellow pilots died in flames. An instant later, the enemy carrier followed them into death.

"Scratch one flattop," an American voice jeered. "We got her!"

Barely, Mahubala thought. *And they still have far more fighters than us.*

She gritted her teeth as the fighters wheeled around to escape the enemy ships. There was no point in remaining close now the bombers had spent their missiles. She had to escort them back to the carriers to rearm before it was too late. The rest of the starfighters fell in with her, a mixture of craft from five different nations. Thankfully, weeks of exercises - and real combat - had smoothed out the edges...

"Here they come," Roberson said.

"Stand by," Mahubala ordered.

The enemy starfighters fell on their formation like hawks on starlings. Standard practice was to ignore the bombers that had expended their missiles, but the enemy didn't seem to have read the manual. But then, there just weren't *enough* bombers to force them to divert their attention to covering their ships. She cursed as two more bombers exploded, then shot madly at an enemy pilot who evaded her blasts with mocking ease. Roberson got him a moment later.

"Hey, you want to have a competition?" Roberson asked. "Winner..."

His voice cut off, abruptly. Mahubala barely had a second to register his death before his killer tried to pick her off too. She threw the starfighter into a crazy spin, then fired back madly in the hopes of scaring her attacker off. But it was too late.

An instant later, there was a wave of heat and pain...

...And then nothing.

———

"The starfighters have taken heavy losses," Regal said.

"Order them to continue the attack," John said. He wasn't too surprised. The enemy had outnumbered his flyers from the start. "Are the missile pods deployed?"

"Yes, sir," Regal said. "They're in position."

John nodded. There would be complaints, he was sure, about expending so many missiles in a single engagement, particularly as most of them would be wasted. But anyone who wasn't a barmy bureaucratic bean-counter would understand. The task force was on a death ride now, he knew, and damned be he who first said *enough*. Besides, unless they got very lucky, escape was no longer a possibility.

"Fire the missile pods," he ordered.

The enemy had placed free-floating missiles in space to augment their forces. *He* hadn't known which vector the enemy would choose, but he *had* prepped the freighters to offload their pods into deep space and fire them on command. Thousands of missiles flickered to life and roared towards the enemy, a barrage right out of a bad simulation or a worse movie. It might have been his imagination, but the enemy ships had seemed to flinch as the missiles launched. So many missiles meant that some - perhaps many - would get through.

"They're recalling their starfighters," Regal reported.

"They'll be using them to take down some of the missiles," Prince Henry put in.

John nodded, concealing his irritation. As a former starfighter pilot, he was *quite* familiar with the tactic. And it would work too, despite the ECM drones and other tricks crammed into the barrage. The enemy would *significantly* weaken his punch before it reached its targets. But they couldn't stop it, he told himself firmly. Some of the missiles would *definitely* get through.

"Order our starfighters to give chase," he said. It would put a hell of a lot of strain on his remaining pilots, but there was no time to do anything else. "Don't give them a chance to adapt."

He paused. "And signal all ships," he added. The missiles were finding their targets now, clumping up as they surged onwards. "The battleline will advance to engage the enemy."

CHAPTER
THIRTY SEVEN

"Signal from the task force," General Ross said, as Percy ran into the command tent. "The enemy has been sighted and a battle is expected at any moment."

"I see," Percy said. "And the enemy on the ground?"

"No sign as yet, but we expect that to change," Ross said. "They timed it well."

"Very well," Percy agreed. It was almost dawn. "At least we're ready to face them."

"Let us hope so," Ross said. "They'll never have a better chance to crush us than now."

Percy nodded in agreement. "We'll stop them, sir."

"Spread the word," Ross ordered. "If they come at us, we hold."

———

We should have had more training on Vesy, Lieutenant Charles Baskerville thought, as the small patrol inched forward. *It would have taught us more about alien worlds.*

He gritted his teeth, scanning from side to side with his night-vision goggles. Vixen was hot, muddy and thoroughly unpleasant, as far as he was concerned. Charles had fought in Mexico, Iran and North Korea, but Vixen was the worst place he'd ever served. There were no friendly natives, no safe bases behind the wire…in hindsight, perhaps it had been a mistake to join the USMC instead of the National Guard. The Guard didn't have to go off-world and fight aliens.

And the aliens are just as devious as the fuckers on Earth, he reminded himself, as he caught sight of an alien habitation. It looked like an earthen hovel, one of the stupid homes designed by freaks who wanted to get closer to nature. The marines had explored two of them, then ruled the remainder off limits after a dozen jarheads had been killed in an explosion. *We can't take anything for granted here.*

He tensed as he heard something moving in the shadows, then relaxed - slightly - as he saw the bird. The local animals didn't seem to be particularly scared of humans, although *that* might be because the humans didn't shoot at them. A couple of the bat-bird creatures had been shot, in the early stages of the landing, and checked by the medics. They'd warned everyone that the creatures were probably dangerously toxic. The marines had joked that that was true of the rest of the planet too.

His earpiece buzzed. "Watch your backs," a voice said. "The enemy may be advancing."

Charles resisted the urge to sneer as he glanced towards the darkened trees and fields. The enemy knew how to sneak around, just like any other reasonably modern combat force. He'd had basic caution hammered into his head at Boot Camp. An enemy that controlled the high orbitals could see a hell of a lot…and what they could see, they could kill. Hardly anyone realised just how sophisticated the military's sensors had become over the last two hundred years. And yet, they *still* needed boots on the ground to actually win a fight…

Something moved, in the darkness. Something too big to be natural…

He toggled his mouthpiece. "Control, I have movement," he subvocalised, as he ducked low and motioned for his men to do the same. The enemy *should* have shown up on his goggles, but humans had been inventing ways to fool them for centuries. "I have…"

The Foxes opened fire. Charles hit the deck, firing a burst in their general direction to force them to keep their heads down. His men dropped with him, one clearly wounded. His comrade slapped a medical patch on the wound, then covered him as best as he could. There was no hope of getting a proper medic out here, not so far from the front line. Charles searched for targets, trying to find the enemy in the shadows. Bullets were cracking over his head...

"Control, I have contact," he said. He peered into the darkness, but the enemy refused to show his face. "Enemy contact..."

Something crashed down beside him. Alarm ran through him as he realised it was a grenade, an alien grenade. There was nothing to hide behind, nowhere to take cover...he reached for the grenade, hoping to toss it away, but it was too late. The grenade exploded...

...Someone was shouting; no, *screaming*. It dawned on him, somehow, that it was *his* voice screaming. He was in pain, immense pain. His entire body seemed to be on fire. And yet...and yet he felt almost as if he was detached from it, as if it was happening to someone else...

...And then the darkness reached up and swallowed him.

————

"Got contact reports all along the line," the operator reported. "Our patrols have been driven back or caught."

Or killed, General Ross translated silently.

He felt a flicker of guilt, but ruthlessly suppressed it. He'd put out the patrols, knowing there was a very real risk of losing them. But he needed as much warning as he could get before the Foxes launched their main offensive. His men were rushing to defensive positions, reinforcing the line...

"General," another operator snapped. "We just lost three of the orbital platforms!"

General Ross swung around. "God damn it - *how*?"

"I think they slammed stealth missiles into the platforms," the operator said. "Three of them are gone. The fourth may be taken out at any moment"

"Shit," Ross said.

He took a breath. They'd planned and trained on the assumption the platforms would be taken out, but...but they'd grown far too used to having orbital support on call. Who needed bombers or long-range artillery when one could call KEWs down from orbit? No one cared much for collateral damage these days. Only one platform meant that they couldn't hope to cope with *all* the problems coming their way...

"Order the fourth platform to be held in reserve," he said. "It is to be used only if there is no other choice."

And if it lasts long enough to help, he added, silently.

———

"Incoming fire," Sergeant Tosco snapped. "Get down and *stay* down!"

George ducked into the trench, silently cursing the rain as the first shells whistled through the air. Dozens - hundreds - were picked off by ground-based defences, but there were so *many* of them that a number were certain to get through. The trench wasn't *that* bad, she knew, yet the rain had pooled at the bottom. It soaked through her uniform as she heard the sound of explosions echoing through the air, the ground shaking moments later as a handful of survivors crashed down. She was grimly aware, all of a sudden, that a shell landing directly on the trench would be fatal. There was no way any of them would *know* they'd been hit before they died.

Mud and water trickled down into the trench as the firing intensified. She rolled over, despite her sodden kit, and peered upwards, spotting flashes and flares of light in the sky. The platforms had been hit, according to a very brief update. Her terminal wasn't useless, but she couldn't call on fire support unless they were in deep shit. And yet, as she felt the ground shuddering beneath her, she couldn't help thinking that they were *already* in deep shit.

Probably literally, she thought. *What's going to happen if one of the latrines breaks its banks?*

It would have disgusted her, once upon a time. Now...crawling through mud and filth was preferable to being killed.

"They're mounting a mass offensive," her earpiece buzzed. "Tanks are engaging the enemy now."

George tensed as she heard engines, the sound rumbling through the air. She'd met a few of the tankers, when she'd been carrying messages for Major Andres. The Royal Marines had sneered at them, yet there had also been a hint of respect too. George didn't pretend to understand it, but she knew the tankers - British, American, Chinese - were good. Maybe, just maybe, they could stop the enemy tanks from reaching the spacehead.

And if they can't, she told herself, *we're all in the shit.*

"The tanks are engaging the enemy," the operator reported. "They seem to be evenly matched."

General Ross nodded. He'd been worried about that - fast-moving tank battles had been a thing of the past for over a century - but his men seemed to be holding their own. The Foxes hadn't had time to muster more than a few hundred tanks, thankfully. They might feel the battering their infrastructure had taken constituted cheating, but it might just have saved the spacehead. If the battle in space was won...

"Route what fire support we can to..."

The shell struck the command tent and exploded. There were no survivors.

"Brigadier!"

Percy cursed, savagely. The *real* command tent hadn't been marked. It hadn't been enough to save it. The Foxes had scored a lucky hit and taken out General Ross, as well as half the command staff. Percy was the next in line to command, but with the network so badly damaged...

"Inform all units that I am assuming command," he growled. The shelling was intensifying as the Foxes steadily located the point defence systems. A hundred shells to take out one of those vehicles would be a better than even trade, for the enemy. "And get me a status report from the tanks!"

"Enemy infantry is advancing to support *their* tanks," the operator said. "They're coming at us from all sides."

"Order the tanks to pull back," Percy said. The original plan had gone splat. *That* much was obvious. He didn't know if he had time to fix the situation before the battle came to a sharp end. "And order our infantry to cover their retreat."

He forced himself to think as the command network rebuilt itself. There was no longer any point in trying to hold back a large force in reserve, even though he knew he'd need it sooner rather than later. The enemy was trying to break through the defences at multiple points at once, making it impossible for him to hold the line for long. He who would be strong everywhere was strong nowhere...he'd been taught that, back in basic training. And now, as his lines contracted, he was seeing the proof of it right in front of his eyes.

"Sir, the tanks are retreating under fire," the operator warned. "But they're heavily damaged."

"Get them reorganised as soon as they're through the inner lines," Percy ordered. The original formations had been shot to hell. "And hope to hell they can work together."

———

"Get up," Sergeant Tosco roared. "Fix bayonets!"

You must be fucking joking, George thought, as she rolled over and stood. Water dripped down her legs and pooled in her boots. *When did we last fight hand-to-hand?*

She snapped her bayonet into place as the marines hurried forward to take up their position in the lines. There were meant to be two other lines before them, but it was clear - as the sound of battle grew louder - that the enemy had overrun them. She caught sight of a smoking tank slowly inching back through the lines...it seemed to be alone. There were no other tankers heading back to the spacehead. She hoped that they'd found other lines through the trenches, but she feared they hadn't...

"Here they come," Sergeant Tosco shouted. "Fire at will!"

Sammy stuck up a hand. "Which one of the bastards is *Will*?"

George giggled, feeling some of the tension dissipate as laughter rippled up and down the trench. Poor joke or not - it was an incredibly lame pun - it had made everyone smile, despite the constant barrage of shellfire. And yet, as she peered over the trench towards the enemy positions, half-hidden in smoke, she couldn't help feeling cold. There was some room behind them, some empty trenches that were probably being manned even now, but there wasn't much beyond them. If the trenches broke at any point, the spacehead was on the brink of destruction.

A hand fell on her shoulder. She jumped.

"Get your terminal ready," Sergeant Tosco ordered. His voice was very cold. "We may need it."

We will need it, George thought, as she pulled the terminal off her belt and linked into what was left of the fire control network. The sheer speed with which the terminal linked to the network confirmed that very few FACs were still alive and active. *They're coming at us out of the smoke. We won't even see them until it's too late.*

The ground shook, time and time again, as more shells crashed down behind them. George couldn't help feeling that was ominous, even though she wasn't in immediate danger. The enemy commanders wouldn't want to shell their own men, would they? They'd certainly prefer to keep any prospective human reinforcements keeping their heads down, well away from the trenches. And…she winced as she saw a number of marines carrying antitank weapons and positioning them on the edge of the trench. Were they going to be needed?

"Here they come," a voice shouted. "Fire!"

George shuddered as the aliens came out of the smoke, running forward and firing short bursts towards the human positions. She couldn't help thinking they were crazy, even as they zigzagged from side to side to avoid human shots. And yet…a machine gun opened fire, its loud *chatter-chatter* echoing over the battlefield. A dozen aliens collapsed, hacked into bloody chunks by the hail of bullets; the remainder dropped, then started to crawl forward, tossing grenades ahead of them as they moved. The marines threw grenades back, firing shots of their own into the advancing enemy troops…

"Tanks," Sammy shouted. "Tanks!"

Three enemy tanks appeared, racing forward with terrifying speed. Their main guns fired, blasting shells into the distance; their smaller machine guns fired long bursts of death into the trench. George threw herself down, hugging the mud as the antitank weapons opened fire, launching three missiles into the enemy vehicles. Moments later, she heard thunderous explosions...

A boot connected with her bottom. "Get up," Sergeant Tosco snapped. He caught her by the back of the neck and hauled her up until she was on her hands and knees. "Get to the next trench!"

George hesitated, feeling too shaken to move. He kicked her again, harder this time. George somehow found the strength to rise and crawl to their escape line, just as more missiles and shellfire echoed over her head. The gunners were practically dropping shells on their own trenches, just to keep the enemy back for a few more seconds. She caught a glimpse of a line of advancing enemy soldiers, wiped out in a second, then turned her head away. The remainder of the marines followed her into the next trench...

She shivered. How many familiar faces were missing? How many marines were dead?

The noise - impossibly - grew louder as the enemy forces continued their offensive. George took up a position behind a prefabricated barrier, sniping at the enemy soldiers. The aliens seemed intent on keeping up the pressure, even as they climbed over their dead comrades to continue the attack. Five more tanks appeared, followed by a vehicle that *had* to be some sort of armoured troop carrier. All five tanks were taken out within seconds, but not before one of them had managed to land a shell further down the trench. A chain reaction of explosions blew a colossal hole in the defences, just waiting for the enemy to charge through it. The force of the impact threw her to her knees...

George stumbled up and continued to fire until her rifle clicked empty. She hastily removed the magazine and searched for a new one, only to discover that she'd used them all without even realising. She turned, hoping to cadge a full magazine off Sergeant Tosco or one of the others, only to discover that they were wounded or dead. For a moment, her mind refused to believe what she was seeing. Nothing, absolutely nothing, could kill the sergeant. He'd been the toughest man she'd ever met; now, blood was leaking from a head wound. She hoped, as she scooped up his rifle, that it had been immediately fatal. A quick death was the best he could hope for...

She turned…and froze. The enemy was taking full advantage of the devastation. An entire line of infantry, backed up by tanks, was pushing through the gap, far too close to her for comfort. Her fingers tightened on the rifle, but she knew it was futile. There were too many of them for her to kill. Numbly, she reached for the terminal and keyed her command code into the system, then added a second code. It wasn't one she'd used before, outside simulations.

Danger Close, she thought.

There was little hope of escape, perhaps none. Calling a strike down on her own position was an act of desperation. The impact would devastate the remainder of the nearby trenches and kill any survivors, if there were any left. She didn't want to do it, but…the situation was desperate.

She braced herself, then sent the order. The terminal bleeped once as the countdown began.

The aliens kept swarming forward, three of them plunging over the barrier and spinning around to face her. George stared back at them, fighting a very primal urge to turn and run as they showed their teeth. It was a challenge, she knew, a challenge she couldn't answer. She allowed her rifle to drop to the ground, knowing there was no point in trying to fight. They expected her to surrender. They thought she was going to surrender…she wondered, suddenly, what *else* they would expect from her. Had they realised, yet, that humans didn't play by the same rules?

"Go to hell," she told them.

The world went white, then faded away.

CHAPTER
THIRTY EIGHT

"They're taking out the missiles," Jean warned. "But *some* are bound to get through."

I hope so, Susan thought. The starfighters had taken out a carrier, but it wasn't the enemy carriers that worried her. They were rapidly closing on twelve enemy battleships. *They have three more battleships than us.*

She gritted her teeth as a flight of starfighters tried to punch through *Vanguard's* point defence, a handful surviving long enough to slam their missiles into her hull. A low quiver ran through the ship, but the armour held. Susan allowed herself a split-second of relief as the enemy starfighters retreated, then focused on the enemy battleships. One of them had taken heavy damage and staggered out of the line of battle, but the remainder were still advancing.

"Signal from the flag," Parkinson said. "All ships are to go to rapid fire."

Expending our remaining missiles, Susan thought. It wasn't really a concern, not now. There was certainly no point in keeping a reserve. Either they won or they died. *And we may do some damage…*

"Fire," she ordered. "And keep firing until the tubes run dry."

"Aye, Captain," Jean said.

The two fleets converged with ponderous speed. Susan watched, grimly, as another enemy ship took heavy damage, exploding into a fireball before she could withdraw from the line of battle. But the aliens were inflicting damage too…USS *Eisenhower* staggered under the weight of enemy fire, while HMS *Rodney* and FS *Foch* vanished into expanding clouds of superheated plasma. A handful of lifepod beacons were clearly visible on the display, but it was clear they didn't have a hope of recovery. They might well be mistaken for something hostile and picked off by a passing starfighter...

"Captain, we will be entering energy range in two minutes," Reed reported.

And then it becomes a battering match, Susan thought. They couldn't hope to escape, even if they reversed course. The two fleets were locked together. *And whoever inflicts the most damage wins.*

"Order the main guns to open fire as soon as we enter range," Susan said. "And stand by all damage control teams."

"They're ready, Captain," Mason said.

Susan nodded as the last few seconds ticked down. *Vanguard* shuddered as a missile struck her hull, but the armour held. Susan started to make mental notes for the engineers, then told herself she was being stupid. If they won, the engineers would learn plenty from the post-battle analysis; if they lost, it wouldn't matter anyway. Another missile slammed home, only to expend itself uselessly against her armour. Susan couldn't help wondering if that was a good sign - the enemy warheads were straight nukes, instead of bomb-pumped lasers - or if the enemy were holding their laser warheads back. The latter might be worrying...

"Energy range in ten seconds," Reed said.

Susan braced herself. The enemy battleships were already falling into attack formation, readying themselves so they could engage two or more targets at the same time. They definitely *did* have a firepower advantage, she thought. Three extra hulls gave them a lot of options. And yet, human battleships were *designed* to soak up fire. Her hull could take one hell of a pounding before it finally collapsed.

Except we had to patch up several sectors, she thought. *If they know where to target, they could take us out.*

She spared a thought, briefly, for the men and women on the surface. General Ross was a good man; Percy Schneider was a war hero. And his sister was down there too...the fleet *had* to win or the spacehead would be obliterated. And yet, she knew all too well there was no way anyone could guarantee a victory.

"Targets locked," Jean reported. "Captain?"

"Fire as you bear," Susan ordered.

"Entering range...now," Reed said.

Susan gritted her teeth as *Vanguard's* forward turrets opened fire. The other battleships fired at the same moment, hurling a vast cloud of lethal plasma towards the alien ships. A dozen starfighters were caught in the blasts and vanished, utterly vaporised. Susan hoped, grimly, that they'd been *alien* starfighters as her main guns started to pound the alien hulls. Moments later, the aliens returned fire. *Vanguard* shuddered as plasma blasts slammed into her main armour.

"Armour holding, for the moment," Mason said. "But they're blasting our point defence and sensors off the hull."

Surprise, surprise, Susan thought, sarcastically. *That happens every time.*

"Link us into the fleet-wide network," she ordered. Being blinded would be disastrous, even if the armour continued to hold. "Tactical, see if you can do unto them."

"Doing it, Captain," Jean said. She paused. "Enemy starships are launching missiles!"

Smart, Susan thought. Launching missiles at short range was against tactical doctrine, particularly with hundreds of thousands of plasma bursts in the vicinity, but it might just pay off for the enemy. *They'll never have a better chance to get a laser head through our defences and they know it.*

"Stand by point defence," she ordered. Her mind insisted on reminding her that a good third of her point defence was already gone. "And order the smaller ships to cover us."

She felt a pang of bitter guilt. *Vanguard* could survive in the plasma storm, but destroyers and frigates didn't have a hope. Their crews would be blown out of space in seconds, if the enemy chose to focus on them. And yet, the battleships had to be protected. Their heavy weapons might make the difference between success and failure, between life and death.

Vanguard shuddered, unpleasantly. "Direct hit, sector alpha-nine," Mason reported. "They struck us with a laser head. Local armour is melted; we're streaming air..."

"Seal off that sector, then dispatch damage control teams," Susan ordered, stiffly. A laser head...it should have inflicted considerably worse damage. Not that she was complaining, of course! Perhaps the warhead had detonated too far from the hull. "Tactical?"

"One enemy battleship has taken heavy damage, Captain," Jean reported. "But she is continuing to fight."

"Understood," Susan said. "Continue firing."

———

There was no point in issuing further orders, John knew. The entire tactical situation had become brutally simple. Either the human ships inflicted enough damage to force the Foxes to surrender - as they were demanding, over the airwaves - or the Foxes crushed the entire task force. It wouldn't be enough to save them, John thought, but...he gritted his teeth as two more warheads crashed against *King Edward*. Their only saving grace was that the enemy seemed to be short on bomb-pumped lasers.

They must have expended them during the advance on Tadpole Prime, he thought. It made a certain kind of sense. The Royal Navy had nearly run out of advanced weapons during the First Interstellar War, when expenditure had been far higher than predicted. But then, the war itself hadn't been predicted either. *And then they found themselves continuously expending their new production, without being able to build up again.*

He cursed, inwardly, as two French destroyers and a Chinese frigate were blasted out of existence. None of them should have been anywhere near such a titanic engagement, but there had been no choice...he told himself, again, that there had been no choice. HMS *Balham* followed them into death, just after striking an alien carrier with her plasma cannon and forcing her out of the engagement. John couldn't help thinking that it was a waste, even though the alien carrier had been dangerous. The battleships were the real threat.

"They're not combining their fire," Prince Henry said, breaking the silence. "Why not?"

"They're smart enough to know that it would give us an opportunity to target them without hindrance," John growled. "And besides, they have an edge. They don't need to gamble."

The damage was mounting rapidly. Losing the point defence weapons was bad enough, but jammed or destroyed turrets were worse. *Bismarck* had lost a forward turret to a plasma explosion, after her oversized containment chambers had been breached. John was privately impressed the damage wasn't worse. He'd reviewed *Bismarck's* design before the task force had left Earth and he'd thought the Germans had skimped on a number of crucial safety procedures. But then, materials science *had* advanced over the seven years since *Vanguard* had been designed. The Germans had taken full advantage of later developments.

"*Eisenhower* reports that she needs to fall back," Regal injected. "She's lost all of her launch tubes."

"Order her to break contact, if she can," John said. Losing *Eisenhower* meant that he would only have one carrier left. "And order *Vikramaditya* to pull back. We need her launch tubes!"

He cursed under his breath as the battering match continued. *Yamato* had taken heavy damage, but - true to their ancestors - her crew were keeping her on course. *Texas* and *Montana* had also taken damage, although their damage control teams seemed to be on top of the situation. *Bismarck* was still fighting, but her damaged hull was an easy target. Judging by the fire heading in her direction, John couldn't help suspecting that putting a nuke through the gash in her armour had just become an alien priority.

Of course it has, he thought. *They'd have an excellent chance of putting her out of action completely.*

King Edward shuddered again, violently. He forced himself not to look at the status display, even though he had access to *all* the data. There was nothing he could do. Captain Tolliver and his crew would either save the ship or lose it. And if *King Edward* was destroyed, or forced out of the datanet, Commodore Hoover would take command. There would be no dispute...not, he suspected, that it really mattered. The battering match had taken on a life of its own.

"One enemy battleship destroyed," Regal reported. "Two more streaming atmosphere..."

Prince Henry clenched his fists. "How much of this can they take?"

John shrugged. The Anglo-Indian War had been genteel. There was no way either Britain or India would expend so much materiel in a single engagement. But the Foxes had to be crushed, they had to *know* they were defeated. And, as long as they had a chance of winning, they would keep fighting. The odds were still in their favour.

Don't they understand what they're facing? He asked himself. *They can't win a war against two separate interstellar powers, can they?*

He studied the display as another alien battleship writhed under human fire. There were plenty of examples, in human history, of cities and nations holding out even when the odds were utterly hopeless. Rome hadn't surrendered after Cannae; Japan hadn't surrendered until two atomic bombs had been dropped; Iran had practically been pounded flat before the remnants of her government had been overthrown and slaughtered by their own people. And yet, the Foxes *shouldn't* regard surrender with utter horror. *Their* defeated were absorbed into the victor's society. It was how they rolled.

"I think we're about to find out," he said, grimly. "And we're also going to find out how much *we* can take."

Texas flickered on the display, then vanished. John cursed under his breath, trying not to think about her crew. Maybe some would have made it to the lifepods in time…it didn't look like it, according to the display. Three thousand American crewmen had either been vaporised or thrown into the inky darkness of space. The battleship had gone down with all hands.

"*Montana* has taken heavy damage," Regal reported. "Her CO is reporting direct hits to her missile tubes and drive sections."

"Order *King Edward* and *Vanguard* forward to cover her," John said. The enemy advantage was starting to take a toll. And there was nothing he could do about it. "And check with *Vikramaditya*. See if they can launch a strike to cover us."

"Aye, Admiral," Regal said.

John forced himself to relax, even as the pounding intensified. The starfighters launched sluggishly - *Vikramaditya* was a good ship, but she was handling far more starfighters than her designers had ever expected - and lanced into the teeth of enemy fire, launching their torpedoes at point-blank range. None of the original squadrons still existed, John noted absently. They'd been broken up and reorganised before the engagement, but now…now they were gone completely. Human pilots from a dozen different nations were hastily thrown together into makeshift squadrons, then hurled at the enemy. Pilots barely had any time to meet their wingmen before going out to die together. It was hell…

He closed his eyes for a long moment. He understood, all too well, why Prince Henry wanted to be out there, sharing the danger. John felt it too, even though he knew *King Edward* was attracting more than her fair share of enemy missiles. There was something cowardly about having millions of tons of battleship wrapped around him…he shook his head, angrily pushing the thought aside. He couldn't take a starfighter and go out to fight, any more than Prince Henry could. His responsibilities lay elsewhere.

"Admiral," Regal said. "*Vanguard* is under heavy fire!"

John gritted his teeth. His remaining ships were heavily engaged. There was no way he could order anyone else up to cover *Vanguard*, let alone pull her out of the line of battle. And yet, he knew just how hurriedly the battleship had been patched up. The aliens might well know it too. And even if they didn't, they might get lucky.

"Order the starfighters to cover her as best as they can," he said, finally. It was almost certainly pointless - and he knew it. But he had to do something. "And see if we can send *Montana* forward…"

Another green icon flickered and died. "*Bismarck* is gone, sir," Regal said. "*Yamato* is taking heavy fire…"

———

Susan clung to her command chair for dear life as the entire ship shuddered. The Foxes had their number now, she thought; they'd punched two gashes in her forward armour and were now trying to take full advantage of them. *Vanguard's* inner layers were holding, but it was only a matter of time before they weakened and allowed the enemy to stab deep into her vitals. Sweat ran down her back - the bridge suddenly seemed very hot - as more and more red icons flashed up on the status display. Her ship was trapped in a nightmare it could neither defeat nor escape.

"Turret Two has jammed, again," Mason reported. "The enemy appears to be targeting it specifically..."

He broke off as another quiver ran through the giant ship. "Turret Two is gone, Captain," he warned. "Plasma explosion. There are no reported survivors."

Susan hoped, just for a second, that the gunnery crews had died quickly. Plasma burns were nothing to laugh at, even if the victim survived. Modern medicine could work miracles, yet there were limits. But there was little hope of survival when one's compartment was opened to vacuum...

Vanguard bucked like a wild horse as two bomb-pumped lasers stabbed into her weakened hull. Susan grabbed hold of her chair as the lights failed for a long second, the gravity field weakening just long enough to make her think they'd lost everything. The status display blanked for a chilling moment before booting back up again, warning of more and more systems failures. She couldn't help thinking, as she looked utter destruction in the face, that the bridge consoles were on the verge of exploding...

"They targeted our weak spot," Mason reported. He looked up at her, his face pale. "Fusion Three and Four are both gone, Captain; Fusion One is showing signs of imminent collapse. We have a coolant leak in Main Engineering..."

He broke off, "Mr. Finch is reported dead," he added. "Engineer Sato is now Acting Engineer."

Susan had to think to place the name. Thomas Sato was...what? *Seventh* in Engineering's internal chain of command? If *he* was the senior survivor, there might not be many other engineers left. Not, she suspected, that it mattered. The damage control teams wouldn't be able to patch the ship up *this* time. *Vanguard* shook, again...

"Direct hit, section alpha," Mason reported bleakly. "They've wrecked the armour."

"Helm, point us at the nearest enemy battleship," Susan ordered. The drives *should* be able to push them forward, just for a few minutes more. "Reroute all remaining power to drives, if necessary. Ram the bastards!"

Reed didn't hesitate. "Aye, Captain."

Susan forced herself to sit back as *Vanguard* limped forward. There was no point in ordering an evacuation, not when lifepods were being picked off by both sides. All she could do was try to take out one enemy ship in a final explosion. They couldn't even keep firing as they closed with their target. The enemy poured shots into her hull, ripping apart the remainder of her armour and stabbing deep into her vitals. And then...

"Captain," Jean said. "They've stopped firing!"

Susan blinked. "What?"

"They're surrendering," Parkinson said. "They're asking to surrender!"

Susan blinked, then looked at Mason. A trick? It could be a trick. But all the enemy ships had stopped firing...

...And then she saw the green icons appearing behind the red ones.

"Abort ram," she ordered, finally. Could they abort ram? Half her control systems had been shot out. "And then inform Admiral Naiser that we need help."

"Aye, Captain," Reed said.

———

"Picking up a signal from USS *William Cody*," Regal said. "It's Admiral Stirling!"

"Put him through," John ordered. The plan had worked, barely. Admiral Stirling and his fleet had followed the retreating aliens back to their homeworld. "And then get an updated status report from the remainder of the fleet."

He glanced at Prince Henry. "And you know how to make the surrender permanent?"

"I do," Henry said.

"Then do it," John said. "Or everyone who died here today will have died for nothing."

CHAPTER
THIRTY NINE

The funeral, back on Earth, was a sombre affair.

Henry couldn't say that he'd known Georgina Fitzwilliam very well. Admiral Fitzwilliam's niece had been twelve years younger than him, even before he'd left Earth for Tadpole Prime; he'd only met her once, as far as he could recall, before they'd met on *Vanguard*. And they hadn't spent *much* time together, not on the ship. They'd only really been acquaintances.

But she'd died well, everyone agreed, even though no one had found the body.

That's not surprising, he reminded himself. *She was at the centre of a KEW strike.*

He forced himself to listen as the vicar droned on and on about a young girl who'd been killed far too soon. The after-action report had made horrific reading, but he'd forced himself to keep going until he reached the end. George's action in calling down the KEW strike might just have saved the spacehead from being overrun, although it wouldn't have stood a chance if the battle overhead hadn't been won. It was a grim reminder that humanity's new allies were savage, at the core. Maybe they had their own code of honour, maybe they had evolved ways to cope with their nature…they were still savage.

The vicar stopped droning, allowing others to stand and have their say. Charles Fraser spoke about a young midshipwoman who had won the respect of her peers; Anne Fitzwilliam talked about a little girl who refused to fit into anyone's plans for her. Anne was the kind of aristocratic girl Henry had always detested - it was clear she was being groomed to marry someone who would advance the family's interests - but she was right. George had fought to find a place where she could be herself, rather than follow her family's will. And even though she had died in the process, she had died as herself.

He closed his eyes for a long moment as Captain Susan Onarina spoke, briefly, about the girl she'd known. It was regretful, in a way, that Captain Onarina *did* know the girl, although Henry had to admit that she had an excuse. She'd been *Vanguard's* XO when George had started her Middy Cruise. And yet, a midshipwoman with George's connections could never be treated as an *ordinary* middy. Henry had gone to considerable trouble to conceal his real name when *he* had joined the navy.

I'm sorry, George, he thought, as the coffin was carried towards the grave. *You deserved much better.*

He looked from face to face, silently counting the number of great and good that had turned up for the funeral. Admiral Fitzwilliam, of course, along with his adopted children; Admiral Soskice and Admiral Brougham...even General Taylor and Ambassador Richards. And, beyond them, the Prime Minister and half his cabinet. It was a stark reminder that politics were never far away, even during the funeral of a war hero. George would no longer be recognisable, he thought, after the spin doctors got hold of her. She'd become the emblem of Britain soon enough, her name cited as justification for all sorts of things. He couldn't help thinking, as the empty coffin was lowered into the grave, that George would have hated her afterlife. She'd rebelled against the establishment, just like himself. And now she was safely dead, she'd been practically canonised by the aristocracy.

The funeral crowd broke up, half heading for the manor where food and drink was already prepared, the remainder heading down to the gates. It was easy enough to distinguish the ghouls from those who were genuinely mourning, now the main ceremony was over. The former were heading out of the estate, hoping to get back home before it was too late, while the remainder were staying to eat and drink. And talk politics, of course.

He fell into step beside Susan Onarina as they walked up to the manor. "I was sorry to hear about the board's decision," he said. "*Vanguard* deserved much better."

"She was a good ship," Susan said. She sounded numb. "And she served us well."

Henry nodded, although he understood the board's reasoning. *Vanguard* had taken one hell of a beating in the final battle, even though her hull had survived. The damage had been so extensive, the board had concluded, that refitting her would be more expensive than building a whole new battleship. And besides, they'd added, *Vanguard* and her sisters were no longer the cutting edge of naval development. There were limits to how many new systems could be crammed into her hull. They might have refrained from scrapping *Vanguard* - the academy had put in a bid for her services as a training hull - but the battleship would never fly or fight again.

He summoned a page as they walked through the French windows and made a special request, then headed down the hall to the Green Room. Fitzwilliam Manor, like all modern-day manors, was more than just a family home. It was a place to do business, a place for discreet meetings to be held. He stepped into the Green Room - a rather unimaginative name. as everything in the room was green - and sat down on a comfy armchair. If he'd read the politics right, he wouldn't have long to wait.

The door opened, two minutes later. Douglas Thomas, Prime Minister of Great Britain, Titan and Britannia - and assorted smaller colonies scattered across twenty different star systems - stepped into the room, followed by a maid in a long dark dress. The Fitzwilliam family, Henry noted as he rose, was thankfully dignified. He'd been in places where the servants wore barely enough to be decent.

"Tea, please," he ordered. "Prime Minister?"

"Tea will be sufficient," Thomas said.

He sat down, facing Henry. Henry studied him with considerable interest, even though it was hardly the first time they'd met. The Prime Minister was a heavyset man, his cragged face slowly turning to fat. His black suit was perfectly tailored, but not even the best tailor could hide his ripening paunch. And yet, the Prime Minister carried himself with an air of stiff dignity that suggested he would be very hard to budge. Thomas wasn't exactly a war hero, but he *had* been credited with organising most of the rescue and recovery efforts launched during and after the bombardment. Maybe not the man of the hour, yet perhaps the man of the decade. Henry disliked all professional politicians with a passion, but he had to admit that Thomas had handled himself well.

And now he's facing deselection, he thought. *The bane of any professional politician.*

"Thank you for coming, sir," he said, as the maid returned with tea. "I know my request must have come as a surprise."

"I had expected some off-the-record discussions," the Prime Minister said, gravely. The maid poured the tea, then bowed and retreated. "Politics infect everything, these days."

"Including the funeral of a war hero," Henry said. He took a sip of his tea. It was perfect, of course. "Did you expect to be meeting with me?"

"I try not to have expectations," the Prime Minister said. He took his own cup. "But I should add that time is not on my side."

Get on with it, Henry translated. He might be a prince of the realm, even though he'd been doing everything in his power to escape the monarchy, but he wasn't the most important person in the room. *I have more influential people to meet.*

He leaned back in his chair. "You are aware, of course, that my post on Tadpole Prime has been filled," he said. "I find that most awkward."

The Prime Minister shrugged. "Britain commands vast influence, yet not enough to keep such a prime post indefinitely," he said. "Our choice of *you* may have worked well, back when you were a global hero, but politicians have short memories. The French were prepared to horse-trade intensely to win the position for themselves."

"And you weren't prepared to fight to keep it," Henry said.

"Quite," the Prime Minister said. He sounded oddly amused. "Resentment at our domination of such matters would not have helped us, not in the long run."

Henry nodded. There was no point in whining about it, not now. The Prime Minister had a point. His position might be rather less powerful than outsiders supposed, but still…Britain holding the seat permanently would put quite a few noses out of joint. Better to swap ambassadors before resentment ended up costing the country more than it cared to pay.

"There will, of course, be another post opening on Vixen," he said, instead. "I want it."

The Prime Minister's eyebrows rose. "And you think you should *have* it?"

"I was the representative who dictated the peace terms, after the fighting came to an end," Henry said. *Dictated* was the right word. The Foxes acted as though they'd been brutally crushed, while the Cows seemed prepared to go with the flow. "They know me. More to the point, they recognise me as a military officer as well as an ambassador."

"That may be true," the Prime Minister said. "And Britain *does* have the inside track on appointing the lead ambassador. But why should we go for you?"

Henry met his eyes. "On one hand, you won't find a more experienced ambassador in the country," he said. "I've handled multinational meetings and conferences as well as talking to three different groups of non-humans. And on the other, if I don't get the post, I'll return to Tadpole Prime."

The Prime Minister's face darkened. "I was under the impression that travel to Tadpole Prime was restricted," he said. "Were my briefers lying to me?"

"It's certainly hard to reach," Henry agreed. He reached into his pocket and produced a datachip. "However, I was able to apply to the Tadpole Embassy here for travel and residency permits. We may control who goes in and out of our embassies on Tadpole Prime, Prime Minister, but we don't control settlement rights. The Tadpoles say my family and I can live there…so my family can live there."

"Getting there might pose a problem," the Prime Minister said, finally.

"It won't," Henry said. He smiled. "There *are* freighters that go to Tadpole Prime fairly regularly. They'll be happy to take on a few passengers, if I pay through the nose. And I do have plenty of money saved up."

"Because the government has been paying your living expenses," the Prime Minister commented.

"My *wages*," Henry snapped. The stipend he'd received as Prince of Wales had long since been cancelled. "First as a starfighter pilot, then as an ambassador. And I dare say I could spend some time on Tadpole Prime writing a book. The publishers would be delighted to give me an advance."

"Assuming you wrote the damn thing," the Prime Minister said. "And assuming it was cleared for publication."

"These aren't the days when there was blood on the streets," Henry pointed out. "You might *try* to have it banned, but would you win?"

There was a long chilling pause. "I do not appreciate being threatened, however indirectly," the Prime Minister said. "And I *assure* you that your absence will make no difference whatsoever to Britain."

"Of course not," Henry agreed. He finished his tea, silently making a mental note to ask for the blend. Nothing, but the best for the aristocracy. "But it occurs to me that my *presence* on Vixen will make a great deal of difference. Particularly, sir, as this isn't exactly an ordinary embassy. And let's face it. There aren't many people more qualified in the world."

He rose. "I would have liked to bring my family here," he said, "but the reporters would have made their lives hell. You can contact me at Haddon Hall, when you have made up your mind."

The Prime Minister scowled. "You're nothing like your father…"

"My father is a bird trapped in a gilded cage," Henry said, as he turned to the door. "I love him dearly, Prime Minister, but he is a broken man. My sister will go the same way, if she takes the throne. Please rest assured that I have *no* intention of following them into a long slow death. I want to do *something* with my life."

"Really, Mr. Ambassador?" The Prime Minister asked. "I'd say you *have*."

———

The flight from Fitzwilliam Manor to Haddon Hall took just under an hour, time Henry spent reading the latest set of updates from the navy and a handful of semi-trustworthy political analysts. He rarely trusted any of the latter completely, but they did have a good record for plotting out the future in general terms. Barring a lucky accident - or an encounter with a *fifth* alien race - the Prime Minister's political future was questionable. Too many people wanted a change.

Particularly now the war is over, Henry thought, as the aircar descended to land on the helipad. *They want to reduce spending on warships and use the money here instead.*

His lips curved into a cold smile. He hadn't lied to the Prime Minister. By any reasonable definition, *he* was almost certainly the most qualified candidate on Earth for the assignment to Vixen. There were others, of course, but most of the best were already assigned to Tadpole Prime or Vesy. And if the Prime Minister *did* manage to get him the post, it might just shore up the Prime Minister's political position too. His party would have problems deselecting him if he scored such an immense political coup.

He climbed out of the aircar, bid farewell to the driver and walked up the lane towards Haddon Hall. Five children - no, six - could be seen on the lake, messing about on a pair of ramshackle boats. Two young women were supervising them…Henry smiled, then hurried up the steps and into the hall. The butler intercepted him, took his coat with practiced ease and pointed to the library. Henry walked inside and stopped, dead. The room was empty.

Strong arms wrapped around him from behind. "Got you," Janelle said. The door slammed closed. "And the kids are distracted…"

Henry turned and kissed her, hard. He'd been away for six months, but it felt as though it had been longer.

Afterwards, they cuddled together on the sofa. "You missed two birthdays," Janelle said, wrapping her arms around his shoulders. "You got Mary a large toy car and Elizabeth a talking doll. They love them both, but the doll gives Victoria nightmares. Try not to look surprised when she insists that you take it away again."

Henry sighed. "That bad?"

"It's programmed to walk around like a real child," Janelle said. "And really…it creeps her out."

"I'll talk to her," Henry promised. "How are they coping?"

"A little better, now they have some vetted friends," Janelle said. "But… no one seems to *quite* know how to handle them."

Henry sighed. "We'll be leaving soon," he promised. "Either to Vixen or back to Tadpole Prime."

"They'll love it," Janelle said. "Earth…Earth is a nightmare for them."

Because they're not normal, Henry thought. *They're princesses of the blood, if not of the realm.*

"We'll be going soon," he assured her. "And then…well, we'll see."

He leaned into her embrace, wondering - absently - if he'd done the right thing. At eight, he'd rebelled against the stuffy outfit he'd been required to wear; at twelve, he'd thrown a tantrum when he'd been ordered to go to a ball; at fifteen, he'd punched a reporter in the face; at seventeen, he'd refused to attend any further ceremonial events after the damned media had picked up some of his words, taken them out of context and used them to paint him as a monster. And the damned palace had refused to back him…

But now he was an adult, thirty-one years old, a husband, a father and an ambassador. He was no longer *young*. And, in the end, youthful rebellion had to give way to adult responsibilities.

I'm not fighting for myself, he thought, although he knew it was partly a lie. *I'm fighting for my daughters.*

His wristcom bleeped. He glanced at Janelle, then tapped it. "Henry."

"Your Highness," the Prime Minister said. "Your application for the post on Vixen has been accepted, at least by us. You may not be Senior Ambassador, of course, but you will be going out there."

"Thank you, Prime Minister," Henry said. Thomas must have spoken to a couple of other ministers at the funeral, just to get an answer so quickly. But then, the Foreign and Commonwealth Office had never had any reason to be displeased with Henry's service on Tadpole Prime. "I look forward to it."

The Prime Minister snorted. "I trust you and your family will be ready to depart within the next four days?"

"Of course, sir," Henry said. The Prime Minister might *think* he was taking a kind of unsubtle revenge in ordering them to depart so quickly, but *Henry* and his family had wanted to leave Haddon Hall from the moment they'd arrived. He tried to sound unhappy, although he had a feeling it wasn't particularly convincing. "It will be our pleasure."

"And report to Nelson Base tomorrow at 1300," the Prime Minister added. "There is a duty His Majesty's Government wishes you to perform."

"Yes, sir," Henry said.

He closed the connection, then grinned. His wife smiled back. They were leaving Earth, again! No more confinement, no more reporters prowling outside the gates, no more threats of being assimilated into the Royal Family...they were leaving Earth! And there would be new challenges on Vixen. Henry felt his smile grow wider. He was quite looking forward to them. They were off on a whole new adventure...

And this time, Henry promised himself silently, *we won't be coming back.*

CHAPTER

FORTY

Susan felt...*numb*.

It wasn't something she knew how to handle, not really. She'd managed to get her ruined ship home, somehow; she'd visited her father after handing *Vanguard* over to the engineers; she'd even, in a blind rage, seduced Paul Mason and spent the night in his bed. But, in the end, she still felt numb. *Vanguard* had been *her* ship...but now, *Vanguard* was gone.

She had been tempted, in truth, not to bother catching the shuttle to Nelson Base. It was unlikely she'd be offered another command, not after everything that had happened over the last three years. She could resign instead, perhaps, but a civilian life held no attractions for her. The Royal Navy had been her universe for the last ten years. Even the prospect of claiming land on Britannia wasn't enough to attract her. She didn't want to leave the navy...

...But she knew, all too well, that the navy might no longer want her.

She waited outside Admiral Fitzwilliam's office, feeling almost like a naughty schoolgirl who'd been sent to face the headmistress. She'd made sure to arrive on time, of course, but the admiral seemed to be delaying matters purposefully. Maybe it was a subtle sign that she was no longer in favour - as if she'd ever been. Or perhaps he wanted to make her squirm in her seat. Or perhaps she was just being paranoid. His last appointment might have overrun.

The outer hatch opened, revealing Admiral Naiser. He'd been promoted, Susan noted as she rose to her feet, trying to hide the flicker of resentment. Admiral Naiser was now a full admiral, although - if he was on Nelson Base - he hadn't been assigned a post yet. Could he go back to NGW as a full admiral? Or was he going to take command of Unity Station? Or...?

"Susan," Admiral Naiser said. "I'm sorry I didn't have a chance to speak to you at the funeral."

"It's all right, sir," Susan said. She'd liked George Fitzwilliam, even though the poor midshipwoman had really been too inexperienced for her post, but she wasn't the only person who had died over the last six months. A third of *Vanguard's* crew had been killed, yet only one of them had been honoured by the great and the good. "I had to speak to her family."

She kept her face impassive with an effort. Lord and Lady Fitzwilliam had been stiff-upper-lip types, calmly accepting their daughter's death in the line of duty, but their sole surviving daughter had been different. Anne Fitzwilliam had broken down when she'd realised her sister was dead. She might have tried to act like an adult - legally, she *was* an adult - but there was something oddly immature about her. Susan couldn't help wondering if Anne's parents had been so determined to shape her in their own image that they'd done permanent damage to her psyche.

"You have my sympathy," Admiral Naiser said. "That is never easy."

The inner hatch opened. "Admiral Naiser, Captain Onarina," Commander Sarah Outlander said. "Admiral Fitzwilliam will see you now."

Susan exchanged glances with Admiral Naiser, then tailed him into the small office. Admiral Fitzwilliam was seated on a sofa, with Prince Henry sitting next to him in an overstuffed armchair. Commander Outlander produced a teapot and teacups, then retreated through the hatch as Admiral Fitzwilliam motioned for the newcomers to sit down. Susan would have preferred to stand - she was very much the junior officer in the compartment - but she knew she had to do as she was told. She couldn't help noticing that Prince Henry wore a sword at his hip.

"Thank you both for coming," Admiral Fitzwilliam said. He leaned forward and picked up the teapot. "Shall I be mother?"

"Please," Prince Henry said. He sounded oddly impatient. "Or otherwise we will be here all day."

"I have a meeting with Admiral Soskice in an hour," Admiral Fitzwilliam said. "And while I'm sure he would be interested in *this* meeting, he may feel rather differently."

He poured four cups of tea, then passed them round. "First things first," he added, as soon as they all had a cup. "The Board of Inquiry completed its inquest into the destruction of HMS *Formidable*, the *effective* destruction of HMS *Vanguard* and the damage inflicted upon HMS *King Edward*, as well as various smaller ships. It was decided that no one was to blame for the lost starships. Both of you *may* be called to testify in other countries as their navies struggle to understand how and why their ships were lost, but His Majesty's Government does not believe that anyone was at fault."

Susan nodded, relieved. She would have made an excellent scapegoat, if the Royal Navy had decided it needed someone to blame. Why not? Depending on how one looked at it, she was technically a mutineer. Admiral Naiser had been in command, but throwing *him* to the dogs would have been politically difficult. The Admiralty would have hesitated even if he *had* been grossly incompetent.

"It was a formality," Admiral Fitzwilliam added, after a moment. "But unfortunately the formalities often exist for a reason."

"Yes, sir," Admiral Naiser said.

"This leads to two separate issues," Admiral Fitzwilliam said. "Admiral Naiser...your name has been mooted as a possible First Space Lord, when my term in office comes to an end. I believe you are not already aware of this?"

"It is a surprise," Admiral Naiser said.

"It shouldn't be," Admiral Fitzwilliam said. "Those of us who have *genuine* experience in command - in all ranks - fight a constant running battle against those who *don't* have such experience and don't understand its value. The number of patently absurd ideas I have had to deflect, during my time in office...you'll discover that half of your time will be wasted keeping idiots from draining the navy's resources."

"You make it sound like a great job," Admiral Naiser said, sarcastically.

"It has to be done," Admiral Fitzwilliam said. "Your work as part of the Next Generation Weapons project has been noted in high places, particularly now that the face of war has changed once again. There are other possible candidates for the role, John, but you are the one with most recent experience. And you have some experience in battling bureaucracies and crazy intellectuals too."

He sighed. "And while it should count for little," he added, "you also enjoy the support of hundreds of officers and men."

Susan nodded, wordlessly.

"War is changing," Admiral Fitzwilliam said. "And we must change with it."

"Yes, sir," Admiral Naiser said. He leaned forward. "Frankly, sir, if we'd delayed the operation for six months we would have lost the war."

Susan wanted to deny it, but she knew he was right. The Foxes had produced some *very* nasty surprises, ranging from a brand-new penetrator warhead to the gunboats and even faster missiles. Given six months to iron out the bugs and put the weapons into mass production, the Foxes could have smashed the entire task force effortlessly. The Royal Navy had copies of the weapons now, of course, but putting them into production would be difficult. In the end, they'd been very lucky.

"That is correct," Admiral Fitzwilliam said. "And while you will no longer be *directly* involved with NGW, you *will* be responsible for picking and choosing which ideas get turned into hardware."

"And God help you if you get it wrong," Prince Henry put in.

"We'll also need to work on the Jump Drive," Admiral Naiser commented. "Everyone will be trying to build their own."

"Now they know it's possible," Admiral Fitzwilliam said. "And, of course, we will be putting together our own FTL communications network."

And dealing with the changes that will bring, Susan thought. *Perhaps Admiral Fitzwilliam is right to want to retire.*

"If I am selected, I will do my best," Admiral Naiser informed him. "But I have not yet received any formal notification."

"You will," Admiral Fitzwilliam promised. "Until then…you'll be kept busy with NGW."

He smiled as he turned to Susan. "Captain Onarina. Susan. You must be wondering why you were called here today."

"Yes, sir," Susan said.

"It was decided, as I said, that you bear no *personal* blame for *Vanguard's* sorry state," Admiral Fitzwilliam told her. "That you managed to get your ship home under such conditions is something of a miracle..."

"And a testament to her designers," Admiral Naiser put in.

Admiral Fitzwilliam shot him a sharp look. "Thank you," he said, darkly. He turned back to Susan. "I understand that you lodged a formal protest about *Vanguard* being struck from the Navy List, but under the circumstances your protest has been rejected. Frankly, the cost of repairs is too high for the beancounters to stomach."

"Particularly as there are newer weapons and technologies on the way," Admiral Naiser said.

Susan closed her eyes in pain, just for a moment. She'd known it would happen, but...she'd hoped, against logic and reason, that it wouldn't. That her ship would survive as more than a training hulk...

She pushed the thought aside. They would understand her feelings of course. There wasn't a man in the room who wouldn't understand her feelings. But so what? *Vanguard* was beyond cost-effective repair. The beancounters had finally won.

"As an experienced naval officer, and one with command experience, there are a number of prospective paths open to you," Admiral Fitzwilliam said, after a moment. "We do not have any large ships currently in need of a commanding officer, but we *do* have a couple of survey ships just coming into service. Given what happened at UXS-469, having an experienced naval officer in command might make the difference between peaceful contact and another interstellar war."

"I don't believe the survey officers made any mistakes," Prince Henry pointed out. "They can hardly be blamed for running into trouble."

"Perhaps," Admiral Fitzwilliam said.

He sighed. "The second option is spending a term at the academy," he added. "Your recent experience includes lessons we'd like to teach the cadets, both military and...and otherwise."

"When to relieve a superior officer," Prince Henry said, dryly.

Susan felt her cheeks heat, even though no one could possibly notice. *That* was not a lesson, she suspected, anyone wanted the junior officers to learn.

But they might need to know it, she mused. *I won't be the last officer serving under a dangerously incompetent commander.*

Admiral Fitzwilliam scowled. "Among other things," he said. "We're going to have to revamp the program - again."

He shrugged. "Taking a year or so off to be an instructor is hardly a career-wrecker," he added. "Your name will be added to the list of officers in need of ships. By that point" - he nodded to Admiral Naiser - "John will be First Space Lord. I'm sure he will remember you kindly."

Susan kept her face tightly composed. Whatever Admiral Naiser might say, now or later, she understood the political realities. The only things she had in her favour were genuine command experience and a collection of various medals from seven different spacefaring nations. She *didn't* have many political contacts, many admirers in high places...and she *certainly* didn't have any powerful relatives. Command experience or no command experience, there was a good chance she would never sit in a command chair again.

Unless I take command of one of the survey ships, she thought.

She wasn't blind to the implications. Survey ships spent *years* poking through the tramlines, boldly going where no one had been before. Or no one human, at any rate. Humanity had stumbled across the Foxes, after all. There might well be other alien races out there, just waiting to be discovered. Part of her liked the idea. Being so far from Earth might work in her favour. There wouldn't be anyone looking over her shoulder...

But it will also allow them to forget me, she added, silently. *And survey service experience won't count in my favour when a new battleship command comes along.*

She sighed. It was the best she was going to get and she knew it.

"Choose one," Admiral Fitzwilliam said.

"I'll take the survey command," Susan said. "I've always wanted to know what's waiting for us out there."

"Others do not, I suspect," Admiral Fitzwilliam commented.

He sat back, sipping his tea. "I was twenty-nine when we heard about Vera Cruz," he said, quietly. "To me, it seemed like an opportunity to jump ahead of my peers and gain a carrier command for myself. I tried to steal *Ark Royal* from Admiral Smith..."

Susan felt her lips thinning in cold disapproval. Stealing a command was bad enough under any circumstances, but worse - far worse - when Admiral Smith was a legitimate war hero.

"I didn't realise how much was going to change," Admiral Fitzwilliam continued. "There was no way to know what would happen - or why. The Battle of New Russia, the Bombardment...the death of *Ark Royal*. All of a sudden, the universe was different. And three years after that, we had a short war with India. The universe changed again. And *then* - now - we have a *Second* Interstellar War."

He sighed. "Right now, there's a strong feeling we shouldn't go provoking trouble," he admitted. "I don't know if the current political situation will survive the next election."

"We may choose to ignore the universe," Prince Henry said. "But will it choose to ignore *us*?"

"Probably not," Admiral Fitzwilliam said.

He looked at Prince Henry. "I believe we have one other thing to do...?"

"We do," Prince Henry said. "My father wishes it to be done before I leave Earth."

He rose, putting one hand on his sword. "Susan Onarina. Please kneel."

Susan blinked as he drew his sword, then put her teacup aside and knelt in front of him. It felt strange to kneel in submission, yet...he was *knighting* her? It changed everything. No one would question her past any longer if the king had ordered her knighted. And by his oldest child, no less.

Prince Henry rested the sword, very briefly, on her shoulders. "By command of my royal father, I dub thee Dame Susan, Lady of the Garter," he said formally. "And I invest you Lady Companion to His Majesty."

He paused. "Arise, Dame Susan!"

The End
The *Ark Royal* Universe Will Return Soon

AFTERWORD

And so we come to the end of the *third Ark Royal* series. If you enjoyed this book, please leave a review. It helps <grin>.

But don't worry. *We Lead* is not the end of the series.

My current plans - which have been known to change - involve two stand-alone stories, both set during the First Interstellar War. *The Longest Day* will be the story of the Battle of Earth, very different from the previous nine books in the series (in that it will follow an *event*, rather than a ship and her crew.) This will be followed by a story following a makeshift escort carrier, hastily refitted and sent out to serve as a stopgap measure in hopes of stemming the enemy tide until new purpose-built warships come online. This crew will be *very* unprofessional indeed, a rag-tag crew of misfits…

Until then, I have many more books in the pipeline. Keep turning the pages for a free sample from *Cursed Command*, Book III of *Angel in the Whirlwind*.

And thank you for reading.

Christopher G. Nuttall
Edinburgh, 2016

APPENDIX:
GLOSSARY OF UK TERMS AND SLANG

[Author's Note: I've tried to define every incident of specifically UK slang in this glossary, but I can't promise to have spotted everything. If you spot something I've missed, please let me know and it will be included.]

Aggro - slang term for aggression or trouble, as in 'I don't want any aggro.'
Beasting/Beasted - military slang for anything from a chewing out by one's commander to outright corporal punishment or hazing. The latter two are now officially banned.
Binned - SAS slang for a prospective recruit being kicked from the course, then returned to unit (RTU).
Boffin - Scientist
Bootnecks - slang for Royal Marines. Loosely comparable to 'Jarhead.'
Bottle - slang for nerve, as in 'lost his bottle.'
Borstal - a school/prison for young offenders.
Compo - British army slang for improvised stews and suchlike made from rations and sauces.
Donkey Wallopers - slang for the Royal Horse Artillery.
Fortnight - two weeks. (Hence the terrible pun, courtesy of the *Goon Show*, that Fort Knight cannot possibly last three weeks.)
'Get stuck into' - 'start fighting.'
'I should coco' - 'you're damned right.'
Kip - sleep.
Levies - native troops. The Ghurkhas are the last remnants of native troops from British India.
Lorries - trucks.

MOD - Ministry of Defence. (The UK's Pentagon.)

Order of the Garter - the highest order of chivalry (knighthood) and the third most prestigious honour (inferior only to the Victoria Cross and George Cross) in the United Kingdom. By law, there can be only twenty-four non-royal members of the order at any single time.

Panda Cola - Coke as supplied by the British Army to the troops.

RFA - Royal Fleet Auxiliary

Rumbled - discovered/spotted.

SAS - Special Air Service.

SBS - Special Boat Service

Spotted Dick - a traditional fruity sponge pudding with suet, citrus zest and currants served in thick slices with hot custard. The name always caused a snigger.

Squaddies - slang for British soldiers.

Stag - guard duty.

STUFT - 'Ships Taken Up From Trade,' civilian ships requisitioned for government use.

TAB (tab/tabbing) - Tactical Advance to Battle.

Tearaway - boisterous/badly behaved child, normally a teenager.

Walt - Poser, i.e. someone who claims to have served in the military and/or a very famous regiment. There's a joke about 22 SAS being the largest regiment in the British Army - it must be, because of all the people who claim to have served in it.

Wanker - Masturbator (jerk-off). Commonly used as an insult.

Wanking - Masturbating.

Yank/Yankee - Americans

Coming in March from Christopher G. Nuttall…

CURSED
COMMAND

(ANGEL IN THE
WHIRLWIND, BOOK III)

PROLOGUE

"Mission accomplished?"

"Yes, sir," Crewwoman Julia Transom said. She smiled rather coldly. "Captain Abraham is dead."

Senior Chief Joel Gibson smiled back. It hadn't been hard to arrange for Captain Abraham's death, even though the IG would almost certainly go through the entire series of events with a fine-tooth comb. Captain Abraham wasn't—hadn't been—*precisely* aristocracy, but he'd had connections at a very high level. Yet there had been no choice. Captain Abraham had also been far too effective. Given time, he might have turned *Uncanny* into a *real* wreck, and *that* Joel could not allow.

He leaned forward, warningly. "And the evidence?"

"Gone," Julia assured him. He didn't miss the flicker of fear, swiftly hidden, in her eyes. "If they manage to recover the black box, it'll look like a random fluctuation in the shuttle's drive field. They can take however long they want to sift through the debris. They won't find anything incriminating."

"Good," Joel said. "And so we are without a commanding officer. Again."

Julia nodded hastily. "You'd think they'd grow tired of losing officers to this ship."

Joel shrugged. *Uncanny* had been in active service, technically, for three years. The first of her class, she'd been intended to serve as both a squadron command vessel and an independent command for a fire-eating captain. But she'd had a run of bad luck that had left her relegated to lunar orbit, well away from anywhere *important*. Spacers believed—or chose to believe—that she was cursed. Given just how many *accidents* had befallen her crew, they were right to be reluctant to serve on her. Joel and his allies hadn't been responsible for *all* of the accidents.

"They'll want us heading out to the war, sooner or later," he said reluctantly. Though the information was classified, he'd long-since spliced a hack into the command network. Given how much time the XO spent in the lunar fleshpots, Joel could honestly say that he read his superior's mail long before Abraham did. "And that gives us our opportunity."

He smirked as he turned away from her. He'd honestly never expected to stay in the Navy, not since a judge had given him a choice between taking the oath and serving his planet or going straight to a penal world. Joel had expected to put in his ten years as an ordinary crewman and then leave Tyre for good, but it hadn't taken him long to see the possibilities inherent in his new position. There was something to be said for being the only effective man in a crew of drunkards, morons, near-criminals, and people the Navy bureaucracy couldn't be bothered to discharge. There were all sorts of other possibilities for a man with imagination and guts.

Julia coughed. "Our opportunity?"

"Why, to take our fate into our own hands, of course," Joel said.

Julia's eyes went wide, but she said nothing. Joel nodded in approval. He trusted Julia about as much as he trusted anyone, which wasn't very much. Julia would sing like a bird if the IG found proof she'd assassinated her commanding officer. The less she knew the better. He'd considered disposing of her in another accident—and he would have done so if he hadn't *needed* her. How such a remarkable talent for hacking computer networks had escaped being put to better use was beyond him, but he had no doubt of her loyalty. She'd done enough to more than prove her credentials to him.

He turned back to face her. Julia's red hair, cut close to her scalp, shimmered under the bright lights. Her uniform was a size too tight, showing every last curve of her body. There was a hardness in her face that warned that anyone who tried to take advantage of her was going to regret it, if he survived. Joel had taught her more than enough dirty tricks to give Julia an unfair advantage over those who thought that mere strength and brute force would be enough to bring her down.

"Keep a sharp eye on the XO's personal channel," Joel ordered. "If the Admiralty wants to send in another CO, they'll notify him first."

"Unless they know what he's doing with his time," Julia reminded him.

Joel rolled his eyes. The XO wasn't very smart—there was only so far that aristocratic ranks and titles could take a person—but he'd shown a certain low cunning in assembling his protective shroud. Unless the Admiralty decided to make a surprise inspection, they shouldn't have any idea that the XO was enjoying himself rather than doing his duty. If they did...Joel found it hard to care. The XO would take the blame for everything and the plotters would pass unnoticed.

Unless they break up the crew, he thought.

He shook his head. *Uncanny* had served as the Royal Navy's dumping ground for the last two years. Even her couple of combat operations in the war hadn't changed that, particularly not after the...*incident*...at Donne's Reach. Breaking up the crew would force the Admiralty to distribute over a thousand unwanted crewmembers all over the Navy while facing stiff resistance from everyone else. No captain in his right mind wanted a crewman or an officer who had served on *Uncanny*. The ship wasn't known as *Unlucky* for nothing.

Julia cleared her throat. "Sir?"

"Keep an eye on his channel," Joel ordered again. "Alert me if anything changes."

Julia nodded, then turned and hurried out of the compartment. Joel watched her go, thinking dark thoughts. They were committed now, no matter how much he might wish to believe otherwise. Whatever he'd said to her, he knew that the IG would not take the death of a commanding officer lightly. And if they started digging through *Uncanny*, they'd uncover far too many oddities to look away...

But by then, we should be ready to move, he told himself firmly. *They won't have time to stop us before it's too late.*

CHAPTER
ONE

HMS *Uncanny* looked...faded.

Captain William McElney wasn't sure just what had prompted *that* observation, but he couldn't escape his first impression of his new command. HMS *Uncanny* was a blunt white arrowhead, like HMS *Lightning*, yet there was something about her that bothered him. Her hull was painted the same pure white as the remainder of the fleet, but it was obvious that no one had bothered to—that no one had *needed* to—repaint the hull. The network of sensor blisters dotted over her exterior looked new, too new. Her point defense weapons, which should have tracked his shuttle as it approached her hull, were still, utterly immobile.

"She doesn't seem to know we're here, sir," the pilot said.

William sucked in his breath sharply, feeling a yawning chasm opening in his chest. A command, his *first* command...he'd served the Royal Navy faithfully for years, hoping for a command of his own. And yet, the more he looked at the heavy cruiser, the more he wondered if he'd been *wise* to want a command. On paper, *Uncanny* was a dream; in practice, the First Space Lord had made it clear that the heavy cruiser was trouble.

"Send a standard greeting, then request permission to dock," William ordered finally.

He cursed under his breath. The Theocracy had shown itself more than willing to use suicide missions to target the Commonwealth, even before the tide of the war had started to turn against them. A shuttle crammed with antimatter, exploding within an unsuspecting starship's shuttlebay, would be more than enough to vaporize the entire cruiser. Even a standard nuke would be enough to do real damage if it detonated inside the hull. These days, no one was allowed to dock without an elaborate security screening to make sure they were who they claimed to be. Even civilians were included despite endless protests. He couldn't help wondering if the Theocracy had deliberately set out to ensure that the precautions caused more economic damage than their attacks.

Careless, he thought grimly. *And dangerous in these times.*

"No response," the pilot said.

"Send it again," William said. He didn't want to try to force a docking, certainly not on the day he boarded his first command. But if there was no choice, he'd have to try. "And then find us a docking hatch."

"Aye, sir," the pilot said.

William nodded, then glanced down at the shuttle's tactical display. *Uncanny* should have been running a low-level sensor scan at all times, but she clearly wasn't doing anything of the sort. The vessel was *technically* within regulations, given how close they were to the network of fortresses guarding Tyre, yet the lack of forethought was careless. *Really* careless. If the ship had had to bring up her sensors in a hurry, it was going to take far longer than it should have…

…And he'd seen enough combat to know that bare minutes could mean the difference between life and death.

"Your commanding officer has written a glowing recommendation, Sir William," the First Space Lord had said. "And so has Rose MacDonald. I'm afraid the combination of recommendations has *quite* upset the bureaucracy."

William had kept his face impassive. He'd been promoted to captain; he'd been promised a command…yet he'd forced himself to keep his expectations low. He was too senior to command a gunboat, he thought; too junior to be offered a cruiser or carrier command. He'd expected a destroyer, perhaps a frigate. Yet, with so many conflicting recommendations, he wasn't sure *what* he'd get. There were hundreds of officers with better connections and only a handful of commands.

"You're being given a heavy cruiser," the First Space Lord had added, pausing just long enough for his words to sink in. "You're being given *Uncanny*."

"Thank you, sir," William had stammered. He had expected a sting in the tail and hadn't been disappointed. He had no reason to be given a heavy cruiser, not when he'd just been made a captain, save for the simple fact that *no one* wanted to serve on *Uncanny*. The ship had a notorious reputation. "*Unlucky?*"

"That's what they call it," the First Space Lord said grimly.

He'd said a great deal more, William remembered. *Uncanny* had lost *two* previous commanding officers to accidents, but that was only the tip of the iceberg. The ship had been deployed to a cloaked fleet lying in wait for a Theocratic vanguard, only to have her cloaking system go offline at the worst possible moment. If *that* hadn't been bad enough, there had been a whole string of incidents culminating in the starship launching a missile barrage towards a *friendly* ship. The events had all been seen as glitches, but they had cost *Uncanny's* commanding officer his career.

And matters weren't helped by the missiles being unarmed, William had thought when he'd reviewed the file. *If she'd been shooting at an enemy ship, she'd have inflicted no damage at all.*

"We need to get *Uncanny* into service as quickly as possible," the First Space Lord had concluded. "And if you succeed in sorting out the mess, you'll remain as her commanding officer permanently."

It wasn't much of a bribe, William thought. There was no shortage of captains willing to compete for a post on *Lightning*—the heavy cruiser was *famous*—but *Uncanny?* He'd be surprised if there was *any* competition for her command chair. And yet, he had to admit, his appointment was a hell of a challenge. A heavy cruiser command was nothing to sneer at, even if she *did* have a reputation for being unlucky. He'd be on the path to flag rank...

Assuming I survive, he told himself. He hadn't felt comfortable airing his concerns in front of his superior officer. *Those accidents may not have been accidents at all...* "Captain," the pilot said. His voice shocked William out of his memories. "We have received permission to dock at Hatch One."

William felt his eyes narrow as the shuttle altered course and sped towards the hatch. Hatch One was located near the bridge—it was the *closest* shuttle hatch to the bridge—but it wasn't where a new captain would board his command for the first time. Normally, a captain would be met by his XO in the shuttlebay, allowing him time to meet his senior officers before formally assuming command. And the XO *was* supposed to be on the vessel…he'd checked, just before he departed Tyre. Commander Stewart Greenhill was currently in command of HMS *Uncanny*.

"Dock us," he ordered, wondering just what sort of hellhole he was about to enter. "And remain docked until I give you leave to depart."

"Aye, Captain," the pilot said.

The hatch looked normal enough, William noted, yet he couldn't help tensing as the shuttle mated with *Uncanny*. Captain Abraham had died in a shuttle accident—the IG had found nothing suspicious in two weeks of careful investigation—but Captain Jove had died in a freak airlock accident. A component had decayed, according to the engineers; the airlock had registered a safe atmosphere when it had actually been open to vacuum. William had been in the Navy long enough to know that accidents happened, but he'd also learned that accidents could be *made* to happen. Losing two commanding officers to *accidents* was more than a little suspicious.

He covertly tested his shipsuit and mask, hidden in his shoulder pockets, as the hatch hissed open. Everything looked normal, but the inner hatch took just long enough to open for him to start feeling nervous. The hatch should have opened at once, unless the sensors registered vacuum or biological contamination. William took a long breath as he stepped into his cruiser and had to fight to keep from recoiling in horror. *Uncanny* stank like a pirate ship after a successful mission of looting, raping, and burning.

Fuck, he thought.

He felt a sudden surge of anger as he looked up and down the corridor. No one had come to greet him, neither the XO nor his senior officers. What were they playing at? Even a *very* busy XO should have come to meet his CO for the first time, if only to explain any problems that caught the captain's eye. And to explain why his ship smelled worse than an unwashed outdoor toilet. It wasn't as if replacing the air filters required a goddamned shipyard! He took another breath and tasted faint hints of ionization in the air, warning him that dozens, perhaps hundreds, of components had not been replaced for far too long. Every trained spacer *knew* that that smell meant trouble.

A hatch hissed open in the distance. William braced himself, unsure what to expect as someone hurried down the corridor towards him. He rested his hands on his hips—it was hard to resist the temptation to draw his sidearm—as the welcome party came into view. A very *small* welcome party. It was a young woman wearing a steward's uniform; she was young enough to be his daughter, yet with a hardness in her eyes that shocked him. Whatever military bearing she'd had before leaving Piker's Peak was long gone. Her salute, when she finally gave it, was so sloppy, her instructors would have cried themselves senseless.

"Stand at ease," William curtly ordered. He took a moment to match the face to the files he'd studied during the flight from Tyre. Janet Richmond, Captain Abraham's personal steward. Blonde enough to remind him of Kat Falcone, but lacking Kat's poise and grim determination to prove herself. "Where is the XO?"

Janet quailed. William suddenly realized that he might have been too harsh. "I..."

William took a breath. Janet was a *steward*. She wasn't in the chain of command. Hell, he doubted she had *any* authority outside her CO's suite. What the hell was she *doing* here?

"Calm down," he ordered, forcing his own voice to calm. "Where is the XO?"

"He's not on the ship, sir," Janet said carefully. She cringed back, as if she expected to be slapped. "Commander Greenhill hasn't been on the ship for the last ten days."

William felt his mouth drop open. "What?"

"He left the ship ten days ago," Janet said. She sounded as if she were pleading with him for...what? Understanding? "He ordered the communications staff to keep up the pretense that he was onboard."

"I see," William said.

He had to fight, hard, to keep his anger under control. He hadn't thought much of Commander Greenhill after he'd read the man's file, but he'd promised himself that he would keep an open mind. Now... Commander Greenhill would be lucky if he was *merely* kicked out of the Navy. Going on unauthorized leave when he was meant to be in command of his ship? Dereliction of duty was a shooting offense in wartime.

"Please don't tell him I told you," Janet pleaded. "He'll get angry."

"He'll get dead," William snapped. Shooting was too good for Commander Greenhill. *Far* too good for him. William had been raised to do his duty or die trying, no matter what curves life threw him. Commander Greenhill didn't even have the decency to resign his commission and totter off to spend the rest of his life in the nearest bar. "Who *is* on this fucking ship?"

Janet cringed, again.

"The chief engineer is in command," she said finally. "But he's in his cabin...the bridge crew are scattered...the crew..."

"Let me guess," William said. He hated himself for taking his anger out on her, but it was so hard to remain focused. "They're currently too drunk to notice that they're steadily poisoning their own fucking atmosphere?"

He saw a dozen answers cross Janet's face before she nodded, once.

William shook his head, feeling an odd flicker of sympathy for Commander Greenhill. He might have had a good reason to throw in the towel, after all. Offhand, William couldn't remember a ship and crew falling so far, certainly not in Commonwealth history. A handful of UN ships had turned pirate, he recalled, after the Breakaway Wars, and quickly fell into very bad habits.

And most of them were small ships, he thought numbly. *This is a heavy cruiser.*

"Take me to the bridge," he ordered, meeting her eyes. "And *don't* call ahead to say I'm coming."

"Yes, sir," Janet said.

She turned and hurried down the corridor, moving so quickly that she was practically running...as if, William reflected grimly, she wanted to get away from him. He hadn't paid much attention to her file, he recalled; in hindsight, that might have been a mistake. A captain had considerable authority over who served as his steward, after all. Had Captain Abraham been motivated by something other than efficiency?

He followed Janet, feeling his anger simmering as he took in the condition of his starship. A dozen maintenance lockers had been left open, their contents scattered over the deck; a handful of overhead lockers had been torn open; the strange smell only grew more unpleasant the farther they moved into the ship. He winced inwardly as he smelled the telltale presence of rats and cockroaches. He'd been wrong, he reflected, as they passed through a pair of solid hatches and entered Officer Country. There were pirate ships from the edge of explored space that were in better condition than *Uncanny*.

Janet stopped and turned to face him. "It wasn't their fault," she said. "Sir..."

William scowled at her. "*What* wasn't their fault?"

"Everything," Janet said. She turned back and opened the hatch to the bridge. "You'll see in a minute..."

William followed her onto the bridge...and stopped, dead. A single officer sat in front of the tactical console, smoking something that smelled of burning grass. William stared at him, and then realized, to his shock, that there was no one else on the bridge. Regulations insisted on at least *three* officers on duty at all times, even when the starship was in orbit around the safest world in the Commonwealth. Where were the other two? It struck him, a moment later, that *Janet* might be one of the other officers. Was she even *qualified* to stand watch?

He pushed the thought aside as he surveyed the compartment. The holographic display that should have showed the system was gone; five consoles were deactivated, four more dismantled for parts. He'd never seen anything like it, at least not outside a shipyard putting the finishing touches on a brand new starship. Creeping horror threatened to overcome him as he keyed the nearest console, demanding a status update. The internal sensor net was down...completely. He'd never seen *that* outside starships that had been battered into hulks by enemy fire.

"It's nonfunctional," Janet said.

"I can see that," William snarled. He strode over to the smoking officer and tore the cigarette out of his mouth, dropping it on the deck and grinding it under his heel. "What happened to the bridge?"

The officer stared at him. "Who are you?"

"I'm your new commanding officer," William snapped. Up close, the man's breath made him want to reel. He had no idea what the man had been smoking, but it couldn't be good for him. Or anyone. "Who are *you*?"

The officer's mouth opened and shut for a long moment. "Lieutenant Rodney Graham, sir," he managed, finally. "I'm officer of the watch."

"Glad to hear it," William said. "What happened to my bridge?"

"The engineers cannibalized it to keep other starships running," Janet said quietly. "They were practically stripping out the entire hull…"

William understood, just for a moment, why one of his uncles had drunk himself to death after his farm had failed. It hadn't been the old man's fault, not really. He'd just seen his investments fail, one after the other, even before the pirates had arrived to threaten his homeworld. Maybe the remainder of the ship's crew—*his* crew—felt the same way.

The First Space Lord couldn't have known, William thought grimly. *Even if they hadn't stripped out essential components, they'd been vandalizing their own ship and rendering it unserviceable.*

He cursed under his breath savagely. It was difficult, sometimes, to get spare parts from the bureaucracy. Even during wartime, the bureaucrats insisted on having the forms filled out before they released the components, despite the best efforts of supply officers. Having a source of supplies they could tap without having to fill out the paperwork would be wonderful, as far as the supply officers were concerned. God knew, he'd rewarded a couple of officers for being excellent scroungers…

It may not be as bad as it seems, he told himself. *Or that could be just wishful thinking.*

"Right," he said, pushing the thought aside. "I want you," he glared at Graham "to recall each and every officer and crewman who is currently not on the ship. If they are back before the end of the shift"—he made a show of glancing at his wristcom—"nothing further will be said about their absence. This time."

Graham looked as if he wanted to object but didn't quite dare. "Yes, sir."

"Good," William said. "I *suggest*"—he hardened his tone to make it very clear that it wasn't a *suggestion*—"that you get rid of any drugs and anything else that could get you in hot water before I hold a search. This is your *one* chance to clean up your act."

He turned and met Janet's eyes. "And *you* are to take me to the chief engineer."

Janet paled. "Yes, sir."

"Good," William said. He wondered, suddenly, what Kat Falcone would make of a ruined starship and a wrecked crew. "Let's go."

CHAPTER
TWO

"You gave him *Unlucky*?"

"*Uncanny*," the First Space Lord corrected. "Her *name* is *Uncanny*."

Kat closed her eyes in pain. She owed Commander William McElney—*Captain* William McElney—her life and career. He'd been her XO on HMS *Lightning* and she knew, all too well, that she would have lost everything without him. She'd called in every favor she was owed and made promises of future favors to ensure that the delay between his promotion and his assignment to a command was as short as possible. Still, she'd never expected that he might be offered *Unlucky*. That ship had killed two of her commanding officers and ruined three more.

"Might I ask," she said in a tone she knew would get anyone else in trouble, "why you gave him *that* ship?"

"Politics," the First Space Lord said dryly.

"*Heavy* politics," King Hadrian added.

Kat swallowed, hard. King Hadrian had sought her out more than once since her return from Theocratic Space, but she'd never been sure why. Perhaps he just wanted the benefit of her experience. The monarch had vast power in wartime, but King Hadrian had no military experience. He'd never been allowed to leave his homeworld, even after being crowned.

"Politics," she repeated finally.

"It's a delicate balancing act," the First Space Lord said. "On one hand, we have noncitizens of Tyre who want postings to the very highest levels;

on the other hand, we have the existing power structure complaining about outsiders being allowed to compete with insiders. And you *know* it. We have to navigate this political storm before it tears the Commonwealth apart."

"We don't have enough ships to go around," King Hadrian said.

"Yet," Kat countered.

She shook her head, irritated. The Commonwealth had a formidable industrial base, but the demands of wartime were pushing it to the limit. Her father, the Minister of War Production, had told her that production was still being ramped up even though countless new starships, gunboats, and missiles were rattling off the assembly line. According to the latest projections, the Commonwealth wouldn't achieve a decisive tonnage advantage over the Theocracy for another two to three years.

But we now know that we overestimated their industrial base, Kat reminded herself. *They're already running hot, while we're still increasing our production rate.*

"Yet," King Hadrian agreed. "But we do not have enough stability, not right now anyway, to risk upsetting the political balance of power."

"And *not* allowing outsiders to be promoted will *also* upset the balance of power," Kat pointed out tartly.

"Quite," the First Space Lord said. "So we promote your XO and offer him a chance to put an…*unlucky*…starship back into active service. If he does well, we can use him as a test case to prove that outsiders should get their chance; if he doesn't…well, at least we have good reason to justify turning down other promotions."

Kat managed to keep her face impassive, but not without effort. The Kingdom of Tyre had never intended to become a multistar political entity, not when everyone had *assumed* that the UN's hegemony over humanity's growing domain would last indefinitely. However, the UN had fallen into war, leaving chaos in its wake. Tyre had created the Commonwealth, a union of stars and planets, with the intention of integrating the newcomers slowly and carefully. And yet the war had blown all of their careful plans out the airlock. The Commonwealth had to square the urgent need for manpower with the political requirement not to sacrifice the ethos that had made the Commonwealth great.

But William deserved his promotion, Kat thought. *How many others also deserve promotion?*

"I am not an all-powerful ruler," King Hadrian said. "We cannot ram through such changes without paying a stiff price."

He cleared his throat. "In any case," he added, "we did not call you here to discuss your former XO."

Kat leaned forward, stiffly. She didn't share her father's obsession with political games—no one had really expected the tenth child of Duke Lucas Falcone to wield political power—but she knew enough to expect trouble. King Hadrian wouldn't have called her to the palace's war room, knowing that it would have displeased some of his ministers, if he hadn't *wanted* her here. And if he wanted her here, he had a reason. He wouldn't have summoned her on a whim.

The First Space Lord tapped a switch. A holographic star chart materialized in front of them, hanging over the table. Kat devoured it, noting with interest the handful of stars that had seen raiding parties from the Theocracy sweeping through in hopes of delaying the Commonwealth's mobilization. None of those raiding parties had taken or held territory, not since the first thrusts into Commonwealth territory. The war seemed to have stalemated.

"As you are aware," the First Space Lord said, "Admiral Junayd defected six months ago, after you embarrassed him in front of his superiors. Since then, he's been singing like a canary in a coal mine. We've learned a great deal about the Theocracy's industrial base, its long-term plans for conquest, and most importantly, how its government actually *works*. Our analysts have been able to confirm enough of the data to discern that Junayd's been telling the truth."

Kat nodded. Admiral Junayd would have to be *insane* to lie. She honestly couldn't imagine the Theocracy choosing to sacrifice an entire super-dreadnought, perhaps more than one, in a vain attempt to prove Junayd's *bona fides*. There was the vague possibility, her father had warned, that the whole thing *was* a con, but Admiral Junayd had been checked and tested extensively.

"Admiral Junayd did not know just what his former allies had in mind to break the stalemate," the First Space Lord added, "but he does know some of their long-term plans. Despite waging war against us, the Theocracy has continued its aim to subvert nearby star systems and eventually bring them under its control. Admiral Junayd believes that the Theocracy intends to continue those plans."

Kat blinked. "Even now?"

"They're committed to spreading their religion," King Hadrian reminded her. "Even if they lose the war, even if their homeworld gets blasted from orbit, their religion will survive."

"Maybe," Kat said. "But they could be wrong."

The thought made her shudder. She'd seen thousands of refugees fleeing the Theocracy and knew there were hundreds of millions trapped on a dozen occupied worlds. She rather doubted that the Theocracy would survive if it lost control of the high orbitals. The level of hatred the Theocracy had unleashed promised bloody purges once the war was over. The Theocracy had meted out savage treatment to their helpless prey and, once the boot was on the other foot, savage treatment would be meted out to them in turn.

"They could be," the First Space Lord agreed.

He pointed to a cluster of stars near the Commonwealth's border. "The Jorlem Sector," he said by way of introduction. "I believe you've been there?"

"I visited briefly, when I was assigned to HMS *Thomas*," Kat recalled. "But I only had a couple of days leave on Vangelis. I never saw Jorlem itself."

King Hadrian looked surprised. "You are not familiar with the sector?"

Kat shook her head. Groundhogs never really comprehended the sheer *immensity* of interstellar space. The Jorlem Sector held over fifty stars and over a hundred settled worlds, ranging from tiny farming settlements to Jorlem itself. She hadn't really seen much of Vangelis, save for a few tourist traps near the spaceport. The idea that her limited experience made her an expert on the sector was absurd.

Although quite a few analysts claim to be experts without ever having left their homeworld, she reminded herself. *At least the king is trying to talk to people who might know better than himself.*

"I couldn't call myself an expert," she said.

"Very wise," the First Space Lord said.

He gave her a half smile as he pointed to the star chart. "The important part, right now, is that the Theocracy is planning to…*seduce*…a number of independent planets within the sector," he told her. "Our defector believes that the Theocracy intends to offer all sorts of incentives to its potential allies, ranging from protection from Theocratic incursions to honored positions within the Theocracy."

"They wouldn't fall for *that*," Kat insisted.

"They might," the First Space Lord said. "There's a great deal of resentment and suspicion of the Commonwealth in that sector, Captain. They may see the Theocracy as the lesser of two evils."

"They'll regret it," Kat said. She shook her head in disbelief. "How can people be so *stupid*?"

"Poor trade policies," the king said. "A number of worlds have expressed interest in joining the Commonwealth, Kat, but their local rivals have been much less enthusiastic. They've actually been trying to arm themselves to the teeth for the last couple of decades. Not enough to be a threat to us on their own, of course, but allied with the Theocracy…"

Kat nodded as his voice trailed off. The Theocracy had poured its resources into building the largest fleet of warships it could but neglected the sinews of war. She'd known, long before Operation Knife, that the Theocracy was trying to buy up freighters and hire merchant spacers in a desperate attempt to solve their problems, yet that hadn't been enough. The Theocratic advance into Commonwealth space might well have gotten farther if its logistics system hadn't collapsed mere weeks after the war began.

"They could tip the balance back in their favor," she said.

"That's not the only implication," the king confirmed. "If the Theocrats open trade links with the Jorlem Sector, they'll have access to markets and traders from right across the human sphere. It wouldn't be hard for them to purchase military-grade gear from a dozen potential sources, mil-spec gear that might be enough to neutralize our advantages. There would be nothing we could do about it. Diplomatic protests won't be enough when vast sums of money are at stake."

"We could buy the gear ourselves," Kat pointed out.

"Measures are underway," the First Space Lord said.

He leaned forward, resting his hands on the table. "HMS *Lightning* and HMS *Uncanny* are being posted to the Jorlem Sector," he informed her. "Our regular patrols through the sector have been withdrawn with the advent of war, so the normal trade routes have become increasingly lawless. Intelligence believes that pirate and smuggler consortiums have relocated themselves after pickings in our territory became rather slim."

"Or the Theocracy may be trying to put pressure on the locals," Kat offered.

"It's a possibility," the king agreed.

Kat scowled as she contemplated the situation. Theocratic forces hadn't hesitated to sponsor pirate activity within Commonwealth space, hoping to weaken their targets before the war actually began. There was no reason they couldn't do the same in the Jorlem Sector, with an additional nasty little twist. If the Jorlem Sector joined the Theocracy, those raiders could be sent elsewhere...but if the Jorlem Sector joined the Commonwealth instead, the Navy would have to divert patrols to protect the sector, putting yet another demand on the Navy's very limited time and resources—just the sort of scheme that would appeal to the Theocrats. Whatever happened, whatever the sector's governments did, the Theocracy would come out ahead.

"Ideally, you'll be doing nothing more than showing the flag and assisting the locals in hunting down pirates and other threats," the First Space Lord told her. "Six months of patrolling should do wonders for our reputation. If you *can* forge a set of alliances, we'd be delighted...but we're not expecting it. Right now, it's more reasonable to simply foster warm relations in the sector; we can worry about convincing them to apply for membership later."

"Because we can't defend them now," Kat said.

"Yes," the king said. "In the long term, yes; we'd like them to join. But for the moment, we'd prefer to keep them at a distance."

"You'll be given specific orders in the next couple of days," the First Space Lord added. "Do you have any questions for the moment?"

"Yes, sir," Kat said. "Why me? Why us?"

The king smiled. "There are several reasons," he said. "First, you have a growing reputation for military skill—you saved an entire fleet at First

Cadiz, practically won Second Cadiz singlehandedly…and then raided deep into enemy space, throwing them back onto the defensive."

"Admiral Christian might have a few things to say about *that*, sire," Kat said. "I *didn't* win the battle singlehandedly."

"No, but that's what the media is saying," the king said. "Are you suggesting that…that they're *fibbing*? I am *shocked!*"

He went on before Kat could come up with an answer. "The point is that you are a military hero, a *genuine* military hero, and you have *very* close links to the aristocracy. Sending you to the Jorlem Sector is an excellent way of showing how important we consider the sector to be. You talking to their rulers on equal terms is a sign of respect. *And* you can talk to their militaries, discussing the exact nature of the enemy threat and how it can be defeated. Your reputation will precede you."

The media will make sure of it, Kat thought darkly. She *loathed* the media.

"Your former XO, your fellow captain, is also an advertisement for social advancement within the Commonwealth, even though he wasn't born on Tyre," the king added. "He was knighted six months ago, which makes him a *de facto* member of the aristocracy, and he was given his own command. A *heavy cruiser* to boot. He's living proof that noncitizens can and do advance within the system."

"Of course, sire," Kat said. "The fact that it was a struggle to get him promoted, after *years* of loyal service, is neither here nor there. The fact that *Unlucky* is on the verge of falling apart…"

"Of course not," the king interrupted. He shot her an annoyed look. "We are trying to fight a war, Captain, while trying to patch over the holes in the Commonwealth's structure. It needs to be handled carefully."

"It does," Kat agreed. "And what do we do if we encounter a predatory merchant?"

"Whatever you see fit," the king said.

Kat resisted the urge to rub her eyes. There was no escaping the simple fact that a number of Tyre's merchants had established trade links that effectively exploited stars and planets *outside* the Commonwealth. Their behavior was technically illegal, but it was difficult to prosecute them when they also tended to have allies in high places. The kingdom's determination to protect its people, even at the risk of war, didn't help. There was no way she could stand back and watch as a crowd threatened to lynch a Commonwealth citizen, but she didn't want to risk her ship and crew to save someone who only deserved a quick trial and a one-way ticket to a penal world.

"I want *carte blanche*," she said flatly.

"Already in your orders," the king said. Kat had the uneasy feeling that someone had anticipated her demand. "We're at war. The normal rules don't apply."

And they just dumped a hot potato in my lap, Kat thought. She was starting to suspect that there were other reasons for her appointment. No one could say she didn't have ties to the merchant sector, not when her father ran, or had run, one of the largest corporations in the sector. *But which way am I expected to jump?*

"Thank you," she said. She'd consider the problem later. "When do you want us to depart?"

"Ideally, a week from today," the First Space Lord said. "But organizing a convoy to Vangelis may take longer. Spacers...are none too happy about the convoy requirements."

"They wouldn't be," Kat said. She'd never served on a merchant freighter, but thanks to her family, she understood the logistical problems facing civilian skippers better than most military officers. "If they miss their due dates, they face fines...perhaps even the loss of their ships."

"We've introduced emergency legislation to tackle the problem," the king said. "But it's stalled in the House of Lords. Too many people are suspicious of how it can be misused."

Kat sighed. "Is there any *evidence* it *will* be misused?"

"Of course not," the king said. "But who needs evidence when there are political points to score?"

"Touché," Kat said.

She shook her head. In all fairness, she could see both sides of the debate. A merchant skipper in danger of losing his ship would run terrifying risks, if necessary, to make his scheduled deadlines. Even with stasis fields, certain cargos were all too perishable; they might arrive too late for anyone to want to buy them, but introducing legislation to override contractual requirements would open up a whole new can of worms. Either deadlines would no longer matter, in which case the merchant skippers could and would cheat at will, or each and every case would have to be decided individually, tying up the courts for years. It would be a political nightmare.

But a collapse of interstellar trade would be a nightmare too, she thought.

"You'll receive your formal orders soon," the First Space Lord said. "Good luck with your new XO."

Kat had to fight a frown. She'd requested that her former tactical officer be promoted, but she'd heard nothing. Somehow, she suspected that the bureaucracy had found a reason to turn down her request. And *that* meant her new XO would be transferred from another ship...

"Thank you, sir," Kat said. She had no trouble recognizing a dismissal. "I won't let you down."

PREORDER NOW!

CPSIA information can be obtained
at www.ICGtesting.com
Printed in the USA
FSOW04n1655280217
31376FS